"Intimate as well as ep... ...... adventure of a young woman's search for her soul while on the run from those who must destroy her to save themselves. Only the fate of the world hangs in the balance. Entertaining and eye-opening."

—Wayne Jacobsen, author of *Live Loved Free Full* and coauthor of *The Shack*

"Tessa Van Wade deftly weaves together so many plot layers in this thrilling story. Once I started reading, I could not put it down! *Deep Trace* will leave you breathless and on the edge of your seat as you await book three."

—Anna LeBaron, author of *The Polygamist's Daughter: A Memoir*

"From the opening chapter until I turned to the last page *Deep Trace* had me hooked. Filled with adventure, suspense, continuous twists and turns, and an unfolding love story... I could not put this book down. Tessa Van Wade drew me in one word at a time and painted a crisp picture that made me feel I was in the story. While I loved Willow in *Out of the Shadows*, discovering Remy made me long for my own undiscovered realities. You hold in your hands a masterpiece and I cannot wait for the final book in this series."

—Julie Williams, Social Media Coordinator

"Captivating and inspiring, *Deep Trace* is a beautiful work of art and love. The world is better for it. As Tessa Van Wade weaves one layer upon the next, she expands our imagination and we come to see our own story inside Remy's. This has the potential to be the next Matrix."

—Harvey Mast, Business Owner

"Tessa Van Wade is a rising star and incredible writer. Her profound way with words that are detailed and descriptive pull you right into this beautifully intricate story. *Deep Trace* is full of incredible characters and twists and turns of adventure and love. I can already see the movie! Check out this book, you won't be disappointed!"

—Natalie Bruce, author of *Aki the Inventor* and *Igniting The Fire*

"*Deep Trace* is a unique, thought provoking adventure into the human psyche. The characters pull you in, and the mystery surrounding their lives holds you captive. It was a wild ride and an intriguing next chapter in the Velieri Uprising Series."

—Jessica Glasner, author of *Voyage of the Sandpiper* and *Saving Grace*

"*Deep Trace* is an adventure that I couldn't put down! Within its pages I experienced Remy's metamorphosis, from the Cellar to Spain. Tessa Van Wade created fantasy, fiction, and mystery, while at the same time coined a new category of its own in self help fiction. Van Wade has a hit in book two. Arek and Remy's love story is one you don't want to miss."

—Jenny Hansen, Business Owner, Kona Swim Lessons

"What a ride! *Deep Trace* picks up right where *Out of the Shadows* left off, instantly pulling me back into this fast-paced fantastical story with thought-provoking underlying messages. I couldn't put it down and now eagerly await book three in the Velieri Uprising Series."

—Cathy Shea, retired Global Campaign Marketing Manager, HP

"I love fantasy that pulls you in with intrigue and high stakes. Tessa is a master at it. Spiritually insightful and action-packed."

—Mick Silva, former editor of Zondervan Books

DEEP TRACE

Book Two of *The Velieri Uprising*

TESSA VAN WADE

Blue Sheep Media
BlueSheepMedia.com
2902 East C Street | Torrington, WY 82240
p. 201.240.7106 | 213.408.9322
email: publish@bluesheepmedia.com

Cover and Interior designs: Lorie DeWorken,
www.mindthemargins.com

Printed in the United States of America
First printed: August 2022

For Ben—my Yovu.

1

The driver peers at Leigh through the rearview mirror. "Ten minutes out to the Cellar."

"Are you ready?" It's been two days since Leigh has spoken anything to me and his words are sharp and moody.

"Could I ever be . . . ready?" I whisper.

He doesn't answer; the rest of the men within the vehicle share loaded glances and I immediately regret my question. Instead of prodding further, I turn away and peer at the vehicle that's following. The tinted windows are too dark to see inside, but Arek, Sassi, and Kilon have been silently following since I turned myself in to Leigh.

In a procession of four large SUVs, we snake our way through the mountainous region of Switzerland. A thick chaotic spread of oak, beech, and maple trees create impenetrable fortresses on each side, only allowing views of where we are going and the empty road we've just traveled.

Just ten minutes away is the Cellar. Now that I'm aware of this, a familiar panic pulses through my veins. *This is my choice. I am Remy, not Willow.* I repeat these words in my head to calm my shaking hands, however, this does nothing to stop my imagination. Leigh stays silent even when he notices my trembling.

Due to the rain when they transferred me from the plane to the SUV, my hair is drenched and it falls heavily over my shoulders while

I fight extreme cold in my soaked black shirt and jeans. Leigh is perfectly dry but his umbrella has left a large puddle next to his boots. Thick beads of water slowly drip down my forehead, and I watch ice form on the outside of my window.

"Can you possibly turn up the heat?" I finally build up the courage to ask.

One of the men reaches for the heater but Leigh shakes his head. "No," he says in the ancient language. "Next thing we know she'll ask for a luxury suite." He rolls his cold eyes as the other guards chuckle.

What did I do to make him despise me? This morning before the sun had even risen, we waited in the Velieri hotel for the caravan of vehicles. Leigh stood next to me, then his men surrounded us like statues with earpieces and guns.

Arek confidently walked between them, took my face in his hands, and whispered quietly in my ear, "I'm right here."

"Enough!" Leigh called out, as Arek's lips fell on mine. This only made Arek grin at his point well made.

During the long car ride, the others speak the Velieri language assuming that I won't be able to understand. "We take her around the back," Leigh says and the driver nods.

"What will we do with her?" asks one of the men, sitting in the seat just ahead.

"Send her to the Cellar and hope she never sees the light of day." Leigh grins, which entertains them and terrifies me.

"How long do you think she'll last?" asks one who resembles both Arek and Leigh. His hair is dark, almost black, but his eyes are the same green. When he speaks, he looks me over.

"I give her a day." The backs of Leigh's fingers make a Velcro sound as they scratch his never-ending five o'clock shadow. For a moment I toy with the idea that maybe he doesn't fully shave because of his weak jaw. I can't help but grin at the thought.

"You seem sure," the green-eyed man comments.

"I've made sure," Leigh gloats, still refusing to speak English.

It's impossible to hide my surprise as my head twists quickly toward him. Instantly, he is uncomfortable realizing that he's made a mistake.

"You've made sure? That I don't last?"

The green-eyed man snarls at me, "You've been lying to us?"

"I never lied about anything . . . you didn't ask." Their game has been upended and the full car is silent. "Tu resema lisol brotare Arek?" My voice comes out quiet, but strong.

Leigh is irritated, which makes his voice drop to a growl. "I thought you didn't remember."

"I still don't remember my life . . . but . . . yes . . . your language . . . came back to me quickly." I keep my attention on the man with green eyes. "Are you Arek's brother?"

He puffs up his chest as if this is a declaration of competition. "Yeah, I am. My name is Dillon, and I am his older . . . more handsome brother." The rest of the men chuckle.

I keep my reaction small but cutting, "I wouldn't be so sure." Even when he seethes, I continue to stare directly at him.

"I'd be careful . . . really careful, Willow," Dillon snaps.

"It's Remy," I whisper, more to myself than to them. I am showing signs of change, I know that. The frightened Willow is disappearing and regardless of how slow it may be, it is still happening. At the beginning, Remy felt like an intruder every time she showed up, but now Willow has moments of feeling like a stranger.

In perfect Velieri, I whisper, "Will we go straight to the Cellar?"

Leigh won't look at me. "Yes."

"What will it be like?" I ask quietly.

"You don't remember?" Dillon asks.

"I was there?"

"Just before you were executed."

"How long was I there?"

"A month, maybe more. Enough that I was sure it made an impact." Dillon grins.

So, I have lived through the Cellar before? I try to think hard, but nothing comes. *Why can't I remember?*

Leigh grumbles. "Don't let that confuse you . . . you are despised there. You will still have to fight, but this time," he picks up my arm, "you are weak and powerless."

"Take a look," the driver warns Leigh.

The Cellar's protective walls stand nearly thirty feet tall all the way around the block. The height of these dense barriers soars to the sky so that you cannot see the actual prison from the outside. They are made of metal and stone with large insets where modern sculptures are displayed every thirty feet. Several watch towers with guns at the ready are staggered the entire distance.

Large sliding doors slowly open to let us in, but a massive crowd, chanting and holding signs, forces the driver to slow down then eventually stop. "I'm sorry, sir."

The masses have now surrounded our vehicle and are trying to see through the heavily tinted windows. They holler, bang on the cars—some even jump on the hood—while screaming profanities at us and one another. Some hold signs that read, "Free Her!" But there are plenty of signs that read, "Kill her!" "Feed the Traitor to the Wolves!" and "Send her back to hell!"

"Don't stop . . . run over them if you have to," Leigh growls. The driver continues at a slow crawl until the mob reluctantly parts. With a high-pitched squeal and a heavy whirring sound, the wall opens up to reveal the Cellar in all its terrifying grandness. It is obviously a city of its own.

Instantly the mob, pressing up against the car, rushes in. I notice guards yelling at the aggressive people, but they are ignored as a SWAT team exits the Cellar to forcibly control the situation.

"Whose idea was it to invite the world?" Leigh pulls out his phone.

"Covey's," Dillon replies.

Prophet Covey is one of the five prophets who has been against me from the beginning. I notice Leigh's agitation, which tells me that there may be a crack in the chain of the Powers, and I take note of it. Covey wants the world to see, but Leigh prefers things quiet—I'm not sure which is more dangerous.

I peer up as we follow the driveway. It's hard to decide whether the magnificent brick building was an old insane asylum or a massive train station. The structure has crumbling towers that I imagine once served as powerful defenses against those hoping to get in . . . or out. Tourists might consider this a sight to see or even visit, however, I know that inside these walls is the secret prison—and somewhere within its darkest dungeons, lies my immediate future.

"Head to the back," Leigh instructs the driver then finally looks me in the eye. "Get yourself prepared for the lowest, most evil offenders because they all wait behind these walls."

Dillon continues when his father doesn't. "Think about the most infamous of the Epheme criminals—Jeffrey Dahmer, Charles Manson, Ted Bundy. They grew old in those prisons. They got weak just as any old man and the evil was no longer able to use them." He tended to pop his knuckles. I'd already seen him do it several times. "That's not how it is here. Imagine criminals never growing old. Never getting weak. Never losing their drive." Just as he finishes, lightning cracks across the sky and the thunder rumbles shortly after.

I peek behind me to make sure Arek is still there—he is.

We take the driveway to the back, which takes several minutes, but the rioters never cease.

"Who are all of these people?" I ask.

Dillon shrugs, "Reds, Rebels . . . anyone who knows about you already. It's against the law at this moment for anyone to share anything about you. The Reds and Powers can't take the chance of the world hearing about your return."

"Aita shared something . . ." I say quietly.

Leigh responds, "She was taken in and questioned, but Kenichi made sure she was released."

Two men suddenly hit my window with their bodies as they turn on each other. "Everyone's so angry . . . so divided."

Leigh shakes his head. "Is the world capable of anything else anymore?" He looks at the driver, "Stop as close as you can next to the door." Dread looms as the car comes to a stop. "Get out," Leigh commands.

The door opens next to me and a soft hand touches my shoulder. I look up and relief floods my soul when Arek is there and whispers, "Hey."

"Hi," I whisper.

Leigh and Dillon hurry toward him. "You shouldn't be here," Leigh says.

Arek ignores his father and leans closer to me. "Come on." I can't move easily with my hands behind my back, so he wraps his arms around my waist and pulls me out. "Stay by my side," he warns. Just as my feet touch the ground, Dillon challenges him. The brothers go chest to chest and nose to nose, while the crowd erupts. "Do you want to fight me right now, brother?" Arek, who stands just a bit taller, with a wider girth of his chest and arms, shows no fear of his older brother and finally, Dillon relents.

The crowd roars when they see me. "Send her to Hell!" the crowd yells. "The Prophecy is now!" the others chant. Clashing sides make the air thick with rage so heavy that nothing will ever see resolve within it. It is more and more obvious how divided the Velieri world is. *If this is what happens within our own kind, how do we ever find a solution with the Ephemes?* A little girl sitting on her father's shoulders holds a sign that says, "I believe in you, Remy." This is another moment when my heart is at odds with my mind.

The enormous crowd pushes Kilon until he falls back against me. Arek tries to hold me upright while Kilon gets his footing. With a guttural roar, Kilon pushes back, moving the masses nearly by himself.

"Firen me gann!" Kilon yells to "let us through," from the depths of his thick chest. There is so much power behind his voice, it startles even me. "Firen me gann, nei!"

The crowd splits as Arek uses his broad body to press through. Arms reach for me, fingernails scratch my skin, people yell vulgar words, and I feel the spray of their spit.

Others cry, "Free Remy!"

As the tensions grow, the two sides lash out at each other. They explode into a brawl. The SWAT team tries to find control, but to no avail. We gain only inches at a time toward the doors.

I notice a man who has climbed atop a lamppost and in seconds jumps over the crowd. He lands on top of me, forcing my knees to buckle. Arek and Sassi angrily rip him away, which excites everyone even more. Sassi easily gains control over him, then passes him off to Kilon as Arek pulls me through.

The fighting continues—men with men, women with women, women with men. Leigh yells to a soldier standing on a high tower who picks up the phone. In moments, the doors we are trying so desperately to reach burst open and several more armed guards run out. They separate to reveal two large fire hoses. With a pull of the lever, the painful blast sprays the crowd. Immediately, people struggle to get away.

This allows us to battle through and we make it inside, leaving the crowd behind. Instantly, I am overwhelmed by the foul stench of these dark halls, but there is something more. It does not apply to my human senses, rather the air is so thick I cannot breathe. Instantly my mind and soul are enslaved to a battle taking place within these walls.

I change my mind . . . I'll deal with what's outside. Everyone's warnings of this place flash back through my mind. There is something bigger here, something more dangerous.

I'm not ready. I'm going to lose this war.

2

The foul smell of the hall forces me to press my nose into my shoulder, as several guards struggle to close the door without catching people's arms and legs. Finally, they lock the doors. Lights flicker above us, which at least hides the dark things in every corner, and somewhere is the sound of dripping water, which casts my attention to the mold covered, stone walls.

Leigh laughs when he looks at me. "Did you think this would be a five-star hotel?" He turns to Arek, Sassi, and Kilon. "It's time for you to go."

"By whose order?" Arek asks. "I am the second in command of the Protectors. It's my job and my right to be here."

Leigh stares at his son for a moment. "Fine. You can stay. They go. Why does a criminal need her bodyguards?"

Sassi takes me in her arms and whispers in my ear, "Don't stop fighting." When she steps away, Kilon places his hands on my face until his thumbs rest at my temples. He looks at me carefully, "We'll get you out of here. I promise you." Then he pulls me to his chest and gathers me into his tight fatherly embrace.

Then, as Kilon and Sassi slip out a different way, a tear drops unexpectedly down my cheek. Without them, without their strength, the hall seems much smaller and darker.

Finally, Leigh marches on without a word, expecting us to follow.

His guards surround us while Arek looks at me and runs his hand down my arm. "Let's go," Leigh barks.

Through a small rectangular window on my right, we can see beyond the mob to where a calm group of people with colorful hair, rings in their cheeks and eyebrows, and black clothing adorned with chains wait.

"They were at the court in Japan." I remember clearly. Each one of them stands with their hands clasped together in front of them. "Who are they?"

"They are the Fidelis. You helped them," Arek says quietly so that no one will hear.

"Fidelis . . . that means loyal," I whisper. The skin creases around his eyes as he grins and nods. "Why did they need my help?"

"Let's just say that they didn't follow the rules . . ." He puts a finger to his lips, warning me to be quiet, then he leans into my ear, "Be careful what you say in here."

"Let's move," Leigh commands.

Reluctantly, I leave the Fidelis, but just before I do one of them points to the window. Together, when they see me looking out, they pound their chests three times.

"They believe in you, because you believed in them," Arek whispers in my ear.

Down the hall there is a cast iron door that looks as though it has gone through hell and back. The farther we go, the more desperate I am for us to turn around and go back outside. Maybe this is hell.

Then I hear something. It is faint at first, then grows. Tormented cries and screams seep through the mold-stained walls and fill the corridor with lamented echoes. My breath becomes rapid until everyone is staring at me.

"Maybe now you're starting to understand?" Leigh says as they watch me hyperventilate. His indifference frightens me.

"You'll be okay," Arek whispers.

"What are those screams?" I ask.

Arek's eyes grow concerned. "Willow, you have to protect yourself. There is no sound . . . there are no screams."

My eyes are wide when I turn to him. The cries are so invasive, I want to press my palms to my ears even though I can't. "Are you sure?"

"I am. Find your rhythm."

"Is it Navin?"

"No. It's the Cellar." There's resolve in his eyes. "You have to be on guard. Do you hear me? As if Navin is in every corner . . . there will be things that you experience here . . . a lot of power . . . a lot of evil. Protect yourself—"

"You have many days, weeks, if not months in here," Leigh interrupts. He hisses through closed teeth and open lips, "If you enter this place trembling, there will be no pity."

Arek raises his hand and rests it on my neck as Dillon knocks on the door with his ring. My chest swells until my ribs ache. From a rectangular peephole at eye level, a piece of metal slides open and two dark eyes look through from the other side. The man peers at Leigh and then the screech of an un-oiled hinge echoes. The door opens and a very large man ducks under the doorjamb to join us. His nearly shaved head is darker than the walls. He closes the door behind him, and it mutes the wails of distress.

"I thought it was a lie," he says with an accent I don't recognize, as he smiles. "But here you are. It's my pleasure to meet you, Remy. I'm Thire."

"Thank you, Thire."

Arek clearly knows him and shakes his hand. "It's good to see you're still here."

Thire places a large hand on Arek's shoulder. "I'll take care of her as best I can."

Arek turns to me. "Stay close to Thire. At all times, do your best to be near him."

I nod.

"Follow me," Thire says. We pass through the metal door, and I am immediately overwhelmed by the rush of earthy, damp, and rotting stench. It upsets my empty stomach.

Thire notices my reaction. "We don't typically have people enter here, but those in charge have asked me to do things differently for you. I'm sorry about that."

The lower levels of the Cellar remind me of a catacomb or dungeon as we follow halls that haven't seen daylight in centuries. It takes everything I have to ignore the sights and smells as each door leads further into the tragic secrets of an underworld. The stink of human rot and waste perforates my skin until I battle the urge to gag. Pressing my face into Arek's shoulder is the only fix.

We enter a large room with cages hanging from every side, where dirty and beaten men and women wait. Guards walk through the room taunting the prisoners with long metal sticks, forcing them to press against the backs of the cages. I make eye contact with one of the women prisoners and instantly I can feel warmth and discomfort in my chest.

"There are rules to how you treat people," I speak out.

Leigh turns. "What about Hitler? Should we have had rules for how we treated him? When he had none for anyone else?"

"These people are as bad as Hitler?" My tone is condescending.

Dillon and Leigh look at each other with confusion. "These people?" Dillon asks. "What people?"

I survey the guards and inmates in cages. They stare at me as though they expect my help. "The criminals in these cages . . ."

Leigh laughs and looks at Arek. "And I'm supposed to believe she's not Remona?"

Arek glances at Thire as we move on, then he leans his mouth to my ear. "There's no one in those cages . . . they haven't used these rooms in a hundred years."

My feet stop, cemented to the ground, while the woman in the cage rocks back and forth, looking at me. The air is thick, but it is more than humidity. A shiver runs up my spine, then down as the room pulses. It is quite possible it's my heart pounding, maybe even my head, but it doesn't matter since I can feel it through my toes. There are forces happening that I can't explain. Evil resides here. There is a fire roaring in the corner, where more than twenty metal rods stick out. Hanging from each wall are chains. There are no windows as two military guards quickly mop the red splatter from the floor. When they squeeze the mops, red pours into buckets.

"You can't see this?" I am breathless.

"No," Arek says softly.

"Even the guards in blue uniforms?"

Thire slows his pace beside me. "Guards haven't worn blue uniforms here in thirty or forty years at least."

It is impossible now to look anywhere else. No one has explained any of this to me. *Why would I be the only one to see this?*

"Keep up, Miss Landolin," Leigh scoffs when they wait for me to exit the chamber.

"I believe it's Mrs. Rykor," I add.

"I wouldn't be so sure of that." Leigh turns his head until I can see his profile.

Arek doesn't explain anything as we continue through several halls and down stairways; the room we enter seems to be cleaner, lighter, and remodeled. It has been designed in the style of the original era in which it was built, but clearly renovated. Green marble floors extend through this room, which has white walls and elegant molding. The cathedral windows are stained glass, and the bookcases are built in from ceiling to floor.

"Where are we?" I ask.

Leigh's aged eyes always seem tired. "The Powers and Prophets are waiting for you . . . through there." He points to the ominous double doors.

3

Several new guards lead us into a grand courtroom that could be in Rome. Painted murals cover the walls between white beams that hold up a forty-foot-high ceiling. My eyes survey the beauty of it all. The majesty of this palace, this fortress, where lives are condemned, holds so much irony as I face the next sentencing.

There are five large ostentatious chairs on a platform with four small steps to ascend. Just in front of these chairs is a wooden barrier that separates them from us. I notice a small podium facing these chairs, then another on the right. There are rows and rows of people seated in pews. The media is there. I recognize faces.

The moment I walk in, the crowd roars, just a bit more controlled than the outside gathering.

"Who is my lawyer?" I ask Arek.

"He is preparing the case in the next room," Arek presses his mouth to my ear so that I can hear him over the anxious throng. "He jumped on a plane last night. He's one of the closest friends we have."

"Well, there's no better time to have a lawyer as a friend, I guess."

"He'll take care of you . . . I promise," Arek says quickly. "He doesn't care that you don't know him . . . he knows Remy and," Arek says with a smile, "she's stubborn. She'll come back. She's coming back."

I watch Arek for just a moment.

"What?" he asks.

"How do I know who is for me or who is against me?"

Arek pulls me to the corner of the room, even though this irritates Leigh. I can't help but feel uncomfortable under my father-in-law's glare. "Look at me," Arek says forcefully. "You have to read people."

"How?"

Arek asks me, "Am I for you or against you?"

"For me."

"How did you know?" I watch him. He wants me to answer the question, but I can't. "When you first saw me . . . were you ever afraid?"

I think back to the stranger staring at me from the sidewalk across the street in San Francisco. "No."

"Why? I was a man you didn't know . . . watching you."

"I don't know. I could tell, I guess."

"How?"

"I don't—"

He interrupts. "Stop saying you don't know. Yes, you do."

"My body didn't get scared. There was just something about you that I trusted from the very beginning." My face grows hot with emotion.

"Everyone has the ability to sense good and bad energy . . . Velieri just do it better—the longer you practice, and the more you listen, the easier it becomes." He breathes in with confidence. "And you will know. You knew that Navin was against you. How?"

"Everything about him . . . I don't know. I could just feel it."

"You see . . . you were already learning to read people. You have been since you were born, and it only grows as you get older. Listen to me, Remy. If you are sent back to the Cellar without us, then you must use this. Do you understand me?"

"Yes."

"Our first instincts are usually right. Trust your gut. And remember how to block your mind. Don't stop doing that. The rhythm will save you."

The doors across the room open, which quiets everyone. The Prophets enter in white robes followed by the thirty-five representatives of the seven Powers.

"Caynan has no more time," Arek whispers to Kilon. With a nod, Kilon runs out.

"Do the Powers hate me as much as the Prophets?" I ask.

Arek grins and says, "Some. The Powers are voted in by the people to represent each territory of Velieri. Each line gets a percentage of vote . . . it's a convoluted mess. But we have been able to get a few with morals and ethics. A few."

When a loud bell rings to quiet everyone, Leigh takes my arm. "Let's go. It's time." His touch is so different—so forceful. We walk across the marble floor, and he directs me toward the podium. "Stand up there."

I obey.

Leigh clears his throat behind me. "Remona Landolin, per your request."

When the Prophets turn to me, I grow desperately uncomfortable. There is so much power staring me down, taking me in. Prophet Covey is already gloating at the sight of me in handcuffs. "We knew we'd get you here. It was only a matter of time," he says.

The large doors burst open, distracting the court. A man in a suit follows Kilon inside. He enters with his head down as he practically devours the paperwork in his hand. He doesn't even notice that he has interrupted the proceedings until he is nearly falling over the podium where I am. Finally, he looks up. His brown eyes command the room, and his umber skin is like silk.

"Remy," he says, smiling with recognition. "It's been too long."

"Hi." The word comes out, but it does not disguise the fear in every cell of my body.

"I'm going to take care of this . . . whether today or tomorrow . . . I will take care of this, okay?" I am pulled in by his kindness and notice the dimples on his cheeks as he smiles. "Remy," he leans forward to keep what he says between us, "just breathe. I got you," he says. "I got you." He turns quickly to the Powers and Prophets. "Your honors, I apologize for the interruption." His words are covered with a thick layer of charisma and a beautiful smile. "But I have been unable to connect with my client before standing here. Might we have a few minutes?"

"Unfortunately, what we have to say will not take but seconds," says the charmless Prophet Covey.

Prophet Jenner is elegant in her white robe. She has wrapped her natural curls in a gele and, while her beauty is evident, I also see her disgust for Prophet Covey. She leans forward and looks past Prophet Zelner. "Have we not come here to figure out the path? To come together to decide what is best for a woman who knows very little about what it's like within these walls."

"Oh, come on, we haven't given her enough time? Really, Prophet Jenner?" Covey shakes his head. "Considering both the volatile nature of this case, and the fact that the news of Remy's return has reached the general populous, we see no other alternative but to incarcerate her immediately."

Prophet Jenner jumps to her feet just as the crowd erupts. "Wait a minute! You do not make the rules, Prophet Covey."

"We've gotten where we are without you." He refuses to look at her—she is the newest of the Prophets appointed by Gyre and Kenichi.

She chuckles, "Well, then . . . thank God I've come along."

The audience quietly laughs. Her nature quickly takes ownership of the room. "Caynan, take a moment."

Caynan nods, "Thank you, Prophet Jenner. Your honors, everyone has the right to council and trial."

Prophet Hawking interrupts. Her red hair hangs loosely down her back and her skin is nearly the same color as her robe. "We are in a bit of an unusual situation . . . might you say, Mr. Tate? Your client has already been tried, found guilty, been executed, and now stands before us alive. We have thousands of people outside demanding justice—you see our dilemma. If we do not take proper action, we might have an uprising on our hands. Is this what you want, Mr. Tate? An uprising?"

Caynan raises his eyebrows and shoulders dramatically as if an uprising isn't such a bad idea. "Well . . . if you're gonna ask me, I—"

"Forget it! No one is asking you." Prophet Hawking's icy voice tells me this isn't the first time Caynan has caused problems.

Prophet Jenner calls out, "Caynan, continue, but make it quick."

"My client is not the same woman who stood before you thirty-three years ago. She cannot remember much of anything. How can we imprison her—in the Cellar of all places—if she has no memory of her past life and lacks her previous abilities?" Caynan looks at me quickly with concern and I'm not sure why until he says, "She will be killed in the Cellar. Not one of you can deny this. And if she isn't killed, she won't be the same."

Zelner, the youngest of the prophets, who looks more like an internet technician than one to Prophesy, shakes his head. "One woman's life is not worth the loss of thousands in a rebellion."

Prophet Jenner raises her voice confidently. "Yes, let's leave it to a man to tell us what a woman's life is worth." Most of the crowd chatters and chuckles from her obvious insult. She stares fearlessly at Covey. "Where's Navin, Prophet Covey? Why are we more worried about Remona Landolin when the rebels have defied every mandate we've tried to place on them?" Half the crowd hollers in agreement.

A loud boom fills the air, forcing the room to quiet. I turn to see Covey has angrily pounded the table with his fist.

"That's quite a talent," I whisper to Caynan, which makes him grin.

Caynan continues, "Let's look at *Hill vs. New Port* back in 1943. They were forced to allow Mr. New Port time." He hands papers to the security guard, who passes them to the Prophets and Powers.

Several people in the court yell and beg for my release, but I don't deny that there is also a palpable loathing and hate directed my way.

"Regardless, Mr. Tate," Prophet Hawking hollers over the crowd. "There is no injustice. I don't believe you need to be reminded of the crime for which she was found guilty, or the lack of evidence proving her innocence." Her face appears to have quite possibly been chiseled out of granite—hardly moving even when speaking with vexation.

Caynan won't budge. His eyes do not blink, and his chin remains upright, and I am moved by his resolve. "No, your honors," he says, his strong voice potent, "I do not need to be reminded of this—that is true. But perhaps you have forgotten that I did not have sufficient time to provide such evidence."

"Caynan, such drama as usual," Zelner plays to the crowd. A faint memory flashes in my mind—almost like a daydream, and I recall Zelner's first name is Mattius. Mattius Zelner, the second to the last ordained Prophet.

Suddenly, Leigh speaks from across the room. His sallow skin looks even more yellow under the courtroom lights. He steps forward with his eyes on Caynan. "Besides, she does remember. On the way over, she made it known that she understands and can speak every bit of Velieri."

Every Prophet, each with his or her own curious or righteous expression, turns to me as blithering fills the courtroom. "Is this true?" one of them asks. Thirty-five representatives of the Powers— the most powerful Velieri in the world—and the five Prophets all stare at me. *No pressure.* My mouth is suddenly so dry it makes a funny noise when I try to use my tongue. I look at Caynan, "They're just waiting for me to make a mistake."

"At this point, you can't make a mistake. Look Remy, they have their mind made up about you. But you have to trust me . . . I will get you out of this . . . it may not be today, but I will." He touches my hand, which forces a breath to escape from my lips. "You can't lie, lies don't work with Velieri anyhow. Just tell them the truth."

I hesitate, then turn to the Powers, trying my best to avert my eyes. "Yes. I do recall some memories of my father, Kenichi, and Mak. I can also speak and understand Velieri. I cannot remember much else. Leigh has failed to mention that this is the extent of it. I know nothing else."

Covey and his white mustache turn all the way around to the Powers with a smile. "Need we say more? She is clearly Remona and if we let her go, she stays in charge of all our people's emotions . . . causing the same trouble she did before."

Arek calls out, "Your people?"

Covey shoots him an angry stare. "I'll have you removed, Mr. Rykor . . . again."

Arek steps forward, to which Caynan responds under his breath, "Here we go again." Caynan jumps over the small pony wall to get in front of Arek. "There's no need for that, Prophet Covey." Caynan looks into Arek's eyes forcefully. "Let me handle this, Arek. Stand down, friend."

Arek glares at Covey but seems to be stalled for the moment.

Caynan finally returns to stand beside me. Just as he is about to speak, Zelner, who pushes up his silver rimmed glasses along his nose, says, "We're sorry, Mr. Tate. We have to do what's best for the people and you must trust that we know what's best."

Leigh tells his guards, "Take her to her cell."

"She will die here!" Caynan yells. "Do you wish to be responsible for that?"

"Mr. Tate, are you suggesting that this prison is not adequately managed?" Leigh asks.

Caynan laughs angrily. "Once again the Prophets rule while we must bow down, and you turn a blind eye to the abomination that the Cellar has become."

"I would be careful, Mr. Tate," Hawking says. "You do not want to lose what good favor you have left. Your actions today may have direct influence on Miss Landolin's sentencing in two days."

"But you cannot possibly leave her without protection. Even you must realize how dangerous it will be for her!" Caynan's eyes are wide with anger.

"Take her!" Covey yells to the guards.

"Covey!" Prophet Jenner yells, as does Prophet Mannon, the man who resembles Santa Claus, but has stayed nearly silent. "Stop!"

Covey looks at Mannon and Jenner. "I will have you stripped, do you understand me?"

The guards forcefully grab me. In an instant, the courtroom is in chaos. People rush from every direction. Caynan stands in front of me with his back nearly wrapped around my chest. Arek is struggling to get to my side, although many of Leigh's men have already prevented him and Kilon from getting any closer.

"What will happen to me?" I ask Caynan as they pull me away. He doesn't hear me in the commotion. "Caynan! What will happen?" I cry out as they yank me away from everyone I know.

The Powers stand paralyzed, as the room explodes into chaos.

"Do not do this!" Caynan yells again and again. Pleading seems to be his only tactic now, but it falls on deaf ears. The judges are resolved in their decision. "Wait!" Caynan bellows. This causes a slight halt to everyone's steps, and he has everyone's attention.

"Tell me now, Covey, Hawking . . . Zelner! Is this not the same woman who you once claimed would bring unity to our world? When she was born, did you not believe that she was the prophesied chosen one? Were your claims about her false?" The vein in Caynan's forehead is protruding. "According to the law, you must make your vote publicly known. Which of you believes she is innocent? Show everyone! Stand to your feet!"

Mannon and Jenner stand. As my eyes connect with Prophet Jenner, my mind suddenly flashes with a memory.

"Remona, you are my greatest concern." She is more beautiful as I draw closer. Her dark skin glimmers under the heat of summer as we walk down a hallway between white pillars. Her black suit fits perfectly as she pushes her large sunglasses on her nose. She has kind eyes and a sweet smile.

I touch her shoulder. "Prophet Jenner, there is no need to worry about me, I can handle myself . . . and anyone else who comes along."

She smiles—although I can tell that this is not what she wants to hear. "That's what I am afraid of. Remy, you are not invincible."

"Maybe not." I shrug.

"I believe in you, but there are many who would like nothing more than to see you suffer."

"Good always wins, right?" I look at her with a smile and nudge her shoulder with mine.

In the courtroom, I see Prophet Jenner with a new sense of appreciation. The expression on her face shows the same concern as before. I nod and she nods back, but ever so subtly so that the rest of the room doesn't see.

Covey shakes his head, "We have the majority; and you, Sir Caynan, know that is all we need."

"And the Powers? Are all of you against her? Or are there some amongst you that have the guts to stand for justice?"

Caynan doesn't stop there. He looks around the entire room and asks the same questions to the audience. Those who support me stand, including nearly half of the Powers. My father, Sassi, Peter, Beckah, and Geo are all tense in the back of the courtroom.

The crowd's yells blend into one consuming roar.

"This is outrageous," I hear a man's voice from my left. "Enough!" Leigh yells to try and quiet the room.

Arek is still fighting to get away from Leigh's men and his chest is rising and falling with the vigor of a wild beast. I can't stop looking at him. His eyes fall on mine.

"Take her to a cell," Leigh commands.

Caynan's voice cuts through the roar: "I ask that I am able to accompany her to her cell and there I will be able to get reacquainted with her since I hadn't the time before this useful meeting." His words drip with sarcasm.

"Do as you like, Mr. Tate. Just make sure that she gets to her cell," Leigh says.

"And I ask that she gets protection," Caynan continues.

"Are we to give every inmate protection now? Special favors for an Electi? I think not, Mr. Tate," Hawking explains. Her eyes are stern and intense, adding a harshness to her many years. "Two days until her sentencing. We will reconvene then."

The Powers and Prophets exit the room as quickly as they came, while guards surround me.

"What will happen?" I cry again. This time Caynan hears me.

"I'm coming with you," Caynan says calmly, as he gathers his things.

The guards push me through the courtroom toward the door. Shouting continues from all directions, but I am shoved through anyway. Kilon yells across the mass of people, "Remy!"

I turn. Kilon pounds his chest three times, as do many others throughout the room. My eyes burn with emotion.

Arek waits in the hall. The guards won't let him through at first, until Thire and Brice—a guard from the courts in Japan—appear and take over the lead.

"They won't let me come with you," he tells me. "Caynan will go. He will stay if he can." I nod. "We'll get you out of here. I promise." His hand is on my face, and I lean into it as tears creep uncomfortably close to the edge.

"I'm sorry sir, but we have to go," Thire explains as he points at the erupting masses behind.

As they walk me through the halls, I keep my eyes on Arek for as long as I can. The loneliness begins the moment I turn the first corner.

4

The farther away Arek is, the emptier I become. My stomach swirls with nerves and fear. I can still hear the cries of the crowd, where Arek and the others remain, but with each step the sound dulls.

Even though Thire and Caynan walk beside me, several unfamiliar guards lead us through the sinister halls of the antiquated asylum. It's hard to tell whether they are there to protect me, or everyone else.

This part of the Cellar has recently been redone with nearly ten-foot-high doors that pass by every twelve feet and I can count nearly seventeen of them. Though the black and white checkered tile floors are newly laid and the ceilings reach high with ducts and pipes crawling out like arms, it is the stained glass, ivy-covered cathedral windows that tell of the Cellar's age.

"This is a fancy place for criminals," I finally say.

Caynan grins. "Criminals aren't kept here. We are walking through the main hall where several government departments have their offices. The Correctional Territory Authority, or what we like to call the CTA, has a home here. As do the Reds, and the Protectors."

"Do the Prophets and the Powers have offices here also?"

Thire and Caynan both laugh. Caynan answers, "No." He turns to me with a sarcastic eye. "The Powers and the Prophets? Be near such vile men and women? No. Most of them sit high on a mountain of cash and gluttony somewhere." He turns to the wall where a painting of a suited man hangs and speaks to it. "Just kidding, Prophet Covey."

I peer around Caynan's shoulder at the painting. "That doesn't look like Covey."

"It's not." He raises his finger and points to the eyes of the painting. When I look closer, it is easier to see the cut-out holes within the eyes of the painted man. Caynan warns me with a severe stare, "Cameras are always watching and listening."

Suddenly, I pay attention to every picture as we pass. Caynan notices and smiles. "You're not quite Remy . . . huh?"

"No. Didn't Arek tell you?"

Caynan breathes in, clearly privy to many of Arek's private thoughts. "He hasn't said much actually."

"But you're close friends?"

"Yeah. Here's what you need to know about Arek. He never . . . ever . . . accepts a fight without knowing he will win. And ever since this all began . . . the fight is for you. You're what he's fighting for right now . . . there's no time for anything else."

"I know he's disappointed that I'm not her."

"Don't confuse fear with disappointment, Remy. This place . . . he's afraid he's sent you off to the wolves. Remy was strong and capable and Arek knows how the Cellar haunts. People don't leave the same. This is the only reason he wishes a bit more of Remy was in there." He stops for a moment, rubs his cheek, then his kind eyes turn to me. "The walls in every Cellar don't just keep criminals in . . . their sins soak into the air until it's hard to breathe. His one goal was to keep you from that . . . and he lost. He hates to lose."

The guards in front of us separate when we reach an elevator. The first guard looks at Thire. "We won't be continuing with you, sir."

Thire nods as the elevator doors open and we step inside. When we turn around, I see Meryl walking through the halls. My mind returns to him pulling me from the water and leading me to the Bryer.

"What is Meryl doing here?" I ask with concern.

There is a moment of silence before I hear Thire breathe, then continue. "Meryl sometimes guards the top floor. It's usually when someone with power has requested him."

"Would Leigh have requested him?" I ask as the doors of the elevator close, but not before Meryl catches a glimpse of me and smiles.

"Anything is possible," Thire says.

After several floors, the doors open to a new hall. It is vastly different than the one we just left. Twenty feet ahead, an extremely tall blonde woman with a pixie cut stands behind a glass barrier. Behind this glass barrier is a computer designed to exist within it. Her hand swipes and taps the display on the clear wall.

"Thire," she says with a smokers growl, "you come first. Then Landolin, followed by Caynan . . . and Brice."

Thire quickly removes all his weapons and sets them inside a clear glass drawer that opens from the wall. He then steps in front of the wall as a blue light appears above his head and slowly runs down his body; a red light scans his valuables in the glass drawer. The woman looks at him when the scanning is done. "You have a slight rise in temp at 98.8. If it goes any higher, you will be unable to continue this week."

Thire rolls his eyes. "It's where my temperature naturally sits, Cal," he says, as though they do this every day. She seems indifferent to his irritation.

"It says you've been in territory eleven within the last three weeks," she says.

"Cal . . . my wife's mother needed—" Thire begins to explain.

I can't hear what Thire says when Caynan speaks calmly in my ear. "Velieri and Ephemes have a marker in our skin that was placed there when we were born. These markers aren't supposed to be able to track everything you do . . ." Caynan shrugs and lifts an eyebrow as if he doesn't believe it. "Only one section of the government should have access to this information . . . or so they tell us . . . and these markers simply connect with towers to inform them when someone has entered a territory too many times. None of us are convinced the government doesn't use these markers for more than just territory control."

"Why does it matter if he's been in territory eleven?" I ask.

"We aren't allowed to go into certain territories if we were there before our last relocation . . . or it's just not looked upon well. Remember, we must relocate every thirty years or so. After three thirty-year periods, this resets, and we can enter territories we've been before. This is only with extremely populated areas."

Thire rests his head on the glass wall with irritation. "Cal . . . let me pass. Arek has asked that I stay with her."

Caynan looks at me. "The security on this level is a bit more rigorous."

"Why?"

Caynan seems uncomfortable. "This level has the most dangerous criminals."

Finally, Cal turns to Caynan and points at a cupboard near the elevator. "Put them on her."

Caynan shakes his head. "Cal . . . no. She won't do anything. Her hands are tied."

"None of you will go past this point if she doesn't put them in." Cal seems to have reached the end of her patience. "She will keep them in until you reach section four. Do you understand?" The tough woman raises an eyebrow.

Caynan relents and opens a cupboard nearby, from which he pulls out some ear buds. The kind I would use to go for a run . . . if I did that sort of thing. He puts them in my ears. "Not too much . . .," he says to Cal. "She's not what she used to be."

Cal swipes and taps the computer in front of her on the glass wall until suddenly sound fills my ears. It starts as just beeping and small enough to handle, until Cal glides her finger up the wall while watching me carefully. It takes only seconds before my body seizes. Every muscle tenses as though I've just been tazed. My fingers turn rigid and curl in. Whatever these earpieces are, they send me to the ground.

"Cal!" Caynan yells.

She pulls it back in a hurry. The shock lessens, until my muscles stop seizing and Caynan can pull me to my feet.

"Whoa, okay," Cal says. "I guess she's not who she used to be."

When Cal is finally able to find the proper setting, I realize what these earpieces are supposed to do—my body can move, but not the same. My brain fogs, my body is tight, and my feet take microscopic steps. Even speaking would be difficult at this moment. After we each stand in front of the blue light, Cal lets us in, one at a time.

We pass through three sections of guards before we reach section four. Thankfully, Caynan takes the earbuds out and hands them to the guard. Once again, I have full control of my body and I shake out my hands. The muscles along my shoulders and forearms feel like blocks of wood from tension.

Caynan sees the discomfort on my face and begins to rub out my muscles. "I'm sorry, Remy. I forget that you don't know what's going to happen and how to work with it."

I look into his kind eyes. "Well, let me remind you . . . I don't know what's going to happen or how to work with it."

Unexpectedly, his face turns into watercolor as tears collect in my eyes. I smile at him, "I've never wanted Arek so much in my life."

He grins, "Yet you don't remember him?"

"Not like a wife should."

He chuckles as though being told of some irony, "Only you two."

"What?" I ask him.

"Only you would still be in love even though you don't remember your life together," he winks.

Thire nods, then begins to place his hand on the biometric fingerprint lock of section four, but stops. "Are you ready?"

"I don't know." The tear escapes down my cheek, but this irritates me and I stand up straight. "I have no choice."

Caynan shakes his head at Thire then turns to me. "Remy, the moment we walk in there . . ." he hesitates, "I don't even know how to prepare you. It affects everyone in different ways. There's no telling what it can do to you . . . just stay close to us and let me get you to your room. If I can do that . . . it's best." He studies me. "I don't mean to scare you."

"Let's go," I say to Thire. "Just get me there."

Thire's hand presses against the glass pad and the door slides open. Instantly, I know I've made a mistake.

5

Several guards line the hall. Each door is black iron and the walls are large cement cinderblock. The vile air hits me as the door rolls away, and it's nearly impossible to pay attention to detail. The best I can describe it, is what it feels for the evil—so grotesque—waiting for warm bodies to enter as they search for the nearest soul to poison. They've been clawing at the door hungry and angry for fresh air themselves. It's like being barraged with a thousand bullets at once. Whether they come from the past or present—it doesn't matter—the horrors that tread my skin don't want to be here and the intense feeling of desperation shakes me to the core. The breaking of men's and women's spirits, whether they are guilty or innocent, resounds in the air so loud that I cover my ears. My heart instantly races and it's difficult to walk. There is no existence of time when fighting these perversions; when you are in the depths it is impossible to know when it may end.

"Caynan," I moan as I drop to my knees.

"Don't look them in the eye," Caynan warns.

It is too late. The small window where food is delivered to criminals is open on every door and eyes peer out. At first it is only feelings . . . of dread, of desperation, and it is impossible to tell whether these emotions are mine or I have been hijacked.

Until I am completely lost.

The darkness is too much, and it pulls me within myself. It takes only moments before I am no longer in the Cellar, rather somewhere far worse . . . in the recesses of my mind. Everything turns to a draining blue and I no longer walk the halls of the Cellar. I am in a disheveled hallway that looks to be in a house. There are no lights, no sun, no windows, the walls are decaying and the floors creaking and it could even be that this place has gone through battle.

The pictures hanging on the walls follow me with their eyes as I pass, and I hear a sound . . . a demonic whisper saying, "Welcome home."

I stop walking when I see a shadow in the corner of the dark hall, lit only by an ominous glow. Something about it has eyes, and my body warns me to beware. Suddenly, the shadow runs along the wall toward me. In a flash, I retreat in terror. With every step the floor breaks. "You'll never leave," the voice whispers again. It could be the shadow speaking.

Racing through the hall, I skid to a stop when a figure, bent at the waist and too flexible to be human, runs out of a room. The shadow comes fast while this bent figure blocks my way. I want to scream, but no sound comes. I rush into a room off the side—my foot plunges into a hole and I fall. The only thing to protect me are my arms, and I throw them over my head to lay in wait. This feels very familiar, like the training with Geo before going to see Navin at the Bryer.

"Remy!" the whisper is gone, but a strong male voice calls out.

I look up. I am back in the hall of the Cellar and seven guards surround me like a shield. I can only see their backs. Caynan and Thire kneel before me as I'm curled up on the floor.

"Get her up!" Thire yells. They help me to my feet, yet there is no relief. Nothing can match this unearthly hell.

"It's too much, Caynan," I weep, unlike anything in years. "It's like it's mine. These demons are mine . . . not theirs."

"Keep a rhythm, Remy. We'll get you there as fast as we can."

There is no hope in a rhythm because I feel no hope at all. The eyes that peer at me, as we hurry through the hall, have no feeling left, but agenda and acceptance of their past sin. It is them. It is who they are.

It is me. It is who I am. Or is it? I can't remember anymore. There is no before and there will be no after, just this . . . darkness . . . forever.

One of the criminals stares directly into my eyes from his cell. I am unable to look away and I can feel him within my brain faster than I can control my thoughts. I look beside me as Caynan turns—his eyes no longer look normal, rather they are gray stone. The only eyes I've seen like this are Navin's, the first night he came to me in San Francisco.

I rip my arm from Caynan so hard that I fall back and hit the cement wall. His face distorts as he comes closer to me, until I have to cover my eyes from its grotesque nature.

"No!" I cry out.

Thire no longer is Thire, but something faceless and voiceless.

"Help me!" I cry out. No one can hear me. *Do I play dead or fight?* The monster Caynan has become reaches for me, but I kick aggressively with my unclasped legs, challenging the enemy in my sights.

The others handle me heavily, ripping and pressuring until my skin has a heartbeat. Just then, one of them reaches out and sticks something in my neck. In only seconds, the hall comes to a dark end and my body stops fighting.

They lift me, each malformed creature taking a foot and hand. The eyes from peepholes continue to watch as I hang emotionless and without fight.

What have I done? I think, as tears fall backward down my temples.

"Hey . . ." someone says to my left and when I turn to his rough and crackling voice, two red eyes glare at me from the nearest door. "Hey!" he calls again, "Look at me, you . . ." and he finishes with a long list of angry curses using my name in the middle.

"Shut your mouth, Luther." Thire hits the door with his stick and immediately Luther backs down.

"I just want to touch her . . . make myself known . . . and I will, Electi . . . I will!" Without a face to go with the voice, it is obvious that this man has little sanity left.

Thire steps close to the peephole with his chest raised, glowering so aggressively that Luther's eyes back away into the shadows and he says nothing more.

The heavy door opens. Two guards stand on the other side with large rifles in their arms. The heavy smell of mildew still fills my nose, and the air has turned cold. Not a crisp pleasant cold, but rather a morbid mortuary type cold. My body begins to shake, then jumps as the crash of the door closing behind me fills the hall.

"It'll be okay, Remy," Caynan whispers.

There are no windows. Heavy banging just ahead knocks a door nearly off its hinges.

"Stop!" Thire yells. "I'll send you to the fires."

Instantly, the prisoner backs away from the door and into the shadows just as Luther did, but not before he digs within my head. The medicine they've given me steals my emotion, which is their only gateway to my subconscious. I learned that from Navin when he held me and tried to use Ian to ride my emotions into the hidden parts of me. Right now, it's a strange combination of feeling the dread and fear, yet my body and mind cannot act on it. I'm numb.

I come to rest on a hard bed and cannot speak.

"Can you get me in here tomorrow?" Caynan asks of Thire.

"I'll do my best."

"We have to fix this . . ." after another moment, the warmth of someone's breath is on my ear. "I'm sorry, Remy. We'll fix this."

Then the darkness sweeps over my paralyzed body, as the door slams shut.

6

If the door remains closed, I am fine. The cell is empty, but for one metal cot, toilet, and sink . . . while the walls and floors are gray. I've done everything to keep myself entertained, yet now my body hurts as I've spent too long on the cement floor lobbing rolled up balls of material from the weathered mattress into a large chip in the floor.

The crank of the lock and squeal of the door fills the room. With swift hands I cover my head and ears and chant heavily. It doesn't matter. As the door opens, the demons sweep in like a rough wind. My voice scratches my dry throat as I chant louder and crawl into a protective ball. A soft and gentle hand on my arm grabs my attention. "Remy," he whispers.

I turn and Caynan's eyes smile at me. I notice the door is closed behind him and release my breath for the first time in what seems like minutes, then I grab his shoulders. He pulls me into his arms, "It's okay."

His expensive suit bunches between us, so I pull away. "I'm sorry, I'm ruining your perfection," I say as I press it back down.

When I look up, I see his eyes have changed. "What?" I ask.

He shakes his head. "You've always said that. Remy's one critique of me was that I took myself too seriously. She used to say, 'Ahhh, well we wouldn't want to ruin your perfection.'" His maroon suit is immaculately tailored. "You like it?" He gives a couple confident and proud poses, then helps me to my feet. "I knew there would be no way to warn you . . . People don't understand this place until they've experienced it."

We talk for a few minutes about his second home, where his Aboriginal ancestors of the Gugu-Badhun tribe called home, and that his love for fashion came from his grandmother. "She would say I chose to be a lawyer for the suits. But it's clearly not my defense skills. I couldn't keep you out of here. I'll be coming back when I can. You can tell me anything that you need, and I'll see if I can get it."

Just in front of us, as we sit on the bed, a leaf falls to the stone floor. It catches both of our attention, and we look up. The ceiling is nearly twenty feet high and there is one window. It is only the size of a piece of paper, like the ones I used to hand out by the thousands to my students. The whistle of a heavy wind rushes in, and again more dried leaves fall to the ground. The window is so high that not even standing on my bed or a chair would allow me to see through it.

"Arek tells me that you've remembered Briston."

"Yeah. Briston and Kenichi are who I remember most, but it's spotty . . . still. For example, I have pictures of my dad's blue eyes . . . with wrinkles . . . without. . . . And Mak, I remember so many things from our childhood to adulthood . . . but just bits and pieces. I want the whole thing. I want to be Remy."

"You are not Remy," he states.

"I know," I say with confusion.

"Just remember that. No matter what comes back to you . . . you are not Remy . . . not yet. You are not capable of what she was, so be careful."

"Thank you, Caynan, I realize this . . ."

"I need to be real with you. It is important that you stay in here. Do not leave. Thire will allow this, but you may need to find excuses with the other guards. There will be times they want you to leave . . . for meals, for exercise . . . but don't. We cannot trust the others in here. Use any excuse . . . I will try to bring you food myself."

A bit of silence hangs between us, as I contemplate how I'm going to make this happen. He sees my wheels turning and bumps his shoulder against mine. "If you really want to be Remy, I never saw her back away from anything in her life."

"So, we knew each other well?"

"You could say that. I loved you for a time," Caynan shrugs his shoulders. "Don't worry. I didn't try and stand in Arek's way, but I did challenge him." When he drops his head with a smile, he lifts his mouth in a very distinct way that I recognize. Caynan quickly scoots closer and wraps his arms around me.

"I promise you just as I have promised Arek . . . that I will find you an answer. You must remember . . . your only option right now is to stay in this room." He lays a hand on mine. "I need to go. Do you have any other questions for me?"

"Shouldn't they separate men and women inmates? I think I'd have a better chance against women."

Caynan laughs. "Be very grateful you are not surrounded by only women. In fact, due to women's natural intuition, they have proven to learn and evolve faster than men." He heads to the door and knocks.

"Thank you, Caynan." My arms hesitantly wrap around my body.

When he sees my reaction to the door, he stops. "Oh, I almost forgot." He pulls something out of his pocket and lays a pair of tiny flesh colored ear buds in my hand. "These will help. They won't be perfect, but no one should notice them . . . put them in now before I open this door."

"I hope these are different than the ones from yesterday," I say as I press the small pieces within my ears.

"Yes, very. Those are called M.F.I.s—muscle function inhibitors—and they're used for protection for other people . . . equivalent to handcuffs for the body. These are . . . well let's just say it's like a white noise for your brain and protection from anyone—dead or alive—that wishes to dig around in there." He touches my head lightly and smiles. "You'll be fine, Remy. Just stick to our plan and Arek and I will figure this out."

Once he's gone, the room feels even smaller. I dread loneliness. Leaves are scattered about my floor, some crisp and others soft. I look up at the one window within this brick prison and its tiny size makes me desperate for air. A dizzy spell sends stars to my eyes and I use the brick wall for stability.

As I'm waiting for the anxiety to pass, something my Ephemeral mom used to say when I was a child comes to me. "Everyone and everything is connected . . . this is important to remember, Willow, as you navigate this life. This world can never be free until everyone is." This place has already shown me that there is so far to go until the world is free of lost souls—within these walls and outside of them.

7

"Git up!" Someone growls from above me in the dark. During the middle of the night, a jagged metal piece from the cot forced me to pull the mattress to the ground. That's where I've slept for the last couple of hours.

Unexpectedly, pain explodes against my shin bones, and I cry out—still half asleep. It takes me only seconds to fly against the wall trying to escape whatever has just hit me. The piercing lights turn on, so I'm forced to shield my eyes. A large man stands in the doorway, as my eyes take a moment to adjust, I can't see who it is.

"Git up." The twist of his Scottish brogue reveals that it is Meryl.

"What?" I ask with my hands still covering my eyes protectively. Finally, they adjust and he's intimidating in his uniform with his gun at his side. His red hair is longer than when we were at the Bryer, and it falls sloppily in front of his freckled white skin. He takes warning steps toward me, grabbing my wrist so that the joint cracks and my skin burns—lifting me easily to my feet.

"Wait," I cry out and instinctively twist my wrist to the inside, almost as though this has been practiced and taught. Before he can prepare, I am free, so I fall back against the wall with a thud.

His surprise shows in his eyes. "Git up!"

I hurriedly climb the wall to standing.

"Why are you here?" I ask. "Not with Navin anymore?"

"Not at this momen'." His rough voice crackles. "Here . . . with ye was most importan'." He grins with his face so close to mine that I can smell his coffee breath. "They told me I git ta do what I want with ye. Whatever I want."

Normally this would terrify me, however today it doesn't and anger creeps up instead. I can't help myself and give a caustic grin, until he grabs my chin with his aggressive hand. My skin smashes against my teeth. "Ye watch yourself, Hen. Ye understan'?"

I say nothing.

"You understan'?" His need to control me surges. Slowly his hand drops down to my neck and his lips come so close they touch my cheek. "This is not th'time ta forget the power I have righ' now," he whispers. "Say ye understan'." His hand squeezes my neck until my head thickens.

"I understand." My whisper is strained.

"Goo'. Time for breakfas'." He finally steps away.

"I'll stay in here."

"That's no' a choice," Meryl smiles, his red beard rises and falls with his cheeks. "C'mon."

He places handcuffs around my wrists that lock tight with his thumbprint. Then he pushes me out of the room. My prison uniform is green with black army font that says Cellar 18 and my pants hang loosely on my hips. The air is suffocating and stale since there are no open windows, or strokes of breeze from anywhere. The world outside has vanished, blocked by thick walls of brick and mortar.

Is Arek nearby? Or the others?

We follow the hall, passing guards that refuse to look away. *In a world where the darkest corners exist, how am I the most entertaining thing walking through these halls?* Meryl saunters everywhere with confidence, untouchable and barrel-like. It is no different than walking with him through the Bryer on my way to Navin. The energy between us is that of hate—deep hate—intensified by years of standing on two very different sides of a story. What I do know of this world is that everyone's story is different, tainted by their own secrets.

Cal, the woman guard with the short hair, waits for us at a large glass door. I'm distracted by watching the wind outside push the trees nearly sideways while a dense gray fog swallows everything—the sweat on my lip makes me yearn for that wind. Another male guard, with long blond hair and wide jaws, waits for Meryl on the other side and stares at me intently. *Do I know this man?* Cal lets us through and the new guard on the other side forcefully grabs my forearm. We walk a few paces away from Cal, then down a hall. When we are far enough away, and Meryl has to enter his code into an alarm, this blond guard comes close enough to me that his chest touches mine.

"Welcome back, Remy," he says with a higher voice than I expect.

"She don't remember ye." Meryl finishes the code.

"Is that right?" the new guard whispers. "My name's Davi. Does that help?"

"No," I say, emotionless. "Should it?"

He whips a knife out so fast that it's against my neck before I can see it. "Yeah, it should."

Just then, a vision comes to me and I close my eyes. Images of Meryl and Davi run through my mind. They have done terrible things . . . to me . . . to women . . . for many, many years. I squeeze my eyes shut as though this will protect me, but they just keep coming. Each one is worse than the next. My hands shake and I gasp.

Davi smiles. "That's all it took for you to remember?"

Meryl nods, "She'll be back ta her ol' self soon."

"That's too bad," Davi states. "What'd ya see?" he asks, excited to hear about his past indiscretions.

"I saw that . . . you belong here more than I do." My words come out in a controlled hiss.

Angrily he swipes the blade across my jaw. Blood instantly pours onto my green jump suit after the initial sting and Meryl cries out, "What ye think you're doin', mate? They're always watchin'." Meryl races to me and presses his palm against my cheek. "Don't move," he warns. After a moment, Meryl pulls his hand away and the bleeding has stopped. I touch my skin with my fingers and there is an obvious slice in my jaw from my chin to my ear. It's barely holding together.

"Davi! Meryl!" Thire's loud voice calls from down the hall as he stomps toward us.

"It's fine, Thire. Just takin' her ta breakfas'," Meryl lies.

My mouth feels clamped shut—my jaws locked. It might be the nerves getting to me, but I watch Meryl and Davi out of the corner of my eye. The tension along my cheeks is firing, and my muscles are paralyzed. For a moment I listen carefully and sure enough, there is someone's unfamiliar Tracing within my brain.

Thire stands like a massive wall in front of us with a concerned look concretely set in his weathered brow. He makes no move to help—because he can't. His eyes tell me of his apology. Then he lunges toward Meryl. Like two beasts colliding in the wild, their chests crash against each other. "I gave my word to watch over her. You do anything and I will ruin you. Do you understand me?" Thire warns.

Meryl smiles, "It's really too bad that I was asked by a prophet himself to be here. Walk on, Thire. Should we end our centuries ol' fight now . . . right here?"

When more guards and inmates pass with subtle glances, the two large men step back from each other. Davi jerks me from the wall and pushes me toward the nearest double doors. Meryl slips away from Thire. "Be movin' along, Thire."

Thire regretfully watches as we leave.

Up elevators, through guard stations, and we pass many hallways in order to reach the cafeteria. Finally, somewhere just ahead, there are hundreds of voices growing louder. The sign on thick metal double doors says "Cafeteria." There are long windows on each door and inside hundreds of inmates carry trays. Guards line the walls, as groups of inmates sit around tables, and workers in the food line slap food onto plates.

My head begins the now familiar ache that forces my eyes shut and I wish desperately to massage my temples, if only my hands weren't tied. When I try to recognize the Tracing deep within, there are faint whispers. No matter how efficient the earpieces in my ear or the small training I have gone through, Davi and Meryl silently control me. It probably began in those first moments in my cell.

I peer at Meryl out of the corner of my eye and recognize his heavy concentration. There's only one option—to do as Geo taught and focus on their hypnotic cadences going through my head. With the Cellar's distractions everywhere, it is difficult to listen, but when I do . . . tiny continuous rhythms flicker in and out, making it grueling to find any breaks through which I can slip in and regain control. At first it seems impossible, but the longer I study them, the easier it is to recognize two defined Traces. After a moment, I know they've lost a bit of control when my fingertips wiggle freely behind my back.

"Walk," Meryl growls.

Davi and Meryl finally remove my cuffs and open the doors. The moment my soles touch the shiny cafeteria tile, all eyes turn to me with curiosity. News of my presence spreads from one side of the room to the other and growing voices create a low hum. Meryl wrenches my spine with his wooden stick, pushing me farther into the room.

We pass by a row of tables, but I am unable to continue when someone sticks their leg out. A bald man with tattoos on every inch of his body grins and stands. He must be more than six feet tall and two hundred and twenty pounds of pure muscle.

"Welcome back," he says as his entourage watches from the nearest table.

"It seems we've got an Electi in our house!" the large man bellows—his voice echoing off the walls. He steps closer until my toes lift from the floor and I teeter on my heels. "Do you remember me?" he asks.

"No," I say quietly.

"You put me in here. What do you say to that?" The tattoos run down his face in a language I don't recognize.

"I don't remember."

"So just because you don't remember, does that mean I have to forget?" His entourage and the others chuckle.

When I turn, Meryl and Davi grin. They head back to the double doors without a word, leaving me there alone. Meryl lets out a whistle and every guard exits the cafeteria; they lock the doors behind them.

"I've been waiting for you," the large man with tattoos says. "My name is Fredo and I'm a good friend of Navin's. I've been in here for one hundred and thirty-seven years and I ain't expected to get out for another four hundred, all due to you."

"I'm not Remy. I don't know you . . . and I definitely don't know what you did."

"Does anyone else in here recognize her?" Fredo asks the crowd. Nearly every one of them raises their hands. "How many of you have lost your lives in this place because of this woman?" Many of them keep their hands in the air.

There are moments when I miss Willow. Remy's overzealous confidence seems to negate rational thought, despite the intimidating audience and the wall-size man standing before me. "I'm sure that if any of you are in here," I say, ". . . you deserve it." *That's it, Remy is going to get me killed.* I can't stop myself and press my chest against Fredo's, staring directly into his eyes. "If you will excuse me."

Fredo's eyes grow wide, and I can see the anger welling up as his chest rises and falls. Mine does not. It sits calmly.

"What did you say to me?" he seethes.

"I said, get the hell out of my way."

I see his fist fly and then darkness, until I wake up on the floor. Blood runs down my head, painting the tile red. Loud voices fill the air as Fredo kicks my kidneys so hard that I instantly fold in half. He rears back to kick again, but I catch his standing foot with my outstretched hands, forcing him to fall back. It takes me only seconds to crawl on him and wrap my thighs around his neck. I lock my knee and foot, stealing his blood flow with my legs.

Several of his men rush forward to pull me from him. It isn't until one of them pries my figure-four from around his neck that Fredo gasps for breath. Instantly, he climbs on top of me as the inmates grow wild with excitement. His punches are painful and fast. I convulse again and again. He grows bored and stands, picking me up and throwing me on the nearest table. The metal is so hard that it knocks the wind out of me, and I sputter to breathe. Blood flies out of my mouth as I writhe in pain.

Suddenly, the pop of a gun fills the air. "Stand back now!" someone yells. With my forehead on the cold metal table, I watch as the group of inmates part. Coming through the crowd is Thire and Brice. "Everyone on the ground! Faces down and eyes closed! Not a soul tries to Trace, do you understand me?"

The thought of anyone trying to Trace Thire seems outrageous. He makes even Fredo look small. Arek, Kilon, Thire, and Meryl all have one thing in common: they are larger than any human I have ever known.

"Take Fredo." I see Fredo smile through my swollen eyes, unafraid of the three guards that run through the metal doors on Thire's command. He doesn't struggle.

The tension in the room is thick. With a finger, Thire points upward. I pull my eyes up despite the pain and find a second set of windows above the first. A second story wraps around the entire cafeteria and behind each panel of glass is a man with a gun pointed below. "Lift the glass," Thire calls out. Every inmate backs down as the glass panels disappear into the ceiling, no longer blocking the guards with guns.

Thire hurries to my side and lifts me to my feet. "Come on." Several guards rush forward with their guns pointed at the circle of inmates. These guards are different than the ones that Davi and Meryl removed from the room. They are dressed in full black body armor.

In only minutes, Thire has carried me into a new room and lays me on a patient's table, but I already feel myself recovering.

"The doctor will be here in just a moment." Thire's eyes tell me there's an apology coming.

"Thire, there's nothing you could do."

Thire nods and crosses his arms in front of his chest. "I told him I would take care of you. I didn't do my job."

I sit up, protectively holding my stomach. "It is not your job, Thire. You are an employee of the Cellar and Arek cannot ask you to leave your responsibilities for me."

"Arek can't. But the Monarch of the Electi can."

"My dad?"

"Your father gave me strict orders, but this morning I was told by the Prophets that I had to do otherwise." He hesitates. "You understand that the Prophets are a much more sanctioned power than your father. I would do anything for your father because I love him. But when the Prophets speak, we all listen, or we lose everything we have, and the Prophets lost their path long ago."

"You've done everything you could. Thank you. I know you've put yourself in a bad position by doing this."

"Just so you know . . . there are more of us. Navin isn't the only one to have his own men in here. Trust me, the Cellar is as divided as the world."

"I guess that's just the song humans sing, huh?"

"Yeah . . . but you're going to change that," he says with confidence.

This makes me uncomfortable and I look away. In just a few minutes, the doctor enters, and he spends only a moment looking me over—as usual, I am quick to heal. We somberly walk back to my cell.

"Being a doctor for the Velieri must be boring most of the time." We pass several doors where prisoners look out with blood-shot eyes. The smell of mold is returning to my nose as we walk the dingy asylum halls once again.

He lifts his arm to reveal a long scar running from his shoulder to his wrist. "It wasn't too bad, but I do get more action here."

I smile. "You've been a doctor?"

He shrugs. "We have many years to do many things. Medicine bored me."

Thire pretends to hold tightly to my handcuffs when guards pass, but the moment we are out of sight he takes them off again. "Remy, why didn't you back down? You have been beaten from head to toe. I saw you . . . unable to back down."

I am quiet for a moment. "At first I wanted to. But then, I couldn't stop."

Thire shakes his head. "Perhaps a combination of Remy and Willow is what you need—what the world needs." He notices that I am still not convinced. "Remy was stubborn. If someone challenged her, she wouldn't back down. She was always in trouble. You come in here and you are definitely not her . . . but you stood up to Fredo. You need to find a combination of the two."

8

I catch a glimpse of my bruised and swollen reflection as I pass a window. By the time we reach my cell, I am ready to lie down.

"What is happening with my case?"

"There is a meeting tomorrow. So long as we can keep you alive." He grins.

As we enter the dark and moldy cell, I hear the faint sound of a delicate breeze outside and instantly I'm swept away to thoughts of the world beyond these suffocating walls. Closing my eyes and lifting my face, I breathe in the ebb and flow of a free world where you can play in the sun. Bitter air bites my nose, reminding me of where I am.

"I'm sorry, Remy. I really am."

I open my eyes and look at Thire. "He'll get me out of here," I assure him.

He comes close to whisper in my ear, "You will have a visitor . . . at this window. It must happen on the hour when the guard changes shifts, which happens when the bells ring." He points to the out of reach window.

"How?"

He takes the metal frame of the bed and, as though it weighs nothing, props it upright against the wall. "Climb this." With a quick foot, he kicks the mattress to the foot of the metal bed.

"You think I'll fall?" I smile.

He shrugs.

My chest tightens at the thought of climbing the bed frame. For a moment I evaluate the height.

"Close your eyes and take a moment . . ." Thire says. "Avoid too much thought and just do."

He's right. My brain is always consumed with all the steps and all the possibilities of what could go wrong. So, I take a moment. Suddenly the air clears and, the best way to describe it is looking into a magnifying glass over the entire room. Every particle that floats in the air becomes vivid. I've felt this before, the Void. Once I'm there, my mind breaks down the parts of the bed. The angle of the metal tells me where its fulcrum points rest, and a clear understanding of the weak and strong places. Thire stares at me, and I pay no attention. My chest rises and falls as this new feeling erupts within. Naturally, every step, I can see its reason—its purpose. I run my hand along the frame and my fingertip brushes past a screw that has loosened over the years. This is the only thing holding a long and sharp crossbar on the bed. If I do nothing to it, someday it will simply release.

Thire sees the look in my eyes and steps closer. "Remy?"

"Give me a second," I say quietly and push the mattress near the right leg of the frame. "This takes the weight away from that side, so it becomes more stable." Thire nods, but says nothing, so I continue. "My foot is thin enough that I will have plenty of room to climb this quickly . . . if needed. If I stay on the left side, because of that mattress the frame should hold without any movement whatsoever. I suppose I'm a bit weaker than I used to be."

"A little, but your mind will calculate for that. Strength has very little to do with anything."

Then, without thinking, I climb. Every movement is deliberate, and my body ascends within seconds. Only when I can stand straight up, do I look at Thire with wide eyes.

"Ohhh," I laugh. "That was fun."

He laughs.

"I could see it . . . the angles . . . the distance . . ." I turn around and look up at the window that is now within reach. "I've felt that before, but not in a while."

"Remy knew better than anyone that strength didn't matter as long as she used leverage."

Strangely, I feel on top of the world as I look over the small bit of real estate I have recently acquired—even if it is dank and decrepit.

Later, in the dark room alone, there is nothing else to think about, but who will come to this window. My hands are still battered and I rub them together to clean the old blood away.

The bells of the tower, that keep the Epheme world blind to what truly sits within this old asylum, begin. I wait. The bells strike one after another. The last one ends. No one comes to my window. The back of my head thumps the brick wall out of frustration as my breath drags out. Just moments before, Thire had been released from his shift. "Stay vigilant," he whispered through the rectangle cutout in the door and only seconds later the cadence of a different boot tapped the hall cement. To protect myself I stuffed my sheet at the base of the door and pressed my body in the corner of the room. Where I now wait.

"Willow?" Beckah's rich voice floats into the room not unlike the leaves. Just then, I hear the click of my door handle as though one of the guards heard her voice. Again, Beckah calls quietly, "Willow?"

I can't move. The bed still stands upright against the wall, ready for me to climb, but fear paralyzes me. My hands move the sheet away from the bottom of the door and a shadow from the guard's boot breaks up the small line of light.

"Willow?" she calls again, this time a bit louder.

Finally, the shadow walks away and my body melts with relief.

Before another second is lost, I fly up the bed with ease and stretch out to see through the small window.

Beckah stares back at me with a smile. She reaches inside and I immediately grab her hand.

"How are you doing this?" I ask her.

"Well, flying is my gift." She shrugs.

Her words hit me in the gut. "Fly? You can fly?"

"Nah, that would be ridiculous," she says dryly. "I'm up on a ladder." Her tomboyish mannerisms make me smile. "I'm just the smallest one and I tend to be fast. Less noticeable, I guess. Can you imagine those other behemoths up here?" She winks. "How are ya, lady?"

"Alive."

She nods but reaches out to touch my face. "A bit beaten I can see."

Unexpectedly, I feel the heat in my cheeks. "I didn't understand this place."

"I don't know how you're doing it," she says. With shaking fingers, I pull one of the earpieces out of my ear and show her. "Ahhh, bless you, Caynan. He'll need to bring you backups for that because they will die. Just be aware. I'll make sure we do that, okay?"

"Okay." Already there is a disturbance within my chest and mind for the few seconds that the pod is out, so I quickly return it.

"We only have a few minutes."

"Where is everyone?"

"We're working on several things. Diem and Gal have their militia in search of Navin, and . . ." she hesitates, "and now we have to find Elizabeth."

"Elizabeth? Elizabeth is missing?" Panic sets in at the thought of this. "My aunt is the only one that knows what happened that night."

Beckah nods. "We know. We'll find her, Remy." She squeezes my hand. "You can't think about anything else, but surviving. You got it?"

"Yeah." I nod. "Beckah . . . where is Arek?"

"He's never too far away from you. In fact, he can see you right now."

I stare beyond her, out into the dark sky. "Close your eyes," Beckah says, so I do. "No distance can stand in the way of your Yovu. Do you feel him?"

At first, I don't. Then, something small builds—a burning within my chest and an ache within my body. My eyes fly open, and I search the woods beyond. A dim light flickers within the trees at exactly the spot my body told me of his presence.

Beckah nods. "He's there." We hear a noise from somewhere below. "I have to go. Stay safe. We're coming."

"They all want to kill me in here," I whisper.

"Not all of them."

"Meryl can do what he wants . . . the rules don't apply to him."

She sighs angrily. "Meryl. He never forgave Rem . . . you, for putting his wife away. She set up several meetings for the rebellion to kill Ephemes." Beckah shakes her head. "And Leigh has a way of getting what he wants."

"Leigh? I thought Meryl served Navin?"

"Sometimes I wonder if there is even a difference."

After a moment's pause, I begin to speak until I hear the jingle of keys in the door and I look at Beckah. With reluctance, she drops out of sight. The door shakes and begins to open. My heart races as I search for the best way down. An idea comes to me. With a solid push against the brick wall behind me, I ride the falling bedframe as it lands in its original place.

I land on stable feet, as the crash of the metal on the cement floor fills the room and the guard rushes in.

"What was that?" the new guard asks quickly.

"I was just trying to move my mattress so that I could be comfortable." Both of us look at the mattress practically falling off the bed.

This guard steps so close to me that I can feel his breath on my cheek. "They've told me about your games, Remy. Be careful."

I lay in silence, devoured by darkness and listening to the agonizing beat of water drops from somewhere nearby. One after the other, drip after drip, my eyes never close. When the wind howls, dry leaves fall through the air. At times, haunting cries of confined criminals seep through the smallest cracks in the door and I am desperately grateful for the protective earbuds.

When I keep my eyes closed, I can picture Arek. Desperate for an escape, my mind plays visions of him touching my face, pressing his body into mine; I replay the feeling of his kiss again and again. It is so real that I touch my lips with my fingertips as though the warmth may somehow miraculously be there. Just for a second, I am no longer in this rat-infested cell, but with Arek.

The sound of boots at my door steals Arek from my mind's eye. I crawl along the floor and press my ear against the door until I can hear voices. It is difficult to keep my breath from covering them up.

"They haven't found him . . . he made a mess in Lompoc and Arizona. Some say he'll continue the killing spree until he kills off every Epheme one by one . . . but I don't know . . . I wouldn't doubt the war happens faster than expected . . . we have no way to calm the fires. Everywhere . . . they know she's alive . . . last night in London, someone started a rift that eventually led to fourteen Velieri deaths. She's bringing hell . . . absolute hell . . . and it won't stop."

Chills come over my body and sweat drips from my forehead as my mind races. "I can't do this," I whisper. The end is too far . . . too removed . . . and any thought of the future leaves more questions than answers, which only perpetuates the fear. I need silence. How do I find the Void again? I calculate a rhythm. Geo's and Arek's faces come to my mind, teaching me the way to find my own battle cry. I close my eyes and count my breath. This time it comes even faster, and I enter an abyss. My body feels weightless, as though I'm floating, my hair falling away from my shoulders. A distant voice, beautiful and rich, her high song enveloping me with comfort until finally, I open my eyes.

I am no longer in the cell, but a night sky full of stars is above, below, and around me—leaving nothing of substance on which to stand. I've been here before—the last time I was with Navin—only this time there is less fear, less ache.

A resonating chorus lightly sings as I gaze at the stars. A woman with short, dark hair, deep-set eyes, and a kind smile grows in size as she comes closer. Her skin is smoother than the snow on the Swiss Alps. Rich dark shades of color outline her eyes and her lips are the palest shade of pink.

"Remy," she calls with a familiar silky voice. It takes a moment for us to drift closer together.

"Holona," I whisper.

Her smile grows. "You remember?"

"Of course."

Within the time it takes to blink, we stand in the middle of the same forest where we met before. Birds flitter, calling out to one another. The perfect afternoon breeze kisses my face. "I want to stay here," I say.

"Of course you do . . . but unfortunately we don't have much time. Close your eyes." I do, then she says, "Open them." We are no longer in the forest but walking on vast green rolling hills. Sheep slowly graze upon the vibrant earth and, far away, the backdrop of mountains captures my eye. In the middle of this valley is a small white cottage, from which we are a hundred feet away. "This might be even better."

I walk through the gently blowing grass, letting it brush against my ankles. To be here for just a moment, rather than the Cellar, is a gift and I lift my face to the sun.

"Get your strength back," she breathes out.

On the wraparound porch of the white cottage, a man with sun-kissed skin lies on the soft pinstriped hammock. When he turns, I recognize Arek immediately and hurry toward him, until an arm wraps around his chest. A woman lays comfortably beside him. After getting a bit closer, I see Remy . . . me. As I watch the exchange between Arek and I, longing rises in my chest.

"I know this place," I whisper to Holona. "This is a memory . . . isn't it?"

Holona nods and gently takes my hand. "An important one."

"Where are we?"

"La Vida Ranch. A sacred place where no one was ever able to find you. You two always made your way back here."

We quietly watch as Arek admires and caresses the woman he so clearly loves. He drops his lips to her forehead as she lies safely on his chest.

"I don't want to wake up," my words barely seep out.

"I'm here for one purpose . . ." Holona and I look at each other. "To give you a moment of rest . . . but to also say . . . It's time to fight, Remy . . . so you can one day get back to this place with him."

Holona smiles, then touches my arm before she begins to walk away.

"I don't want you to go."

She turns back, this time her green eyes sparkle from emotion. "Remember that falling is necessary and a climb is vital." She starts to walk away, but stops. "And Remy, tell him hi when you see him."

I nod. The weakness within me is boring a hole in my chest, desperate not to return. There is no telling whether I will even get to see Arek again.

"Will I get out of the Cellar?"

She nods.

"When?"

"Soon. It's coming."

Suddenly, I am back in the Cellar, still lying on the floor in my own personal hell. A mouse squeaks just above my head and I quickly pull the blankets over me.

9

A collective tap of boots in the hallway just outside my door wakes me from a dead sleep and I am on my feet before I'm even fully awake. My heart pounds beneath my ribs and my fingers squeeze something hard between my fingertips. Looking down, I recognize the metal bar from the cot, sitting like a weapon within my palm. *How did it get there?* There's no time to figure it out when the door swings open, letting blinding light pour in that forces me to cover my eyes with my free hand.

"Hello?" I ask.

They say nothing.

"What do you want?" I ask again.

Suddenly, four figures rush in. They wear tight black masks with red Xs at the eyes, nose, and mouth, and the material is strangely molded to their faces like clay. I fight back and slice two of them near their face and neck, but soon, they hold me down and the leader swiftly stuffs a rag down my throat until I gag. My shoulders scream when they pull my hands to be tied behind my back after they yank me to my feet. As the rag in my mouth absorbs my saliva, it turns into a heavy brick, dangerously deep, and I fight the urge to wretch, which makes my eyes water. The eeriest thing is that, whoever these people are, they make very little sound as they toss me around like a rag doll and aggressively drop a heavy sack over my head.

A glimmer from the hall light is all that I can see beneath the sack, so I'm forced to trust their rough hands as they push and pull me through the halls. Inmates hoot and holler, creating such an uproar that one of the men hits the wall with something hard until the chaos lessens. My breath turns to whimpers, to gagging, to desperation.

We've descended far after a few minutes, taking staircase after staircase underground where we no longer hear the bellow of the other inmates or feel the cement beneath our shoes, rather the floor turns rough and edgy. The smell of mildew and stagnant air continues, but now, there's a new foul stench penetrating my nose. At first I can't place it, but the farther we tread, the easier it is to recognize sewage. I see nothing beneath the sack over my head, but in this place—in the darkness of the Cellar—sight is the last thing needed to know that you are surrounded by an infernal presence. When the hairs on the back of my neck rise, I aggressively protect my mind more.

Even the temperature has dipped quite drastically, so my body shivers and my teeth begin to chatter.

I must be moving too slowly, for after a moment, one of them comes to my side and throws me over his shoulder. The blood rushes to my head as I hang lifeless while his bones dig into my abdomen. Tears well up in my eyes, but don't fall . . . yet.

Finally, the swing of heavy doors, the cry of a lock, tells me that we have reached the end. He sets me down, but I can't find my footing and fall to the hard floor.

"Ia nushe call stil naun?" One of the men asks if he should take off my mask. His voice doesn't sound human; it's distorted and warped.

"Kav el." Another tells him to wait—his voice is also disguised.

One of them violently yanks me to my feet. When I stumble, this makes him growl with irritation. He doesn't remove my handcuffs, rather drags my arms above my head and attaches me to something else. I hear the ting of metal as he closes the ring. My hands are now locked to some sort of pipe above my head that I touch with my fingertips—it is wet and slick. When I move my body to the left or right, the sound of metal-on-metal screeches throughout the room.

They pluck the sack off, sending my hair flying. Four men of all different heights stand in front of me, still hiding behind black masks that move when they speak, as though it is their own skin. Two of them have brown eyes, one has grayish blue, and the last is almost black. With the eyeholes so severely small there is no way to tell who they are, even if I knew them.

The lights flicker in this dank room, until it gives the strobe effect. Although Caynan's earpieces help, these men are constantly poking and prodding within my mind. My breathing vacillates from shallow to deep, ever inconsistent as I struggle to control my fear. When they see that I'm contained, they turn away and whisper. My eyes survey every inch of the medieval room, from the mold-infested brick, to the damp floors, to the rusted metal cages along one wall, and a chair with leather straps at the arms and feet. *I'm okay . . . I'm okay . . .* I chant to myself. I close my eyes and breathe . . . until I hear a strange sound. My eyes bounce open and anxiously search from left to right.

Someone is near, incessantly whispering, and it only grows louder and more frantic the longer time passes. I look behind me. There, curled up against the wall, his head shaved, his hands covering his face, his bony, malnourished body covered in bruises and dirt, a young man cowers—crying. Just his anguish alone sends chills down my spine. Then he begins to moan, a horrible cascading moan. *I'm okay . . . I'm okay . . .* I repeat for several moments with my eyes shut, hoping that he'll stop. Finally, he quiets.

When I feel someone's breath on my cheek, I open my eyes. The gaunt young man now stands just inches from my face, staring intensely at me, his chin down, and eyes squinted. His eyes are red and pulsating, veiny and inhuman. His body writhes and bobs abnormally, as though led by the evil that permeates this room. I pull away when he shows his black teeth and steps a bit closer. My movements are limited by the pipe overhead. "No!" I cry out.

The men with masks turn to me, as I unsuccessfully retreat. This evil Being who presses against me seems to be stuck in this strange existence of fear paralleled with the power of his own demoniacal energy.

Breathe.

Finally, he backs away when the masked men take his place. They pass by him, completely unaware of his presence, just like Arek and the others couldn't see what I saw in the first moments here. *What are these people that display themselves only to me?* He writhes and babbles around them, coming close to their faces, but they are undisturbed, even as he breathes down their necks. Nothing is worse than his tortured voice; even his sallow skin does not jar me as much as the sounds escaping his lips.

What do I not understand? Is everything that I thought I knew about life and death confused? They don't see him—this tortured man— yet I do. How can this be real?

Perhaps this is my curse—perhaps a sentence to hell simply means eternally shackled to this earth.

"Remy," the warped voice of one of the masked men whispers. I look at him . . . he takes several moments of silence to Trace, but I counter as best I can. Soon, he shakes his head in frustration. "I'm not getting in."

The vile young man with black teeth now walks around me, pressing his filthy skin on mine and smiling from my scent. It is difficult to pretend that he doesn't exist. Whatever lives within his soul is so foul and immoral, it strips me of anything good that is left after being in this malevolent place.

The leader of the masked men comes closer. "It's time, Remy, to tell us what you know. We don't leave here until you do."

"What I know?" I tremble.

They dig and search, invading my mind, trying to force me to say what they want me to say.

"There are secrets . . ." he says, "and we need them."

In this world, the Velieri world, our thoughts are never our own. They pry until you are weak, and when you are weak, they attack. The longer I exist within these walls, the more fragile I feel. Despite this, my training helps me distinguish my thoughts from theirs, and I seek out their unique rhythm. *How do I battle four, and especially with the demon boy at my shoulder?* The masked men rip at the fabric of my consciousness, leaving me to wonder what I would do without Caynan's earpieces. The mental toll is still so torturous that it is tempting to just give up and drown—let my head drop beneath the water and breathe in.

"I don't know anything," I cry.

"You lie!" One of them loses his temper and comes so close to me that the demonic boy laughs and jumps away almost joyously, still invisible to the others.

"I don't. I swear."

"We don't believe you. We can get the truth . . . it's just how hard you wish to make us work for it." He stands so close, the smell of his sweat wafts through my nose. Instead of pulling away, a familiar confidence returns, and I lean into him with challenging eyes. I suppose there is a bit of pleasure that I feel from his surprise.

"The truth . . . that Navin killed my mother? Or the truth that he wants my child because he believes I'm the one." I tilt my head to cast an angry stare. "You don't scare me."

Silence follows. Which only makes me smile. Then, he grabs the back of my hair and rips my head back. He begins to say something but stops.

"Just get in," he calls to the others.

They circulate within my mind, swarming similarly to birds over a carcass. They try to peck their way in, but I battle, forcing myself to beat them and block their Trace. It is easier than I expect—especially when closing my eyes and forgetting the distractions. After I focus, I notice four succinct and different hums.

Four different beats, different styles, different paths, should be more than I can handle, but instead, my mind is able to categorize them until I can follow one, all while keeping the others at bay. So, I follow, descending into the dark recesses of the one I choose to follow. Without truly understanding how, I ride on top of his chant rather than compressing below it. Like any mathematic formula, it becomes clear how to add to his cadence, by tone, beat, or rhythm, in order to take over. He doesn't know . . . not yet. He doesn't hear the extra note. Until his power weakens, and there are only three vultures instead of four.

"What are you doing?" the man bellows, and the others turn to him. "She's in," he says with confusion.

"What do you mean, she's in?" one asks.

"That's just what I mean. She's gotten into my Trace," he growls.

"That's impossible with four of us."

The gray eyed man rushes to me and grabs my face. "What are you doing?"

Before I can say anything, he turns my head to the side and pulls the ear bud out, then he turns my head the other direction and pulls the other out.

It is instantly clear what Caynan's protection has been saving me from. The vacuum begins, directly pulling every sound of torment, every layer of spirit, every cry of the weak, and they bear down on me so heavily, that I gasp. My hair stands on end, my bones instantly ache with tension, and my eyes roll. Suddenly the room is full of more than just the demon boy and his tortured soul. Now, there are more tortured souls, aimlessly walking around, never acting as though they are aware of anything but themselves. Rubbing their hands together, whimpering, cussing, overall seething in their anguish.

The four men seem to understand what they've done when I cower from their sight, and they smile—instantly taking advantage to now dive, hell deep into my memories. Just like before when Caynan and Thire turned into monsters before my eyes, these men with masks do the same. That's when it becomes clear, the demented now control my mind—both the living and the dead.

***

For hours, I battle.

"No!" I refuse to give them any confession.

They strap me to the wooden chair when I am weak, fastening the leather straps tightly around my ankles and wrists. Hot coals are pressed against my skin while the spirits surrounding us cry and wail as though reminded of their own moment in this chair.

When I have no energy left, they lay me on a table, tie me down, and roll the medical equipment beside me. A tormented woman, with sunken eyes and blue lips, stares at me from across the room. She looks on with curiosity, then walks to me, one slow step at a time. The blue veins beneath her skin are easier to see the closer she comes. Finally, she bends down beside me.

"You can see us?" She's unhinged with ticks.

"Yes." My voice is barely audible.

She comes closer. Something is not right about the way she looks at me, yet I can see her desire for my attention. She reaches out with her feeble hand as though she is afraid to make contact, then touches my cheek. Instantly, she rips her hand away and tears come to her eyes. "I can feel you . . . you're real," she whispers.

I am so weak, I cannot answer.

"I want out of here . . ." she whimpers.

Switching quickly from anguish to a strange maniacal laughter that spews from her, she then calms and brings her mouth so close to mine that I ache for her to back away. I can feel her insanity ripping at my mind's framework until I am unable to have even one coherent thought.

"Do you want to know if I deserve to be here?" she asks just before she reaches out and touches my hand. Instantly, I am sucked into her nightmare—what she felt when she stole babies from their mothers because she couldn't have children of her own. "Stop!" I cry out as the progression of her crimes grows to unimaginable heights. "Stop!" I yell again.

The four men stand over me as one of them grabs a knife. They believe my cries are to them, but the clutch of this woman's savage disregard for humanity has made me forget the torture I am going to receive for just a moment. The sobs billow from my chest before I can stop them. It is depleting to feel someone's hate . . . it is too much to accept it, even for a second.

"Willow," one of the men speaks to me in his distorted voice.

"No," I cry, refusing to look at his terrifying masked face. "Enough . . . please . . . enough . . ."

"It only takes a moment to give us what we need."

Each man grabs a limb and carries me across the room. In the corner, there is a cement square on the floor smaller than a match-box. They work together to tie my hands above my head and set my feet on this small box that is only big enough to support the toes of one foot. The other foot rests on the opposite ankle and already I can feel the edges of this sharp square digging into my skin.

"You will say what I need you to say, even if it takes all night. I've heard it's haunted in here . . . we'll let you join the dead for a while."

With that, the men, distorted and grotesque without the ear-buds in my ear, exit the room and shut the lights off, which makes all the left-behind tortured souls wail and beg to be let out. It grows to an overwhelming decibel, although I cannot see them anymore in the dark. This only makes their desperation worse.

The warnings of the Cellar are true. Moment after moment, I lose more of myself to this place.

Each time the men come in throughout the night to check with only a flashlight, to see if I've changed my mind, they repeat themselves, "This could end if you just say what we need to hear. Sleep, comfort, freedom are all yours, if you just say the words."

I want all those things more than I've ever wanted anything in my life. My strength is waning and in my weakest moments, my lips actually mouth the words. Just as I am about to give up, something stops me at the last second—call it strength, call it divine . . . whatever it is, I am somehow able to hold on.

Soon the ante is upped when they burn the Cellar's symbol on my bare skin with a branding iron. The symbol consists of the letter C and the letter I—for Cellar Inmate—intertwined. One of them lifts my shirt as they press it to my ribs.

If I say I killed my mother, then all of it will stop. The words dance on the tip of my tongue like stubborn children playing where they shouldn't, and my body shakes uncontrollably. My eyes catch sight of the earpieces from Caynan laying on a nearby table and I'm desperate for them.

The night passes and I have no more energy to even stand. My body is limp when they finally release my hands and I fall into their arms, then they lay me once again on the table. One of them picks up a large knife.

"Nooo . . . please," I beg—my voice is hoarse.

"Just tell me what I want to hear, and it will all be over."

My head rocks back and forth uncontrollably. Tears cascade down my temples. If they want the words, I will say them. Nothing can be worse. They haven't proven my innocence anyway. My breathing is labored, and I feel pain in every joint. For the first time my hands are free and dangle lifelessly off the sides of the table. As one of the men presses the knife to my sternum, playing the game with me, I look away from his terrifying masked face. The woman with blue veins comes close to my side; her awkward eyes and crazy movements no longer scare me. "The table next to you," she manages to babble. The table she speaks of is by my left hand and a scalpel taunts me as it lays there. She points at it. "Take it," her voice rises and falls strangely.

Do I have the energy? There is no option. I have no other choice but to conjure up the ability to fight back. Otherwise, this night continues.

With quick hands, I grab the scalpel as one of them leans over me. I swing my hand around and connect the metal piece with his throat. It punctures his windpipe, and he falls back in surprise. Before the other men can rush forward, I reach out to the table where the scalpel once laid and grab Caynan's earpieces. Instantly, when I put them in, the men in black are no longer distorted.

Unexpectedly, as though the help of the earpieces is enough, I feel the shift as my body and mind sync. I gather my wits again and increase my attention to my rhythm. The air becomes clear and I can read the room. The men attack from different directions, but I know which foot carries their weight and which arm will reach out. In mere seconds I grab a man's hand faster than he can end a punch. Even with fresh wounds, I move fast. The technique shows itself. I strike an elbow at the joint, breaking the bone. He cries out as his arm bends the wrong way. The other men try in any way, but they come up short. I pull the scalpel from the first man's neck and he collapses to the floor while the next man throws his fist, and I duck out of the way. I slice the scalpel across his gut and he falls. Before I know what has happened, they are all on the floor writhing in pain.

Instantly, I run to the double doors and struggle with the handle for only a second before racing into the hall. The doors crash together when I shut the men and the tortured inside. It won't be very long before they recover, so I must hurry. Looking around the long empty hall I see a broom not too far away. It slides easily within the handles of the double doors, instantly locking them inside.

My adrenaline wears thin and my knees buckle. I struggle to pull myself back up using the wall as the men shake the door behind me and yell at the top of their lungs. Finally, I press on.

Through halls and up several stairways, I stumble. The bottoms of my feet are trying to recuperate, but the pain is still excruciating. *Where do I go? I don't know. Where is Thire?* Rooms pass to my right and left, but there are voices within, so I try to go unnoticed. *Should I head back to my cell?*

It takes me too long to know where to go and the sound of an army tearing down the halls echoes behind me. They yell, "Find her!" The pounding of their boots is loud enough to echo through the Cellar's labyrinth of corridors and cavernous rooms.

My limp is debilitating, but I press on.

A large dead-end door takes every bit of energy to push open, and it extends these halls into what now looks less dungeon and more clinical. Windows line the walls between doors with name plaques beside each one. When peering behind me, my heart plummets when noticing blood from my feet giving away my direct path.

Behind the metal door, through its window, my eyes catch sight of the men in masks gaining ground. My body still takes a longer time to heal. Panic strangles me. "Go!" I yell at myself.

They burst through the door in seconds and sprint toward me.

I push, limp after limp.

"Stop!" the men yell. Just close enough for their fingertips to touch my arm, but a door opens ahead, and I lunge toward it.

Leigh emerges from the door, as though he knows nothing of the chase.

"Leigh!" I yell, "Please." I drop to my knees with relief. Several officers enter the hall behind him and stare at us with confusion.

"What is going on?" Leigh asks.

"Help me!" I cry.

None of the four men say anything. I notice the one with gray eyes looks at Leigh with a strange expression.

"Get out of here," Leigh tells them, with a gesture of his tense hand.

The gray-eyed man shakes his head just before he walks away. His raspy voice is still disguised, "She wouldn't."

I look at Leigh in terror, but he ignores me and grabs my arm. "There's nothing we can do now. The Powers are waiting."

As the men scurry away, leaving me broken on the floor, Leigh nods at the officers behind him and they lift me by the shoulders to walk me through the hall. Leigh calmly leads the way as my feet drag.

We enter a large hallway, and this time officers, as well as inmates, stand around. They all stop what they are doing to watch.

"Where are we going?" my voice cracks.

"To convene with the Powers and Prophets for your sentencing. Get ready." Leigh grins.

10

As the doors open to the courtroom, I am on display and the crowd erupts. The loudest are those against me, and the others look on in horror, as my broken and bloodied body is dragged in. The Prophets are already in their places, seated in the high-backed white chairs, waiting patiently just in front of the Powers.

The first person I see is Caynan. He stands with his hands clasped in front of his pressed striped suit. The expression on his face does nothing to give me confidence. Leigh's men take me to him, and he quickly grabs me.

"What did they do to you?" Caynan whispers. As he assesses my injuries, I scour the room for Arek, but he is not there. Sassi, Kilon, Geo, Beckah, and Peter are not there. My heart sinks lower than I thought possible. I am alone.

"Where—" I begin, but just then the doors open, and several guards enter followed by my father. Briston looks more handsome than I remember him. His blue eyes are piercing beneath the chandeliers. Following him are Mak and Kenichi and I've never in my life felt so grateful. Briston comes to my side and reaches his hand out to my face. One of the officers of the Cellar begins to step between us, but Leigh stops him.

Briston turns angrily toward Leigh and calls out to all who might listen, "What the hell is this? Look at her! Look what they've done to her!"

"We have been told that she has not been the easiest inmate to care for," Prophet Covey says.

I shake my head. "That is not true," I whisper.

Caynan nods at Briston, and then he speaks to the Powers. "Do any of you have proof?"

"Mr. Tate, we haven't the time to discuss anything other than the case at hand. Please Briston, let us proceed." They encourage my father to sit down, but I can see that he doesn't want to. After a moment, he finally complies.

"We, the Five Prophets," Covey begins, "with no new evidence to acknowledge, hereby sentence Remona Landolin to death once more. This is to be carried out immediately. Guards, take her."

The room explodes. My eyes fly to Caynan, and I can see that he is caught off guard and is grasping for an argument. Briston jumps up and yells something, but the room is in such chaos that I can't hear what he says. Several guards grab me and slap cuffs around my wrists, but Caynan desperately tries to keep me behind him. Briston reaches for me but the officers make a blockade. He pushes against them with all his strength, but ultimately to no avail. They pull me from Caynan's protection, needing to nearly carry me with my lack of strength.

There is no more struggle within me. I can't fight anymore. Perhaps death is better? The more I try to accept this, the more I can't wrap my mind around an execution. Then suddenly, I remember. My mind flashes back to a time when I was dragged away from this very courtroom.

The hall looks the same. The guards are different, and even my stance is different. I watch as Remy keeps her chin held high and her shoulders back. She shows no fear.

Today, it is not the same. I can barely walk without help. My shoulders are stooped, and my head is low. Tears well up in my eyes as I search for the people I know. Caynan and Briston are so far away, there is nothing standing between me and death.

"Where's Arek?" I yell at Briston. My arms burn from the guards dragging me, but I struggle to keep my eyes on my only comfort in the room, my father. "Where is Arek!?"

Briston tries to reach for me over the guards, but our hands can't even touch. "Don't worry! We'll figure this out! I promise!"

Caynan yells at the Prophets, his flailing arms forceful, and his voice carrying over the court. "Stop this now! Prophet Jenner!"

Covey and Hawkins stand like stone, clearly watching the outcome of which they had so instrumentally worked, and they pay no attention to Caynan. It is Prophet Jenner who steps to the edge of the platform, her strong African features clearly showing her opposition to what is taking place. Mannon walks up behind her and rests his gentle hand on her shoulder, as his chest rises and falls with a disturbed and stoic nature.

Everything seems to play out in slow motion.

Even though Briston and Caynan are still yelling, the guards rip me from the court room and nearly carry me down the hall. The chaos echoes loudly behind us.

The hopelessness returns, storming through my heart greater and more powerful than depression, anxiety, or more. It is everything all at once attacking the corners of my mind. How had Remy been able to survive this before?

More men wait thirty feet away at the end of the hall. Davi and Meryl are among them, which devours me in panic.

"Please! Please!" I dig my bruised feet into the cement ground even though there is no way for me to overpower them, but the terror gives me no choice.

"Keep walking," one of the guards threatens. "Get—"

Just then, a cacophony of explosions and pops fill the hall ahead of us. We can see nothing—only hear painfully loud cracks that whip flashes of orange light somewhere down a hallway to the right.

The guards intensify their hold on me, as they glance at one another with confusion. "What do we do?" one of the younger ones asks.

Blasts hurt our ears again, as the same light flashes orange. It is so loud that I wish to cover my ears, but I am the only one who can't.

Boom!

Boom!

Boom!

BOOM!

The guards take defensive positions preparing for something they cannot see. Nothing. One of the guards uses a window to check outside, but soon shakes his head. Nothing.

The explosions stop.

We wait. Many seconds pass empty of sound. Unexpectedly, from the hall off to the right just ahead, a heavily armed man, wearing all black SWAT gear, a hat, and glasses, bursts into view as he fires automatic weapons from both hands. Instantly the hall turns to pandemonium. The barrage shreds the walls around me. Glass and mortar fly, followed by a cloud of white dust. The guards waste no time and fire back. It takes my reflexes only seconds to drop out of the way and press myself flat against the floor.

Men fall with their hands pressing against parts of their bodies—blood is pooling on the cement. I cover my ears from the piercing sound.

Minutes pass as I breathe into my sleeve. Then I feel someone pull on my arm. Despite the pain, I try with everything I have left to fight them off. With my body still weak, I cry out as he turns me over.

"Remy!"

My eyes pop open. Arek is kneeling above me with one gun pointed straight out at the enemy down the hall. He reaches out to my swollen face. The hall is bursting with light and sound, so intense that it is hard to hear him.

"Can you walk?" he asks.

I nod. As I stand, I see Sassi, Kilon, Peter, Beckah, and Geo all dressed in pure black SWAT gear. My heart has never known such relief. They're here. My brain is still battling the unseen, but at least they're here.

Their casings fall to the tile floor.

"Come on!" Arek yells.

Despite everything, I get up and run. It isn't long before we hear yelling from what seems to be everywhere. Arek grabs my hand to lead me through halls where I have never been. He can tell that I can't run fast and that I am struggling physically; he has no choice but to push me to hurry anyway.

Kilon, Sassi, and Arek circle around me and seem to know exactly where to go. Then the Cellar's sirens begin. The sound is painful to our ears. Several times as we push through doors, they fight off groups of officers. Arek, Kilon, Sassi, Geo, Beckah, and Peter are strong and trained. They fight as a team.

Down we drop, past the deepest and darkest chambers of the Cellar and into an underground parking garage where the transport vans are held. Arek pulls my arm, but I cry out in pain.

"I can't run anymore."

"Faltyn hun nai!" he yells to Kilon. Kilon nods and pushes faster than everyone else. Before long he disappears between the vehicles, following Arek's order.

A shot whizzes past my ear and I duck. My cuffs are still tightly pulled behind my back and clang together as we run. Arek shoots, immediately catching the first man who entered from the stairs. He slumps over and falls down the last few steps. Several men push past him, knowing that a gunshot wound is not lethal to any Velieri. Arek forces me to run.

More shots echo. Sassi, Arek, and Peter all take bullets to their bodies and cry out in pain. Finally, the roar of an engine comes close. A new SUV, one that I have never seen, pulls around the other cars and stops between the pursuing officers and us. Arek rips the door open and pushes me inside. I crumble on the seat as bullets hit the windows, but the glass does not shatter—they only leave jagged marks.

Arek jumps inside and slams the door shut. He places his body over me as he drops the window just an inch to shoot a few more rounds. Finally, everyone is protected by the bullet-proof SUV and Kilon screeches away. The sirens can't even be heard from within the car.

Finally, one of the worst days of my life is over. I close my eyes, desperate for us to make it out in one piece, desperate to never have to go back to the Cellar ever again.

After several twists and turns, I can finally see gray sky through the moon roof overhead. We are traveling fast out of the massive Cellar walls, but they are closing.

"You can't make that!" Sassi yells.

"No options," Kilon quips as he presses on the gas even more. We speed toward an opening that doesn't seem wide enough for the vehicle. My chest begs for air, before I realize that I have been holding my breath.

"Come on. Come on," Kilon says under his breath.

"You're not going to make it!" Sassi yells again. "Turn around and we'll try the back!"

"No! There's no time."

I close my eyes as the opening diminishes. The walls already seem to be too close together for the SUV.

"Kilon," Arek says with concern.

"Come on!" Kilon yells.

Shots ring out behind us and again bullets hit the windows but leave no holes. Arek covers me despite knowing that they will not break. Sassi yells commands at Kilon and Peter, while Geo and Beckah stay quiet in the back.

Just as the gates are about to close, Kilon twists the steering wheel and the car swerves to the left between them. The SUV scrapes and sparks between the closing cement walls. The sound is shrill and the scraping shakes the car. Kilon hits the gas and works to break free of the screeching metal jaws. He grips the steering wheel tightly, trying to keep control. The SUV suddenly stalls, and no matter how much Kilon pushes on the gas, the vehicle won't budge. More bullets ascend. This time, Peter sticks his gun out of a small window and fires back.

Only when I peer over the back seat do I see Leigh running out of the Cellar followed by three of the Prophets and several other guards. The major rulers of all the Velieri, the leaders over an entire race of humanity—they are all here to witness my fate. And now, my name will be slashed with even more slander and hate. Everyone in this car made a choice to be here. They are now criminals—no different than me.

The car squeals and hitches.

"Come on!" Kilon yells again.

Officers race to the back and side windows to bash them with the ends of their weapons. I crouch down more in my seat, still feeling the pain of the cuffs around my wrists.

"Get us out now!" Arek yells.

Kilon shifts into reverse, pulls just slightly away from the closing gate, and this time he presses the gas, sending it straight. Tipping to the side, the car nearly stands on two wheels as it passes. Cracks and screeches fill the air. The car shakes and trembles.

I watch as Leigh waves on several officers holding massive weapons that could take out the SUV with one shot. The officer at the back window finally breaks through. Instantly Arek and Peter are in the back seat, holding and fighting the officer that wants in.

Then, suddenly, the walls start to open again. All of us are surprised when Kilon can easily get through.

"Look!" Peter points to the Cellar, where Mannon and Jenner stand with smiles. "She did it. Prophet Jenner. I know she did." Peter laughs.

An officer is still hanging on to the back of the SUV, and I watch the veins in Arek's biceps bulge as the guard tries to get in. Finally, with a swift push, the guard falls from the back window.

"Go!" Arek yells as he climbs back into the middle seat—almost on top of me. Kilon steps on the gas, knowing that it won't be long before they chase after us.

Finally, we are on the open road, leaving the crowd behind.

After a few moments, Arek turns to me. For the first time since I have been put away in the Cellar, he is able to touch me and place his hands on my face. He lets my hands out of the cuffs. My arms are finally free, but one of my shoulders is not in place and I finally feel it. Pain sears my bones.

"My shoulder!" I cry out with my eyes squeezed shut.

He can tell instantly what has happened. With one hand on my shoulder and the other behind my clavicle, he jerks quickly, and I cry out as the bone shifts back into place.

For the first time since this all began, relief floods every cavity of my soul and I cover my face with my hands as I melt into him.

"It's over," he whispers as his hands cover my ears. "It's over."

11

I wake to Sassi driving while Arek's and Kilon's eyes are on the road behind us.

"I noticed them about fifteen minutes ago," Sassi breathes out in irritation. "I'm afraid to speed up and let them know we see them."

Kilon nods, but Geo's voice breaks in. "No Sassi, get us there. They know you see them and there are four more."

Sassi looks at Arek in the rearview mirror. "Arek?"

None of them seem to be aware that I am awake or maybe they don't care. Arek waits a moment to say anything as he studies the streets. We are in an unfamiliar city with beautiful modern architecture interspersed amongst old European influence. The streets are narrow, with some cobblestone here and there, walls of graffiti, and high-rise buildings.

Sassi keeps her eyes closely on the computer in the console. "Arek, I either take them closer to our place, or I take them farther away."

Finally, Arek nods. "Lose them."

She presses her feminine foot on the gas until the car growls and sneaks up on the traffic ahead. Her eyes are steady and focused as she weaves in and out.

"Yep, here they come." Kilon shakes his head and turns back around to face forward.

With every corner, the car screeches and threatens that it's too tight, but Sassi is defiant and seems to tell the car what it can handle. Several vehicles come closer, so she aggressively swerves down a skinny alleyway, then another, and another, until the chasers disappear. Finally, she whips around one more corner, narrowly gliding into a garage beneath a twelve-foot-high rolling metal door. In seconds, Arek and Kilon jump out of the SUV and use their strength to roll the old rusty door down.

The garage seems to be an old repair shop. Once the light from outside disappears, Kilon and Arek stare out the tinted windows.

"There they are." They wait a moment to see that the cars pass and when they do, Kilon looks at Arek. "Good enough?"

Arek grins and places a hand on his friend's shoulder. "Good enough." The rolling door has triple locks and I watch as Arek checks each one twice.

Beckah peers into the SUV once everyone is out, and I've not moved. "This is sort of the time we leave the vehicle," she jokes. It's possible that my face gives her nothing, since now, that is what I feel. Then her smile disappears. "Oh damn." She climbs into the car next to me and sits down and faces ahead just as I am. "It'll go away. I promise. What you saw? It'll go away."

Again, I have no response.

Arek walks over and they look at each other. Before she walks away, Beckah kisses my cheek, then she leaves us. Arek leans in. "I'm sorry," he finally whispers. His hand reaches out to touch mine; the stroke sends vibrations through my skin, so I close my eyes to soak it in. It isn't until I do that, that small tears escape the corner of my eye. "First . . . sleep. Just sleep," he says.

After a few more moments, I struggle to pull my aching body out. Everyone else has disappeared behind a door as I step onto the oil-stained floor. He gives me room, but just as I pass, he takes my arm and pulls me into him. My lifeless body melts into his.

After a moment of silence, he pulls away slightly and reaches behind him. "First things first." He brandishes what looks like a touchless thermometer gun, or something similar.

"What are you doing?" I ask.

Arek begins to trace my body with this gun. "We have to make it so they can't turn on your V-tap and track you." Methodically, starting with my arm, he searches my body. "Wherever the V-tap is, the body rises in temperature just slightly." The thermo gun beeps suddenly as it glides down my oblique. With two fingers he pushes heavily into the skin, then he unwraps and presses a clear bandage across the area. "These are especially made to disable it."

"That's how you've always been able to find me?" He grins but says nothing, so I continue, "If you can find where the V-tap sits in the body, why don't you just take it out?" I ask.

"Because it's not what you think. This isn't a microchip or anything like that. We carry phones that tell of our location at all times and we do it freely. This is only used for very specific purposes and only the highest in the Protectors have access to it. It's an injection that we were given at birth. It slides down the blood stream and eventually your body absorbs the solution. There's nothing to take out. We simply mask the signal with this bandage. If the bandage is removed, we're back to square one."

12

My body is cold and hot at the same time, vacillating from shaking to sweating. I walk the cement halls of the Cellar alone as the lights flicker within the gray. It is reminiscent of an old film—forcing my eyes to work harder and adjust more. I wrap my arms around myself as the reality of where I am exacerbates my fear. What lives here is unmentionable, what lives here is untethered, catering to the filtered lies that appear to be truth but fall lightly so as not to awaken one's inner intuition. Angst constricts my breath, while my eyes survey the morphing shadows. Inmates within their cells watch me, through the peepholes of the doors, as I walk past. Their vacant eyes never leave me. Just at the end of the hall, something slithers into view, bigger than human, no arms or legs, just body. My feet stop and retreat until I run into a door that has opened behind me. The inmate with yellow teeth and hollow temples emerges from around the corner, and I am trapped between that which slithers, and this criminal. My head pounds and I back away, hitting the wall behind me as both entities pursue me . . . the scream holds onto the walls of my chest until I must cough it out . . .

I am covered in sweat when I fly to a sitting position and a cry escapes my lips. My swift eyes quickly study the room. The sheets on a soft bed are all the way at my feet and the breeze blows a white curtain up and away from the window on the other side of the room. I press my hand to my pounding chest and beg it to calm down.

"It's okay." Arek's voice carries from nearby. The moon and stars outside illuminate his body as he walks to the bed from somewhere across the room. "Are you okay?"

Still, I am not ready to speak. The layers of ache are too thick to sift through now; he rests his hand on my face as he sits down close to me. "It's okay," he says again.

The darkness is so alive that the broken souls within the Cellar live in my mind as if they are in the room with me. Have they attached themselves to me? Have I brought the demons? How will I be the same? The rims of my eyes hurt and as I close them, tears fall. Arek's hand cups my face then travels to my neck. This is the invitation that I need to drop my head to his shoulder. "It's okay," he whispers again as he pulls me tighter to him.

Only now my chest starts to calm. I awake hours later, lying beside Arek as the morning sun fills the room with a yellow glow. He is looking at me, studying me, his hands running down my arms where burns are healing from the four men.

He doesn't say anything, nor do I, and for just a moment, I am free of the remnants until I stretch my feet and they still have pain.

"You came for me," I whisper.

"I will always come for you."

"I don't know how to tell you what happened." I brush my hair back with my burned hand.

"I already know."

"How?"

He reaches out for my hand and when he does, that is all the answer I need. He is my Yovu, whether I remember or not. My skin lays the groundwork for the tethering of his spirit to mine. Wherever my memories have been hiding, some of them ignite from his touch.

For a moment, I think about those tortured souls left behind in the Cellar. The crying and wailing of the lost begins again within my mind. It is too much to bear and I pull the pillow to cover my eyes. Arek draws closer.

"If I have climbed into the darkest part of someone's soul, how do I return to just me?" I breathe into the pillow, not hopeful for an answer that will suffice.

"You may have visited their hate, but that isn't their soul. No one's true self facilitates that damage or darkness."

"It surrounded me, day and night. It was a wading pool of pain and damage, which is the very reason they are there."

"The people in there are not the pain and damage. Release them in your mind, see them as they were truly born—free of any of that . . . and when you can see the separation, the difference between their damage and who they were meant to be . . . it will release you. I promise."

The vision of the woman with the blue veins comes to me. I close my eyes and think of her youth—or back even further to her birth—and of the innocence that is inherently hers. The heaviness in my chest lifts. I breathe out as Arek waits quietly.

When I open my eyes, he takes the chance to let me see a small smile.

"Did it work?" he asks.

"Yes," I say, as one last tear steals away from my eye. "What now?"

"Protect you and clear your name. Only now, we have no timeline . . . we just run from the Prophets and Powers. Every one of us blocked our trackers before we came to get you."

"All of you put yourselves in this position for me."

"And we would do it again . . ."

He pulls my palm to his lips and kisses it gently. For another hour, we say nothing, but let the sun and breeze speak to us as we rest.

13

We walk through the large apartment that looks to have once been a firehouse. The morning is quiet as Arek leads me by the hand. When we pass a window, I notice the tall buildings lining the streets as the sun shines across the pale wood floors. A soft breeze hits my healing skin. I stop for a moment just to take it in.

"Where are we?" I ask.

"A friend of Caynan's is letting us stay here, just until a doctor can look at you. We can't stay long."

I nod. We climb up two flights of metal stairs. My aching hand slides along the railing, helping my sore body rise step after step. We reach the third floor, where everyone sits around the living room. There are several monitors, a police scanner, and radios lined along a skinny table under several pieces of modern art in one corner of the open room.

It takes a moment for everyone to notice us, but when they do, Kilon turns the volume down while everyone stands. They clearly don't know what to say, or how to act, but neither do I.

It's as if they know that the Cellar might have changed me forever and the jury is still out. When I lost my mother, I was tightly wrapped in a fog and felt it was nearly impossible to find my way out. This is a bit like that, but worse. It's one thing to recognize the worst in humanity, it's another thing to experience it.

Arek looks at me as I press closer to him. Everyone is quiet. I clear my throat, before I speak. "Thank you."

Sassi pulls her long sweater down over her jeans as her feminine fingers fidget. She reaches out and places both her palms on my cheeks, from which I instantly feel a childlike relief. "Can I get you anything? Tea?"

I smile. "That would be great."

When she passes, she touches Arek's shoulder and they have a moment. Still, he never lets go of my hand.

"What are you listening to?" I ask.

Kilon speaks up, "This radio is tuned to the encoded channel that Leigh and the Protectors use. We've been listening to their pursuit to make sure we know that they aren't on top of us, and so far so good," he says reassuringly.

Beckah uses her tomboyish body and steps forward with a smile. She then dances toward me, until I can't help but smile. When she is so close I can feel her energy and warmth, she winks. "There's that beautiful smile . . . I made it happen . . . don't you forget it."

Her sunshine is impossible to resist. She then takes my hand in hers and sympathetically looks over the fingers that the men worked over.

"Wait till you meet my uncle Hugh," Beckah grins. "You think I'm a character . . . well let's just say he was always my source of inspiration."

Arek looks at the clock on the wall. "Where is Hugh?"

"He'll be here." She turns back to the room. "Uncle Hugh has never been one to work on anyone else's time and if he even thinks you're hurrying him, he works harder and more diligently to take longer. I love that guy."

After a bit of tea, and an hour past when he said he would show, Uncle Hugh—out of breath and sweaty—stops at the last step breathing heavily. He has a large nose, double chin, and spiky hair despite its receding line. "Could you have found a taller building?"

Arek laughs as he walks to the older man. "You're a doctor . . . you should be in better shape, Hugh."

"Son, it's a lot easier going back down those stairs."

The men laugh and shake hands. When Beckah hears her uncle from the kitchen, she jumps out of the doorway with a growl. "Ahhh!" He yells back at her in the same way, until they both get serious and unexpectedly robot dance their way to each other.

"Uncle Hugh!" Her voice is guttural like she's yelling at a football game. "Remember Remy?"

"I sure do." He turns to me with a friendly smile. "Arek said you would come back . . . but I suppose I'd lost a bit of hope. Yet here you are . . . my dear, my hope is restored."

I don't know how to respond, so I simply say, "Thank you."

"Let's check you out, dear. You all right with that?" he says kindly. "Yes."

We walk down the hall and he carries a black leather bag in his hand. We round the corner into a large room; I notice Arek's shirt hanging over a chair and his bag sitting in the corner. Several firearms are beside it and, next to that, his computer.

"Is this Arek's room?" I ask.

Arek enters just after me and concern fills the creases around his eyes. Hugh and Arek look at each other.

"This is where you slept last night," Arek says easily.

Moments later, Dr. Hugh looks over the healing wounds. I take him through my personal warzone, answering the "how" questions. He sets my fingers and wraps my feet. "Anything else?" he asks, as Arek waits by the window.

"Just this." I lift my shirt to show where they've branded me. The burns are still just as bright as when they were first done.

I can see the look on Dr. Hugh's face and in Arek's eyes. Arek comes closer to look at the branding. "Why do you both look like that?" I ask.

Dr. Hugh suddenly tries to pretend it is not as bad as it seems and clears his throat. "These won't go away. Burns are the one thing that have the largest possibility of scarring Velieri skin. Some of these may go, but these . . ." he points to several along my arms and stomach, "these are more than likely permanent. And this," he touches just below the branding, "this will stay."

"Well, I guess, proof that I lived through the Cellar." I smile. "I don't care about my body . . . it's here that scares me." I point to my head.

Hugh smiles. "Dear, don't be confused with here," he points to my heart. "That is what may take the longest, but mark my words . . . it will heal."

"I feel like I could sleep for a week."

Hugh stops what he is doing, places a hand on my arm, and drops his head to catch my down cast eyes. "Then you should sleep. Every bit of healing requires sleep. You'll never find your sense of humor without it." He winks. "I'm off to help your father chase the world."

"Please tell him hi for me."

"He'll be happy to hear it."

As he leaves, I crawl into bed. My eyes open and close, taking mental pictures of Arek as he moves about the room, pulling the shades down, then turning the lights off. I assume he will leave, but instead he crawls into bed and wraps his arms around me. His lips come close to my ear and his closeness takes my breath. "I'm sorry," he whispers again.

This is everything I need. My eyes close and I draw from the rise of his chest to guide my own.

14

My eyes flutter open. One single ray of light from a near window shines across my face and warms my skin. The handsome figure sitting in a chair on the other side of the room interests me more. Arek stares out the window with a gun in his hand. I sit up and realize my pain has decreased when my fingers easily wiggle in front of my eyes, yet when I peek at my stomach, the branding is still there, just as Hugh said it would be.

"What are you doing?" I ask him.

He quickly looks at me, seemingly pulled from whatever trance he was in. "Just thinking."

"About what?" Before he says anything, I throw my hand in the air to stop him. "Wait," I say. "You were thinking about where Navin might be."

Arek grins.

"What?" I ask.

"You know me."

I smile. "At times . . ."

Finally, he continues, "Navin's my brother . . . you would think I would know where his favorite places to hide are, but . . ." His voice fades away and he chooses not to finish his thought. After a moment he stands, stretches out his long body, then walks to me. He places a palm on my cheek. "How are you?"

"Pain free."

"Good."

After we've dressed, my hands run along the smooth walls as we walk quietly through the hall. A vision of the Cellar flashes in my mind; instantly, I'm overwhelmed until sweat runs down my forehead and my body slightly shakes. I squeeze my eyes tight. *Still with me, huh?*

Arek comes close when he sees that I'm struggling. "Remy?" His rests his hand on my neck with his thumb at my jaw.

"I'm sorry . . . I don't feel right."

"Just breathe." He waits a moment before speaking, letting my nerves calm one breath at a time.

Finally, the moment passes, and I let out one staggered breath. He takes my hand as we continue through the hall. I concentrate on a large hanging picture to my right. It's a six-foot-long canvas of four large creatures—neither human nor animal, perhaps a mixture of both. "What are these?" I ask him. "I've seen them before, maybe in my other life?"

"They should be familiar. This is the Velieri crest. These are the four effigies representing the downfall of the Ephemes. It's to remind us how to live." He points at them one at a time, "The first has no armor. It represents how the Ephemes do not teach their young to protect themselves, but every Velieri learns protection in our mind, body, and spirit from a young age. The second creature has two heads, which represents that the Ephemes can't seem to agree on anything."

"To be fair, the Velieri don't seem to be good at agreeing either."

"You're right. However, I believe that one day we can get there. I also believe that Velieri began with the intention of peace. Velieri were willing to go into hiding simply to appease the jealousy of Ephemes. We have it in us to believe in a Utopian society." His hand runs along the canvas as he continues, "This third one, here, has no neck, which represents the Ephemes inability to look behind him and learn from the past. Then the last creature has a massive gold necklace that weighs him down till he cannot move. The Ephemes spend their lives in gluttony, but Velieri learned long ago that money gives no one happiness."

I chuckle. "So far, I've only known Velieri to have a lot of money."

"Many of us have chosen at different times to live without money—to be happy with or without it." He steps closer to me until our chests touch and his hands run down my hair. Slowly he lowers his head until his lips hover over mine. Finally, he kisses me, sending the vibration and electricity through my skin. Just for a moment I am free of the Cellar, until the moment he pulls away and it is back, dragging my spirit to the floor.

"Arek!" Kilon calls from the living room. We head to where everyone else has gathered. All eyes are watching the news. Kilon notices Arek, so he quickly speaks. "There have been more incidents. Boston, Montreal, Pervise, Liberia, and San Diego territories, among others, have noticed an increase in Ephemes finding out about Velieri. The Reds have gone in and taken care of what they can. No one is blaming Navin . . . yet we all know who cares the least about Ephemes knowing about us."

"What can we possibly have to do with Ephemes finding out about us?" I ask.

Kilon speaks, "Over the years, some Ephemes have discovered our existence, while many others have heard theories or rumors about us. Reports are constantly being made around the world about Velieri. However, when Ephemes see too much, Velieri must cover it up somehow. So Ephemes are often taken in to go through a long treatment of hypnosis and tests to forget what they know. Leaks happen here and there, but there seems to be an alarming increase since you came back. The Reds and the Correctional Territory Authority are working their asses off right now. If there are too many, it will at some point be out of control and we all know what happens when people are afraid and don't know enough. Panic." Kilon smiles and walks to me, then kisses me on my forehead as a father would. "Sorry

. . . all this is too much, too early in the morning. Good morning, sunshine."

Arek crosses his arms and says, "We should be heading out soon. We can't linger. Twenty minutes."

15

Traveling across the world Velieri style is easy. Far above miles of land and sea, I peer out of the window of the Gulfstream jet, surrounded by every ounce of luxury and overabundance that life can buy. The jet—checked for trackers and logged under an unknown name—glides over a half moon shaped airport that, once again, I know I've been to before. The others have been busy on their phones and in meetings for most of the flight, leaving me alone with my thoughts. A severe discomfort and fear twists and turns in my belly, as though it has arms and legs. Sweat falls from my brow and tells me that the Cellar is not gone. I rush to the bathroom to throw water on my face. Warm water wraps around my cold hands, and when I look up at the mirror, I gasp. The tortured woman with blue veins and lips stands behind me—she is so close to my ear that I feel her breath as she whispers in a raspy voice, "I'm here." I swiftly turn. No one is there. I clumsily rush out of the bathroom and fall into Geo.

"You okay?" he says with his hands on my elbows.

"I'm fine," I whisper as I head back to my seat.

All of us cover ourselves with glasses, hats, jackets, and bags as we hurry to waiting cars. We drive along the winding streets of the city, dwarfed by tall buildings and hugged by beautiful beaches. At first, I have no idea where we are, but soon I read a sign: "RIO DE JANEIRO." A stuttered breath escapes me as the car emerges from behind buildings and the blue sky opens behind the Christ the Redeemer statue. It is grander than I ever could have known.

"I'd never been anywhere before all of this," I say to Peter, who sits next to me.

Peter laughs. "Kind of. That's actually not true."

I laugh. "Yeah, I guess not."

"This place is big and overpopulated. Finding us should be difficult," Sassi explains.

The city pulses with life. Ten people vie for every square foot, but it is easy to understand why since it is beautiful beyond what I have ever known. Brazil, a place that before would have been only an idea or a dream, is now surrounding me with culture more alive and unrestrained than my imagination could create.

The sleek cars maneuver down an alleyway, where the drivers stop, directing the line of fancy vehicles behind us to do the same. We jump out and take a moment to look up at the tall buildings surrounding us.

"Up there?" I ask.

Arek nods. "Up there."

"Okay."

We enter a parking garage and ascend several flights of stairs before entering an elevator that takes us up seven more. The elevator doors open to a large golden sign that says "Gianda." I take two steps before I stop and turn to the rest of the group.

"I know this place well . . . don't I?"

"Yeah, you do," Sassi agrees.

The walls are covered with the most beautiful graffiti so none of the brick is untouched. My hand runs along the antiqued letters of Gianda that are engraved in a large four-foot sign. Two men see us from within and quickly hurry to open the well secured French doors.

"*Gianda* means Guard in Velieri?" I ask.

Sassi nods, "Et tui empasias pae vi Gianda."

I translate, "It was important for *me* to name this place Gianda?"

Sassi nods and places a hand on my shoulder. "We'll explain everything. Let's just get settled and safe."

The double doors lead directly onto a loft . . . lifted high above the biggest open building that looks nothing like I expected. It reminds me of a very large and open mall, except without the stores. Vegetation and life grow in a large park underneath a sunroof in the middle of this massive real estate. People zip in and out of rooms, into the park—some even go outside onto a fourth story rooftop that looks like a backyard. I walk to the railing, from where we have the perfect view over all of this. "I've never seen anything like this before."

Beckah comes to stand on one side of me, while Sassi is on the other. "Yeah, I remember the first time I saw it too," Beckah says. "Wait till you hear the story of how it got here. Talk about Remy and her power to persuade."

The people within these walls are covered in tattoos from head to toe, piercings all over their skin. Many of them have shaved heads, even the women. I recognize them from the men and women I saw outside the Cellar as I was heading in. "The Fidelis?"

Arek nods at me, then shakes the hands of the men who brought us inside. They look at me with wide eyes and wait just a bit too long to speak before I grow uncomfortable.

"I'm sorry," one of them says. "It's just that you hear rumors. But it's another thing to see it for yourself. We can't believe that you're back." The man smiles. "We hope you're okay after the Cellar."

"Me too," I say quietly.

He continues, "Nothing has ever been greater for the Fidelis than to have you back." He reaches out to shake my hand, so I do. "You protected us for so long . . . now it's our turn to protect you." He is an imposing figure with tattoos that I recognize to be representative of the Navajo tribe. His Indigenous heritage shows through his pronounced eyebrows and thick heavy black hair that is shaved on the sides. "My name is Hok'ee, but people call me Hok for short."

Suddenly a matrix of some language I know well runs through my mind. "*Hok'ee* means abandoned in Navajo?"

Hok smiles, "That's right."

"Ya'at'eeh," I say hello.

"Ya'at'eeh abini," he says, good morning. "We've met before. In fact, you and I had meetings together nearly every month for many years. I helped you begin the Gianda in San Francisco in the seventies until it was taken over by two sisters. A decade ago, I came to Brazil to help this one thrive."

"Then there are more of these?"

Hok smiles and his lip piercing moves with his skin. "There are . . . many. You built them for years . . . all over the world. Nearly forty to be exact."

I turn to Arek. "That's why you figure no one will know where we are?"

"Well . . . and we are all criminals now . . . and Hok isn't afraid to take us in."

"That's right," Hok proudly says. "The more rebellious the better. In fact, we have a saying here, how else do you find how big God is without breaking down the walls."

I smile.

"It's good to have you back, Remy," Hok says.

Just beyond Hok, I notice an open window with an astonishing view of Rio de Janeiro. The city continues for miles.

"Welcome to Rio de Janeiro. A place to blend in and disappear," Hok says. "Let me take you around and show you the place. Did you take care of your trackers?"

Arek nods. "Well before today."

In a few minutes, we walk through the city within the city, where there are apartments, restaurants, doctors' offices, yards, and gardens, but from the outside it simply looks like apartment buildings. The façade is unbelievable.

"We own several blocks," Hok explains. "Giandas are set up for the Fidelis to never have to leave, if they don't want to. If they never want to step outside these doors, then they are free to do that. We have everything we need. To pass from one building to the next, you don't have to go outside, rather— look up there," Hok points above us, as we have traveled down to the floor with the park. Just out the window where he points are multiple passageways from one building to the next all at different levels. "From the outside, no one can see anyone passing from building to building because the windows are tinted. It's important that we keep the Gianda as secret as we can."

People begin to gather as we pass, whispering and pointing at me. Hok leans over to me, "Wave at them and watch what they do."

So, I wave at a group of kids who stare from the story above us. Instantly they giggle and their eyes burst with excitement.

The sunlight from outside creates a natural glow and the scattered clouds cast slow-moving shadows on the adjacent walls. Every door is blue, and the colors are vibrant in true Brazilian fashion. Just outside a wall of windows is a massive courtyard.

"This is incredible," I whisper.

"Come on," Arek finally steps forward to intervene. "Let's go sit somewhere and help her understand this place."

We shortly find ourselves in a large room built on the roof. The ocean is just a mile away and all I want is to jump in.

"Where do we start?" Hok looks at Arek. It is obvious they know each other well.

Arek stretches his neck, Kilon scratches his head, while Beckah hums and Geo cracks his knuckles. Peter stirs enough sugar in his drink to make it solid. Sassi rolls her eyes, "It really is irritating that you always leave the hard stuff to me." Sassi says thank you to the woman who brings her tea, then she turns back to me. "Just after the Methos and Ephemes war, when the government decided that we would all stay hidden and become Velieri, the government had to somehow make sure that everyone followed the protocol. So, they put measures in place. At first everyone was given a number no different than our social security numbers. They were written on parchments, in books, and as we've become more advanced, we keep track of everyone with the V-tap."

I touch the bandage over mine, as Sassi continues the story. "As with anything, there were many people who refused to be a part of the system—for themselves and for their children. They risked their lives to make sure their pregnancies and births were kept quiet. They would have babies in places that the Powers and Prophets wouldn't know. All for the sake of anonymity. When the government found out that this was happening, they created a task force to handle the situation. Many of the parents and children were killed, if they were ever found. If they were found out, they faced prison, or worse . . . all because their parents had chosen for them to be unattached to the government. The challenge was, if you don't have this connection to the government, how do you live, how do you work? Because of the target already on their back, they couldn't open businesses, couldn't get jobs, so they starved and found it nearly impossible to live. You refused to let that happen, so for many years you traveled, gathering wealthy donors, whom you trusted to never say anything to the government, and create Giandas all over the world. Here, the unwanted can thrive. No one thought this would work, except you. Here we are, and the economy within these places is better than ever."

There was silence for a while as my brain computed this idea. "Are they stuck here?"

"No," Sassi says easily. "Not at all. However, if they want to make a living at something, the Gianda helps them."

"And the Powers or Prophets have never found this out?"

"I believe they have inklings, but we are very careful. And besides, we have grown so large and have created our own army so they may be afraid to rock the boat," Hok explains.

"The government should know by now," I say looking to Arek and my friends, "that your trackers have been blocked."

Arek interjects, "That's why, from here on out, we will have to work harder at getting around. They know we've stopped our trackers.

None of the Fidelis ever had one. The government doesn't even know these people exist." Arek turns to Hok. "Thank you for taking us in. I recognize that this could create a lot of trouble for you."

Hok laughs. "We're here because someone named each one of us 'trouble' when we were just kids. Our destinies were decided by something we were never even a part of, and Remy stood up for us. It would be wrong to do anything but accept you all with open arms. Besides, my people, all my fellow Navajo brothers and sisters, believe in restoring balance and harmony."

"I just have to say it though," Arek nods with a grin. "We are criminals. You are taking in criminals."

Hok laughs even harder, then takes a drink. "I believe I've been a criminal longer. You just may have a thicker noose around your neck at this moment."

Kilon whistles and grins.

Hok turns his attention to Peter. "Peter, you're growing fast. It's like seeing a young Arek." Arek roughly rubs his little brother's head with a smile. "The GoLightlys are back at this Gianda, just thought you'd be interested."

Instantly, a red glow lights Peter's face as the table lets out small cat calls.

"Who are the GoLightlys?" I ask.

Beckah, who is sitting on the other side of Peter, nudges him. "Peter, tell her who the GoLightlys are. Come on . . . butterfly . . ."

Peter can't look at anyone, however his lips curve in the hint of a smile. "It's just a family . . . they're nice."

"A family with two beautiful daughters, one named Lily who has a special interest in Peter," Beckah explains.

Finally, he looks me in the eye. "Yeah, she's interested." He shrugs. "We'll see."

16

Hok provides us with a five-bedroom apartment and even places the "in-house" security at our door. I am tired from still wrestling with the remnants of the Cellar, which is growing worse by the hour. My brain is getting foggier—not clearer—and now, in each mirror or window that I pass, she's there with her terrifying empty stare that makes me feel as though the roof is caving in.

After a shower, I stare out the window while I comb my wet hair. The views of this beautiful sprawling city beside mountains and ocean should be mesmerizing, but at this moment, I am blind to it. In my reflection, she is there. Her blue veins are bright beneath her skin and her eyes are so empty. Her pain and torture sit on my chest until I rest a hand there out of concern. My mind returns to the halls of the Cellar, again fighting the oppression and ache of tormented souls. The sin that was once confined to the walls of the Cellar feels shackled to me. To live this daily, in all pretenses, forces me to feel as destitute as they.

I squeeze my eyes shut and grab my water with hands that shake uncontrollably. Something or someone touches my shoulder, which makes me jump, and the glass slips from my fingertips, breaking into a thousand pieces when it hits the ground.

"I'm sorry," Arek says quickly. "I was calling your name." As he helps me step over the mess, his eyes never leave mine. "Where were you?"

"Lost," I whisper.

I can see on his face that he isn't surprised. "You'll learn to let them go and be free. We're going to teach you."

"Can all Velieri see what I see?"

"No. You and Sassi were always connected to things from another realm . . . another world . . . unlike anything I've ever seen. Everyone has their unique gift. This one is yours."

"I don't want it."

He grins, "Too bad. I suppose you can try to put it to bed, but it won't be easy. Turning away from your gifts is harder than just accepting them and learning what you can do with them. Those souls you saw in the Cellar, they don't have to stay there. They can leave. Yet they've chosen or been manipulated into becoming a slave to who they once were. After a while . . . it becomes too late. They camp out between this world and the next, never really living or dying."

I am quiet. My mind is sifting slowly through what he just said, but not having the energy to react. With his forefinger and thumb, he twists a piece of my wet hair. "There is a party tonight. I couldn't stop it . . . Hok does what he wants."

The world suddenly gets heavier, and I breathe out the weight of what this means.

He continues. "You'll be fine. I promise . . . you may actually enjoy yourself."

The "in-house" guards walk me through the halls, ride the elevators with me, and lead me through mirrored passageways where we can see out, but no one can see in. I learn how massive the Gianda truly is—it seems to be several blocks before we reach the crowd on the roof deck. The football field–size rooftop sits high above the city. Lights hang in a zigzag pattern over long tables. Arek stands out above all the rest as he chats with a group of people I do not recognize. He is wearing a white button-up shirt, gray slacks, and a brown leather belt—that fit him in all the right places—and I stop for a moment just to stare. Sassi's long statuesque body is perfectly curved in a tight pink dress and three-inch heels. I look down at the black dress she loaned me. I had wondered if I would be overdressed, but clearly everyone took this time to revive what we had lost over the last year. When I look up, Arek is staring at me. For a moment, we simply watch each other, then a slow grin comes to his lips.

Moments later, we sit around the large banquet tables while chatter and laughter fill the air.

Hok looks at me from across the table. His piercings shine under the lights as he smiles, "I invited a hundred people to see you tonight. Hundreds more would have come if allowed."

"Thank you," I say quietly.

The awestruck nature I feel when the people of the Gianda glance at me makes me fidget in my seat until Arek, while still in conversation with others, takes my hand in his.

After so much food is brought to the table that we cannot finish it, Hok takes a sip of his beer and sits back, so I lean over to him.

"It's hard to believe the government does not know this exists."

Hok nods, but then shrugs. "Let's just say, I'm not convinced they don't know. The Giandas have grown to an insurmountable amount of people who could make a lot of trouble for the Powers and Prophets. So, someone up there probably thinks it's best not to wake the beast. But I do think trouble started happening for you as this grew."

"I get the feeling I didn't do much to get on anyone's good side," I admit. He chuckles, but his eyes study me. "What?" I ask.

"I'm sorry, forgive me. It's just strange to be speaking with the woman who gave so much of herself to help us, and now she knows nothing about doing any of it."

"I wish I did. I'm sorry . . ."

"No, on the contrary, I think it's been good for us. We always worried that this place would fall apart without you. I mean, after all, we were always told that we were criminals and unworthy of a normal life. You were the only one to fight for us and tell us otherwise. I suppose we had it in our minds that if something happened to you, we wouldn't be able to make it on our own. Yet, you died more than thirty years ago and here we are. We're still safe. The Powers have let us be."

Kilon turns to Hok, quickly joining the conversation. "We didn't see much of you or hear from you until . . ." Kilon hesitates, "until Remy was back."

"Keeping quiet is what we do best. I suppose we fought for so long just to be treated fairly, that once we achieved peace, we desired to keep it—"

A shorter Latino man named Jace, who was with Hok earlier in the day, interrupts him, "—losing you was horrible. A part of all of us died with your execution and none of us believe what was said about you."

"Thank you, but . . ." I study the crowd and rub my forehead aggressively. "We shouldn't be here." The conversation from our table halts until the clink of glasses and discussions from the other tables fills our ears. A sweeping breeze lifts my hair and cools the sweat on my neck. It's the hottest time of year in Rio and my black dress sticks to my body.

"We want you here," Hok assures me. "We can take a little danger."

"Remy . . ." Jace waits until my eyes meet his. "We have an army that the government would never expect. I say bring 'em. I welcome the opportunity to fight."

Arek speaks up. "Our people are actively monitoring where the Powers are deploying their forces. If we get any notion that they have tracked us here, we will leave. There is a reason we have come."

"There is?" I ask.

Before anyone answers, a small bit of commotion pulls our eyes to the glass door entrance to the rooftop. Briston enters with Mak and Kenichi by his side. I jump to my feet and rush to Briston's side as he pulls me in with a smile. "It's good to see you. Are you okay?"

I nod, but I want nothing more than to tell him how I'm not. Nothing feels as though it will ever be the same. Until I look into his eyes and see that there is no hiding from him . . . he already knows that things are quite different. The pain and torment from the criminals, past and present, within the Cellar will not leave me alone.

Mak peeks his head around Briston's shoulder and he, too, provides me with familiarity that I so desperately need. There is no better gift than history with someone. I grin and wipe my tears before accepting Mak's hug. Everyone around us is basking in a joyful reunion, so Mak and I have a moment together.

"You made it," he whispers.

"Did I?"

He touches my face with a concerned expression. "That's why we're here. We have some work to do." His comfortable hands take my cheeks as his eyes seek mine. When I finally connect with him, my heart calms. "We're here for you. Anything you need." Finally, Mak drops his hand to my shoulder as other people come to say hello and that is when I notice Arek watching us from across the table. He takes a sip of his beer as a woman I've never seen before tries to steal his attention.

Most of the party dissolves leaving our core group, now including Hok and Jace. We sit at the table for hours. Peter is huddled in a corner with the sweet fifteen-year-old Lily. Here and there, in the Gianda's private corners, Peter has done his best to find quiet moments with her. My shoulder leans against Beckah's, who is sitting next to me with her water resting on her knee. "If Lily is Fidelis," I say, "even if they have the same blood makeup, will they be able to be together?"

Beckah breathes out heavily. "No," she laughs, "but you know what? Screw the Prophets. Freedom is what we're fighting for, right?"

Beckah and I watch as Peter sweetly kisses Lily's cheek. Her dark hair falls heavily over one eye, showing just one of her rich brown eyes.

Briston's salt and pepper hair looks less pepper and more salt than ever before as he tells everyone of their travels. "We did our best to keep the scent off us. Multiple flights, multiple cars, keeping no one in the loop but us," Briston explains. "The search is on for all of you. Covey is aggressively managing it. We need to be careful. They have the Reds involved and so many more. Remy's old contacts have all been grilled—"

"And they haven't caught you, sir?" Sassi says with a wink and smile.

Briston grins, "It's hard to catch a ghost." My father looks at Sassi. "And may I say you are beautiful Sassi, as always."

"You absolutely may say that," Sassi says, as she nudges Kilon's arm.

"Leigh is on a rampage," Briston continues.

"I'm sure he is." Arek runs his hand through his hair, which is a habit I now notice when Leigh is mentioned.

Briston shakes his head. "No, you don't understand. He has called in all assets, including Geretzima's men."

Arek's grin disappears. It takes a moment, but Kilon and Arek look at each other. The heaviness looms.

"Geretzima?" I ask.

Peter begins, "You remember. I told you about Alfonzo when Arek went missing. Arek and Navin both went through his training. The Umbramanes . . . the Shadow Ghosts."

Arek finally speaks, "Men led by Alfonzo Geretzima are the world's most elite trackers." His voice shares the gravity of the situation.

Hok speaks with an authority that explains why Remy chose him to oversee the Gianda. "This means that you will be found eventually. It's only a matter of time."

"Can we keep track of Geretzima's men?" Peter asks. "If we know where they are, we can stay one step ahead."

Briston shakes his head. "I hadn't anticipated this. My assumption was that Alfonzo would refuse to do as the Prophets asked. He has no contract with them, but they clearly offered him something. You know him best . . ." Briston says to Arek. "No one will tell me anything at this point, so by the time I knew what the Powers and Leigh were planning, a group of Umbramanes were already gone."

Beckah speaks up with concern. "So they could already know we are here?"

"We've done everything we can." Briston shrugs.

"You're second in command of the Protectors—and you're the Monarch of the Elite," I say. "That has no power?"

Sassi shakes her head. "We lost our titles the moment we decided to get you out . . . including your father."

All because of me.

"But Arek," Peter begins, "you worked with Alfonzo. You know what they know."

Arek shakes his head and takes another sip of his drink. "No. I didn't spend enough time—"

Peter interrupts, "Didn't spend enough time? That doesn't matter . . . you caught on quicker than anyone else. Alfonzo himself said you knew enough."

"Peter . . ." Arek warns his little brother to stop.

Peter continues, "I get that you don't want to say anything, but don't lie to yourself. . . you know just as much as Alfonzo."

Briston interrupts the brotherly spat. "Look, we'll be fine. We won't stay in the same place for too long. But we have to start training Remy immediately."

17

No matter how many times I blink, my eyes don't get used to the darkness. Not even the light from the clock on the nightstand, which reads midnight, is enough. My heart pounds against my chest as though I've just fallen several stories, but never hit ground.

When I close my eyes, I see her—the woman from the Cellar. She stares at me, as her veins pulse beneath her skin, and she shakes with anger. This Unyielded woman is not the only one taking up space within me. It feels as if multiple people have found residence in my body and soul. Their vibrational angst and crushing sorrow are in constant war. *How deep does this hell go?* My muscles strain and my head aches with an unexplainable panic.

The apartment that they have given us is quiet as everyone sleeps, however my room is heavy—the thick air grinds my temples. I tell my arms and legs to move, but they don't. In fact, my fingers stay pasted to the bed. Somehow, I can roll over, but I fall to the ground with paralyzed limbs and the thud against my bones sends shooting pain through my hip and shoulder. There is a pressure so intense on my chest, that my ribs might crack.

What is happening?

Quick feet enter my room and draw close, but I'm paralyzed; I stare at the ceiling fan turning round and round. Two voices become clear. "Remy?" Arek and Sassi are there at my side and drop to their knees. Sassi cradles my head, while my muscles spasm. Arek leans over me.

Every part of me is frozen, which makes speaking impossible.

Sassi and Arek look at each other. "We knew this would happen," Sassi says to him as she caresses my cheek. "We need Kilon."

"We got you, Remy," Arek whispers in my ear.

In just minutes, Kilon kneels in front of me and gently touches my face. "Hi darlin'. It's okay. Look at me." I look into Kilon's eyes, desperate. "Just breathe. I'll take care of you." Somehow, somewhere within my chest and head, Kilon manages to reach whatever has me paralyzed. His gentle hum, relaxing and pure, directly blocks the voices that have remained with me since the Cellar and my mind begins to go blank until all I desperately want is to sleep. It doesn't take long until his powerful gift sends me there.

I don't wake till the morning sun sprays across my room. Arek sleeps peacefully on his side with his thick arms crossed in front of him. My heavy eyes follow the lines on his brow.

"Why are you staring at me?" he whispers with closed eyes.

"What happened to me? Why couldn't I move?"

He reaches out and gently places a hand on my cheek. "The Cellar doesn't leave us easily."

"Have you been there?"

"Not as an inmate, but with the Umbramanes during our training. And even then, Alfonzo took us through a 'cleansing' from what we experienced. We will do the same for you."

"The Umbramanes . . . why is everyone so afraid of them?" He stays quiet and wipes his tired eyes. "You don't want to tell me?" I whisper.

"Alfonzo teaches people how to disappear . . . how to live in the shadows. He doesn't just teach anyone—he scours the world for the best. There is one thing they teach that I was never able to justify though. You are not allowed a conscience. From the shadows, to cutting someone's throat in seconds, never knowing or caring whether they deserve it . . ." He pauses. "They complete their missions, in any way they can, long before anyone knows they are there. Assassins without rules."

"Assassins."

"Gone before you can blink."

"So, you learned to be one of them . . . to disappear?"

"I did, but I didn't stay with Alfonzo . . . mostly because I was given the position as Second-in-Command of the Protectors, but I would also have to sign a contract to never get married."

I grin. "A woman held you back?"

He smiles. "No, I wouldn't say that. A woman set me free."

18

Today on the first day of training, as we make our way through the Gianda, Kilon stuffs his mouth with a white powder donut, leaving residual white sugar everywhere.

"Where'd you get the donut?" I ask, as chunks hit the front of his ripped chest and stick to his shirt.

"They were delivered to my room this morning." He grins with a quick lift of his eyebrows.

"None were delivered to me." I look at Arek, then Sassi, who are both smiling. "Why are you smiling?"

Sassi looks at Kilon. "I told you not to eat that in front of her."

Kilon can't help but chuckle. "It's a good lesson."

Sassi hands me a bottle of green juice. My eyes get big as I look closely at the pond water. "This is your breakfast," she says. "We don't want you puking with what's ahead. Sorry." They've also made me dress in leggings and a tank top.

I open the lid of my green drink, try not to breathe, and take a sip. It barely goes down. "Are you kidding me?" I choke.

Kilon laughs as he shakes his head. "No one can stand that bloody drink but you, Sassi. Give her something better than that."

Sassi looks at her husband with a raised eyebrow. "I'd be quiet, or you'll be drinking the same thing tomorrow. Remy, make sure to drink all of it."

My stomach lurches at the thought. Arek smiles as I try to take another sip but fail miserably. We reach another rooftop—different than the one from yesterday's party. There's green turf across most of it, and a large warehouse with two fifteen-foot-tall doors. Hok is waiting outside the doors.

"Good morning." He looks at the drink in my hand. "Sassi, I'm pretty sure you're trying to kill all of us with that drink."

"Just open the door, Hok."

Hok opens the doors to reveal a large open space. One side is covered with thick black mats on the ground and the other is set up for working out. We step inside.

"We've closed it off, just for you." Hok turns on a giant fan nearby.

"Great," I say sarcastically.

Several voices catch our attention through the doors of the warehouse. When we turn around, I instantly recognize a rough and edgy man. His name is Atum. He is older, but still handsome and built.

"Atum," I say, as he draws near.

Atum steps back with surprise. "I was told you didn't remember?"

Everyone else is also caught off guard. "I trained with you. I remember well actually . . . in fact, being in Egypt with you is clear to me."

Atum puts a hand on my shoulder and says, "I'm honored." I look at Arek, who winks at me. Then I take in a shallow breath as Atum continues, "Don't look so nervous. If you lived through training with me once, you can do it again."

From the opposite side of the gym, Mak yanks a large handle that turns on all the lights. Mak explains, as though he's put it together, "Kenichi and Arek are here to teach you to fight . . . tae kwon do, jujitsu, karate, among many others. Atum will build your strength. Geo and Sassi will train you in mind control and connection, while Kilon, Arek, and Beckah will work on your weapons training. Sassi will also teach you to drive."

Briston steps within the circle. "Thank you everyone for meeting here. If anyone sees anything unusual, please do not hesitate to tell us. Unfortunately, we need to be more careful than ever. Alfonzo Geretzima and an undisclosed amount of Umbramanes disappeared yesterday. We don't know where they are."

Hok speaks up. "Please feel at home here. We are prepared. Every person in the Gianda knows where they belong . . . so please do not underestimate the power that we hold. We are here to protect Remy no matter what trouble comes."

"Thank you, Hok," Briston says with a nod.

"I'm curious about her ability to learn quickly," Beckah says. "She's only months into her rebirth, usually it takes, even at best, seven years to recoup."

Out of the shadows, Dr. Hugh—wearing a tailored blue suit and his hair an absolute disaster—enters the conversation. "She is quite young, and it does take seven years to reach her full potential. This makes her more vulnerable to pain, to wounds, to mental anguish; she will take longer to recover. But," he begins, "Remy was . . . *is* very strong. She will do well and we will simply provide better care for her since she is at such risk . . . right Kilon?"

Kilon nods. "She is mine and Sassi's to protect. We've done it for six hundred years and we will continue to keep her safe. If we say she has had enough, then you will stop your training. If anyone sees anything out of the ordinary, we are the first to be notified."

Everyone nods.

"Atum, you are first," Mak instructs. "Dr. Hugh will be checking in periodically to monitor her health. It is time to get started."

19

A pool of water beneath me makes my feet slide. I have never known my body to sweat like this. As I stare in a mirror, Atum makes sure that every move I make is done with the greatest technique.

"Without technique," he says to me as I hold dumbbells in each hand, straight out from my shoulders until the burn is more than I can handle, "your body has no backbone. Without technique, your body has no strength in your base, in your feet. If you can learn to use your entire body when you step, instead of just your feet, you will not falter. Every hit, every punch, and every toss of your body means nothing, if you cannot back it with your core and mind. Therefore, in the next few days," he continues as I cry out from pain, wanting desperately to drop my hands, "you will be pushed beyond your limits to create new mind, body, soul."

Every muscle is screaming as I shake all over. The moan that escapes my mouth is unrecognizable. Then finally, when my arms drop just a bit, he nods. "You may let them go." The dumbbells fall to the floor and bounce on the rubber mat.

Based on my memories, I had expected Atum to train me with throwing rocks, swinging hammers, and lifting logs; but instead, he uses modern techniques and combines them with old principles. He is training me for power and endurance, as I jump onto boxes and toss around weights.

My heart races to keep up with my body, and I notice Kenichi and Kilon in the mirror. Kenichi comes forward between my sets to stand by Atum. In his broken English, he points at my body—first at my shoulders and then at my legs.

They speak for a moment, then Kenichi walks back to Kilon.

"What is he saying?" I ask.

"You have weak shoulders, but large legs. He wants your shoulders to be as strong as your legs."

Atum smiles, until I smile back at him. "Okay, then. Fix my weak shoulders, Atum."

"As if I cannot see these things . . . but Kenichi is also not someone I care to offend in any way. He wants you to move well and be strong enough to hit hard . . . I understand that . . . and we'll make it happen."

Nearly two weeks later, when Atum has ground me into the floor until I cannot speak, repeatedly, I walk into the dojo barely able to keep my legs beneath me. My quads, hamstrings, calves, and every other muscle scream for rest. They are stiff and sore, even though I have gone to a masseuse every night. It is the kind of massage that rips and pulls at my muscles until they bruise. My hands tremble, as I grip my water bottle. It also doesn't help that every night I have woken up paralyzed. I haven't told anyone about the woman from the Cellar, who stares back at me in every reflection.

When I reach up to pull my hair back, my triceps barely let them rise above my head. By the time I reach the mats, Kenichi and Arek are already practicing. They don't notice me enter and it gives me a chance to watch what I might learn. The style they are fighting isn't something I recognize. They are masters in so many forms of martial arts that they all seem to blend.

Just the day before, Kenichi explained it by saying, "You need not worry what it is . . . you only worry about how to make it yours."

In other words, we don't have the time. Their job is simple: make me a good fighter—grappling, striking, kicking, submitting, and controlling whoever is my enemy in whatever form I can learn.

Arek and Kenichi are both sweaty and shirtless. Kenichi has the typical pants worn by martial artists. The pants are black with a high waist, and they are loose around the legs to allow for unhindered movement. Their size difference doesn't seem to matter as they spar. From the small bit I have learned, they are practicing muay thai—a form best known for its striking and kicking.

Their fluid, fast, and unexpected movements are mesmerizing. They move so rapidly that I wonder how either one blocks the other. Next to Arek's tattooed body, Kenichi has only two markings. On his back is a dragon and on his chest is the lion, an emblem I often see on his clothing. The old man moves like he is still a teenager.

Neither of them can catch the other in any mistake. They travel from one end of the mat to the other, never stopping. Their hands slap each other, their legs tangle, and they exchange positions like a puzzle—each one is trying to solve it best.

Suddenly Kenichi throws his hand in the air and stops the fight. He turns his eyes to me, as though he already knows I am standing there. "You are late."

"I have been standing here for some time," I answer.

"Come." Kenichi calls me over and forces me to stand in front of Arek. "You remember what we taught you the other day?"

"A bit. I fear everything has fallen from my brain. It's all too much."

"Nothing is too much," Kenichi answers. "That is your choice to think this. Nothing is too much."

I don't look at Arek. We have spoken so little since the training started. I suppose this is on purpose, but my body and mind also shut down quickly once nighttime comes. We simply pass each other in the hall, he touches my face for just a moment, then leaves me to fall in bed, only to wake up by the alarm once again the next morning.

Kenichi takes a towel to his sweat as he talks. "You not understand what it is to be a true warrior until you understand Bushido." Kenichi walks to the other end of the mat and looks away.

"Bushido?" I ask.

"My ancestors, and many of yours, though they did not call their way of the warrior the same, lived by a code . . ." His voice is the normal thick Japanese accent, and I've come to understand it almost completely. "If you are warrior, you must have a code . . . without it, the line is not drawn . . . you are simply taking life with no compass. When you question your actions go back to the code. I am sure your father will teach you his code . . . but for now . . . you will learn mine. We live by a code of seven virtues. The first is Gi, which means justice. Do right, make right choices ethically and morally. You must be honest when dealing with others." Kenichi turns to us. Arek stares ahead, as though he is also being taught. Perhaps this is what makes him such a powerful fighter. A master knows there is always more to learn.

Kenichi walks to me. He is short enough that his eyes are at the level of my nose, but his presence is greater than the Christ the Redeemer statue standing above the city. "Next is Respect. A true warrior does not bully or intimidate. Number three—Courage. You must face danger with determination to prevail. The virtue that I believe is your greatest quality, one that you, Remy, believed in more than any warrior I have trained . . . is Honor. No matter what trials you face . . . your courage, justice, and kindness were guided by your commitment to honor. You always pursued the right path, even when others challenged you, and you fought for the wellness of the less fortunate. This is what made you a great warrior.

"Every warrior must be strong in body. But strength is useless if one fights for no purpose. Compassion gives you purpose. Standing up for the good of others, when others are in need, gives us just reason to exercise our strength.

"Number six, Makoto—Honesty and Sincerity. Do what you intend to do. Never will you allow duty to shadow your responsibility to do as you say. And lastly, Chu—Duty and Loyalty.

"Remember this code, and always seek knowledge. When you think there is nothing more to learn, then you become unteachable. But when you know you always have more to learn, you will be unstoppable."

Kenichi pulls a paper from his pocket and hands it to me. It has the Japanese symbols of the moral code.

"Gi. Yuu. Jin. Rei. Makoto. Meiyo. Chu."

I read them three times. I have done this before. *In one memory, I am covered in armor from head to foot. Sweat cascades from my face and my heart pounds against my chest. I am so exhausted that I can't lift the heavy armor.*

"We've done this before," I whisper.

For the first time since this all began, I see a hidden grin on Kenichi's mouth. "Many times," he says as he nods. "Turn to your partner," Kenichi orders.

My heart turns over. They have only taught me movements and patterns. Techniques have been drilled into my head for weeks now. I wonder what he expects of me as I stand in front of Arek, who is undoubtedly one of the fittest and most skilled fighters.

I quickly set the paper down and turn. Arek stands solid, straight, and controlled in front of me. So I do the same.

"You must be ready to defend yourself," Kenichi quickly explains. "Are you ready?"

Just then Kenichi makes a motion with his hand, and I turn my attention to him. Unexpectedly, Arek grabs my arm, turns his body into me, and sweeps me to the mat. It happens so fast that I lose my breath. When he is done, he steps away without touching me again. Kenichi motions for me to get up with a nod. It takes me a moment to get my bearings and finally stand.

"You look at me. Why?" Kenichi asks. "He is your opponent. Do you turn your back on the ocean? Will the waves be kind if you are not observant of them?"

I shake my head. It is my job to listen without explanation of why I do things. They don't care for meaningless excuses.

"Again," Kenichi says as he backs off the mat.

Arek is my opponent. This is hard to reconcile. At first my face runs hot with fear, but there is something else there. Somewhere below, almost out of touch. Is it the heat of competition? At Kenichi's instruction we each resume our fighting stance.

"What is the first thing you have learned?" Kenichi asks.

"Close the distance," I answer.

"If you do not, they will do it first," Kenichi agrees.

I never take my eyes off Arek. He steps toward me and I back away.

"Do not back away," Kenichi demands.

Arek gives me no time to think. He closes the distance, my body pounds the mat, and I lose my breath.

Kenichi shakes his head. "Close the distance."

The fight is in me. I can feel it. No matter how small, I slap the mat with my palms in frustration and jump to my feet. With each loss, it is as though the flame is lit just a bit more. At this point it is not about winning, just a desire to do what Kenichi is telling me to do. *Close the distance.*

Arek and I step in front of each other. I give him no time to ready himself. In just seconds I wrap my arms around his waist. I cannot take him down, but I keep him from throwing me.

This is enough to satisfy Kenichi . . . for a moment.

Arek never lets this happen again, but I give him a decent fight. Out of respect to Kenichi, Arek continues to be my partner and teacher, rather than my husband. There are only moments, when Kenichi is not looking as I get up from our recent grapple, that Arek touches my neck as he passes.

Soon I can counter Arek's movements. He is not moving at his normal speed, or aggressively training, and with each moment Kenichi seems to grow more frustrated.

Finally, Kenichi yells out, "Stop!" Kenichi pulls out his phone and walks away.

"Are we done?" I ask Arek, as sweat drips down my face.

"You aren't, but I have a feeling I am." He walks to me, presses his palm to my cheek. "Are you okay?"

I give a short laugh. "Besides the bruises everywhere and everything aching? Sure."

In just minutes, Kenichi comes back with Mak, but following them is another Japanese man with army pants and a shaved head. Kenichi speaks to him in Japanese, until he nods and joins us on the mat. "Arek, come," Kenichi orders. Before long, Mak and Kenichi watch us, while Arek towels himself off. I can see him calculating the situation.

"Perhaps someone a little smaller?" I say with sarcasm.

Kenichi shakes his head. "And that would teach you?"

"I guess not."

"This is Kenta. Together you will fight."

We slap hands as opponents, then ready our stance. My heart pounds as I wipe the sweat from my chest. Closing the distance is my only job, yet it is also his. For several moments, all I do is retreat from his advances. Only when Kenichi growls do I stop running, but this quickly ends with Kenta slamming me to the floor so hard my breath is knocked out of me. For the first time, the difference between how Arek was fighting against me and how it could be, is clear. I can feel it in how long it takes for my breath to return. I lay flat on the ground for several moments. Finally, I roll over on my knees to gather myself.

"Again," Kenichi calls out. He walks to me, "You lose because you think of how good you need to be. Pay no mind. Your only job is to accept where you are, take small critique for small growth. You understand?"

I nod then stand again in front of the man with hard eyes. After a second and third time of getting thrown to the mat, my back and head ache.

"Close the distance. Commit!" Kenichi says again, but I am so tired.

It is difficult to even stand up straight and I fear getting thrown to the mat again. In a moment of clarity, I notice the man step to the left as he comes at me. He has done the same thing every time; he first reaches out with his right arm then grabs my left. This time, I counter to the opposite side. Instantly, I can connect to his body, wrap my arms around his hips, and tuck my head close to his chest.

"Good . . . again!" Kenichi nods.

He steps again, only this time with the other foot since I caught him on this the last time. So, I adjust and quickly grab him and squeeze tight.

"Again, but finish," Kenichi calls out.

As he tries something new, something connects from my brain to my body. As Kenichi asks, I stop thinking and just feel where my opponent might go. This time my arms wrap around him, my head hits his chest, and my right foot kicks his leg out from under him. He slams to the ground just as I've done so many times before.

Clapping fills the room as I turn to Mak and Kenichi, even Arek smiles.

"Again," Kenichi repeats.

Again and again, I can anticipate his moves. Kenta shakes his head but grins. He raises his arms in question to Kenichi. For the first time, no matter how angry my body is, I want to continue. I can feel it. The ability to know where he's going to go and get there first is intoxicating.

Kenichi nods and then, with one of his hands, he pushes Arek out onto the mat. Arek gives him a questioning glance. "Don't take from her what you can teach," Kenichi growls.

Arek is obviously uncomfortable with what is next. He takes his position in front of me while Kenta walks away. "Go," Kenichi calls out. He closes the distance, but I adjust. The only difference between Kenta and Arek is how quickly he also adjusts. My back slams against the mat as pain radiates through my spine. Once again, my chest is constricted. My breath is gone.

"I'm done," I wheeze and roll over onto my knees.

"You are not done," Kenichi says quickly.

"No more today, my body is done," I say with aggravation.

Kenichi sees the look in my eyes and the way I stand in pain. Finally, he relents. "Tomorrow."

20

On my way to bed my body aches, but it is also accruing strength. During this entire process, the most difficult thing to regain is not within my body, but my mind and spirit, where there seems to be no clarity or focus, rather the constant chatter that is not mine. So, as I walk back to my apartment, my mind betrays me, telling me there will never be an end to any of this.

"Remy?" someone calls out.

I look up, the rims around my eyes stinging from fatigue, and find Beckah coming from the opposite direction. Her excitement grows just from my presence, but she raises her brows with concern. "Whoa, someone needs a drink."

"I don't think I'm allowed to do that."

"Look if you ever want to get back to the respect Remy had, you're going to have to learn that Remy just did whatever the hell she wanted to do. Nothing was going to stand in her way of anything . . . even a drink. If her body told her she needed a drink, then for the love of God, she had a drink. Besides, I'm meeting my uncle at the Idiota Risonho."

"The Laughing Idiot?" I immediately translate the Portuguese, and surprise myself.

"Yes!" Beckah does a small dance to celebrate this piece of my growth. "Come on! Oh man, it will be like old times."

"I'm gross and sweaty."

She looks at my clothes. "Yep. Okay, thirty minutes. Let's go."

An hour later, we walk into a packed bar that is mostly the same as any other bar, although the people appear tougher and have shaved heads, piercings, and tattoos. A local band plays up on a stage while cultural dancers holler and shake their hips. Immediately my energy rises. Beckah holds my hand and pulls me through the people. Many notice that I have arrived but they leave me alone, until someone grabs my hand, refusing to let me pass. I turn quickly. A man points a phone toward me, takes my picture, and won't let go of my hand.

"Remy!" he says, as though he knows me. Faster than light, Beckah's tiny body blocks mine from his. She rips his hand away and calculatingly knocks his iPhone out of his grasp into hers.

"Oh, so sorry," she says to him. "Let me get you a picture." She deletes the one he took of me then, before he can object, she takes a selfie with him. As she hands the phone back to him, she winks. "Enjoy that. I don't want to toot my own horn, but it's something special."

Her large personality forces everyone to let us pass without problems, then she yells at the bartender for two cosmos and points up some stairs. The bartender nods. We climb a winding set of metal steps to the roof, where we see a large group. Instantly, I recognize everyone. Kilon, Sassi, Geo, Peter, and Lily GoLightly are there, along with my father and Mak. Dr. Hugh is there, Hok and Jace also. When my eyes fall on Arek, my heart does a small flip. They seem to be distracted by something and Beckah places a hand in front of my chest. "Wait, you need to watch this."

Jace and Kilon sit across from each other, staring intently. Everyone else watches with such intensity, you would think this was the World Cup. It isn't long before Jace's body drops heavily to the side and slides off the chair like a rag doll. Kilon shrugs with confidence as the crowd laughs.

"How about more than just one person?" Peter dares Kilon, as he stands next to Lily.

Kilon takes a swig of his beer as Hok places smelling salts under Jace's nose and he comes to life.

"Do it!" Sassi laughs.

Immediately, Peter sets up three chairs facing Kilon instead of just one. Peter sits down, and Lily follows. Then Hok sits in the last one, while he and Peter high five—ready for the challenge.

"Ready?" Kilon asks.

"Come on!" Hok yells, psyching himself up for the task.

Kilon whistles and claps his hands together with a grin. Carefully he looks from one person's eyes to the next to the next, then back again. I can see that he is chanting something under his breath, and the others look meticulous and focused as well. It takes no more than a minute before Lily's eyes close and her head drops down. Soon Peter slinks to the floor still holding his drink. Sassi quickly grabs it from his hand before it spills. Hok is the last to fall victim and his head rolls back with his mouth open, dead to the world.

Kilon laughs. "Anybody else?"

This time Briston uses the smelling salts. "Wake up, sleeping beauties."

Peter wakes up with a yell of frustration as his cheeks are extra rosy. "Come on!"

"At least you made it longer than I did," Briston tells him.

"Arek! Arek's next." Peter points to Kilon.

Kilon chuckles. "This is the one thing . . . the one area Arek has never been able to beat me."

Arek rubs his hands together in competition, "Well, then maybe today's the day."

Just then, Beckah calls out to let everyone know we are there. "This we gotta see." The door behind us opens and the bartender hands Beckah two drinks—she passes one to me.

Sassi shakes her head, "Did I say that you could drink that?"

"Come on Sassi. One night ain't gonna hurt anything," Beckah bumps Sassi with her hip, although this is practically at Sassi's knee with the size difference. As we walk over, Beckah finds the energy infectious. "Nobody tell Kenichi about Remy being here. Y'all hear me?"

The energy of the group and its exuberance makes me realize how lonely this training has been. It is hard not to stare at Arek in his black T-shirt and jeans. From across the way, with the loud group between us, he looks at the drink in my hand, then at me. I shrug.

Soon, he chugs his beer and claps his hands together. "Let's do this." He walks to the chair directly in front of Kilon and sits down. "'Kay, let's go."

Both men take a measured stare at each other. They seem to be sitting there for nearly ten minutes, with nothing happening, while they are clearly working hard. Then the small droop of Arek's eyelids flicker as we all hold our breath. Within thirty seconds from that moment, Arek's head drops and he's asleep.

Peter throws his hands in the air. "You have to be kidding me."

Briston quickly brings Arek back to life. Arek shakes his head, "Again."

The crew laughs when five minutes later he is asleep. "Again," he says upon waking. Again and again, they try. "Ahhh!" Arek growls with a laugh. "I'm going to figure it out."

"How is anyone supposed to beat him?" I ask Beckah.

Beckah looks at me with pursed lips. "Actually, Remy, you were the only one who was able to do it. You said that it had something to do with grounding yourself in the chair and inner body, and blah, blah, blah . . . you know all that stuff. Kilon couldn't stand it."

Just her words alone sound familiar—not just familiar but strangely resonant within me. It brings goosebumps to my arms and a twinkle to my eye.

"What's going on?" Beckah asks.

"Have you ever felt something within your gut that feels closer than a memory, but more like . . . I don't know how to explain it."

"Like the universe has empowered you with something that sits above skill. It has its own locked door that only you can open?" she says with a grin.

"Yeah."

"Nope, I have no idea what that feels like." She hesitates a moment. "Just kidding. Wait until this grows and becomes so close to you that you don't turn it on and off, it just is." Beckah turns back to the group. "I think Remy should try."

My eyes grow wide. "No, that's okay."

Beckah leans in close. "You have to listen when it calls. Believe me, you can learn more from this than any other teaching moment."

Everyone looks at me, in question. Finally, I nod. "Okay."

Quietly I walk over to the chair from which Arek stands. He gives me a questioning look then walks back to his drink. I sit in front of Kilon. My heel bounces uncomfortably on the ground while Kilon gets comfortable.

"You ready?" he asks.

"I have no idea." Yet something tells me that I am.

Instantly, Kilon starts to connect. In just moments, I can see why this is different than Tracing. It feels lighter and strangely more energetic between his body and mine. He seems to be sourcing to steal my energy, which makes sense for what he is trying to do. So, in some way, it's about making my energy heavy so that it sits with me. Several times, I can feel him stripping pieces of it, but it doesn't take long until I find a way to access it, starting with my hands, then my toes, and so on. It is no different than placing weight in my core—rather, extending it to the space around me.

"Remy . . ." someone says. I ignore them since conserving my energy and never allowing his sourcing is more important than paying attention to them. Perhaps it's Kilon. Is he in my head? "Remy . . ." the voice says again. "Remy!" This time they yell and it snaps me out of my heaviness. Everyone is on their feet with a ton of excitement, and just ahead of me Kilon is asleep. He's halfway on his chair and halfway off.

"How did you do it?!" Peter, whose excitement is beyond anyone else's, laughs.

Briston wakes Kilon. For a moment Kilon looks at me and we share a moment of disbelief. "I remembered," I say quietly.

"I see that," Kilon quips.

Everyone joins in the excitement, as Sassi places her hands on my shoulders. "I think he was hoping you wouldn't remember how to do it."

Geo raises his glass with a smile. "Cheers to your progress, Remy. We realize it isn't easy, but this is just proof that it's all well worth it."

Everyone lifts their glass and drinks. For the first time in what feels like eternity, the night is free of fear. Even the pieces of the Cellar within me have taken the night off.

Later, as the group descends the metal stairs and enters the bar where the crowd is still thick, someone pulls me back into the dark stairwell. In seconds, I am pressed against the cement wall while Arek is so close that our lips almost touch.

"Tonight . . . you . . ." he doesn't continue, but his fingers run through my hair. The way his eyes devour me is new and it makes my breath increase until both of us can hear it. I am sure that the pounding of my heart can be felt through my shirt. "I saw *you*, Remy."

I don't say anything, out of fear that it will push him away. If it takes pretending to be everything that Remy used to be, I will do so just to bring him closer.

"I've waited so long, sometimes it feels like it will never happen."

"I want nothing more," I whisper.

With power and emotion that can only come from a man who knows what it is to love and lose, he kisses me. My lips come alive as though already swollen, before I wrap my arms around his neck.

It feels as though it will last forever and I'm desperate for that. I've been so lonely over the last week, that to feel his arms hold me so tight makes the waiting almost worth it. Almost. When he finally pulls away so we can both breathe, he presses his forehead to mine. "It is coming," he says confidently.

21

On a warm but breezy day, Geo and I hike up a mountain just outside of the city. I'm sweating profusely while he seems to be barely
working.

"It's been weeks, why are we only just now working together?" I
ask as my tennis shoe kicks some rocks up the trail.

"Briston didn't want to overwhelm you. It can be just as fatigu-
ing to work with your mind and spirit as it is with your body . . .
actually, even more so. Are you ready?" He smiles back at me.

I grin, even though, somehow, I know this is not going to be
easy. At the very top of the mountain, we reach a rock that juts out
over the ocean. When you stand on it, you cannot see anything but
the vast ocean and land miles down, and I quake with fear while Geo
steps out onto the edge.

With his back to me, as he closes his eyes and breathes in the
salty air, he raises his arms out as though he will jump. "Are you ready
to take the leap, Willow?" Still, he does not turn to look at me.

"No one has called me Willow for a while."

"That's who you are, right? Not quite Willow, but still not Remy,
either. You are going to have to leap. If you trust me, I promise, we'll
do it together. Do you trust me?"

"Yes," I say confidently.

"Come here," he speaks quietly.

When looking out over the cliff, it is nearly impossible not to picture myself tripping and plummeting straight to my death while I question my decisions on the way down. My skin rises, my steps are slow. Geo reaches out his hand and takes mine while I quietly stand beside him.

"Close your eyes," he says. "Be aware of this moment. The sounds, the smells, the breeze against your skin. Let every word I say resonate. Just listen and breathe."

At first, the fear of the edge is all consuming. My eyes squeeze tightly until the muscles in my face cramp. Loud, high-pitched screeches from a swarm of birds surround me, and they seem so close that I could quite possibly reach out and touch them. The salty air doesn't just flow into my nose and along my taste buds, but it leaves a layer of moisture on my sweaty skin.

Geo continues, "You need to learn the truth about time. Ephemes are always chasing time as though the fear of death forces them to never surrender to the moment they're in. Instead, Velieri recognize that time is just an illusion. If we are enslaved to the future or our past, this tells us that we are not living with our spirits, but our minds. Your protection, Willow, is this. When you can let go of day and night, minutes or hours, up and down, in and out, and just Be, nothing can touch you."

"How do I get there?"

"I'll teach you. Layers . . . one at a time. Open your eyes."

When I do, I am shocked that we are no longer on the edge of the rock, but kneeling beside a stream where several deer pass. My hand feels like ice as it dangles in the flowing water. "I've been here before."

Geo smiles. "Many, many times actually."

Just then, Arek's mother appears from the nearest ledge. Holona stands above us with her hands on her hips and a smile on her face. "I've been waiting for this," she says.

"I'm not sure she's ready," Geo admits.

Holona makes her way down the side of the rocks and through some trees to come stand with us by the stream. Her beauty radiates from within through eyes that remind me of the man I can't love, even though I do. She places a palm on my face. "Do you wish to stop the nightmares?"

My eyes grab hers with surprise, which makes her nod in a *yes, I know* fashion.

"They won't let go, will they?" Unexpectedly, I understand exactly what she means.

Heat rises to my face, until my eyes are blurred from tears. "I'm afraid to feel this way forever, just like they did."

"The Cellar is a place where they try to put evil to death. Those who have lived there, wait there for someone like you . . . because at some point there is no more space left in the pit. You gave them a place to go."

"Someone like me?"

"You were always sensitive to anything spiritual. That's how you and I found each other again. Spirits of all realms. Your empathy always cast its net and pulled the biggest fish . . . some good, some bad. Even Remy, one of the most powerful women I ever knew, had a hard time shaking it off."

"I wake, paralyzed. My muscles so tense, they are in pain. The feeling of those people in the Cellar and their hate, and the emotions of those who don't know why their spirits haven't left . . . but they have left the Cellar." My breath shakes. "They're with me now."

Geo comes forward. "Remy knew that she was more susceptible, more open to things beyond us, and that is where the real work was put in. Once she figured it out, conquered it—I will never forget—nothing could ever touch her again. Better than I could do myself."

"Then let's do it. I'm ready. How do I get rid of them?"

Geo looks at Holona with a smile. "First step, help you create your best rhythm, which is why Holona is here."

Holona takes my arm, "Let's walk."

We begin our path next to the stream, yet within the time it takes me to blink, our surroundings change, and I am in New York on one of the busiest sidewalks. People are forced to turn sideways to clear each other. All colors, shapes, sizes, moods of people cover every square inch of the sidewalk. In fact, everyone seems to be dressed from the World War II–era. The cars that pass are also from the same time in history.

"New York?"

"We need busy, jam-packed minds and streets to teach you fast enough," Holona explains.

Geo nods. "You can't get more minds colliding than in the streets of New York."

Even though we have stopped in the middle of the crowd, people slide by us as though we don't exist. Holona starts to explain, "In order for you to find your rhythm, I have to help you sift through the muck, for lack of a better word. So, for just a moment, we are going to make it so that you can hear what's going through everyone's minds."

"Everyone?"

"Everyone," they both say at the same time.

"At first it's going to be overwhelming, but I need you to do your best to listen," Geo explains. "See if you can isolate voices. This isn't like Tracing—no one is digging within your mind. This is a different skill."

After a moment, the reverberation of hundreds of voices rises in the air. Slowly it grows until it's so loud that I squint my eyes and cover my ears with my palms. Geo walks to me and gently pulls my hands from my ears while shaking his head. He leans forward and whispers in my ear, "Listen closely. Separate the nuances."

At first, it is absolutely overwhelming, and I accomplish nothing. I look at Geo with wide eyes and he simply laughs. He twirls his finger in the air, telling me to keep going.

I posture my body but look down at my shoulder, trying to hear the closest bystanders. A woman with a purple dress and red shoes yells at her husband for not doing the dishes. It takes me a moment, once I connect with her conversation, to move to someone else, but then it happens. I realize it's as easy to move to the next person's thoughts as it is to move the direction of my head. So I do both. A man passes by with a bright smile and says, "I can't wait." Someone else is discussing their stress and workload . . . no, *many* are discussing their stress and workload. I quickly get the hang of it. Different conversations, different voices, different inflections.

Suddenly, the world goes quiet again and my body and ears instantly relax. Holona nods. "Good job. Now that you have the hang of that, it's not just enough to understand the unique voices, you must know within the depths of your soul how to separate *one* from the *many*. How do you listen just to one and quiet the others? No voice is solid. We are not talking about people's rhythms . . . that is the end goal. But here, we are simply teaching you to make your attention to detail hyper aware. There are holes in everyone's voice. You climb subtly into those holes and that voice will never leave you unless you want it to."

"Okay." For a moment, I almost feel a sense of . . . intrigue.

The voices rise again. This time it takes me only a moment to capture one voice and keep my attention on it. It's a man with a fedora who speaks in Italian. I understand him as he talks about his daughter's wedding. He begins to move out of my sight, so I follow him down the street in New York. Geo and Holona stay not far behind. Sometimes I lose his voice and the other voices cover it up, but I get better and better at returning to his specific conversation. Then, listening to his voice for a while, I recognize the holes that Holona spoke of, and I dive in. For the first time, all other sounds completely disappear, and it is as though he and I are in a soundproof room—just us.

"I got it!" I yell.

The old man stops and looks at me with surprise. With a rich Italian accent and a pleasant smile, he speaks, "She's a sweet girl, my granddaughter." I look around with confusion at the invisible echo chamber he and I have found ourselves in as the rest of New York continues their fast pace, but in complete silence. "She looked so beautiful there . . ." he pulls out his wallet and shows me an old-fashioned picture of a young bride. "I got to dance with her to Bessie Smith."

"She's beautiful," I say to the sweet old man.

Geo walks up and shakes the old man's hand with a grin. "Hi, Robert. Good to see you."

Robert tips his hat to us and walks away.

The other voices are still muted. "Who is Robert?" I ask.

"Robert is an Epheme I was friends with in the early forties," Geo explains. "He's here because in order to teach you, we used a memory from one of my trips to New York in the forties. It's easier to use someone's memory than the present moment—less emotional and better judgement."

"Oh. So, I'm not really in New York?"

"You're in my memory of it. Okay, now that you can be hyper focused on just one, we need you to search for their rhythm. A person's voice or even their idiosyncrasies are the easiest way to understand their rhythm quickly. Ride their voice like it is the path to their mind."

"Wouldn't it just be easier to search for mine?"

Holona and Geo laugh. "You would think. However, it is most difficult to hear our own. Let's try this again."

I blink and in that second, we are back where we started. The woman in the purple dress and red shoes passes, just as she had before. I close my eyes, searching through the voices, and find Robert's. When every other voice quiets, we are once again in the echo chamber. In seconds, I hear his rhythm.

Moments later, Holona, Geo, and I are back in the forest together. "That was the fastest I've ever seen anyone get that," Geo assures me. "You were able to search, listen, quiet a crowd, follow someone specific, then truly listen to him, and you found his rhythm. Everyone has one. It's like our fingerprint. It is what makes us unique, but also guides us. Keeps us safe. You need to learn yours until it is innate. Like your signature on a piece of paper—that easy, that connected to you. If there's any separation between you and this, someone like Navin can get in." Several chipmunks run across the ground and up the nearest tree. "Now that you've ridden a voice to find the rhythm, you've found the key to a quicker Trace. And a quicker Trace means everything."

"Okay." I look at both of them. Just like the night before, something within me tells me that I can do this. "I heard Robert's and I know what I'm looking for. Let's go."

"Close your eyes and find your rhythm," Geo says.

The sounds of the quiet forest soothe me, and in just moments I find the rhythm. It's been a while since I've heard it, but once it becomes clear, I am reminded of the last time.

"I know it," I say quietly. "The last time I heard it was with Navin, at that house."

"Yes," Geo says. "Do you remember what happened?"

"Yes." My eyes are still closed, and while I hear my rhythm, getting to know it more, I see the room where Navin had me. "I saw things differently."

"How?"

"Everything looked different. All colors, depth perception, thoughts, feelings, all my senses came to life beyond anything I ever could have imagined. It just didn't last long."

"It never does at the beginning. But it will grow," Holona says sweetly. "Open your eyes." We are back on New York's busy street. Holona continues, "Find it again."

It takes me a second longer, but soon I do.

They increase the amount of people.

"Find it again."

Again, I do.

They raise the sound until it is deafening. "Find it again."

I do.

"Find someone else's."

"Now, go back to yours."

They lead me through many different scenarios, changing my surroundings several times, but it doesn't affect me. I continue to get faster at finding my rhythm.

"Now this," Geo says.

This time when my eyes open, I am in the halls of the Cellar. Back in my nightmares. Instantly my heart starts racing and my rhythm is nowhere to be found. Holona and Geo are there, yet it doesn't matter. The dark hall shrinks me back into just the shell of who I know I'm supposed to be.

"You know how to do this," Geo says firmly.

"No. I've lost it. It's too much." My chest constricts and it's hard to breathe.

"Willow—"

"No! It's too much." Just then, the woman with the blue lips and veins is there, passing Holona and coming so close that her tormented eyes bore into me. My breath is caught until I'm dying. I try to breathe but can't. Again and again, I try.

Holona shakes her head as I fall on my knees, unable to speak.

"It's too much, Geo! Take her back," Holona cries out.

I am choking unlike anything I've ever felt. My fingernails scratch my skin as I claw at my throat. Geo reaches out and takes my hand.

Instantly, we are back on the rock jutting out over the ocean. I suck in a painful gasping breath, and fall. Geo sits on the rock and pulls me in his arms, while my breath slowly returns. "It's okay," he says as he holds me. "It's okay. That's enough for today."

22

My eyes are barely staying open as I sit at a table in the back of the Laughing Idiot. Nobody knows I'm here and I want to keep it that way. Atum will be first tomorrow, then the rest of the day with Geo. My body and mind reserves are empty. I pull my light hoodie over my head and sip the straight vodka.

Hiding is easier than Velieri like to make it seem, until I hear the soft clearing of a throat at my table. I look up just enough to reveal my eyes. Arek stands there with a grin, for which I'm grateful since I'm not supposed to be alone, or drinking, or up this late.

Without saying anything, he sits in the booth, scooting in so close beside me it pushes me over just a bit. He wraps his arm over the back of the booth, then grabs my glass and takes a sip.

"Straight vodka." He raises his eyebrows as he chokes it down.

"Maybe it will help me sleep."

He nods. "How many does that make?"

I purse my lips together. "Ummmm . . ."

The music starts playing as the new DJ begins his set. The tall and lanky waiter comes by. "Can I get you anything?" he asks.

"How many has she had?"

The waiter looks at his paper, "Five."

"Five?" Arek looks at me with wide eyes and a smile, which makes me shrug clumsily. My brain is a bit foggy, but not as much as

I thought it would be. "Here," Arek says as he hands the waiter some cash. "We're good, thank you."

"How'd you know I was here?"

"I told you, I always know where you are. Are you ready to go to bed?"

Unexpectedly, tears fall from my eyes like they've been sitting there for hours. I don't remember being close to crying. "No. I can't."

Arek takes my face in his palm so I have to look up at him. "Geo told me about today."

"I can't," I cry.

"Come on," he pulls me to stand, but that's when I realize how impossible my feet are at the moment.

"Is it the working out or the alcohol?" The slurred words leave my mouth before I even know they're there.

"Definitely the alcohol," he says as he dips down and grabs me in his arms. "Do you remember this is what you did the first time I met you." He smiles as he walks me through the Gianda and heads to our apartment. Before I realize it, I crawl on top of my bed, but when I look around, it isn't my room. Arek throws his wallet and watch on the table next to the bed, then sits beside me. "Sleep tight, sleeping beauty. We finish this tomorrow."

His hand on my face is everything to me at this moment, but it lacks in comparison to when he leans down and kisses my cheek.

"Your mother was with us all day today," I whisper.

Something passes before his eyes, reminiscent of sadness. "I know."

"Geo told you." I reach up and try to move a piece of hair from his eyes, but my fingers miss it at first. "You're my husband . . ." I whisper, "but not. It's so confusing," I say with dramatic frustration that makes him laugh.

"Yes, although this is very familiar to me."

"Really?" I sit up suddenly till our faces are within inches of each other, which makes him hesitate and glance down at my lips, and I'm grateful when he doesn't back away.

"Yeah, this is Remy for sure. She could never handle her liquor."

Without thinking, I press my lips against his and treasure every moment of the vibration that we share. He doesn't pull away but presses harder.

After a moment we come away for breath, and he gently encourages me to lie back against my pillow. "Sleep."

"Yes, my husband," I whisper.

Once again, Geo takes me out of the Gianda to experience the quiet parts of Brazil, only this time Arek and Sassi follow closely behind. My head pounds from a hangover as my legs burn with each step of the climb. Large green leaves brush my body and leave a trace of water from the morning rain that just passed. For a moment, I look through the trees and take in the beautiful view above the city. Arek reaches my side.

"Why are you coming?" I ask.

"Geo might need help," Arek explains.

"It's that bad, huh?" I whisper.

He doesn't answer, but instead takes a moment to look at me.

When we've entered the rainforest, we reach stone steps that are covered with years of plant life and ascend at a steep incline. Vines crawl along the carved stone, making their own path without care of what may come upon it. While mosquitos buzz in my ears and I bat them away, I can also hear trickling water from somewhere nearby. A gentle scent from the myriad of flowers fills my nose, as my foot tries to miss the mossy rocks, knowing from experience that they'll be slippery. Once we've reached the top, Geo points ahead to a bridge that tells its age by the cracks and chips along the corners. As we draw nearer, the sound of trickling water turns to a rush. Coming around a large native tree known as a walking tree, since it shoots roots into the ground that create a large trunk, we finally see the waterfall just a few hundred yards away. Once we've climbed onto the bridge, all four of us pause for a moment to enjoy it. The jungle around us continues to play its symphony. Just for a moment, I forget what we are there to do.

There is never a moment when I am not aware of Arek, but it still surprises me when his fingertips gently run down my skin and take my hand. When I look up at him, his face, mostly his eyes, tell me that he has a question. "Do you think you'll see her again?"

It takes me a moment to realize what he is asking, but once I do, I nod. "I've seen her many times." It is subtle but hope fills his eyes. "She seems to come whenever there's something to learn and I certainly have that today."

Geo's calm voice can barely be heard over the waterfall. "She meets us in the forest. I'd never seen her until Remy took me there."

"Then let's go there," I whisper.

"Are you ready, Willow?" Geo asks, still refusing to call me Remy.

"Yes." *Am I? I think I'm going to choose . . . yes.* Any other day might have been no.

"Just a bit farther and we are there." Geo leads us higher for a few more minutes, then into a large echoing cave. Flowing water drips from above. The air has dipped at least twenty degrees and the water that splashes on my shoulder is icy.

"A cave?" I ask.

As Geo sets his backpack down, he explains. "Thousands of years ago, Gyre and others began working with people in caves. It's the very reason he lives within walls made of rock. They began to make great strides with people, believing that it was due to the natural state and the density of the walls. Our energy stays around us, creating what we call Elan Vital. Or in other words, a barrier of our life force. It can be greatly healing and an amazing place to learn."

For a moment as everyone remains quiet, a unique hum hits my ears forcing me to take a few steps into the cave. The more I listen to the sound, the more my skin comes alive and my chest expands with breath.

Sassi's rich voice echoes, "What is it?"

"There's a hum, do you hear it?"

Sassi comes to my side. "Pay attention. That's how we'll get you there. It's calling to you . . . listen."

Within my soul, I know it is time. Time to finish this. To break free of the Cellar's hold on me. When I turn back around, just in the split second of a blink, we are back in the forest by the stream. Once again, I am kneeling beside the water with my hand in the flow. Only this time, Geo, Sassi, and Arek are there with me. The same deer pass by, and several pinecones fall and bounce on pine needles in the distance.

Together we walk through the trees at a time that looks to be dusk—the sky is an orange glow. Arek places an arm about my shoulders as we soak up the peace. It is not long before I see the sway of her blue dress coming our way. Arek doesn't notice at first, until I raise my hand and point in her direction.

"Arek," I say gently. "There."

I can feel his chest rise, as the small wrinkles around his eyes lift when he grins. Holona stops walking toward us when she sees him and her hands clasp just under her chin. It takes only a fleeting moment before tears stream down her face. Arek rushes forward and grabs her in his arms. Sassi and I look at each other.

"Look at you," Holona says, as she runs her hand down his face.

He smiles. "I missed you."

Soon, Sassi comes to embrace Holona, her words genuine and crisp. "It is a great moment to see you again, my friend."

After several minutes, Holona takes one last look at Arek, then shakes her head. "Okay, we're here for a purpose. You," she says to me, "let's finish this."

"I'm ready," I say to all.

In only a short time we practice what I learned before. It is easier than I expected it to be. My own rhythm has become as fluent to me as breathing, collecting within my soul so richly that I feel the protection it has created, within me, around me, and through me.

"It's time, Willow. You have one job and it's the only way to do this," Geo explains. "You have to find them, revisit the halls of the Cellar."

I chuckle a bit, until realizing the serious look on everyone's face means this is not a joke. "How do I do that?"

"We send you into a dream-like state," Geo explains.

Geo turns to Holona, who nods and smiles, but says nothing at first, her hesitation speaking louder than words. "Remy, we are all connected. As humans we like to make separation where there truly should not be. Just as the stars . . . it takes millions of years for us to see the light . . . yet that time doesn't break. It still reaches us, giving us a sky filled with diamonds. This connection, the thing that makes us all one, is the way that you will break this. We can teach you in dreams, but it is these true souls that are waiting to be released. They don't know why they're here; they don't understand it's not where they're supposed to be. And it isn't even what they've done that has kept them from the after. Somewhere, life told them they were no longer connected, no longer accepted. For them to release you, for them to leave the walls of the Cellar, all you must do is get them to be aware."

"Aware of what?"

"They don't see where they are, or anyone or anything . . . rather only the soul they're trying to take from—that is all they see. That is why you feel as you do. Whatever state they exist, it is only to seek, but never find. We teach you ways to free them. It's called Yielding. Ephemes never learn to do this, so many times they walk about wearing the heavy coat of others."

It won't be long until night falls and we will be surrounded by darkness. I run my shoe across the pine needles, making a small hole. My mind races.

"Will it be like last time?" I break the silence.

"Yes," Geo says honestly. "Until you get it."

I breathe until my lungs completely refill, then release. "Okay. Let's go."

The dark and grungy halls have not changed, they have not been redeemed. If anything, there are more shadows, more darkness, and the air is so thick my breath feels like molasses down my throat.

Sassi and Arek have come with me, yet Geo and Holona must stay back to keep their minds clear. Sassi shakes her head and rubs her neck. "I never knew," she whispers. We pass more eyes staring at us through peepholes. "I just did not know," she speaks again of the anguish that I understand well.

Even though this is my memory . . . my spirit . . . I can feel the heavy burden of pain and the digging within me. "It feels the same," I whisper.

Arek nods. "It's your memory and spirit . . . in fact your mind or imagination could make it worse. So don't drop your guard."

Sassi hands me a gun and then places a knife in my belt. When I look at her with confusion, she answers, "We're here to teach you what you can do beyond helping them Yield. It is important to know what can be done in one's psyche. What you learn to do here, will help you beyond this place. Just watch."

We begin walking down the dark halls, passing eyes, battling the heavy spirits that attack my mind. It's no different than an unbridled emotion controlling your every thought and piercing your self-protection with more pain and sadness. The walls appear to be solid until something begins to pound against them so hard, they move and sway. Arek pulls me away just before the brick-and-mortar wall crashes to the ground. Instantly, there are a dozen inmates climbing over the rubble toward us. The lights flicker overhead, the yells devour my strength as they direct their attention toward me. Arek and Sassi instantly begin fighting. One criminal after another, the big and the small, they take their feet out from under them and try to control the chaos.

"You can change this!" Arek yells at me.

"How?"

"Did this happen? Is this a memory or your imagination?" he says as he tosses two criminals at a time over his shoulder. Sassi sweeps one's feet from under him and presses her gun to his chest and pulls the trigger. "Concentrate. This didn't happen."

I picture what the halls truly looked like. It takes a moment, but as though on rewind, each criminal reverses what has just been done. They move backward, taking every step, every jump, every yell on rewind. The wall rebuilds into existence and, once again, we are in the dark hall alone.

"That," Sassi says quickly, "is exactly what you should do. We battle our imaginings of what is taking place more than the actual truth. Now . . . take us directly to the place you found those who won't leave you. The Unyielded."

"Down here." I point to the end of the dim hall. After several stairs down, just ahead, I recognize the door behind which they tortured me. I can feel the paralysis coming on, just as it has every night, and everything in me seizes.

"Remy?" Sassi says as she comes to my side. I can't say anything. I can barely even shake my head. "Arek . . ."

Arek stands directly in front of me and holds my face in his hands. "Look, Remy, listen. Your rhythm is your protection. If you allow your fear, it will overrun anything that can help us. I'm here. I got you." He stares into my eyes, and I can soon feel him Tracing within my mind just to give a little nudge to help me find my beat. Soon, he can see that I've returned, and he steps out of the way. I walk to the door, reach out, and turn the knob.

Inside they wait. The four men and their terrifying masks, and the tortured souls. Whatever it is that I have, they want. My chest aches as my heart races and my muscles tense. I want nothing more than to be somewhere else. I close my eyes and look up, begging to a higher power to release me. Take me from this place. The Unyielded rush me, their veins pulsing and their teeth chattering.

"Did this happen?" Sassi asks, with her guns raised, prepared to battle.

"Yes," I whisper.

The moment I let out the word, the four men surge forward and grab me. Arek doesn't do anything to help, nor does Sassi.

"What do I do?" I beg as the men act as though they cannot see Arek or Sassi. They repeat every step from my memory. Ripping at my arms just as they did before, they cuff me to the pipe overhead and force me to stand on the small cement box.

"Remy, listen," Sassi says quietly. "If we don't let them do this, then the Unyielded don't have the chance to become aware. Which of the Unyielded are the ones who have stayed with you?"

As my feet cry out in pain, and the smell of rot permeates my nose, my eyes search about the room. In the corner, facing the wall, I see her drab hair. The four men leave, just as they did that night. "Over there in the corner."

The woman with the blue veins is eerily facing the wall, her body ticks and bounces without control. A quiet whimper escapes my lips when I feel her angst more than before now that we share the same room.

"And this one," I squeeze my eyes shut as the boy with yellow teeth and eyes maniacally dances about me.

They both seem to naturally repeat everything from that night . . . until the woman does something different. When she turns and sees me, with her veiny eyes and gray skin, she jumps to her feet and rushes over to me, getting just as close as the boy.

I can't help myself and keep my eyes closed as she walks about me like a wild dog.

"Open your eyes and look at her," Sassi warns.

Slowly and methodically, I force the breath in and out of my lungs, but she strangely gobbles it up, stripping me of the ability to breathe.

"Remind yourself that you are alive and that is what she desires. It is a bit of your actual breath, but in truth, it is that you have dimension—not living with one emotion. She seeks to attach to you, change your prism of emotion into stagnancy. That is where she lives, able to perceive only what she can accept—guilt, sadness, anger. Find your rhythm, open your eyes. She can steal nothing from you if you don't let her."

I believe Sassi and open my eyes again. The woman comes closer. She smiles, although it doesn't mean she is happy—it means she wants something. The aura of the room with so many Unyielded makes the walls start to shake again. This excites the Unyielded until they begin to yell at the air, their bodies violently reacting to the noise and quake. This only increases the aggressive shake of the walls, until cracks form and dust billows. The chaos builds and the Unyielded get angry with me, the only source of Being in the room. They begin to yank and pull me, sending pain through my arms and wrists. I cry out, unable to fix it.

Sassi yells to be heard over them, "This wasn't the way it happened. You can change this!"

"I can't breathe!" I yell. "I can't—"

Then it all stops. My hands release and I fall to the soft ground of the forest. When my eyes open, Arek is there kneeling in front of me while the others stand behind him, looking on.

"Give her a moment. Then we try again," Geo says, as he walks away.

Holona stands beside Arek, who sits on a tall rock. Geo crosses his arms in front of him, but patiently waits for me to recover.

"Did anyone ever tell you why stars dance?" Holona asks.

"No," I respond.

"When the light pierces through our atmosphere, it is manipulated—bending and refracting due to the disruption. The thicker the film of atmosphere, the more this becomes the barrier to our sight and the stars brilliance. Just the same as this is for stars, this is also what is happening to you . . . in there. Your fear interrupts your strength."

"Even though it is just memory?" I ask.

"Do you feel like it is just a memory? What we live through never really becomes memory unless we free ourselves from how it affected us. It is your fear and inability to break free of this memory in order to live in the present, that keeps you stuck to the Cellar," Holona explains.

Sassi walks to me and continues for Holona, "You are believing too much in what you have to do in there, and not enough in recognizing the space, the room for what it is. If you concentrate too much on what is next . . . it will be too big. Stop there, recognize the fear as only fear, and recognize the room in its state at that moment. You are not there to try and change them . . . your awareness will help them be aware."

"Let's get this done, Willow," Geo says as he offers his hand to help me to my feet. I accept.

I attempt to wander through the halls several times. They tell me that with practice, I will have more control, but for now this will have to do. Repeatedly, we fight off criminals. Repeatedly, the walls crumble releasing the hounds onto us.

This time, I lay on the table, the four men doing just as they did before. The look on Sassi's and Arek's faces grow concerned. "This happened?" Sassi asks.

"Yes."

Sassi walks around the men. She looks at Arek with a raised eyebrow. "Meryl and Davi. But I don't recognize the others."

The men speak to one another, letting Arek and Sassi hear their warped voices. The monstrous growl of these men yanks me back as sweat beads on my forehead.

Only now, the Unyielded woman walks around me. "You can see

us," she says, just as she did that night. Her cold hand reaches out and touches me, swiftly pulling it back in surprise.

It is obvious now why she helped me. It was not for my benefit, or for my protection; rather she knew, somehow, that she could be carried out of these walls with me. A new destination for a spirit that can never feel the joy of something new, yet she tries anyway.

I try to connect with her eyes that wonder. "What is your name?"

A noticeable trait of all the Unyielded is a continuous rubbing of their hands and whimpering of unintelligible language. She can hear me, I see from a quick glance, and even tries to respond, yet her mannerisms grow angrier and terrorized. "Name?" she spouts quickly. "Name?" Frustration and anxiety rush through her until I feel it rise within me—just more of the same I have felt for weeks now.

"Keep asking things," Sassi whispers.

"Your name?" I ask again. The four men are in discussion, although my memory was not able to retain what they said so it sounds like gibberish. She is my concern at the moment. "Please," I reach out and touch her hand, "your name."

"My name . . ." Something appears to catch her attention as her lifeless eyes take on a bit of thought. "Ka . . . Ka . . . Kati . . . Katia."

"Katia was your name?" I say again.

"Keep going, Remy," Sassi orders me.

"Can you see me, and them?" I point to the four men.

She closes her eyes and shakes her head as her fidgeting becomes more intense.

"No."

"Can you try?" I ask.

The men begin to pick up the hook that they threatened me with that night. Sassi and Arek grow concerned and they come swiftly to my side.

"What happened here?" Arek asks.

"Katia told me to see the scalpel and I took it," I answer, as one of the men comes close to me speaking nothing that I can understand.

Arek shakes his head, "You have to do that."

"What happens if I don't?"

Sassi leans close to my ear and whispers, "Just finish this before you find out. Trust me. Remy, get her to be aware. Now!"

Katia is agitated and flailing her arms as though the small bit of awareness has made her darkness worse.

"Katia," I cry out.

Katia leans toward me until again, I want to pull away. "Look over there," she suggests to me, just like before. I reach out and grab the scalpel.

"Katia, I need you to see them. You're in a room with me and these men."

She is rattled at the new bit of information as though she is comfortable in her torment.

At first, she does not respond, so I ask again. This time she shakes her head, but I can see in her eyes that she's not telling me the truth. She does remember. The room starts to shake, and I quickly look at Sassi and Arek.

"No fear," Sassi warns me sternly.

This is only a memory. Nothing can happen. The room shakes even more until the wall begins to break apart. I try desperately to not fear the situation, yet here they are and I can feel their attachment to me, stealing what little of me I can be aware of within these walls.

Arek comes closer but not too close. "This was not your memory—it didn't happen. The more you focus, the less it can be manipulated."

The ceiling starts to break apart as rubble falls on us.

"Now, Remy!" Sassi yells through the collapse of the building while the Unyielded grow in intensity. "Get yourself right, find your rhythm, this did not happen, and get Katia to understand!"

Arek dodges a large piece of the ceiling as it collapses where he stands. The walls, piece by piece, separate, and on the other side, more of the Unyielded pace back and forth, reaching over the broken wall like zombies. "We might need to get her out of here!" he yells to Sassi.

I don't want to return. I don't want to start over. So, I close my eyes and find my rhythm, which has now become second nature. Returning to this brings clarity, and once again the succession of events retracts. In reverse, the walls rebuild, the ceiling returns, and the Unyielded and four men repeat what they have just done, only to return to minutes before. Just this alone helps me breathe.

One of the men grabs the hook again, as Katia comes to my side. "Katia," I say, as I grab her hand in mine. For the first time, her eyes connect with mine. Despite that, when I touch her, a flash of her tragic life descends upon me. I keep hold, fighting the desire to let go. "Katia," I say as she tries to pull away but I won't let her. "See me," I tell her. "Look at what's happening," I beg.

Katia closes her eyes and shakes her head, her skin gathering a bit more color.

"Katia, look at me," I yell. The man with the hook, speaking in his gibberish, grabs my arm and raises the hook. Katia opens her eyes, so I continue. "The Cellar is not where you belong." Just then, I realize I have to make a move. I sit up in place and stab the man in the throat, just as I did before. Unlike before, though, Katia watches as he falls. My feet slam the floor as I jump from the table and the other men move to attack.

"Get her to leave the room," Sassi yells.

We rush out, entering the hall just as I did that night, only this time something new begins. Katia watches me. She looks at the men then at the walls, as though she's never seen them before. I wave my hand at her to follow, and it takes her only a moment before she does. When she steps out into the hall she circles about, still a creature, yet her absolution seems to be set in motion. No longer blind to her actual surroundings, no longer plagued by just her thoughts, but rather her ears accept the noises in the hall and she walks to me one more time to touch the skin on my hand with her own. Even the boy with the black teeth slips out of the room just after Katia. He howls and moans, while rubbing his hands together.

"Is he another one?" Sassi asks.

"Yes."

Once we are all out, Arek fights to slam the door shut, then he sets his foot against it, to keep it closed.

Sassi nods, "She's doing it."

"How do I know when it's enough?" I ask as Katia looks around.

"You'll know," Sassi yells as she is forced to run over and help Arek when he is no longer enough to keep the door closed.

Like a child seeing the world for the first time, Katia continues to search. At moments she seems happy, at moments unsure. She catches her reflection in a glass door, which seems to intrigue her.

"It's happening," Sassi says as she and Arek grimace. They are forced to conjure up all of their strength against the Unyielded and the men in the room.

Katia slowly walks to her reflection, touching her face as the young man paces just as he did before. Whimpers escape her lips as she steps closer. She reaches out to touch her reflection as the color returns to her skin.

Just then, the agitated man notices that Sassi and Arek are blocking his way back into the room. I can see that his agitation is only growing, as he talks incessantly to himself and slaps his own face. His face distorts, then his body, as the rage builds. Suddenly he runs at me, his face turning to something inhuman and grotesque. My body slams to the ground and Katia jumps away, a bit of her face losing what life she has just gained. The man scratches at me, his mouth growing in size and showing sharp pointy teeth. His teeth snap at me, as though he will bite if I allow him too close, so I stretch my arms out, barely able to keep him away. I cry out, as his eyes turn blood red.

Suddenly he is ripped from me and flies in the air, hitting the wall behind us. Arek reaches out to me while Sassi continues to block the door from opening. We watch the black toothed man, his shape increasingly changing. He angrily hits the walls then retreats . . . nearly crawling away with arms and legs that have stretched and thinned.

When I turn back, Katia is no longer the monster who has haunted me. She drops her head and, in the blink of an eye, she is gone.

"Out now!" Sassi yells.

In seconds, we are back in the cave with Geo. I suck in a tense breath as I lie back on the hard, cold, and rocky earth. My chest heavily rises and falls.

Arek hurries over to me. "How do you feel?"

I take a moment to accept all that just happened, and what I feel. My fingertips run down my chest and stomach. "Free." I smile, then so does he as I say, "And that's how you get it done."

Sassi breathes out and rubs her smooth skin on her cheeks, and Geo winks at me.

"So Katia's released . . ." I sit up. "But he's not."

"It's his choice . . . in the end. As long as he's no longer with you. We've done what we came for," Geo says as he throws his backpack on his shoulders. "Come on, time for a swim."

With my newfound freedom, I jump into the water and swim under the waterfall until it is dumping on my head and shoulders. Arek swims close to me and, although I want him to touch me, he doesn't. Instead, he passes by, only allowing our shoulders to graze, but when I reach for him, he's gone.

23

I'm tired—physically, mentally, and emotionally. Living in a world of questions when I'm desperate to understand the nearly eight hundred years that are just gone. Whoosh. Just like that. The bits and pieces that have resurged make me desperate for it all. It is Arek, him alone, that has me aching, even as I train and find myself again. I am not his wife; I am not his love. The longer this continues, or the closer he stands to me, the more I ache for him.

As if my thoughts manifest, Arek passes, while I sit hidden in the Gianda café in the early morning. He doesn't see me, so I watch him. What is it like to love someone for so long that you don't remember not loving him? The smell, the feeling—to experience every moment with the remnants of the past. It colors our world and, without it, I feel like a child. I squeeze my perfectly healed hand in and out. Every morning I wake up without bruises, every night I have fresh ones. Maybe Remy loved training? Maybe she caught on to things faster? The hot tea slides down my throat and when Arek disappears from sight, I close my eyes.

"All alone?" Sassi says from somewhere near me.

When I open my eyes, she smiles. Her beautiful muscular body is statuesque within her leggings and running shoes. "For the moment," I reply.

She sits down and before we can even speak, the waitress brings her coffee. Sassi exists in peace. It embodies her every step and surrounds those who are near. Even when the enemy is within yards of us, her presence tells the world, "Nothing is too big."

"You will get through this," she says as she takes a sip of her coffee.

"You seem sure."

"I am."

"Sassi, why was Remy so special? Even the hate that some felt for her seems to be created by fear of what she could do. You all are great. You all have trained until you are the best fighters. You see the spiritual world, Arek sees strategy and ways to succeed, Geo connects the worlds, Beckah is fast and light, Kilon . . . puts people to sleep . . ."

We both laugh. "My husband does more than that," Sassi admits. "It's just his favorite part. Kilon sees the world with Big Eyes and it allows detail like I've never understood. He hears people's rhythms better than most. And Remy . . ." She takes a moment to think. "Besides being part of the Elite line, it was very clear to Kilon and I as you grew up . . . even when we did not know because they hid the prophecy . . . we knew."

"But why?" I rub my head with tense hands.

"There was nothing you lacked. Everything we were good at; you were also good at. And the speed at which you learned new things . . ."

"Wouldn't it be possible that I lost that while living as Willow?"

"Maybe," she answers honestly. "However, what you don't hear is what they are saying when you aren't there . . . like right now. Kenichi, Atum, and Geo have all pointed out how quickly you are learning. For instance what you did yesterday, Remy. It takes other people years to learn how to dive into their memory and release the Unyielded. Some Velieri never know how to truly release themselves from the crush of their grasp, so they must learn to simply never allow them in. Seeing those who already passed to the next life is a gift. You might not understand that now, but the dead . . . they can sometimes help, love, and see what we cannot because they don't have the constraints of this tough world. Don't you think Arek would fight to have the gift that you do so that he could see his mother?"

"Holona is not Unyielded though, right?"

"No, Holona is free. The Unyielded died unaware that they were no longer weighted by their own choices. They identified more with their pain in this world than the freedom that was always theirs anyway. Their trauma made them feel whole. Without it, they would have to deal with the discomfort until they could find out what filled the gap of their pain."

"It's taking too long for my memory to return."

"Is it?" Sassi smiles. "That's your problem, my darling. I think maybe the one thing standing in your way is that you believe you know what's best. Do I want you to be as you were? Of course I do. Of course Arek does . . . more than anyone. I guarantee that. One of the most important things to learn, that most Ephemes never do, is that what you want and what is best are rarely in harmony. You had labels and limits to who you thought you were for thirty-three years, and it formed a girl named Willow."

"How do I . . . detach?"

"The answer to that is that we are not our past and we are not our future. We are this moment." Sassi finishes her cup and stands up. "Come on. This is too heavy for the morning. We have work to do."

The thought of spending another day getting yelled at and beaten down makes me wrap my hands tighter around my hot drink. Days upon days, I go to bed tired and wake tired, knowing that the next day will be the same as today. My body is transforming. In all my thirty-three years as an Epheme, I have never been so familiar with the muscles under my skin—regardless of how badly they ache.

Hours later, on the mat with Mak, I am losing repeatedly. Sassi walks by and kneels in front of me while I bend over catching my breath. "Count your breath, find your rhythm, and forget about what you feel the next move should be." I nod, even though my body and mind are desperate to quit.

As we stand, ready to start again, I do my best to silence the world around me. Counting my breath, listening for my rhythm, paying as little attention to the projections of what might come next.

Then it happens.

I've felt this before . . . the air suddenly becomes infinitely clear. Distance and time no longer distract me. Rather my body, mind, and spirit flow into one rather than working like conflicting parts.

We begin. Within six moves, I take Mak down. Kenichi calls for it again, which I quickly do. He hollers for someone else. Time and again, with different and stronger opponents, I leave them on their back or compromised. I can read them—every move is broadcast before it is done.

Kenichi calls Mak back to the mat. Within three moves, Mak loses his upper hand and I throw out my foot to catch the back of his ankle. He flies to the ground, and I drop my knee to his chest with my straight palm at his neck. If he had been an enemy, I would have cracked his windpipe. Instead, Mak's handsome eyes reward me with surprise. We smile at each other.

"You see," Mak says as he touches my arm.

Kenichi laughs and claps his hands. "Yes."

Sassi smiles.

Later, as we walk through the Gianda with my bag over my shoulder, several large screens have been rolled from each balcony. Crowds have gathered around and are watching what looks to be the news. Mak and I take a moment to watch.

Andrew Vincent, the journalist, speaks in a serious tone. "Several bombs have devastated the Reds from Mumbai to Florence, to New Jersey. They were planned and perfectly coordinated attacks that have killed thousands. While we've done what we can to keep the Ephemes believing this to be terrorists, what we have is terrorists of our own." He turns to a man he is interviewing, and I roll my eyes at Prophet Covey in a button-up shirt. "This has to stop," he says. "There are criminals at large. A group that has helped Remona Landolin hide. If anyone knows where Miss Landolin and the others are, speak up."

The Fidelis begin to peek in my direction. *Is there anyone here who would turn on us?* There are many here who could lose everything for having me here. The murmurs rise through the crowded hall in the Gianda. I quickly rush away, knowing that it will only get worse.

"Remy!" Mak calls, as he rushes after me.

He catches up as we reach the elevator that leads to our apartments. Just as the door opens, he pulls my arm back until I am up against the wall. His caring eyes search mine, as he places a hand on the wall behind me—showing me that we are not leaving until I explain.

"Mak, how many are we going to put in danger?" I ask.

"You gave these people everything."

"To say that they owe me goes against everything Remy stood for . . . you know it and I know it."

Mak smiles. "What Remy stood for was fighting for the underdog, releasing the ego, and choosing good. You, my friend, are the underdog. At this moment, every Fidelis has traded places with you. Certain Powers and Prophets want nothing more than to end you before you can make this world believe, once again, in the Prophecy."

"What if the Prophecy isn't real? What if God never intended this? And we are flying all over the world trying to save something that never really was possible to save?"

Mak bends lower in front of me, to catch my eyes. "Remy, we have to believe. Peace and hope are all we have."

For a moment we are silent, and with the emotion stirring within me, I am so grateful to know him. It is natural and comfortable when he leans in to kiss my lips. When he pulls back, he looks at me with careful eyes. "I'm sorry. I shouldn't have done that."

"Where's Aita?"

"I've not forgiven her for the trouble she put us through. She is in Japan, sulking." Mak smiles, and I can see him battle whether to kiss me again.

"It's probably best that you don't," I whisper.

"Look at you, learning people's thoughts," he says, still not retreating.

"You're not making it too difficult."

Peter, Lily, Arek, Sassi, and Beckah appear as they are heading to the elevator that has closed again. They notice us. Mak steps away quickly, yet I can see the concern in Arek's eyes.

24

"Meet me in the club?" Mak asks just a few hours later on the phone. "You need it." When he hears my hesitation on the other end, he says, "Come on, Remy. It's time to just be free. If only for a moment."

Minutes later, I can see the extra-large moon from the window in the ceiling of the club as Mak and I walk in. Our bodies vibrate to the loud and pumping music, which instantly grabs hold of me. It's impossible to think about anything else as I watch the people give in to the beat. Multicolored lights move about, sending rays of the rainbow from one side of the room to the next. Mak looks down at what I'm wearing and raises an eyebrow. "What?" I ask.

He shakes his head. "Nothing. You just look beautiful is all."

"Your wife really needs to come keep an eye on you." I roll my eyes and he chuckles.

"Remy, you were my first love, there is no changing that. I understand that you're married to Arek, but you know what . . ." he nearly has to yell to be heard, "where is he now, Remy? The guy passes by you without a glance. It's like he pretends you're not here. I hate to say it but just because my father asks for you to be left alone while you're training . . ." Mak leans closer to my ear. "Nothing in the world would be reason worthy enough for me to stay away from you. I'm just saying." He takes a moment, then winks. "Come on, let's dance."

"I don't dance," I yell in his ear.

"Sure you do! Just let go. Come on." First, he pulls my silky shirt's hood over my head to hide who I am. "There." He takes my hand and leads me to the middle of the dance floor where no one pays attention to us. It takes me a moment, watching everyone around me, afraid to even begin. Mak pulls my face to his. "It's not about them. They don't care. And you shouldn't either. They can't tell who you are. Don't worry."

Finally, the infectious song takes hold of me, and I let go. I remember . . . my mind flashes to dances from all different centuries . . . they aren't with Mak. Ballrooms, speakeasys, among so many others, one at a time, pop up in my memories. Arek's smile and his eyes as he pulls me through each crowd. When the memories stop, I am in the middle of the crowd with Mak, feeling the freedom of dance. The crowd grows bigger, the songs more addicting, the movement intoxicating. For so long I have been so constricted, so controlled, and for just a moment, I let it all go. After several songs, a slow one begins and Mak pulls me in to him. It takes no time before I rest my head on his shoulder.

Just as the song is about to end, Beckah, Geo, Arek, Sassi, and Kilon enter the club. As though he already knows I'm there, Arek's eyes instantly catch mine. Within my chest, I can feel his discomfort that I'm already there. Mak is right about Arek's obsession with the rules. *Could they be more important than what we have? What is he trying so hard to protect?*

"Should we join them?" Mak asks, taking a step away from me.

Sassi whispers something in Arek's ear, which brings a calm to his eyes that I wish I could give him.

"No. I want to go back."

Mak hesitates. "Are you sure?"

"Yeah. I'm sure."

Walking away is the only way for me to wrap my head around everything. Just as I'm about to leave, I look back for a second and catch Arek's eyes. Finally, Mak walks me home.

An hour later I am unable to sleep, so I sit in the chair beside my open window. A breeze lifts my hair as I stare at the stars and the giant moon. For the last hour the new memories of dancing with Arek replay in my mind. Again and again they repeat, when our love was less complicated, when he did not hesitate to pull me in to him—when there was nothing to protect and no secrets. The only sounds I can hear are large waves crashing in the distance.

Unexpectedly my calm is broken when a hand slides down my shoulder. It takes only seconds before my instinct takes over. Before I can even understand what has happened, I have twisted the hand until the person attached is forced to roll to get out of it to keep their wrist intact. In the dark room, I drop my knee to his chest and his hands catch my hand just above his neck.

I realize it is Arek, and that he is smiling at what I've just done. "I'm sorry!" I begin to pull away, but he grabs my leg to keep my knee on his chest.

"It was perfect." He lays there for a moment under the moonlight. Finally, he pulls my hand—that nearly cracked his windpipe—until it lands on the wood floor beside his face. Before there is a chance to question it, he wraps me in his arms and my knee slides down to the floor. His face is so close to mine that I can read every curve, his full lips, and even the heat in his cheeks.

"Why are you looking at me like that?" I whisper.

"Like what?"

"Like . . . you want me."

His hands hold my face near his. "'Cause I do."

He sits up until my legs envelope his waist, then one hand travels from my eyes, to my lips, then down my neck and onto my chest. Suddenly, I realize the sound I hear is my own breath shaking in and out. I press my palms to his face, ready for him to give in. There are many experiences with Arek that I will never get used to, but one of them is the fire beneath my skin from his touch.

"I'll fight for you, Remy," he whispers. "Do you know that? With every bit of my soul, I am fighting for you and everything we have."

"Yes."

He opens his thick lips to grab mine, leaving behind a trail of heat and nerves. My arms entangle in his as I pull at his shirt. For a moment, I stop and let my fingertips glide from his collarbone to his thick chest. Everything about him is perfect. He takes my hand in his and kisses my fingertips. Again, we lose ourselves in the deep in and out of the kiss, leaving behind pieces of us with each touch. He kisses each shoulder.

Suddenly he stops and places a finger to his lips. He listens carefully, even though I hear nothing. I am on fire from his touch and want nothing more than to continue, but he pulls back with concern.

"Did you . . ."

I hear the pop just before I feel the pain in my neck. When my hand flies to the pain, blood flows from the wound beneath my fingertips. Arek swiftly rolls us over on the hardwood floor, covering me with his body, but he also pulls my gun from the nearby table. Several more pops and strikes of bright light fill the room. My windpipe has been hit, and I am suffocating. A man jumps from the shadows, but Arek has him down to the floor in seconds. With my finger I try to plug the hole from the bullet, but the pain is so intense my entire body shakes.

Arek climbs on the man's back and wraps his arms around his neck. As the man fights, he grabs his gun and tries to direct it behind his head at Arek. With one arm Arek keeps his stranglehold, and with the other he blocks the gun as bullets puncture the ceiling.

I am not getting better. My head grows cold, my hands as well.

Finally, Arek wrestles the gun away from the attacker's hand and an orange flame flashes when Arek pulls the trigger. The man drops still and lifeless. Arek races over to me and drops on his knees. Instantly he checks my wound when I wheeze with panic.

"I have to get the bullet." It takes only a moment, but the pain is intense as he pulls the metal from its shallow position relieving the pressure on my windpipe. When he does, I am instantly better and able to breathe. "Put your hand there. It will heal fast now." He grabs his phone and presses speaker. Soon I hear Sassi's voice on the other end.

"Arek, they're here." She sounds as though she's running and out of breath.

"Meet us in the basement. Now!" he says. Then he reaches down and scoops me up to my feet. "Come on, Remy. We've gotta go."

He grabs weapons from my closet that I have been training with for the last few weeks. Kilon has been teaching me about his favorites and those that aren't. The last training session, I was able to prep three guns in thirty-seven seconds. The fastest time yet. Now, my hand holds one with power and precision while my other hand holds the wound in my neck. Arek lifts my shirt and pushes two more weapons into the waist band of my jeans.

Arek wraps his arm around my waist and helps me through the hallway toward the basement. The group waits quietly for us in the dark.

"What happened?" Sassi rushes to me and looks over my wound.

"He was in her room," Arek answers, as he presses the buttons in a keypad on the wall.

"Let's get her in the holding room until we figure out what's going on," Kilon suggests.

"I can stay with you." My voice is still weak.

Kilon shakes his head. "Are we here again? Is that what this training has done? I have battled with you, girl, your entire life. Just do what I ask one time."

Sassi agrees, "Beckah can stay with her. Remy, this is what it means for us . . . for what we do. Let us do it."

Hok and Briston come barreling around the corner just as Arek gets the door open to the basement. We swiftly enter the soundproof and windowless room, not much different than the basement at Arek's home in Switzerland.

Arek shouts orders to Hok. "Take a group and go to the southwest and search that ridge from the end of Turn Pike to Tulane.

Briston and I will take the curve of Beel's Alley through to the Epin Ridge." These are all landmarks within the Gianda.

"Sassi and I will catch the rest," Kilon nods.

Arek stops Beckah when she, he, and I are the last ones in the room. He warns her. "Stay here. I'll let you know what we find."

"Of course."

"Arek . . ." I call out.

He walks to me. "Stay here, stay safe. Guard your mind always, do you understand?"

I nod as he closes the door, leaving Beckah and I alone. Together, we barricade the door.

25

"How are we supposed to know what's going on out there?" I ask Beckah. The wound on my neck is still there but has already begun to heal.

Beckah is pushing the clip in and out of her gun from where she sits on a gray counter across the room. "You know, Arek's always been in love with you." The gun quickly bores her, so she pulls at a string on her jeans, twirling it around the tip of her finger. "He's always been in love with you. He told me once, before he even knew who you were, that he couldn't keep his eyes off you. Then you met, and he never spoke of anyone else. That's how it's always been and that's how it always will be, I guess." She shrugs and continues quickly before I have a chance for rebuttal. "I believe Mak loves you . . . but it's not the same. Don't tell, but I see Geo with someone else, too."

I watch her with surprise. When she sees my eyes, she shrugs with a nod.

"Yeah. I don't mean, I *think* I can see him with someone else . . . I mean I was shown a vision of him with someone else. Someone important."

"Beckah . . ." I shake my head. "Come on. Geo absolutely adores you."

Beckah smiles. "Yeah, he does. But if I'm honest, I'm Geo's Mak . . . not his Arek. I'm with him now, but it's simply because he hasn't felt what it's truly supposed to be like. And I guess you could say, I had a prophecy about him when I was with Gyre once . . . but Gyre said I would know the right time to tell Geo."

"So you believe in the prophecies?" I finally build up the courage to ask after some loaded silence.

It takes her a moment to respond. "I think . . . we need to believe in prophecy. Sometimes when things are so bad in this world, even the glimpse of hope can make the difference between diving right into the ocean or just dipping your toes. Hope gives people the push . . . you know?" She shrugs but moves on quickly. "I'll never forget when Arek came home to England with you, and I couldn't get enough. This young Swiss girl who could barely speak our language, but by the end of the night you had taken all our money from Alquerque."

"Alquerque?"

"A game from that time . . . sorta like checkers." She quiets for a moment, and I watch her profile as she thinks. There's something in her eyes that I've never seen before. "Yeah," she finally says quietly, "sometimes you just know when certain relationships are only for a time or when they're for a lifetime." She stops for a moment, as though the idea is painful. Then continues, "I watch Arek squirm when he thinks of you with Mak. However, I've never seen him squirm nearly as much as when he knew Navin wanted you. Navin could never love anyone more than himself. Do me a favor though . . . would you?"

"What's that?"

Beckah raises her hand to silence me and her face grows concerned. "Did you hear that?" She jumps from the counter and walks to the door where she places her ear to it; suddenly it shakes when someone pounds on the other side.

"Ready your weapon," she warns me as she pulls hers. It takes me only seconds and both guns are in my hands. Beckah comes to my side and together we look at her phone. On her screen is present footage of the hallway outside the door.

"What is that?" I ask.

"This is an app that shows what the security cameras can see. Hok gave us the password." Standing in the hallway is a man, covered in a long coat and hood. He tries to shoot the door with no luck, then throws his body against it. "There's no way he can get through this door. That's why we're in here. I'll call Arek—" She begins to switch the screen but stops suddenly, when the man in the video pulls something from his pocket. "Wait, what are you doing, dude?" she whispers and zooms closer. "What is that? Wait—" Her face grows panicked. "Oh my god. He has a UKD."

Beckah becomes frantic, quickly calling Arek, with her hands shaking as she rubs her forehead. "Oh my god, oh my god. Get behind the couch. Now!" she commands.

"What's a UKD?" My voice strains as I rush to make the couch my only barrier.

"It means he can open any door, any high-tech system, it can override." Her voice changes, "Arek! Someone's here and he has a UKD. I—"

The door starts to open and Beckah rushes over, throwing her body against it. She is so tiny that it doesn't do much. With swift hands she points the gun within the crack of the door and takes several shots. The door slams shut.

"Help me!" Beckah yells. "Push the couch over!" Already the door starts to open again. The tip of a gun sticks between it and shots hit the couch and walls. We duck but continue to push the furniture against the metal door.

"If they get in, shoot them between the eyes," Beckah explains. "It won't stop them completely, but it will take the most out of them, which will give us time."

Beckah cries out as she battles the strong man behind the door. Even the couch seems to not be enough weight. She grabs her larger gun and pulls the lever to chamber it. Just as she does, the couch slides across the floor, the door bursts open, and she is thrown against the wall.

A figure rushes in like a ghost. He is so fast I can't catch sight of him. Beckah starts shooting. Even I find the ability to pull the trigger. I nearly hit the moving target, but not before he and Beckah fight. The dark figure moves so fast it's hard to follow. I've never seen Beckah have to work so hard. They battle, their hands swiping the air, and I watch her gun fly away. She quickly replaces it with a knife, then sends his gun flying. He stumbles back, and she tries to take advantage of it.

Until suddenly she loses ground and falls back.

"Beckah!" I yell. I rush forward. His arm flies out to try and clothesline me, so instead I roll out of the way and wrap my arms around his ankles. He falls with his ankles tethered together by my arms but catches himself in a push-up. This gives Beckah a chance to step away, but only for a moment. He wriggles a foot free and kicks my face, moving faster than I've ever seen. With a thick hand he grabs my neck, but Beckah immediately takes the attention back, as she slices him across the cheek. He throws her to the floor. I try to help, but his hand contacts my jaw at just the right point and my sight blurs.

While I struggle to regain my mind, he stands over Beckah with his knee on her chest and his hood still covering his face. I can only see the tip of his nose. He isn't the biggest man I have ever seen, but there is something about him that is terrifying. I have never seen as much fear in Beckah's eyes as there is now, and this sends my heart racing. She shakes her head to warn me not to come and tears fall from her eyes.

"Tell him what I told you," she whispers. "Run!!!!" she yells at the top of her lungs, as he pulls another gun from his back. Instead, I run toward them, my footing still not beneath me as the stars have not gone away. Before I can reach her, he sets the gun to the back of her ear and pulls the trigger. The blood splatters the wall.

"Beckah!" I scream. As though her power fills the room, I am overcome by memories. The years we shared; thousands of moments that we spent laughing and playing; the memory of Geo and Beck-ah's love affair. Each picture is a dagger slicing away at me since it is too late. In just mere seconds, I am reintroduced to my best friend but lose her all at the same time.

Something rushes through the room as mysterious as the soul, but as consuming as fire. Swirling about me in a way that I've never felt before. My heart cries but also distracts me from my pain with the new experience. In a strange way, whether it's in my mind or actually there, the air appears crystal clear and her spirit enters it with an inferno of brightly colored flames. Power that I've never experienced builds in my gut, rising to my chest, and beyond. It is born from my rage and, just seconds after he takes her life, I face him with my gun pointed between his eyes. However, even though Beckah said to do this, something within me doesn't wish it to end so quickly.

He stands over Beckah and comes up with his hood hanging so low over his eyes that I still can't see him. He works to Trace deep into my subconscious, but I swiftly gather my rhythm.

"You're stronger," he whispers, his voice not far from a raspy growl.

I say nothing.

He takes a step over Beckah's body—his boot landing heavily in the pool of blood that has already spread across the uneven floor.

My gun is pointed, but the closer he comes, the more I want to lower it. With pulsing skin and heat unable to escape my tense body, my breath releases rapidly in and out from my lungs. Something has taken over and the sound of my gun hitting the ground fills the air. I stretch my arms out wide telling him that I am ready.

His bloody boots leave red footprints with every step. He throws his gun away and smiles.

For the first time, I know I can kill him. This isn't just an inno-cent man on an opposing side in training—I can sense his evil. He wishes to kill me. In fact, he likes the kill. For a split second, I can see and taste and experience the awful things he has done in his lifetime. It sends chills down my spine.

He runs toward me, his boots slamming against the concrete. I keep the knife in his hand in my sight, but I listen to the pattern of his steps and calculate the equation. Standing tall for as long as possible to let him believe that I haven't the instincts to do what is necessary, at the best moment, I drop to the ground and roll out of his way as he slices his knife through the air. From the ground I reach behind me with my left hand and grab his ankle, sweeping him to the floor. Taking his toes in one hand and his heel in the other, I twist, rupturing his knee and everything within.

He cries out. Sitting up, he whips his arm around and cracks my cheek with his fist. I immediately taste blood. My foot connects with his ear and his head turns at an unnatural angle as the knife flies out of his hands.

He is on his feet too fast and grabs my neck until I twist his wrist. I spin around him, jump onto his back, and wrap his neck in my arms.

Feet pound the hallway outside and their voices carry. His gag continues as he scrapes at my arm to release the rear choke. My strength is waning, but it doesn't matter. Despite my head just beside the attackers, before I see it happen, I hear the gun. Arek confidently lifts his gun and shoots him between the eyes. I feel his arms go limp as we both fall to the ground. To finish him off, Arek shoots again behind his ear when he comes close.

For a second, my body is drained, and I lay on the floor to breathe. I hadn't even seen or heard Arek enter the room . . . nor had the man. This is when I know—Arek is more dangerous than I expect.

Only when Arek reaches out to me, do I dare move. I take his hand and, as I do, I realize that I have blood spatter all over my skin, all the way down to my fingertips—Beckah's blood.

Geo kneels beside Beckah. She is gone. The anger seethes within him until the air about him is toxic. His knuckles are white, wrapped about the gun in his hand, and his chest expands with emotion. Arek's phone dings and he checks the text.

"Geo, we have to go," Arek warns. He is calm, but stern. "We have to go."

Again, Geo nods.

"We will come back and take care of her. We will make sure it is done, but right now you and I have to move."

Geo stands as Arek places a hand on his shoulder. Then, together, they pull their guns as we walk to the door. They are laser focused, and as we head out into the hall, just the nerves alone sharpen my eyes and ears. Something has changed and I feel it in the way I hold my weapons, the way I am able to control my fear. My eyes see clearer than ever.

The only lights left on in the Gianda are blinking, sometimes for long moments, until we are forced to reach out for the wall's guidance.

Bullet holes riddle the walls as we climb the levels. One by one we reach bodies lying about the Gianda. It is impossible to take in all the carnage, as there is so much in the wake of a trained killer.

"Are there more?" I ask quickly.

"We don't know. All it takes is one of the Umbramanes to do this," Arek whispers.

"One man did all of this?"

Arek shakes his head. "Umbramanes are taught to never work with another unless they have to, but they often come with an army of their own."

"You were able to kill him so easily," I whisper, contemplating just how dangerous Arek is.

Arek lifts his gun as we come to the edge of the hallway leading to the staircase to the main entrance. Just ahead, there's a recognizable face lying on the ground. "Jace," I say. He has fallen down the stairs and now lies awkwardly with his feet above him. Blood seeps from his neck and head.

As we continue, we keep close to the wall and step over debris from the decimated cement and drywall. Arek stops with caution as we near a corner, listening intently. A whistle vibrates through the air, not too far away. Arek nods at whoever has made themselves known. I can't see as I stand behind him.

"Do you see anyone?" Arek calls out.

"No," they respond. "Come to me . . ."

Arek pulls me behind him as we hesitate before stepping out into the open Gianda. We walk slowly at first, making our way through the park. Besides the dead scattered about, the Gianda is empty. "Where is everyone?"

"Most are protected, hidden within their homes. These are just the few who risked it."

Across the open floor, hidden in the corner of the café, Mak waits with Kenichi and Briston behind him. His eyes fall on me and he mouths, "You okay?" I nod. Everyone looks disheveled, sweaty, and uncomfortable with the idea that anyone else might be there.

Mak points above them to the second story. Just then a shot rings out, passing between us, and I fall to the ground. A turned over table is nearby, and we slide behind it, ducking for safety.

"Geo," Arek says, "if you take the left, I'll take the right."

The fire in Geo's eyes is untamed, and perhaps untamable. He doesn't need to respond to confirm his intentions. Together, they count to three, then with multiple guns collected from those laying about, they split in opposite directions, immediately firing from both hands. When a gun is empty, they drop it and grab another. It takes only seconds before the attacker from above makes himself known by firing back. Both Geo and Arek get shot and wince, even fall, only to continue. The second story of the Gianda explodes in increments, the dust never settling as they continue. Then, the man from the second story manages to move fast and perfectly, jumping from one level, using a railing to glide, then land on the next floor. Arek and Geo continue to push forward. Mak and Briston jump out as they come closer and join in the line of men sending a barrage of bullets up to the higher level.

Nothing stops this man.

Until a bullet from an entirely different direction hits him. Finally, he drops to the floor. Standing at the attacker's side, just behind a corner he would never have known, Sassi still stands with her gun out in front of her and her jaw tense. Her shot was perfect.

Everyone looks at one another, but it is Geo and Arek who sit in pain. Their arms and chests are riddled with at least four bullets each. Arek grabs his chest and lets out a groan of pain. Blood seeps through his shirt, but it doesn't take long until he is back up on his feet and telling us all to hurry away.

"More are possibly coming . . ." he says as pain hardens his face.

Sassi takes her fingers and squeezes out a bullet from Arek's forearm, which makes him growl. She quickly shrugs, "No other choice, my friend."

Arek ignores it and engages Hok, "Look, if we leave now, you can close things off and get everyone situated. If we stay . . . they won't stop. Let's keep the Gianda safe."

Hok comes to him and places a hand on his shoulder. "I can help you out of here quickly. But you all must promise, that when you need us . . . all of us . . . every Gianda there is . . . that you will call."

Arek nods. "Of course."

Just then more attackers explode through the door.

"It's time to go!" Kilon yells.

"Come with me," Hok beckons as he runs toward a hall nearby. Neither Geo nor Arek are fully healed, yet they keep up the best they can.

The hall is bright and modern following suit with the rest of the Gianda, yet a quarter of the way down, Hok stops and swipes his hand to unlock an unmarked door. We all rush inside, only to be instantly transported to an industrial stairwell that looks neither inviting nor representative of the place we've come to know.

"Down, this way." Hok races on, his feet pounding the metal stairs sending echoes that all of us hope are far enough underground to not be heard. We descend three flights of stairs and I find myself wondering how we could be so far underground. Again, at the bottom, we reach another metal door with a lock that Hok must use his fingerprints to open. Only this time, when he opens it, a rush of cold hits my body that feels good after all that has happened.

Before us is an underground body of water, running beneath the Gianda. The cave has been carved out of the ground and lined with dim lights. Just like the swaddling cold of the cave from the days before, this too cools my cheeks and lips. The sound of running water drips nearby, and echoes of our voices reverberate smoothly. Strangely the only way to describe the smell is that of earth.

I shake my head, "What is this?"

"Follow and I'll explain." Hok hurries along the wall on a small lip carved out of the rock that runs on each side of the passageway. Although there is not enough height for sails, the width of this underground passage is that of two small boats side by side. Each of us must hug the moss-covered wall since there is no railing to keep us from falling in the water. Luckily if we did, it does not flow too fast and it is not too far to drop. In a single line we move quickly—careful not to step on the heels of the person ahead.

The dim light begins to disappear the farther we go, so Hok pulls out his phone and uses its flashlight.

"Back in the fourteenth century when gold and diamonds were found in the mountains, this was built to transport them closer to the villages, but without the knowledge of pirates and thieves. This," he looks back only for a second, "is why Remy and I chose this place to buy and build the Gianda. She knew at any moment things could change, that the Powers or Prophets could find out about the Fidelis, and she wanted to make it easier for us to escape."

For a moment, a strange sensation travels through my body—my skin puckers and my spine shivers. My feet have walked this exact path before, and my ears have heard this same vibration. The déjà vu sweeps across me, riding the cool chill in the air. Somehow, I know there's a boat ahead. I can see it in my mind. Then it comes into view just ahead of us. The boat is small and more modern than my memory, though. It can carry eight to ten people and that is all we need.

Hok turns to us. "Take it, all the way. It leads underground and you'll exit through the manhole into the heart of Main Street. Leave the boat there and I'll pick it up later. I'll call now and have cars waiting for you on the other side."

Arek places a hand on Hok's neck and shoulder. "Thank you, brother. We are grateful."

"Call us . . . when needed."

"Of course."

Kenichi is the first to get on as others help him. He grumbles the entire way, "One day you will all get old. Don't be so smug."

The rest of us pile on. It is only then that we are all aware of the one who is missing. For a moment everyone can feel the heaviness. Beckah's vibrance is gone.

Finally, as the boat roars to life, Hok places his hand on his chest and pounds three times. "The Fidelis stand with you."

Then we are off, driving beneath the city.

26

"Stop the boat here," Sassi says with certainty.

Arek slows the boat down until it comes to a stop near the ledge. Along the rock wall to our left are metal bars that lead up the thirty-foot wall we must climb. Kilon begins first and pushes the heavy manhole cover out of the way with his strong arms. One by one we make our way to the top, where Kilon helps each of us out into an alley that is tucked away from the main thoroughfare. Finally, Arek pulls himself up and onto the street, then they move the cover back to its resting position.

A robust smell of food is intoxicating, while we listen to the percussion of music and the city buzz on Main Street. Peeking out from the alley, we find a busy plaza with bustling shops, food carts, and a large water feature where a crowd sits along the white stone.

"How are we supposed to get past this?" Sassi asks.

"I guess we have no choice," Arek says, as he looks back at the dead-end behind us. "Stay here."

He and Kilon stealthily make their way out to the crowd while we watch.

Hundreds of people flurry about all dressed in bright colors and yelling at one another in order to hear over the music. A peddler with fifty puppets hanging from a wooden cross haggles money from people's pockets.

"Actually, this isn't too bad," Sassi whispers. "We could definitely disappear in this." Sassi looks at me, then back at Peter. Peter was just forced to leave Lily and the disappointment is written on his face. "Peter," Sassi says quickly, "give me that."

Peter has a black shirt with a hood wrapped about his waist. "This?" he asks.

"Yeah." Sassi instantly throws it over my head and then pulls the hood low over my eyes. "Keep it low."

Arek and Kilon separate, taking opposite sides of the crowds. After a few minutes, Kilon nods our way and one by one, we disperse. Kilon stands against the corner of a building, as he tells each one of us, with a subtle pointed finger, to look to the right. About a hundred yards away are two black vehicles parked beside a bank with drivers leaning against the hood of their cars. Clearly that is where we are supposed to go.

Sassi stays close until a large party of loud, teenage girls cut us off as they head toward a café nearby. Soon I am by myself, zigzagging through the café's tables and chairs. Mak and Briston help Kenichi to the cars, Peter makes his way to Arek's side, and Kilon maintains distance behind us all.

The black hood over my head throws off my peripheral, and I run into someone. "I'm so sorry," I say quickly without looking up. When I hurry to pass him, he steps with me, refusing to let me by. I look up. The man stares at me with confidence. He raises his hand and places it on the gun in his belt.

"Back to the Cellar, Remy," he says with a grin. Just as he reaches for my arm, I duck out of the way and under one of the balloon handlers before he can stop me.

Sassi yells at Kilon, who is the closest to me, yet there are still too many people between us.

I escape into an alley between two buildings. He chases me.

In one alley and out another, again and again, I snake my way through, hoping that I don't get lost. Until suddenly, a dead-end stops me in my tracks. I turn around to see the man staring at me. Behind him, two more of his men appear to back him up.

My mind races. There is no way out of this. For the first time, my instinct is to protect my mind first so I quickly rebuke their Trace. They point their guns in my direction and I lift my hands in surrender.

"Keep still, Remy!" one of them yells.

"I'm not Remy. I can't do what you think I can."

"Just keep those hands up," he warns me. "If you move, you will force me to shoot, do you understand?"

"Yes," I say quietly. "I promise you, I can't do anything. Are you a part of the Umbramanes?"

"No. We work for Prophet Covey."

I raise an eyebrow and feel the sarcasm burst from my mouth. "Prophet Covey has his own team?"

None of them back down, rather they take short steps toward me. I beg, under my breath, for Arek and the others to find me. The men inch their way closer, never lowering their guns. He comes near enough that he hesitantly reaches out to take my arm, and I see the others holding cuffs for me.

"I haven't been in cuffs since the Cellar," I whisper.

"The Prophets are waiting for you."

My chest rises and falls at an unnatural level when something clicks. Once again, the air becomes crystal clear, and I can hear each individual sound of the city. Succinct calculations run through my mind, as he pulls my arm. My path is clear.

It takes thirty seconds altogether. Suddenly I am standing in the alleyway, looking at all three men lying lifeless on the ground. I have one gun in the front of my belt, the other in the back, and one in my hand pointing at Sassi and Arek, who are staring at me.

"Remy," Arek says, as though he has already said it once before.

I drop my hands and look down at the bloodied men. It is not like I have blacked out, as I remember every crunch and groan, but it is more that there was simply no thought. Arek's hand rests on mine that holds the gun and he looks at me carefully at first, but then his smile builds into a grin. As does mine.

"Do you remember what just happened?" he asks.

"Yes. Every second of it."

"Good. Okay, it's time to go. Let's get out of here before they wake up," he says as he takes both guns from my belt.

"I don't get to keep those?"

"Ummm, normally . . . yes, but it might look a bit too much as we head to the cars."

Kilon suddenly runs past the alleyway only to slide to a stop and return. "Let's go, let's go, let's go!"

The setting sun starts to paint the town pink and orange as it settles upon us. We reach the cars swiftly and jump inside. Sassi opens the door to the driver's side. The driver looks at her with confusion as Kilon gets in the passenger seat.

"Move," Kilon says quickly.

Still, as though the driver is worried for his car that belongs to the Gianda, he shakes his head. "I'm supposed—"

"Now!" Kilon growls.

The driver jumps out and Sassi quickly gets in. Soon, she pushes the car through the streets, aware that anyone can be following.

"Briston, Mak, Kenichi, and Peter will meet us later," Arek explains. "They're going a different way to throw anyone off."

"We're all damned anyway . . ." I say. "All of us. It doesn't matter whether we find something to clear my name or not. They've made a choice. We're all at the mercy of the Powers and the Prophets."

"Not necessarily. There are still those we can trust. If we clear your name, they will have no choice but to let you be free," Kilon says.

"And if we can't clear my name? We run forever?" I ask.

For the first time, no one says anything. Geo stares out the window, his eyes lost, and his chest compressed. Beckah is the first one lost. How many more will follow?

27

An hour later, in the belly of a jet, we are all quiet and look just how we feel—as though we've been through battle. Everyone carries the sadness of losing someone so close to our team. The memories of Beckah and our friendship continue to pass through my mind as well as her last moments on earth.

I look around to find Geo, but he's disappeared. Arek turns to me when I unbuckle my seat belt. "I'll be right back," I say.

There are a few conference rooms in the back of this smaller jet and I open doors until I find Geo sitting with his head in his hands. He doesn't look up when I enter, rather his tired voice rumbles out the sadness, "She knew that was going to happen."

The gray chair beside him squeaks as I take a seat while placing my hand on his back. There is nothing to say that will help, so the silence lays heavily between us.

He continues, "I should have listened to her." We look at each other. "She did what she was there to do. Protect you."

The pressure of being the *One* seems to build every day. I shake it off and finally know the most important thing to tell him: "I felt her . . . the moment she passed. I felt her power. I still feel it."

He nods. "She's not gone for good. I promise you that."

"Yeah. She told me something. That she wasn't the one for you . . . there was someone else and she knew it."

It takes him a moment, then he nods. "Yeah, she told me the same thing. I didn't want to hear it."

"When my mother died of cancer, she said something I'll never forget. She said, 'Willow, I'm supposed to work for the other side. I'm not meant to be here anymore.' I still don't know what that means, but what I've learned in training with you . . . is that I know now more than ever that we will never understand how much truly goes on in a realm we cannot see."

"That's right," Geo says, just as he takes my hand. "You, Remy, could feel that more than anyone I ever knew."

"So, I've graduated to Remy now with you?"

"Yeah." He squeezes my hand and smiles.

The door to the conference room opens and Sassi peeks in. "Geo, come with me. It's time."

A few moments later we all stand together in the belly of the plane. Gathered in a circle with a glass of scotch in our hands, everyone prepares in their own way to say goodbye. Arek, who stands the tallest of the group, reaches out his glass to the middle of the circle and clears his throat. "This . . . is for Beckah. We are grateful for her sacrifice and while she is not present in our eyes, the truth is that she is now more powerful than any of us could ever be. Cheers to our friend and one of the strongest, smallest people I ever knew."

The group smiles, and Sassi wipes a tear from her cheek as she speaks, "Cheers to our beloved friend."

"Cheers!" everyone says in unison as we clink glasses and gulp down the brassy colored liquid that burns my throat.

After a moment, Briston takes a breath. "As we move on from this, we have to remember what's at stake. We must keep an eye out for one another and understand there are massive risks to fighting Navin, or the Powers and the Prophets. I never thought we would be here . . . feeling orphaned from a regime that I, at one time, would have placed all my trust in." Briston shakes his head, then continues, "Elizabeth is still missing."

All of us look at him with concern.

He continues, "While I cannot assume who has her, she is the only one who knows what happened that night with Remy. Unfortunately, this just adds to our fight. I will have to continue my search for her, which divides us even more." It is obvious how much he loves her, and I am reminded of the years that Lyneva wedged herself between Briston and Elizabeth all in the name of Power. "Everyone take a seat," Briston says as he pulls out his computer to share a video on a large screen that slowly drops from the ceiling. His movements are tired.

From the screen, we see a news conference beginning. Prophets Covey and Hawking stand behind a podium with many journalists waiting to hear what they have to say. Camera flashes pierce the scene as Prophet Covey begins. "Good morning, ladies and gentlemen. This will be quick. Commander Arek Rykor, Sassi and Kilon Pierne, Peter Rykor . . . Beckah Hammonds, and Geo De le Croix have warrants out for their arrest. Monarch Briston Landolin has been removed from his seat on the council and stricken from his place in the Powers. Each one will face the harshest penalty and are hereby stripped of their appropriate titles. If anyone has any information on any of these men and women, they are to act and call the number at the bottom of this screen. If it is found that anyone has not complied with this mandate, there will be ramifications. I'll take questions now." He points to one of the reporters to his right, "Yes?"

A male reporter with gray hair calls out, "There are many rumors out there about the return of Remona Landolin. Nothing has been verified, yet there have been many possible sightings. Can you say anything about these rumors?"

Covey laughs it off. "Well, I can tell you that I don't know who they think they have seen. It is not Remy Landolin. Let's be clear, they want you to believe. You understand that? Remona Landolin was executed more than thirty years ago, as a criminal. That is where that road ends."

Briston mutes the press conference even though Covey continues to speak. Everyone seems to have nothing to say, so Briston continues, "Covey's running the show."

"That's nothing new," Sassi whispers.

"No, no it's not. However, he's angry and doing his best to turn everyone against us."

Arek nods, "Then perhaps separating isn't such a bad thing." Everyone seems confused by this suggestion and many postures shift uncomfortably in the room.

Briston nods. "Look, here's what we're dealing with. The Umbramanes will come. Several of them will show up and we don't know what Covey has told them. Now that he's done this conference, every Velieri will turn us in. From now on we do not go out unless our identity can be covered. Elizabeth is still missing, and she is the link to our puzzle. She's the only one who can testify on Remy's behalf. Diem and his group are searching for any information to clear Remy's name. Not to mention Navin's rebels are growing in numbers as the years progress, and with Covey leading the pack, Navin has the freedom to do anything he wants. And frankly it's uncomfortable that we know nothing of his plan. We're losing here and that's the truth. None of us have any power, which means no covering. We're on our own."

After a severe pause, laden with confusion and fear, Arek speaks up. "Diem will find it. If there's anything to find, he will. He and Gal have their ways and a loyal tribe. Mak and Kenichi should return to Japan."

Mak smiles with annoyance. "And why is that, Arek?"

Arek's chest rises with an irritated breath. "I can't guard a massive group."

Mak stands abruptly to his feet. "So, you use our resources, draw us in, Arek, until our names are questioned and then send us off when you're done."

"It was never my choice for you to be here, Mak," Arek's voice rumbles.

"Is that because your ego can't handle me here? Or the way that she looks at me still? Maybe that she remembers our life together and not yours."

Mak takes several steps to Arek, forcing Arek to his feet, until Kenichi grabs his arm yelling, "Urusai! Both of you, urusai!"

Sassi stands up and lifts her phone in the air. "Jenner wants to meet us."

Everyone stops suddenly. "Prophet Jenner?" Briston asks.

"Yes. I've told her where we're going, and only she and I know where we will meet. Let's not make any big decisions until then. And one more thing . . ." She hesitates with a clearly heavy soul. "One thing Diem and Gal did find out . . ." She pulls papers from her bag and throws them across the table. "My first thought when we found out that Lyneva was back, was that Lyneva might not have truly returned as Velieri. If so, her awareness would be weak and therefore easy to access. So, I asked Diem to do a bit of research. I'm going to let him explain. He's on the line."

Diem and Gal show up on the screen, sitting in an office of their own. Without all the cold clothes, they look quite less rugged and a bit more normal. His ears, which are pointed at the top, still catch my eye. "Diem, tell them what you found."

His Irish brogue twists and pulls. "We found her papers. It seems someone notified Navin of her birth before sending the information through the correct lines. So, she's been with Navin since she was just a child."

Briston throws his pen across the room—it hits the wall of the plane and bounces into a basket of papers nearby.

"So, what does that mean?" I ask, although I think I know.

"It means that he's had years to do whatever he wants with her memory, with her strength . . ." Sassi explains. "You see, it's against the rules. We allowed you to live your Epheme life until we knew for sure that you were truly going to return Velieri."

"Wait," I say suddenly. "So this could possibly mean that she's not Velieri, but that she'll simply go through an Epheme existence and die within that boundary."

Sassi nods. "It's possible. Navin would be using her for different means if that's the case."

"Is there a way to find out?" Peter asks.

Diem joins in, "Aye. If I can get her DNA and we'll search for any MRI that could have been done in her lifetime that might show her hypothalamus. The Fellows might have done one when she was a child. But I think until we know, it is best to believe that she is Velieri and has every power that we have."

Briston touches Sassi's arm, since he sits next to her. "All right, Sassi, we leave where we're going to you. I'll stay with you until after the meeting with Prophet Jenner."

"Thank you, sir. We'll be there shortly."

"Well, at least we're safe in the sky from the Umbramanes," Peter says with a grin.

I stare out the window while Sassi reads beside me. Memories of Briston with my mother, Lyneva, have continued to run through my mind. The mother who somehow made clear she was the special one and not me. The mother who barely touched me when I needed her to.

Just before we land, I lean over to Sassi, "Sassi?"

She looks at me, "Yeah?"

"Did you know my father was in love with Elizabeth?"

She nods, then looks around to make sure Briston is not listening. "We all knew. We also knew that Lyneva wanted the prestige of the Elite line more than she cared about her sister, Elizabeth. But back then, Remy . . . back then we questioned nothing. The Powers and the Prophets spent years indoctrinating us to never question them or their connection to God."

"There seem to be so many rules to who can marry verses who can't marry. Everyone understands that Yovu does exist. Wouldn't that have been the wake-up call Briston needed, when he couldn't marry his true Yovu? He had to know that Lyneva was not."

Sassi nods. "Remy, I wish it were that clear back then. None of us knew that the rules the Prophets force on us change with the weather. The rules change with what they need from us. If they don't want two people to be married because they fear their power together, then they won't allow it. For the longest time, I did not realize that so many decisions were being made for the wealth of the few at the detriment of the many. At one time, all of us believed the Prophets had truth to guide them. And at one time, I believe they did. As the years have progressed, we found all of us were gravely deceived. That is why I choose . . . no matter the outcome . . . to make things right. This world needs to be taken back to the original hope . . . the balance of freedom and unity."

28

Outside the window, the clouds are a nasty slate gray and angry lightning strikes below the plane. One of the stewardesses brings me hot tea, which shakes on the table next to me when she sets it down. I look up at her with surprise and she smiles. "Arek suggested you might want it."

"Where is he?" I ask.

"He's in a meeting in the back. Can I get anything else for you?"

Just then the plane shakes from the storm's turbulence, which turns our attention outside. For miles beyond, we see a light show that jumps from one ominous cloud to the next. My skin rises, the hair on the back of my neck stands, and a memory tucked away from somewhere rolls out.

The memory is a part of me. Not separate, not over there . . . but mine—real . . . with smells, sounds, and all the yumminess that nostalgia brings.

It is a cold night. The bottom of my kirtle dress is so heavy over my wet and ice-cold feet that my shaking hands pull it above my knees to run. My lungs ache under the heavy rain and flashes of lightning.

I am afraid of who chases me. Just off to the right is the large dark brick house for which I have been searching. It is exactly as I remember, with a large brigade of trees, a cemetery next to the pasture, and rose bushes cascading over the stone steps. It belongs to Bartholomew

Hedlow—an Epheme who has been heavily involved with my father. He was one of the original ambassadors to promote civility between the Velieri and Ephemes, despite the concealment of our society.

This is the only place nearby for protection and I'm growing tired.

Thank God, it is where I remembered.

My very cold and muddy hand knocks on the door and I constantly check the road behind me. No one answers. Repeatedly my fist hits the weathered wood, while with every passing moment my breath is strangled by fear. Off in the distance, the whinny of horses barely seeps through the muffling fog and, in an instant, I test whether I can open the door myself. It isn't locked and I rush inside, quickly closing it behind me. Everything is dark, but for an orange glow somewhere down a hall to my right.

"Hello?" I call quietly, hoping those chasing me cannot hear.

My icy hand runs along the bumpy stone wall toward the lit doorway at the end.

To my left is a mirror. Mud covers my young face, my lip is bleeding, and my hair steadily drips on my already soaking and ripped dress. A noise escapes from within the dimly lit room.

"Hello? Mr. Hedlow?" I call out again.

The storm reverberates outside, and the lightning illuminates the hall again and again. My body is so cold that it aches.

Suddenly someone jumps from the room, pinning me against the wall.

"Mr. Hedlow!" I cry.

The man lets go and quickly grabs a candle from inside the room. Finally, we can see each other, and I am surprised to find that it is not Mr. Hedlow, rather Arek Rykor. We have only met each other a couple of times, but I certainly know who he is.

"Mr. Rykor?"

"Miss Landolin . . . I'm so sorry. I didn't know it was you. Are you okay? What has happened?" he asks, quickly coming closer.

"I'm sorry to bother you, it's just that I was riding home when my guard and I were attacked."

"Attacked? Are you hurt?" Arek asks.

"Nothing that isn't healing, but they've killed him . . . they've killed my guard."

Arek quickly grabs his sword. "Are they out there?"

"I think so."

Just then, we hear a group outside yelling for me to come out. Arek looks through the window and shakes his head.

"Give me a moment." He sets his sword down and picks up a crossbow that hangs to the left of the door. Quickly, he grabs a lit torch and flings the heavy front door open. I follow. Just as he steps out, he whistles, bringing the group's attention our way. He aims the crossbow directly at them, and when they see it, they pull their horses backward a few steps. "I suggest you leave," Arek says confidently.

They look at one another with fear in their eyes. "That's Leigh Rykor's son."

"Sir," the main culprit says, "Miss Landolin is capable of taking care of herself. Do you see us? Two of my men can barely ride on their own because of her." Each man is covered in his own blood and perhaps a bit of mud. Two of the men are hunched over; one is missing a limb from the elbow down. This does not grow back, despite being Velieri.

Arek looks at me and quietly says, "It is good to see Atum is doing his job well."

I shrug. "Tell them to keep their hands to themselves."

He chuckles, then continues with the men. "You have till I count to ten to leave and if I hear of you coming near her again, I will finish you." Arek waits, still aiming the crossbow at the group.

"Come on," the fearful one says.

"Eight . . ." Arek begins, with no need to start at one. "Nine . . ."

They race off just as the lightning strikes again.

"Well, I guess they had nothing more to say," he says as he finally drops the crossbow. "Come in."

We enter the drawing room where he provides me a place to sit in front of the fire, wrapped in a blanket and drinking hot tea.

"It's no wonder your father always surrounds you with protection," Arek says as he leans against the fireplace.

"I've never understood it, actually. The Elite blood. You'd think they believe they can do something with it."

He shrugs with a smile. "Maybe they do."

I take a sip of tea and it nearly scalds my tongue. "Where's Mr. Hedlow?"

"He's visiting a cousin and has allowed me to stay here while I'm in Switzerland."

"And my father invited you and Leigh?"

"Yes."

"Why?"

"It seems a small group of Ephemes have discovered some artifacts that have piqued their curiosity about us here in Switzerland. The Prophets want it squashed and we are meeting to discuss with the Reds what should be done."

"So, you'll leave after it is done?" Immediately there is tension in my chest at the thought of him leaving and it's possible that I sound a tad bit too disappointed. I scramble. "It's so quiet. Where are Bartholomew's servants?"

"I sent everyone home since I knew that it would storm, and I didn't want them caught in it. Why were you out in it?"

"My mother needed me to meet someone for her materials. Yet nobody came where she set up our meeting."

Arek walks to the table where there are glasses and port. I watch him closely. Since he arrived in Switzerland, every girl has learned his name.

"You and Mak are to marry? Is that right?" he asks confidently.

Instantly he has my attention, not that he didn't have it before, but I didn't expect him to know that information. "No, actually, the Prophets have denied us twice."

"And you agree?"

"The Prophets can say what they want, but they know nothing about me. Why should we believe that God speaks more loudly to them? They

*were chosen by man . . . they are human . . . and humans are fallible."
I pause, take a sip, before telling the most important part. "But I have
chosen to end our engagement."*

*He pours himself a drink quickly followed by a second one. I can't help
but admire the breadth of his back. There is no wonder why he is already
considered in line to gain control of the Protectors—he could intimidate the
most intimidating. He fills the glass again and brings it to me. "Something
to calm your nerves . . . are you sure you're all right?" He reaches out and
touches the skin beside my ear where there is blood. The cut from a sword is
gone, but in its place is fresh pink skin. An electric jolt shoots through me the
instant his skin touches mine. Both of us pull back with surprise.*

What just happened? *My heart continues to race.* Neither of us
speaks, while he looks at me with wonder. *Can we try that touch again?
I want to ask. It is addictive. I reach out and touch his hand, sliding
down to his fingertips. Again, the power charges through my body and I
gasp for breath.*

*"I thought it was just a rumor," I whisper. It is every Velieri's dream
to find their Yovu, yet so many don't. There have been stories of some who
search forever for this mysterious feeling.*

*This doesn't make sense. Arek and I cannot fuse. We wouldn't be able
to have children. The Prophets would never allow it. When the sensation
becomes too much, there is no other choice but to let go.*

Suddenly the memory ends and I am back in the belly of the
plane. The stewardess is still beside me. "Anything else that I can get
for you?"

I shake my head. "Where did you say Arek was?"

In just moments, I find a small office toward the back where
Arek stands with his phone to his ear. When he sees me, he quickly
ends his conversation. I am silent, which makes him grin. "What's
going on in that head of yours?" He sits on the edge of the desk.

"Bartholomew Hedlow," I say quietly. Instantly his eyes tell me
that this name has brought back the same memory. Walking closer
to him, I let my hand touch his knee.

"Is it my turn . . . finally?" he asks.

I raise my crossed fingers in the air. "I hope so."

"Remy, I need you to promise me something." He takes my hips in his hands and pulls me close—our faces just inches apart.

"Anything," I whisper.

"No matter what you remember, whatever it is . . . don't tell anyone but me."

I smile. "Are you jealous?"

"No, worried. No one should know everything that Remy knows. Not even Sassi or Kilon." For a moment I'm quiet, as I read the seriousness in his eyes. "Remy knew how to keep people out of her mind and keep her secrets close. You aren't there yet."

"What secrets can other people not know?"

He reaches out and his strong hand wraps around my face. "Just trust me. Our secrets are ours."

"I do trust you. More than anyone in the world."

He kisses me slowly and tenderly as though he hopes the memories he holds can pass between us. Perhaps they do. There is something rich and protected that travels from his body to mine, an energy surging—with no ebb, but only flow. "Just come back to me," he whispers as he pulls away.

29

Sassi drives us through Johannesburg, South Africa. The city feels like it runs on springs with lights, cars, and winding streets pulling it tighter and tighter. Something in me tells me that I spent much time here, and the feeling that it gives me is pleasant. Arek is next to me in the car on his laptop.

"Do you ever stop or sleep?" I ask.

He thinks for a moment then grins. "Not lately."

"I believe I had a memory come to me last night." He shuts his laptop and looks at me. "You were with me at a farmhouse. It's in the middle of nowhere only surrounded by green pastures and fields."

"That could be anywhere . . . we've been many places together," he says quietly.

"I saw this place when I was in the Cellar. Holona took me there. This place feels different for some reason. Like it means something more. It is a white house with a sign above the gate that says "Vida." So, I'm assuming it must be somewhere in Spain, perhaps, or anywhere Spanish is spoken." His face changes subtly, but I notice it. "What?"

"Anything more?" he asks.

"Not really. I'm not able to see myself, but I'm happy. Strangely happy."

He smiles, yet this is just the layer on top of what's truly going on in his head. The only way I can interpret how he feels is a slight distance, as if he's in a far-off place. Also, the hesitancy when he peeks at the others to make sure no one is listening. Kilon, Sassi, and Briston seem unphased and in their own conversations.

Then finally, when he turns back to me, the connection between us is obvious, as though this conversation has returned a bit of Remy to him.

"Are you going to tell me where this is?" I devour him with an endless hunger and although I don't know anything more from this memory, his eyes make me wish I could go on forever.

He shakes his head. "Nope," he says simply.

"Wait, really?" I smile.

He wraps his arm around my shoulders and pulls me in with a smile as he kisses my head. "When it's time, you'll know."

It is nearly evening, but the sun leaves an orange haze just below the clouds. "Cover up," Sassi says as she pulls into a parking garage under a hotel. Each of us disguises ourselves quickly. "Just follow me."

Sassi leads us up several flights of stairs, using a key card to get into an upper floor in the hotel. "There are cameras on the right," she warns us, so we drop our heads to the left. After several laps zig-zagging through the maze of hallways, she stops in front of a door and uses the keycard. The green light flashes and she opens the door to an empty hotel room. Once we are all inside, she knocks on the adjoining door, and we wait. Soon, the lock shakes and finally the door opens. Prophet Jenner and a bodyguard emerge from the next room. Briston smiles and hurries to her with a swift hug.

"This is a nice reunion," he says.

She walks to me with her arms out. Her natural hair is out today, and her beautiful smile is calming when she hugs me. "How are you holding up?" she asks as she places her hands under my chin in a motherly fashion.

"Okay," I answer.

"Good." She makes her way around, greeting everyone individually, and I get the feeling this is normal for her. She has wisdom that can only be attained through a oneness with the source. I feel it and see it around her. "Let's sit."

Just then a knock sounds on the door, and in seconds Sassi, Kilon, and Arek have their guns in their hands. Prophet Jenner places a tender hand on Arek's gun, pressing it down and out of the air. Then she walks to the door and opens it. Caynan, in perfect attire, as usual, saunters in with a smile.

Caynan and Arek quickly step to each other with laughter and embrace in a hard hug. "It's good to see you," Arek whispers.

Minutes later we sit about the room. Arek begins by addressing Prophet Jenner, "You've risked everything to be here."

Prophet Jenner breathes in deeply, then out. "I have. It is against everything in me to continue in silence. Covey and Hawking will never let you be free."

The words hit us all. Sassi shakes her head. "What do you know?"

"When the Powers and the Prophets were created, it was to give the world a chance at peace. Prophets were chosen because of their God essence, their robust discernment for all that love could be. I was ready to become what God created me to be. Seen for something I could give to the world. Yet quickly it became clear that it is not a universal chain that we all carry, rather it has been broken by the lust and need for power and money," she explains.

Arek runs his hand through his hair with a heavy breath. "It has been clear for as long as I can remember that the original intention of our government has not been the outcome. We understand this."

"Yes, I know you do. However, we also all know that there is no way to fight this . . . not easily. I don't know how far the rabbit hole goes. And I've asked Caynan to help me find the source of Covey's power."

Caynan speaks up, "Which we believe is somehow connected to Navin."

"You mean, like, why they don't touch him, yet *we* are all considered criminals. Why *you* would go down first for meeting with us, before an obvious dictator like Navin can continue to build?" I look at Prophet Jenner with concern. "You are our only hope for sanity in all of this. Be careful."

She smiles and pats my hand. "The universe is on my side. I believe that."

Sassi pulls some papers out of her bag and throws them on the table. Everyone looks up at her. Prophet Jenner seems to know what they are. Sassi explains, "The Manchester books have been taken. This is the statement by the Manchester Protectors about when and how it happened."

Kilon wraps his thick arms around his chest and smiles at his wife. "You've been busy."

"While you're sleeping, I've got things to do." She lifts an eyebrow in a playful way.

"When were the Manchester Books taken?" Geo asks in surprise. Suddenly my memory tells me that Geo's grandfather was a leader in the pursuit of these valuable pieces of history.

"Two nights ago," Sassi says.

Arek is confused. "And we haven't heard about it?"

With calm hands, Prophet Jenner taps the papers and looks up at Arek. "That's exactly right. Arek, what would it take for this to remain quiet?" She waits a moment, then when she sees something of recognition in his eyes, she nods. "If you read the Manchester Protectors report, it cannot be what truly happened. Caynan and I did our own research. Somehow these books have just vanished. The vault was not hurt, no guard was hurt, yet these reports say they were stolen. With no consequence?"

"What does that mean?" I ask, a bit lost. "What does it matter if these books disappear?"

Kilon growls, "It means all the proof someone needs to expose our existence is in their hands. And many of us know who would want that."

"But don't the Prophets and Powers want us to stay hidden?" Everything seems so backward in my mind.

"That was the decree from ancient times and we've always followed it. What would happen if we decided to expose the Velieri society? War. It's inevitable. Ephemes are not capable of sharing their world with diversity. Or at least that is what our original government believed. And to some degree this understanding of remaining hidden has given us the ability to live our lives. Gain wealth. Have friends, family, and dreams. However, the more I am immersed in this realm of the Prophets, the more I see who is really getting rich from this and who is being so secretive that I worry over their plans. So, the answer is that I don't know at this point which of the Prophets remain entrenched in the old ways. What I do know is that regardless . . . the old ways are no longer working. We are slipping further toward ultimate control faster than we can break free."

Caynan looks at me. "I have many jobs, but the biggest one is finishing what I started. Remy, I will clear your name. Believe me on that. I promise you."

I nod. "Thank you."

"Prophet Jenner and I have many things to work on. The Manchester Books, clearing your name, and digging into Covey's black hole," Caynan explains.

"There's one more thing." Prophet Jenner is somber, her words falling like a weighted bullet. "Have you heard what Alfonzo has created in the Umbramanes?"

Arek shakes his head.

"He's managed to teach Tri Planum." Prophet Jenner says nothing more, as she lets this sink in.

No one has to say anything for me to understand that this is beyond bad. Kilon and Arek look at each other with tension in their shoulders and jaws. I can see the lines of their bodies working overtime.

"What does that mean?" I ask.

No one says anything.

"What does this mean?" I ask more urgently.

"Tri Planum," Sassi explains, "is a level of warfare that very few Velieri have reached. It means multi-level war. At the same time someone is physically fighting, they are also warring in their minds, on multiple levels."

"I thought that's already what every Velieri is doing with Tracing?"

"No." Geo explains, "We've learned to battle in our minds . . . yes. And people can Trace us, making our movements labored, or taking us deep within ourselves, but . . . do you remember when I took you into the forest and eventually it turned to whatever your fear created?"

"Yes."

"Okay, now imagine that you are in a different dimension battling someone within the confines of dreamlike worlds and situations, but at the same exact time you can physically fight in this world, at this moment. Your mind and body working separately but as one."

Sassi looks at Prophet Jenner, "Some believe this can't even be done."

Prophet Jenner looks at Arek with confusion. She cocks her head to the side and stands. "You have never told them?"

"There was never any need," Arek admits. We all look at him, waiting for him to explain, yet true to his form, he doesn't.

"Arek was able to learn Tri Planum. He's been able to do so for years."

"I haven't perfected it. I can't turn it on and off, rather, when I go there, it's hard to find my way out," Arek explains. "Navin learned it too."

Kilon shakes his head. "How do we know he's not teaching every one of his people?"

"We don't. You and I both know that this can't be learned by just anyone. It does make me afraid for Navin's plans. The reason no one has ever tried to take over the Ephemes is because they know we are outnumbered. Yet if Navin finds a way that is more powerful and numbers don't matter . . . then we are all in trouble. Besides, because we have been hidden for so long, this is the largest population of Velieri that the world has ever known, even though we still do not outnumber the Ephemes . . . therefore *now* is the best time for Navin to attack."

As the air continues to thicken in the room, Prophet Jenner takes a step to Arek and places a hand on his face. "Listen, son. Two of the Umbramanes are prepared to use this. And they're after you . . . now. Not eventually . . . but now. Get away, don't touch anything that would allow them to track you, and keep her safe. You and I both know she is needed. Let us take care of everything else. Do all of you understand?" she says as she looks at each one of us.

We nod.

"Good. It's time that I go."

Before she can stand, I feel the urgency within my chest to ask something. "Prophet Jenner, did you know my mother, Lyneva?"

She settles back into her chair as if she can feel that there is more to come. "I did."

"Would you tell me what you know? I need to understand her story."

Prophet Jenner takes a moment to think and adjusts her bright dress. "When Lyneva was young she was brutally attacked by the leader of the Reds." The room is silent for a moment, letting the truth fall over us with an aggressive wave. "She sought comfort and guidance under Prophet Covey. I wasn't a Prophet just yet, but I watched how she changed. She grew obsessed with the Prophecy, but it was strange . . . she never believed in it. She wanted the power of it. Which was why she set her sights on Briston even though he was in love with Elizabeth. She worked hard and I thought it strange the amount of time she still spent under the tutelage of Prophet Covey."

Sassi sat on the bed next to Prophet Jenner's chair and quietly broke in, "May we ask about the Prophecy?"

"Of course. What I know . . . is that old texts refer to a fusing between an Elite bloodline with an entirely different bloodline. It's never happened before. My belief is that Lyneva spent her entire existence trying to sabotage the Prophecy. She had no desire for peace. She also hated that people believed it was you. That you were chosen."

"This would be the reason she made me meet with Covey all my life," I realize.

The Prophet nods, ". . . and why she never ever was a good mother. I don't believe her to be capable of that after what happened to her."

I look at the others. "So Lyneva didn't want to be the Prophecy, she wanted to end the Prophecy."

Briston nods.

Prophet Jenner continues, "My entire purpose as Prophet is to change this system. To weed out those who don't care for truth, but for power. I'm only one woman, but there are others on our side. Others who believe we can find a new way. Ultimately, Covey was the reason for your mother's demise because he pushed her into the arms of Japha and Navin, who ultimately used her to get to you. But here's my truth . . . if we fall, we fall together. While there have been and may be more moments of this, I also see that we will rise, and we will rise together. We just can't lose our true purpose."

"And what is that?" I ask.

"To be one," is all that she says, then she stands, touches my hand, and walks out of the room, but not before she looks back and smiles a rich, confident smile. "Don't forget where you come from and why you're here."

"Thank you, Prophet Jenner." Arek takes her hand and then they hug. She embraces me with the nurturing of a mother and then she and Caynan exit the room, closing the door behind them.

Kilon rubs his face as though this is the recoil from his anxiety. "Tri Planum adds a whole new dimension."

Arek nods, but then looks at him with resolve. "But nothing we can't handle."

30

Prophet Jenner is gone. I can tell from their heavy faces that Kilon and Arek are uncomfortable with everything she told them. The air feels claustrophobic because of a crushing wind, and it is obvious while walking to the jet with heads down that my questions about Tri Planum will need to be answered later, once there is time for the team to settle. I place my hand out into the storm and, as my fingers battle the heavy gale, I am unexpectedly swept into another memory. It comes fast within one step to the next, and I am suddenly on the pastureland of Spain. Instantly the smell of fresh rain, the feeling of tall grass against my legs, and a hope so overwhelming erupts within a memory that I've now had multiple times. Only, every time it comes, I am shown more and feel more connection than before.

My hand brushes atop tall grass until it bends and sways under the sun. Flowers bloom with the essence of spring. Rolling green hills smile at me from every direction and I turn around breathing in the music of nature. The small white cottage sits alone but quaint under a large umbrella tree. Then I see Arek, chopping wood near the shed, his sweat glistening despite the wind that blows my dress in waves about my legs. He smiles when he sees me and throws the ax aside, confidently walking to me with dirty boots. Without a word he picks me up in his arms and carries me inside the cottage, all the while unbuttoning my dress one dainty button at a time.

"Good morning," I whisper as he lays me on the bed and kisses my neck down to my chest.

"Good morning, sweet Remy." His gentle hand runs down my stomach as the sun sprays light through our open window.

It is disappointing when the memory ends, but I continue up the jet's airstair without missing a step. When my eyes land on Arek, who is already talking with Sassi and the pilot within the plane, a smile lifts the corners of my mouth.

Just a few minutes later, he sits beside me and the look on my face gives me away. "What's on your mind?" he asks.

I shake my head. "A tiny white cottage in the rolling fields of Spain . . . this same memory keeps returning."

His lighthearted grin slowly disappears as he checks the seats around us to make sure no one else is listening to our conversation. Everyone is within earshot, which makes him even more uncomfortable. He touches my face with his hand, "It could be one of many that we've stayed in."

"I don't get that feeling. There's nothing around it for miles but rolling hills. There's no Sassi or Kilon or anyone else who would normally be there. It's just you and me." The doors close and the plane begins taxiing along the tarmac.

Sassi furrows her brows. "A time when we weren't there? Was there ever?"

Kilon scratches his face. "I don't remember a small cottage. I try to avoid living in small places with the amount of people chained to our sides."

Arek shrugs. "We've been thousands of places in our lifetime."

Something suddenly comes to Sassi. "Wait a minute. I vaguely remember Arek telling us to go home and take a few months off once." She laughs. "Kilon, you remember that?"

Kilon shrugs, "Nah. Not particularly."

Arek smiles uncomfortably. "Well, I must have needed some time with just my wife."

Briston is listening but says nothing. Something on his face tells me that he might know the place in Spain or the time when Kilon and Sassi weren't around.

As we are still awaiting takeoff, one of the pilots runs from the cockpit. "We have a problem—" Instantly an explosion sends the pilot flying forward and a ball of fire fills the belly of the plane. My body is consumed with heat, my skin instantly charred, my hair singed, as I fly back, still attached to my seat. Shards of glass and metal shoot into my skin. I lose consciousness when I hit the back wall, only to wake up moments later on my side, trapped between the wall and heavy debris. The plane is in ruins. My body is hammered and broken, having sustained several injuries. I look around at the carnage where only just now people are starting to move about and call out for others. Kilon yells for Sassi, while Geo is to my right. He crawls over to me, just as Arek climbs over the mess to reach my side. They are both bloodied and burned as they work on the metal shards keeping me pressed so my ribs ache.

"The belt!" Geo yells at Arek over the loud ruckus.

Arek pulls with all his strength, using his legs as leverage, while the sounds of popping metal and the crackle of fire grows, and smoke fills our lungs. Geo grabs a knife from his belt and while Arek pulls, he slips it between the clasps. Finally, it bursts open, and when they move the seat I can fully breathe.

"Navin's out there," Kilon yells from the direction of the cockpit. "I can feel it."

Strangely, so can I.

"Here," Arek says as he wraps us in a heavy cargo blanket to pass the fire to the right. Finally, we are upwind of the smoke and huddled just between the cabin and the cockpit. Everyone grabs their weapons, paying no attention to their pain.

I feel the familiar rummage through my mind, which shows my abilities have grown to know who is Tracing. Just like the thumbprint, and what I learned in Geo's memory of New York, I have memorized Navin's powerful Trace. Instinctively, I protect myself. Someone else is also in my mind. That's when I notice Geo staring directly at me with intention in his eyes. He is worried. I nod. "I've got it," I whisper, and he nods back.

"We're not that far away from the hangar, but I can't see where they are," Arek says.

"What do we do?" Peter asks.

Arek turns to Briston and they share a look, but it doesn't last long before we see flames climbing the walls. From every window on every side, orange, red, and blue flames lick the paint off the damaged jet. The smell permeates our noses; the smoke makes it nearly impossible to take in a breath. The most unsettling of all is the sound of the curved metal splitting and popping—which sends a splattering of dangerous shrapnel.

Mak says something to Arek that makes him nod, yet I cannot hear anything over the fire. Mak disappears with one of the other men. I look back just in time to see Arek rip at the carpet on the floor. A square of blue wool flies away to reveal a safety hatch.

Before he opens it, he presses his hand against the metal, but pulls it back instantly. He shakes his head as he turns to Briston. "Too hot. The fire is beneath . . . check the cockpit."

With that, Briston hurries inside the cockpit with the other pilot—the first pilot is nowhere to be found. Although we can see flames encapsulating the airplane, there is a flat surface on the nose of the plane that has not been touched.

Arek and Kilon both kick the two large front windows out as several bullets puncture the walls; they duck out of the way.

Geo starts to climb out. "You're the best shot," he says to Arek. "I'll go first, and you keep me covered."

Arek nods. Geo pulls himself up on the dash, as the sweat darkens his shirt. Before he continues, he pulls his gun from his belt and checks it carefully. Meanwhile, Arek grabs all the weapons from everyone. "Get everything ready. Kilon, stand on that side, I'll stand on this side. And we'll cover. I see them to the right, Geo."

The fire is beginning to overwhelm us, so we press materials to our noses and do our best to touch nothing.

Arek yells at Geo, "Run as fast as you can to the outer building. Once you get there, lay cover fire for everyone else."

Geo takes a few deep breaths in preparation. Finally, as the flames climb higher, there is no more time to wait. Geo slides down the nose of the plane—covering himself with his arms. The fall isn't a small one, and everyone loses sight of him once he drops.

Arek's eyes squint as he kneels on the nose of the plane while smoke surrounds him. From where I am standing, I can see the small hole in the thick cloud where Arek's eyes are fixed on Navin's men. They are so far away; it seems impossible to reach them. Until, one by one, Arek shoots clean and hits his target. When he has no ammo left, he hands it to Kilon who switches it out for another. Meanwhile, Geo rushes across the tarmac toward the nearest vehicle. Repeatedly, Arek shoots, sending someone to the ground each time.

"We can't stay here. The fire . . ." Kilon yells.

Geo is hit by a bullet and Arek growls. He fires the gun and again drops the shooter. Geo peels himself off the ground with his gun in the air and he crawls to the nearest escape. A bin of luggage is high enough to cover his entire body as he slumps to the ground.

Arek pulls his hand away in pain from the metal beneath him. "Let's go."

My eyes widen.

Arek shakes his head. "We can't stay here. We have a better chance with bullets than fire. Trust me. Stay to my right and hopefully everything will hit me instead of you."

"Wait!" one of the stewardesses yells. She throws open a cupboard nearby. "There's three of these vests for the pilots and the marshal."

The pilot shakes his head. "Give them out."

Briston hands one to Sassi, one to me, and then leaves the last with the stewardess. As the heat of the plane continues to increase, I throw the heavy bullet-proof vest over my shoulders as Arek stretches the Velcro tight around my waist.

"What is he doing?" Kilon asks.

Every one of us peers out. Geo jumps onto the luggage cart and drives it across the tarmac. "He's getting it closer," Sassi says.

By the time he reaches us, one last bullet hits his head, sending blood all over the luggage, and his body falls forward.

"Oh my God, Geo," Sassi cries out. We watch as he drags himself behind the luggage car.

Finally, every one of us exits the plane, doing our best to make it to the luggage. Bullets whiz past my face, neck, and shoulders. We run. Arek fires with his left hand while covering me with his right.

"Remy!" The holler comes from behind us. It is a man's voice— one that I have never heard before. "There's nowhere to go," the voice threatens.

We panic when several men bring out semi-automatics. "Arek!" Sassi yells as she shoots at a man and hits him in the cheek. He falls to the ground.

Before any of us can stop it, these weapons begin to roar. We fight to keep moving, but it becomes impossible as the bullets dig within our bodies. I get the least of it all when the others do everything in their power to protect me. Arek's body, Kilon's . . . Sassi's . . . and everyone convulses with deadly bullets. It will take time for even a Velieri to undo the damage being done. I fall to the ground, holding my body in pain as Arek's body falls on mine.

When we are all down, they stop shooting.

Even though it won't be fast enough, I can feel the reconstruction of each cell sending chills up my spine, and it makes me claw at the blacktop beneath my fingers, like insects crawling under my skin. Arek bites his lip through pain as he reloads his gun.

Soon they surround us, and when I look up, there is an army— their guns pointed our way. The main officer looks at Arek, "On your knees, sir."

"Sir." I hear the name he calls Arek. All of these men were at one time his subordinates. Arek was the Second-in-Command of the Protectors, outranked only by his father, Leigh. Now here we are, guns in our faces, and Arek can do nothing but raise his bloody hands and surrender. He gets to his knees and within seconds they have him in cuffs.

My father follows.

A vehicle drives up and Navin emerges with a smile on his face. He speaks Velieri to one of the soldiers as he looks down at me.

"Yes, sir," the main soldier answers as he comes to my side and pulls me to my feet.

"Don't touch her," Arek yells.

Navin looks at his brother, no dramatics, just with serious eyes. "I'm sorry, brother." He is wearing a suit and his hair is brushed back—I have never seen him so put together.

Without saying another word, he walks to Briston and pulls a needle from his pocket. Quickly he injects my father. "We have about twenty minutes before it spreads to his brain and kills him. So, you have to listen."

"What did you give him?" Geo yells as he jumps to his feet pointing his gun at Navin. "Kill me if you want," Geo yells, "but I will get a shot out before I go down and it will hit you where it needs to."

Navin doesn't seem worried. "Where is Karine?"

"I don't know." Arek shakes his head with aggravation. "You'll have to talk with Leigh. I don't have anything to do with him or his case."

"That's not what I was told."

Briston cries out in pain. Sassi tries her best to get close to him, even with her arms tied behind her back. "Arek, look," Sassi says. Her eyes point out Briston's arm. The veins have turned to almost black, and his hand seems to be lifeless.

Navin continues, "You were the last to see Karine, to talk to him, and now you tell me that you don't know where he is?"

"What's happening to him?" Arek asks.

Navin breathes out. "He was shot with a chemically altered form of mercury and there is a very short time before it reaches his brain and starts shutting down his body. Even Velieri can't stop this, even someone as powerful as the Elite blood. There are a few minutes before his heart stops. Arek . . . I'm trying to get you to understand that we have a way to take over. No longer will we have to listen to the government or be forced into hiding." He pulls a needle from his coat and raises it in front of Arek's face. "We've been told our whole lives to stand back and let everyone else make our decisions . . . and now, I see it. There are ways to take as many people out as we need to in order to live free. You've never understood. When you see the way this rips through his body . . . maybe you'll understand the power we have. Tell me where Karine is, and I'll tell you how to help him."

"I don't know where he is," Arek says as he looks at Briston with urgency.

My father's strained voice gasps, "You won't be able to get to Karine. He's surrounded at all times."

Navin swiftly plunges the second needle into Briston's tense arm, but just before he can press the double dose of mercury into his system, Arek stands to his feet even though seven guns are trained on him. Navin raises his hand to stop the men from shooting. Arek speaks gruffly, "The Cellar in the Sudan."

"Thank you, brother." Navin looks at Briston, then pulls the syringe out. "You'd best get him to Gyre. And if I find out that you are lying about the Sudan, I'll make sure you feel it." He turns to his men, "Get her to my car."

Some of Navin's men keep their guns pointed at Arek and the others, while the rest of his guards drag me to the car. Soon, Navin jumps in beside me.

I scramble to sit up and look out the back window. The army of men are beginning to back away from Arek as another car swings around to pick them up. As Sassi and Peter rush to Briston's side, Kilon, Geo, and Arek stare at Navin's car as we drive away.

It isn't until I turn back around that I see Lyneva sitting across from me. Suddenly I am staring straight into the eyes of the woman who hated me, only now we are the same age.

31

We drive for an hour. Neither Navin nor Lyneva try to talk to me. Occasionally, they say something to each other, although even that is minimal. Lyneva, who is dressed warmly with a black puff jacket and red scarf, her hair pulled back in a tight ponytail, looks put together, unlike I who have just been through hell. Her eyes fall on me, which I can see in my peripheral, but I refuse to make eye contact. My memories of her are through the eyes of a child and they are never kind.

Arek and the others have trained me well enough at this point to protect my mind and in a way, it happens almost naturally. Meanwhile, I keep track, as much as I can, of where we are going.

Finally, Navin decides to speak. "I thought I'd wear you down. Yet we've been driving an hour and I can't get in to see what's going on."

I smile and finally look at him. "Yeah, well, you can stop trying because I haven't even noticed." It's strange to see his face with the familiar Rykor look after so long. The driver pulls us into a new city after leaving Johannesburg. The city sprawls out in all directions, with powerful lights, while nighttime descends on us. We've reached a bit of traffic along the highway.

For whatever purpose, I finally give myself permission to study Lyneva—the woman who has paralleled my journey. Only, we now know she has been fed the world through Navin's eyes.

"He's raised you," I say.

Navin shakes his head. "You don't need to talk to each other."

"She's my mother."

Navin chuckles, "I suppose she is."

Lyneva grins, "I'm nothing to you."

The nightlife within this city is getting busier on what I can only assume is the weekend. It's been so long since I have felt normalcy or known what day of the week it was.

"Did he tell you why he wants me? That he wants my child?" I ask.

"I know everything," she says.

"How about . . . did he tell you that he never really wanted you in the first place? Or that he killed you, to get to me?" I smile, yet my cheeks are flushed from anger pulsing up my neck.

I see questions pass through her eyes. She looks for just a second at Navin, but Navin instantly flies across the car and presses his large hand against my already tense neck until my vision warps from the lack of blood. "You don't need to speak. If you say something else . . ." He pulls a syringe from his pocket and threatens me with it.

"You need me healthy. We both know that," I say as a tear runs down my cheek and my head presses against the headrest from his weight.

"I do. However, this can make you very sick for a while. You don't want to be miserable." He lightens his grip but continues to stare at me. Lyneva watches the scene, and I can see there is a slight difference between this woman and the mother I knew.

Outside I notice a break in the crowd of people due to a bridge coming up fifty yards ahead. A dangerous idea comes to me. I can't let on or Navin will know what I am up to. So, carefully my rhythm grows to protect my thoughts. Mistakes are not an option as I stare outside, waiting for the perfect moment.

I check my seatbelt while turning my attention on the driver. His eyes stare straight ahead and for a moment I sift about his thoughts. Just as Geo and Holona taught me on the streets of New York, I focus on his incessant thinking and separate him from everyone else in the car. I press my weight down and dive into the abyss of our energy. It doesn't take long before the driver's eyes get tired, and he begins to fade. My heart races knowing that there is no way to see how this will turn out, but there is also no other option. Navin suddenly reads my eyes and shoots forward—without a seatbelt.

"What are you doing?" he growls.

It is too late. The driver's eyes shut completely, and his chin drops to his chest. My body tenses as I prepare for the pain.

In only seconds, the car crashes into the median and flips over again and again, slamming into the front of another car and then missing the rest of the traffic. The world spins, my neck whips, and a cry escapes my mouth. It lasts only moments, yet it feels like forever. I lose consciousness, but when I wake, Navin is not in the car, which is upside down. In fact, his awkward body has been thrown several feet from my door and he's lying lifeless on the street as the sun finally sets. Lyneva is bleeding from her head and starting to come to, but her seatbelt saved her. Suddenly, I reach out and rip some fabric from my shirt. Before she knows what is happening, I press it to her arm and soak up some blood, then I stuff it in my jean pocket.

Groaning the entire way, I pull myself from the window and limp away, as fast as I can, although my foot and my rib beneath my shirt feel broken. Luckily the falling light of dusk is on my side.

For nearly thirty minutes I run through neighborhoods and alleys, without any direction.

As the shock of the accident wears off, more pain emerges from my stomach. I lift my shirt and know instantly that I shouldn't have. One of my ribs has broken through the skin. This is when I notice the bandage keeping my tracker silenced has been ripped off. Suddenly, in my imagination there are ghosts in every corner . . . ghosts in the shadows.

I have to find a phone.

I realize, in a divine moment, that I stand on the corner of a four-way stop across the street from a house with a sign above it: "Dr. and Dr. Foe, Pediatrics."

Carefully but painfully, I hobble over and knock on the front door. With blood on my hands, I lean against the doorway just trying to breathe. Again, I knock.

The porch light turns on and the door opens. A man in his sixties, with skin that is a russet, reddish-brown, and kind eyes, is there. He doesn't need to ask anything as my appearance tells him everything. "Gabriella!" he yells behind him. "Open the office!" He helps me inside. "Are you okay?"

"I was in a car accident."

He looks out at the street, trying to find the cars, but stops after a few seconds when his wife rushes in with her keys and opens the door to their duplex. On one side is their home and on the other side is their doctor's office.

"What happened?" she asks as she throws the lights on.

"I was in an accident. If you could just fix my rib, I'll be okay. Can I use your phone?" I ask as I feel myself getting drowsy. Blood still seeps from my wound and as it pours out onto the floor, my temperature plummets and my body begins to shake. Even my skin under the light of the doctor's office has a gray tint, just as my mother's before she passed, but it is still a surprise when my vision disappears. Just as I fall back, the husband and wife rush forward to grab me.

32

I wake up suddenly, gasping for breath, with an intense pain in my side. The woman is bending over me, but it's the man who holds me down so I can't jump off the table.

"Just a moment. Wait . . . we're almost done," he says to his wife. "Patti, hurry."

I look around. "I need a phone. Quickly."

"This is the last one," Patti says as she ties off the sutures.

As soon as she's done, I push my way from the table and hobble in circles searching the room for something to use. It's obvious that they think my behavior is strange.

"How long have I been asleep?" I ask suddenly. My body heat has returned, in fact, sweat is beading along my forehead. They look at me with concern. "How long?!" I ask again, this time my voice commands their answer. There is no time to play.

"I . . . I . . . Jay?" Patti says. "What time did we start?"

He hurries to a desk and grabs his watch. "It hasn't been long. Just thirty minutes maybe?"

"Are you sure about that?" I ask.

"Yes. I am." He nods.

Their faces are kind and while I wish to slow down and give them a proper explanation, it is for their safety that I cannot.

"A phone? Can I please use your phone?"

"Okay." He grabs one from the pocket of a jacket nearby and hands it to me. My shaking hands dial Arek's number, with surprise that I even remember it.

It rings only twice before he answers. His rich voice makes me close my eyes and breathe. "Arek, it's me."

"Remy!" He quickly talks to whoever he's with, then returns to me. "Where are you?"

"I'm not sure." I turn to the couple as they patiently wait with concern. Then something stops me from asking their address and I shake my head. "Wait, Arek, my bandage is gone. The one that Hok gave us in the Gianda." I'm careful to keep it vague, even though it won't matter what they know if the Umbramanes find us.

"What?" His voice rises with concern. "How? How long has it been gone?"

"For an hour?"

His silence on the other end sends chills down my spine. Then he finally responds. "Listen Remy, you can't sit still."

"How long do I have?"

"There are Umbramanes in every city within an hour of any-where. Hopefully, it will take them time to realize that your tracker has come back on, but we have to assume they know. They will send the closest ones."

"The closest ones? Multiple?"

"Yes. Multiple. Not to mention, all of the Protectors will be notified."

"I am in a doctor's office, is there anything that can cover it?"

Again, Arek speaks to someone, then returns. "If there is any numbing solution you should inject it into the site, then topical numbing cream, and a thick surgical bandage over it. It won't be perfect, but it may blur the signal."

The doctors' eyes tell me instinctively that they are ready and willing to help. If only they knew what we were up against, I'm pretty sure they would run. "Do you have an injection for numbing, and also topical numbing cream and a surgical bandage?"

"Yes," he says. Then they move about the room collecting the items, as they softly talk to each other so that I cannot hear, which makes me nervous.

Arek quickly reacts, "Who's that?"

"It's the doctors who helped me."

"Remy, don't tell them anything. They are most likely Ephemes, you cannot tell them anything and you need to get out of there."

"I understand." I lift my hand to the doctors, telling them to hold on for just a moment. "Arek, what do I do, where do I go?"

I can hear the others on Arek's line as they talk excitedly. Finally, he continues, "You have to get out of the city. We're nearly three hours from where you are."

"Three hours?" I breathe out heavily as I rub my forehead.

"How am I supposed to get out of the city?" My messy hair covers my concern, but I still turn away from the doctors. "Where do I go?"

Before Arek can reply, the man interrupts from behind, "I know somewhere you can go."

"Arek, wait," I turn to the kind doctor.

He sees my curiosity, raises his hands in the air for peace, and nods. "My family owns an abandoned piece of property with an old gas station. No one is around for miles. I can show you how to get there."

"Arek, he says there's an abandoned gas station that he can get me to."

Arek's hesitation is apparent even through the phone. "Okay, send us a pin drop before you leave."

"I will."

"We'll be there."

When I hang up the phone and turn back to the doctors, it is obvious that they are expecting answers. "Listen," I say kindly. "It's best that you don't know. If I can just ask you for one thing and get out of here . . . everything will be fine. I promise."

"Who are you?" Jay asks. "There were no accidents for miles. We called around. There was an accident thirty miles from here and they found no one at the car."

"I can't tell you," I say softly. "It's important that I go, for your safety."

He shakes his head. "You're in no shape to run around."

"I know. I need you to give me a shot with that . . ." I point at the needle in her hand, "here," I rub my side. "I wish I could explain, but please just trust me."

Patti shrugs. "Okay, get on the table."

Already feeling better, I climb on the table and pull up my shirt. "Here." I point to the spot on the opposite side of the recent wound. "Give me one here, here, and here." She injects in a circle about the size of an orange and before long everything begins to lose feeling. She rubs on the numbing cream, but after a while I catch her eyes looking at the other wound. The cream instantly falls out of her hand and sprays thick white ointment all over the floor and cupboards as it bounces.

"I don't understand!" She looks at Jay then back at me, her skin starting to shine from sweat. "How is it healed already?" Jay sees a red line of healing, where just minutes before was a gaping hole; his eyes widen. I scramble off the table and pull down my shirt.

"I've got to go!" I rush to the door but stop suddenly as my hand drops to the gold handle of the front door. I close my eyes and breathe out. "I need to know where to go." Finally, I turn around. Clearly, neither of them know whether to stand far away or draw close. "Listen," I say, "it's okay. Just help me know where to go and let me leave. You'll never have to deal with me again."

"How has your skin healed?" Patti says forcefully. "Just tell me how that happened?"

"I can't," I whisper. "It is safer for you to just pretend that you never saw this."

The room settles for a moment, then Jay's rough voice escapes a tight chest. "You know we've been doctors for a very long time." He places a hand out, calling for peace with a genuine, but careful grin. "One time a boy came in with his family after having fallen from a tree. It took only an hour before he healed."

"Yeah." I nod.

"Another time, during my residency, a patient had bleeding in the brain. By the time most people would reach the point she was, they have only a few minutes. In the middle of the night . . . alone . . . I watched as the damage started to reverse itself."

"Miracles happen," I say nervously.

"Yes, they do. Is that what this is?" When I don't answer, he continues, "They weren't that different from you . . . were they?"

"Jay," his wife asks with irritation, "what are you saying?"

"It's okay, Patti." He turns back to me. "Were they?"

I let the silence tell him too much. *How do I explain in a matter of minutes?* "Can you help me? The longer I stay here, the more this is a problem . . . would you please . . . help me?"

"Okay." His eyes soften telling me he'll give up the line of questioning. "Do you need protection?"

I nod. "Yes, more than anything."

"Okay." Suddenly, he exits the room with a quick, "Come on." We move through the well-kept house until we stop at a cupboard in the mudroom near the back door. He throws it open, showing a safe. It takes him only moments to turn the knob and he pulls the metal door open, revealing several guns inside. "I'm guessing these will help."

I look at him with surprise, but he shakes it off confidently. "You're willing to help me?"

"Of course." He nods and grabs a gun. "Of course." With his thick brown fingers and strong palm, he places the gun in my hands, and I noticeably terrify both of them with how quickly I am able to check it.

"Thank you." In the shadows behind Patti, my eyes catch something. A swift figure runs by the window. My head begins to ache, which has always been the first sign of someone digging, even though now I protect myself easily and instantly. "Get down!" I yell.

The ghost appears just behind Patti without a sound. My gun raises quicker than they can drop. Whoever this is, his face is covered with a black mask just like the ones they wore in the Cellar. This yanks at my insides. Patti and Jay cry out.

Then, my thoughts stop and the air turns crystalline. I pull the trigger. The gun warms in my hands as it unloads bullets. They hit the ghost, sending him against the back wall. "Get out of here!" I yell and the couple quickly scrambles across the floor and away.

I rush out the back door and see a detached garage. Before I can reach it, some pieces of the garage door explode from the Umbra-manes' bullets. I yank it open, jump inside, then push against it just as he reaches me. His fingertips slide along the wood and catch the edge. My shoulder rams against the door again and again, and each time, grunts escape my lips. Then finally with one last shove, it clicks in place, and I quickly twist the lock. He wails against the door, shaking the hinges, then pummels the stucco with bullets, so I shield myself behind a nearby refrigerator. A golf bag leans against the wall, so I grab it with a block of wood and stuff it beneath the metal han-dle. Just one more obstacle for him to pass.

When I'm able to scout the room, my eyes widen at the museum in front of me. There are two rows of classic sports cars, shined and pristine. *Where would he keep the keys?*

I rummage through the shelves, searching. "Come on," I whis-per. Several car parts sit upon a table. Just above this is a lock box, with the key to it hanging from the lock. A gas and oil can sit on the ground nearby. *There it is.* I rush over and pop the door open. Multi-ple keys hang from metal hooks. A keyring says "green 1956 Porsche 550 RS Spyder." There's only one green car and it's a small convert-ible. Just next to that one a keyring says "silver 1955 Jaguar D-Type."

It occurs to me that it is quiet. The pounding and shooting have stopped. *How long has it been quiet?* I run around to the driver's side of the car. As the door swings open, my hair rises and falls from someone's breath behind me, and the musk of his skin wafts up my nose. In complete silence and with no warning like a true spirit floating above the ground invisible to my eye, it is only now that I know he is behind me. Just as I turn to look, he wraps his arms around my neck in a choke hold, but I am fast and grab his forearm, which puts distance between his skin and mine, then I drop my weight forward and send him over my back. He pounds the ground on the other side of the car door. But he swipes with a knife beneath it and cuts the front of my ankles. I fall in pain. He tries to crawl beneath the door as I kick his face and chest. He hits me across the face with his weapon. In seconds he has me pinned. The world is in slow motion, as he pulls a gun and presses it against my head. *You know what to do.*

In three moves I kick his knees out from under him, rip the gun from my head, and roll. I jump to my feet. Just as before, the training from centuries of memory roll within the dark room, within my body, and I stomp on his hand as he reaches for his gun. My fist hammers the side of his face. All of this is happening faster than humanly possible.

After grabbing the gun, I twist my body as he reaches for me, and I shoot him between the eyes. This incapacitates him, but it is the bullet behind his ear that solidifies my safety. He and the others won't stop until I do.

When I stand to my feet, Jay and Patti are at the door with horrified looks. My hand swipes at the blood on my face, hoping they haven't seen it. But in the car's side mirror, I can see a long thin line of blood from my nose to my ear. There is nothing to say. "I'm sorry," I whisper. "You don't understand, he would have killed me and then killed you."

Jay shakes his head. "I've never seen fighting that fast."

"I have to borrow your car."

Jay steps forward but Patti quickly stops him with a hand on his arm. "Patti," he says. "It's okay." He turns back to me.

"Let me take you . . . wherever you need to go." He walks to a free-standing metal closet and unlocks it. Large intimidating guns hang from the back, and he begins to pull them out and place them in the back of the green Porsche.

"Jay!" Patti yells at him.

"Patti, listen. She clearly needs help. Let me do this. I'll be okay."

I shake my head, "You really don't have to."

"Yes, I do." As we finish loading the guns, I notice the heavy pile in the back of the car and look at him inquisitively. He shrugs. "I hunt."

He hurries to Patti and kisses her sweetly.

"There will be more," I warn quietly.

He hands Patti a gun. "Go to the basement and lock it until I get home." She looks at me, then back at him. "Go," he says.

After she rushes out, he grabs the keys from my hand and points to the passenger side.

"Why are you doing this?" I ask as I climb in and the garage door raises after he presses the button.

"Two reasons . . . this is my favorite car. And second," he twists the key until the engine growls, "if anyone gets to race through the streets in this thing, it's me." He shifts it into gear and jets out of the garage, down the driveway, and onto the streets beneath the now dark sky.

33

"We have a full tank. Do you think if we just stay moving, we will be fine getting to the address I gave you?" Jay asks.

"I think so." I say, as I send the pin to Arek from the doctor's phone. For a moment, I put my head back and watch the streetlamps pass. *Could it be that the last time I paid attention to streetlamps was back in San Francisco?* It's possible. Just above them stars are sprayed across the night sky. It's tempting to fall asleep to the display until Jay starts talking.

"What's your name?" he asks.

"Remy."

"Remy, my grandmother used to be my favorite person in the entire world," he begins. "She would tell stories better than any book I could get off the shelf. There was one I would ask for again and again . . . she said it was passed down from many generations before . . . I'm sure I'll get it wrong, but apparently there was a group of people . . . still human, but they had the ability to live a long life." I can see out of the corner of my eye that he's looking at me, but I keep my attention on the road. He continues, "Because of that they're forced to blend in . . . stay unknown. I mean . . . knowing this world and its inability to accept differences . . . it made sense to me. She said that they had abilities, not superhuman, but simply empowered because they healed . . . faster than any human. She said that she hadn't met any, but her grandfather told her that one of his sisters fell in love with one. But they couldn't stay together because he was one of them." Jay continues trying to study my reaction. "As a kid, this story stuck with me . . . it felt right or something. A little bit like maybe this could really happen?" His eyes fall on the bit of my stomach where my shirt had been cut away; the sutures were still sitting within my skin, but not even a red line remains. My hand quickly covers the evidence. "Is that why they're after you?"

I keep my voice quiet beneath the whoosh of air blowing my hair all around. "Sounds like your grandma had a good imagination."

"That's the thing . . . she didn't. Not a lick of one." For a moment, he's quiet. "Look, you may as well tell me."

"Jay, for everything that I tell you, I put you more at risk. Trust me, there is no turning back . . . once you know."

He grins, "My grandmother, she was the best lady in the whole world, and she told me, 'Son, to think that there is nobody different than us on this planet, it is just plain ignorant. There are powers bigger than we can ever understand.' And I believe that."

"I'm human, Jay. That's all you need to know."

"Okay. Okay. Just tell me one thing . . ." He turns down a quiet street but keeps his eyes on the car behind us. I, too, notice it has been consistently taking the same route as us for quite some time. "If I undo both of our seatbelts and crash this car, what will happen?"

I shake my head with a grin. "Are you thinking about doing that?"

"No. Just wondering." His eyes still haven't left the car behind us, and he's increased the speed to well over the speed limit.

"Let's just say, for your sake, I don't think you should do that." I start to look behind, but he grunts to grab my attention.

"Don't." He shifts and presses the gas a bit more. "Don't make them aware you know they're there. They've been following for a while. Hold on." Suddenly he turns onto a street that has nearly passed and my head strains to stay upright due to the speed. The following car screeches around the corner, climbing the sidewalk and nearly taking out a fire hydrant. By the time they can correct themselves, we are nearly to the next street and flying around that corner barely missing a woman walking her dogs. From a passing street to the left another car joins and stays beside Jay's window. Whoever they are points a gun out the window and pops, taking the sideview mirror off the door. Jay shifts gears and jets forward—harder and faster. By his expression, I can see that his car is living up to his hopes, and this chase is fulfilling every boyhood fantasy.

Jay does his best to lose them, but I know that if Sassi were here she'd already have outdone them. Just around the corner, when they've lost sight of us for just a split second, he spins into an underground garage. When he presses a number on his phone, a garage door begins to slide down.

"What is this?" I ask.

"The garage beneath my second office. Give it five minutes. Then we'll leave the city." He pulls his phone from his pocket to display several camera angles from many cameras around the building. His vintage car idles high after the chase, and a faint smell of burning oil fills the small garage. The cars outside stick around until, finally, they roll away. The streets are empty, and he pulls out. "Let's get out of here."

Soon we are passing the city limits with no one following—at least for now. We head out onto the open road, with nothing but land and stars beyond. The fresh air fills my lungs with a slight chill. I wrap my shirt tighter about me and lean my head back with a sigh. For the first time in a long while, I let my guard down. All I can think about is whether Briston is okay. Memories come to the surface of plenty of moments when Briston, throughout the years, was the target. An Elite bloodline partly because of the longevity, but also partly because of the attached Prophecy, but whatever it was, the interest of others was not unusual.

My eyes close and I fall asleep, trusting that Jay is on my side and will drive us without any trouble. Hours later Jay is waking me with a hand on my shoulder. "Remy?" he says.

I sit up quickly and wipe my eyes. The view has not changed, except for a small dot on the horizon. "That's it." He points with a strong hand. "That's my family's old gas station. We'll be there in five minutes."

Minutes later, we pass an old rusty sign that stands quite tall above three separate abandoned buildings. "What are the other two?"

"Storage. But not anymore. I'm sure it's all rusted junk now. It's been a long time since I've been in there."

He pulls around the back of the gas station where he jumps out and opens the door to a small shed, then drives in and parks. Carefully he closes the sports car inside and we grab the guns before we enter the gas station. After setting everything down, he searches his backpack and pulls out a syringe.

"Is that more numbing?" I'm hopeful.

"It is." He nods.

"How did you know to grab that?"

"It just seemed important. I was in Iraq during the war." He shrugs. "It was my job to bring what someone might need to the lines."

I take it from him and quickly reapply the numbing solution. We wrap it again, then he looks at me. "What do we do now?"

"Wait, I guess."

After an hour, he and I have found comfortable positions on the floor against the walls. He's told me more of his marriage and career.

"What about the cars? You restore them?" I ask.

He smiles. "I think my wife wishes I was normal, but damn it, I just love the art. There's a group of us . . . men and women . . . when we come together for a show, it helps me realize that it's not just me, you know. There are plenty more who have the same obsession. We call ourselves the Panel Beaters."

I chuckle. "The Panel Beaters?"

"Yeah," he grins. "It's just a term used to describe someone who knows how to shape metal, bring things back to life. There's thousands of us." He hesitates, takes a big breath, and then looks directly at me. "You still aren't going to tell me anything?"

I hear the tick of something nearby, moving much slower than the beat of my heart. Windows line every wall and it occurs to me that there aren't many places to hide. There are supplies still left on the shelves and it feels strangely apocalyptic. "Have you ever heard of the Methos or Velieri?" I ask.

He shakes his head.

"Centuries ago, when people evolved, there were two kinds. Ephemes, people that would have a hundred years, and Velieri—if allowed—people that could have quite a bit more than that," I simply say.

"Like how much more?"

"A thousand . . . two thousand, maybe more. I don't really know, and I think it's different for everyone, just like humans."

"You'd think that longevity would make one more powerful than the other? Why would the Velieri?" I nod when he looks at me with question. "Why would the people with more life go into hiding?"

"I've thought the same thing. From what I gather, on top of the Velieri having more trouble procreating . . . it's more than that. There's something internal—a characteristic, if you will, that makes many of them more compliant . . . perhaps despite that they're more confident . . . if you can believe that. Politically, it will take too long to explain, but from what I've experienced and been told of the Velieri government . . . I get the feeling they pushed and portrayed it in such a way to convince everyone that hiding was the right thing to do . . . and behind the scenes they were getting rich off the deal."

Jay gives a heavy whistle and shakes his head.

"Jay, there's not enough time to explain, but just trust me when I say, I've been where you are. It's hard to understand at first. Who knows what else is out there? I mean, I now know about Velieri, but I will never underestimate the universe again." Just as I finish, I notice a black speck along the road about five to ten minutes away. It is still night, but the stars are fading. I get to my feet so that I can walk to the window and Jay follows.

"Is that your people?" he asks.

"I don't know. Jay, listen!" I look at him carefully. "The others, they are dangerous. You cannot fight them."

"We have the guns." He's an intuitive guy and seems to know this answer is too simple.

"If you shoot them in the head, you will have some time, but it will not kill them. And it's more than that . . . they don't play with the same rules. If they want to take you out, they simply start with here." I touch his head and wait for him to acknowledge what I've said. "That's why you need to hide. Don't try and help, just hide . . . okay?" He nods. "Is there a place you can hide?"

Soon, he throws aside heavy pieces of wood from the cement floor, revealing an oil change pit. After he climbs down the ladder and I hand him two of his guns, I kneel over the dark rectangle where old grease covers the walls and a table of oil cans tarnish. "Thank you, Jay. Listen, if there ever comes a time when you must choose whether Velieri is something to accept, or something to fear . . . would you do me a favor and remember me? And help others too as well . . . okay?"

He nods with a grin. "Of course. Be careful."

I gather the wood planks and return them over the pit. But before I can place the last one, he stops me, "Wait, Remy."

"What?" I notice the black car driving in.

"There's a lot of us . . . we have a big group that can help if you ever need it. They all think like me."

"Thank you, Jay."

As the last piece of wood is laid, we look at each other while sweat drips down his forehead. "Be careful up there," he says as it drops into position. Soon, sawhorses and empty boxes cover the oil pit.

The car is close enough that I slink behind several shelves of old newspapers and magazines. Luckily the windows haven't been washed in years, and the mud splatter from storms has cemented a hard shell on the outside. It is difficult not to become intoxicated by the fumes burning my nose as my breath rises in anticipation. A large bag for hauling wood is nearby, so I throw the guns in it, making them easier to carry. Once ready, I notice an office in the back with a rectangle window that overlooks the main entrance. The office will cover me but allow me to watch what they do. Outside, four men step out of the car—none of them are recognizable. My knuckles are white, and my palms are clammy as I hold on to a Glock pistol.

They split up, sending two men into the main building where we waited. When they enter, their guns are drawn. My hot and sweaty skin pulses, while my brain is constantly fighting the Trace. They stealthily check every inch but miss where Jay is hiding. When it comes time to search the office where I am, I press myself against the wall. The man is so quiet that I instantly understand . . . this is one of Alfonzo's men. Not only that, but the Tracing is heavy and incessant. As quiet as a mouse, he walks toward me. If I do nothing and let him enter the room, I'll be forced to use my gun, which will call the second my way. In my left pocket is a switch blade. As if a thousand times before, it is ready in my palm in a flash. Instantly, hundreds of memories are there, in different times, different centuries, for all different purposes of me doing this exact thing.

Several drips of sweat fall from my temple. My breath is a bit loud, so I try to calm it to not be found. He practically floats inside. At just the right moment, I throw my arms around his neck, kicking the back of his knee till he falls against me. With as little sound as possible, just a few gasps from him while he fights my choke, I carefully lower him to the ground. Finally, his body is limp.

"Marco?" the other man says as he lifts some papers from the nearby table to read. When Marco doesn't respond, he drops the papers, lifts his gun, and slowly walks over the wood planks of the pit toward the office. Again, my heart races; only this time I wonder if it will be as easy. His gun enters first, but he throws his body in swiftly, leaving me no choice but to lunge at him. I knock his gun from his hands, and it clangs to the floor. He throws me against the wall, knocking the wind out of me. With my right leg, I sweep his feet out from under him, but he then does the same to me before he's even reached the ground. My head hits the corner of the table so hard my eyes blur. These men, they move fast and precise. I lag just a second and he wraps his legs around me, leaving his arms free. Before I'm aware, his gun is in his hand, and he presses the tip of it behind my ear. I hear the shot, a loud pop as I squeeze my eyes shut. When nothing happens, I open one eye first, to see blood dripping from his forehead. Jay stands in the doorway with his gun tightly gripped. The man falls to the floor.

"Come on!" I yell at Jay.

"He's not dead, right?" Jay asks.

I place my gun to the back of his ear and pull the trigger. "He is now."

Jay nearly trips over a pile of rubbish as we race to the back door, but I grab his arm to keep him steady. We stand on both sides of the door just as we hear the men in the office coming to life. "Stay behind me, Jay," I whisper.

The door makes a high-pitched squeal as we step out onto the dirt. Little green tufts of succulents are scattered about, while the light brown and dry earth has a continuous lace of cracked dirt. The guns are heavy in the bag over my shoulder, while I point the Glock every which way. With slow steps, one by one, we tread the last bit of distance back to Jay's car. I press myself against the splintering side of the building, as does Jay, until I round a corner, running directly into one of them.

Instantly, I am not equipped for his psychic abilities. A spider works fast, spinning her web, attaching the silk to strategic places in order to capture. The way this man's Trace spins about my mind is no different—deeper than the subconscious and stronger than the best of my strengths. He plays the game confidently, distorting my reality. Pain that I haven't felt in a while shoots down my forehead. Every move he makes feels foreign, like he's using a back door into my energy—perhaps something locked away.

We fight for a moment, but it doesn't last long since my mind is moving too slow. He catches my fist, as my other hand presses against my forehead in pain. When I look up, nothing is as it was. It isn't a man that I fight—his face deforms, one side of it melting, the other side of it looking just as I assume a demon would appear. He has grown in size and his head pulsates until I close my eyes.

It is so terrifying that I rip my hand from his and fall back. That's when I notice the ground has joined this other realm. It has turned to sludge and is now alive with things that crawl and slither. Insects that are bigger and look like nothing I've ever seen climb my clothes and onto my neck. I cry out, but there's nowhere to go.

"Remy!" Jay yells, but when I turn to look at him, he too is a monster. He reaches out for me: his mouth stretches from one ear all the way to the other and black drips from his mouth.

There are moments, just seconds, really, of breakthrough rhythms, that I try desperately to separate from everything else. *If I can just grab one. Come on, Remy.*

Their trick is to make you feel that this is real, and if it's not . . . is it me? Am I crazy?

Three more men appear, including the ones that Jay and I fought off. Everyone fits in this nightmare from head to toe. My heart pounds as I hide my head in my arms.

"Remy!" Jay yells again.

The four men point their guns at Jay. "No!" I yell.

Out of the darkness, two cars speed in. They run straight into the men, sending them flying. Instantly, the pressure lessens in my head and a bit of the fog lifts. Sassi, Kilon, Arek, Geo, and Peter all jump from the cars, their faces still minorly distorted. Arek places himself between us and these men as they get to their feet. The fight is thick around me and I start to emerge from whatever state I had just been in.

The gun bag is not far away. I pull out the first that I feel and instantly point it at the man that Sassi knocks to the ground. "Sassi!"

I yell. She looks and jumps away just in time as I pull the trigger. The bullet hits him directly behind his ear and he instantly falls lifeless to the ground.

Arek finishes one of them, then joins Kilon, while Sassi takes care of another. Unexpectedly, one runs. He manages to reach the car and peel away before anyone can stop him.

When it's all over, Arek is standing over the last man, but he doesn't look like himself. I try to walk to him, but Sassi stops me with a hand. "No," she says. "Give him a moment. He just had to go deep."

"Go deep?" I ask.

"Yeah. That's what makes everything turn to fiction for you . . . Tri Planum. They're messing with your unconscious . . . one level more than your subconscious. If you remember what Arek said . . . he knows how to do it, it's just hard for him to come out of it."

We watch him stand there in a daze for a minute, then he walks several yards away from us and angrily hits the shed in the back, yelling at the top of his lungs.

After a while, he seems to come back to life. He comes to my side, still recovering from whatever he has just gone through. "Are you okay?"

"I am." Jay has remained quiet behind me, but I call him forward. "This is Jay. He's been helping me." He raises a hand to say an insecure hello as Arek stretches out his hand for a handshake.

"Thank you, Jay."

"Of course. What should I do now?"

"Let's get your car," I say as I brush the dirt from my clothes.

When we pull the Porsche out of the shed, Kilon whistles. "I used to have this car when it was brand new." He looks up suddenly with the revelation that he's given himself away to Jay. I shake my head and smile.

"It's okay. He knows."

Arek pulls a clear bandage from his pocket and quickly covers my tracker. He hands Kilon the tracker gun, who starts to search Jay's body.

"What are you doing? You think I have one of those?" Jay asks.

Kilon grins and raises one eyebrow, just as the gun beeps. "No, I know you do. Everyone does." Kilon lifts the leg to Jay's pants and covers the area with a clear bandage. "Keep it on for a week. Go off grid and when you come back, they'll have moved on. This is for your safety." Kilon hands him another bandage and a tracking gun to keep. "Run this over your wife's body and when it beeps that's where you put the bandage."

"Let's go," Arek says, and begins to walk us back to the vehicles.

"Wait," I say and hurry back to Jay. I reach out and touch his arm, "Thank you, Jay."

His smooth voice enters the world in a quiet hum, "Just remember what I said. I have a lot of friends." For a moment, we simply look at each other and he's easy to believe.

He then jumps in his car and races away.

Before long, my body slides next to Arek into the comfort of the leather seats.

"What will happen to Jay?" I ask.

"If he does what I told him," Kilon says, "he'll be fine. Usually, I would call the Correctional Territory Authority, but obviously that's not an option right now. So, he's on his own." Kilon sees my concern. "He'll be okay. He just needs to listen to me."

"And Briston? How is he?" Sassi pulls one of the cars out into the main highway and soon we are under the stars heading west, away from Jay.

Sassi looks at me in the rearview mirror. "We're going there now. But it will take us a couple of hours."

I lay my head back, watching the infinite number of tiny diamonds in the sky, until suddenly I remember the bloody shirt in my pocket.

"Kilon," I say as my hand reaches around his front seat headrest. "Here." He furrows his brow as he takes the dark material. "It's Lyneva's."

Kilon laughs, then reaches back to give me a high five. "That's my girl."

34

Briston looks to be near death. Doctor Hugh has set up a make-shift hospital room in a dank apartment where no one can find us; monitors are beeping, fans are blowing, and people are whispering. Beneath Briston's gray skin are dark and raised veins, his eyes are sunken, and in all my memory, I have never seen him look so weak. He is the reason we are still in Africa, as Dr. Hugh has been unsure if he is okay to travel.

"How is he still here?" I ask as Dr. Hugh checks the closest monitor.

"Well, I was able to take some of his blood to break down the elements of Navin's injection. It came out to a combination of mercury, actual powdered cement, and several amino acids in peptide form, which make it move quickly through the blood. We were able to break down the peptide . . . however, we still have to finish the job. I've been on the phone with other doctors, but so far no one has the exact answer."

It suddenly occurs to me that I haven't seen him since Beckah died. His naturally funny and flamboyant lightness is missing. "I'm so sorry about Beckah," I say quietly.

His face lightens just a bit. "Thank you. I'm sorry about your father. Let's go out and talk with everyone. We have some big decisions to make," Dr. Hugh suggests.

Rain begins lightly, but within a few minutes it pelts the roof so heavily that we must gather closer in order to hear one another speak. From the table a laptop is set up so that Diem and Gal can join us remotely. It must be cold where they are, since their noses are red and they are covered in fur.

"Does anyone know what Navin needs with Karine?" Geo asks before anyone is settled.

Gal yells to be heard from the computer, "Karine?! Navin was asking for Karine?"

Arek's voice is more fatigued than usual. "Karine is one of the most deranged criminals who's ever sat within the walls of the Cellar . . . of course Navin needs him."

Dr. Hugh nods, "Not to mention a brilliant scientist. And after what has happened with Briston, I do not doubt that we have a better idea of Navin's plan."

Sassi steps forward. "I've already told Prophet Jenner to send someone to the Cellar in the Sudan . . . hopefully they'll keep Navin from getting anywhere near Karine." Sassi changes gear, knowing that we haven't much time. "Listen, we can't run forever. Not only do we have the Umbramanes searching for us, but we also run the risk of being seen and turned in by any Velieri after Covey's press conference. Even Leigh has sent his own men out. There's not a place on this earth that I feel safe to stay for too long. So, what are our options?"

"First we figure out what to do with my father. Right?" I ask quickly.

"Yes," Sassi agrees. "Kenichi, I believe you already have a plan?"

Kenichi nods, his voice emerging quietly. "No options . . . only Gyre."

"That's all the way around the world," Peter blurts out.

"Yes . . . Dr. Hugh, Mak, and I, . . . will travel with Briston," Kenichi explains.

Sassi crosses her arms in front of her and rocks on her heels. "So that breaks our group up."

From the computer, Diem speaks quickly with his thick curled accent, "I have a team of men who will jump at a moment's notice to help. But listen to this . . . we've also found a trail of emails and letters between Navin, Japha, and Lyneva about the Red Summit. Just a little more searching and I believe we've got what we need to clear you."

Like a roll of thunder through the room, smiles begin to grow on everyone's faces. "Are you serious?" I ask.

"Yes. We don't have it all yet, but once I do, the first thing we do is go straight to the top. We call a meeting with everyone and clear it . . . clear your name. Besides, someone felt they saw Elizabeth the other day. I have a group chasing down that lead."

"If someone finds Elizabeth, and we can get her memory to tell the truth, then it's done." I look at Arek, but I can see he isn't convinced. My assumption is proved right when he speaks up.

"Diem, tell them also what you already told me." Arek rubs his cheek the way he usually does when he's stressed.

Diem clears his throat. "They've decided to put every Umbramanes on the job. It's no longer just four or five. Alfonzo Geretzima has signed a contract to refocus all their attentions on finding you. You must understand this means at least two hundred of the best trackers in the world are on this. There will be no place you can go that they will not find you. The first thing you need to do is to move on to somewhere new every couple of days. But look, if Gal and I can do our job, we will find what we need within this week. I feel it. We've jumped far in just a short time."

Sassi hesitates, breathes, then hesitates again before she speaks. "Okay, so the question is this: Do we make our group smaller, or do we call in the big guns and get more men for protection?"

No one speaks for a while. The air in the room is moist from the rain—it even smells of wet grass—and mixed with our anxious energy. It pumps through the room like a vibration so high, none of us can match it.

Kilon is the first to speak. "The more people, the less control. Would we trust everyone there? Also, Arek and I have some work to do. Prophet Jenner told us about Tri Planum. We have to work on this."

Diem speaks up again. "Kenichi, Hugh, Peter, and Mak head back to Gyre and see what you can do with Briston. Gal and I continue to search and follow these leads. Meanwhile, Arek, you and the others find a place. If you need back up, you call. But otherwise, you are on your own so fewer people know where you are. We will be ready at a moment's notice."

Sassi nods as she walks to the computer. "Okay, Diem, I agree. Find it and fix this. We'll call you if we need anything."

"Aye. Will do."

With that, Sassi closes the meeting, then looks at Kenichi. "Tell us what you need for Briston."

"We leave tonight."

Sassi takes a sip of water. Her beautiful lips perk up with shine. "Even traveling is getting more difficult. We know fewer and fewer people who we can trust. Arek, do you have an idea of where we can go?"

Arek looks at me. "I do."

35

There is an instant smell and feel as we drive the roads of Spain that tells me I was once in love with this place. From the airport, we drive for several hours until we stop quickly for some food at a small medieval town in the Catalan countryside called Besalu. Besalu remembers me, just as I remember it. While Arek puts gas in the rental car, I walk inside the very first small store we see but forget to cover my hair with a hat and wear sunglasses. A small old woman with silver hair and thick dark eyebrows stares at me in shock. Immediately, I know that I've made a mistake.

She smiles, her graying teeth showing all the way back to her molars. In a thick Castilian accent she says, "I thought I'd never see you again?" Her frail body moves faster than expected from behind the counter, as she runs to take my hand. "Remy. You're back!"

At first, I try to think of a lie to tell her, but I stop, as suddenly a memory pours over me like fine wine. Evette and her husband Gyelle own this tiny turquoise blue shop where I would often stop on my way in and out of Spain.

"Evette," I say.

"Yes. Yes. What a lovely thing to see you. It's been so long." She doesn't act as anyone else in the Velieri community has been. It's as though she hasn't the faintest idea of Remy's death. "Will you be here for long?"

"Not for long."

"Well, let me give you this." She laughs. "I realize it has been a lifetime and you may not remember, but I do." She disappears into the back of the store so that I cannot see her, then reappears with a worn and torn book. "Here. You left it on the shelf nearly . . . what was it . . . thirty years ago?"

"At least," I simply say.

The bell over the door rings as Arek steps inside. He must duck under the door frame and instantly catches me in his sights. He has my hat and glasses in his hands and a sour expression on his face. When he gets close, he presses the cap over my hair and sets the glasses in place. "Sorry," I whisper. "Evette remembers me."

Arek turns to the old lady with a manufactured smile and nods. "Of course she does, we stopped in here often." Suddenly he begins to speak in Spanish, "Evette, How's Gyelle?"

"He is well, thank you."

"Evette, if you wouldn't mind, we are trying to stay low right now. Rest time," Arek explains. "We'll stop by, of course, but can you keep us quiet? Don't let others know we're here."

"Claro que Si!"

Before long we are back in the car and I stuff the old book into my bag. Twenty minutes later the roads are greatly familiar.

"We're close . . . aren't we?" I ask.

Sassi looks at me with confusion. "I don't remember this place at all."

Arek looks at me. "Yes, we're close."

Just off the main highway is a dirt road and a dark wood sign with antiqued letters that says "Vida." It has been well kept, just like the neatly manicured fields and a tall wooden post fence that wraps around the fields for miles.

Sassi stops the car beneath the sign and looks back at Arek. "I don't remember this place."

"Let me drive." Arek opens the gate, quickly switches places with her, then heads down the dirt road.

Clouds of dust billow out behind our car. We run into a hundred sheep crossing the road, which take their time while we wait to let them pass. Several are stragglers and even stop just in front of the car to bleat at us. Kilon's irritation grows. The minutes pass, until finally I see a strange look in the sheep's eyes. One by one, the last four sheep slowly rock back and forth until their soft wooly bodies drop to the ground asleep.

"What are we supposed to do with them now?" Sassi growls at Kilon. "Those sheep are heavy!"

"It's fine, I'll move them." Kilon jumps out of the car and we laugh as he struggles to lift the heavy beasts out of the way. Finally, the road is clear, and we move on.

The car slowly rocks up the hill and then, once it reaches the top, we overlook a large meadow with one small cottage in the center. This is not just any cottage; it is the one—the one that I have been dreaming about since the Cellar. Now that we look at it in person, I can feel the spirit of this place holds something special. A pounding pressure in my chest begs me to remember the details, but they just don't come. The perfume of earth and grass wafts through the windows and for just a split second, the memory plays cat and mouse through fractures, only to dive back into hiding.

Arek continues down into the valley where the meadow rests. The moment he pulls to a stop, I get out of the car. Now it is the scent from scattered flowers that wraps about me the memory of dewy mornings and lilacs wafting through the open windows.

Arek turns to Sassi and Kilon. "Can you give us a moment?"

Sassi nods, "Of course."

Arek takes my hand as Kilon and Sassi start pulling our things out of the car. We walk up the porch steps. "Remy, I need to remind you . . . whatever comes back to you, you must keep it quiet. Sassi and Kilon can't know."

"Know what?"

"It's best that your own memory brings it back. Just listen to me. You can tell me but that is all . . . for now."

"Okay."

He turns the key to the front door and lets it swing open so that I can walk in first. As soon as I step onto the creaky floor, my breath is stolen by an intense spirit. I close my eyes when heat flushes my cheeks and unexpected tears fall. Before I can open my eyes, Arek stands in front of me with his hands on my face.

"This place . . . was yours and mine." He grins. "Just us for the first time."

Feelings sweep about me like smoke from a fire until my skin burns with pain and happiness all rolled into one. Quietly, we walk through the rooms, my fingertips seeking the stimulation of tactile comfort. Everything is covered in plastic and, as we remove it, the small space becomes a home. Just off to the right is a bed . . . our bed, mine and Arek's. The window where the morning sun rises sits at one side of the room and I look out.

Arek walks up behind me and presses his lips to my neck. The warmth in my chest builds until my body shakes. "It's time to come back," he whispers in my ear.

Later, as the sun sets, I crawl into bed beside Arek, as though I've done it my entire life. We lay quietly, looking at each other in the dim light. My eyes grow heavy.

"Is that why you brought us here?" I whisper.

"To get you to remember us? Maybe. I also know this is the only place you and I kept between us. No one else knew we lived here. It's the safest choice."

As my eyes close, I nod. "It's coming. I can feel it. Somewhere close . . . our life together is somewhere close."

36

The sun is out on the open fields, rolling for miles, a mixture of green and yellow grass. Slow clouds pass with the light breeze. Everyone seems to wake this morning with a mission. Our breakfast on the porch is quiet while we sip our drinks and listen to the nearby animals.

Mid-morning, we stand out in the field in a circle. Geo, Arek, Sassi, Kilon, and I. The grass tickles my bare feet.

"How do you prepare for this new way of fighting?" I finally ask over the quiet hum of nature.

Sassi looks at me with strong eyes. "Do you understand the many levels we have to our consciousness?"

"I'm not sure," I say honestly.

She continues, "We have our conscious level. This is you and I, here. We are talking, engaging, aware of all that is around us. Our senses are heightened from new smells, our eyes aware of new sight. The second level is our subconscious mind that holds those conscious moments in time. As you sleep, your dreams are made up of what your conscious has taken in and your subconscious has stored. These subconscious moments create layers of what many think is their true self. But our true self isn't living within our subconscious, rather in our true consciousness.

"Most of us can't find true consciousness because it is influenced by the third level—our unconscious. This is where we stuff and store.

Where we've learned things that have become a part of our identity, good or bad. The reason we don't visit the unconscious often, or if ever, is because it's usually made up of things we refuse to let rise to the subconscious and especially the conscious. For most of us this would mean more pain, fear, or even responsibility for learned hate."

"Because the unconscious is simply what we recognize as our identity?" I ask.

Sassi smiles. "Exactly. And we never question that. Even Velieri have a hard time delving into their unconscious. Facing what lies in our unconscious will show us what compromises our true freedom. Yet, it can also be dangerous to fight someone here."

"Why?" A gentle breeze caresses my cheek and I watch a bird pass overhead, but I'm locked in on every word Sassi says.

"It's where we carry our demons, our deepest wounds, our most covered judgements on ourselves and others. It's where we carry our hate." Sassi looks at Kilon, sharing a moment of understanding. "Call it indoctrination or simple ways we were taught to believe, or abuse that was so horrible we had to forget. People learn hate; it becomes such a part of their makeup that they are unaware of the hate even when they are spewing it. It is one thing for Navin to hate Ephemes because of what he has gone through, and another for him to teach Lyneva from the moment that she is born to hate them. He will mold her before she can even choose for herself. That's how it becomes part of her unconscious.

"Unless she learns to face it, it will control her. We know that at least two of Alfonzo's Umbramanes have studied how to fight in their enemy's unconscious, which gives them the perfect gateway to control them."

I turn to Geo, "So, when you were teaching me those places that I feared most, was that my unconscious? If that was it, I think I can do it."

There's an awkward pause as most avert their eyes to the ground. Arek stretches his neck uncomfortably before answering. "No . . . all of that fear was still your subconscious. It would have been too dangerous to let you experience your unconscious. In the subconscious your enemy is external . . . it's the monster made by your fears and imagination coming toward you. In your unconscious, the monster is you." He hesitates, then clears his throat. "The unconscious fight begins with parts of you that you didn't even know existed. Perhaps the places that if people knew about you, they'd fear you. When your enemy can delve into this and manipulate it . . . they can affect . . . your sanity."

"The Cellar affected my sanity," I say confidently.

"In some ways, yes. Some of the smartest criminals seem to have learned Tri Planum naturally. They aren't afraid to go there or get lost in it. So, they were using a bit of your unconscious," Sassi agrees.

My shoulders grow tight. "So, Tri Planum is worse than that?"

"It can be, but there's hope. Arek and others have been able to be there and keep control. Not only that but imagine the unconscious *good* that's never retrieved. The spiritual awakening from releasing the unconscious until your consciousness is free. Remy lived much of her time there. Many of us do. That is the difference between Ephemes and Velieri. Yet, to fight within this all at the same time . . ." she doesn't continue.

"Okay. So how do we do this? How do we learn?"

Geo steps to the middle of the circle. "We visit each level. Do it one at a time to see how far each of us can get. Arek and I will go first . . . to make sure we can truly do this."

Several minutes later, they are prepared. Arek and Geo sit across from each other in wooden chairs that we placed in the grass just beyond the house. Arek has a long thick rope in his hand. Geo explains before they delve deeper, "Rolling this rope around his hand and elbow works with the same part of his brain from which he fights. If he stops rolling it, then we know he's lost the ability to fight in all three. The conscious fight will be the first to stop, which is why it is so dangerous. I'll go into his unconscious and dig around."

We watch silently. Arek rolls the rope without stopping while they stare at each other. For fifteen minutes we watch until Arek's body begins to struggle. His hand begins to move in slow motion, then little by little it stops wrapping the loop, and his chest begins to rise and fall. Geo snaps out of his Trace and quickly stands. "Stay back," he says.

Suddenly, Arek roars to life. His muscles strain as he yells from the top of his lungs. He walks away cursing and growling with clenched fists.

"Can I go to him?" I ask.

Geo shakes his head. "No. He won't be himself for a moment."

A hundred yards away, Arek yells to the open sky again. Then leans over, placing his hands on his knees, and sucks in heavy breaths. It takes him nearly twenty minutes to come back to us, although his eyes are not fully recovered, and I swallow fear from the look in them.

"Again," he says the word, even though he obviously does not want to do it again.

He picks up the rope and sits down, instantly rolling it around his hand and elbow. It takes a bit longer after Geo digs, but the same thing happens. This occurs at least five times, until finally his hand never stops feeding the rope. Finally, Geo opens his eyes at the same time Arek does and they grin at each other.

"Yep, you've got it. Two more times?" Geo suggests.

"Yeah, let's go."

Each time Arek fights Tri Planum without an issue. When they are done, they come back to the rest of us who now rest on the porch. "Arek," Geo says, "will work with me now. We'll work with the rest tomorrow."

Kilon shakes his head. "I don't know that I can."

Everyone turns with surprise. Geo asks, "Why?"

"I've been taught before and was never able to," he admits.

Sassi stays quiet, but she keeps her eyes down.

Hours later, when all of us have gone on to other things, Geo is still working with Arek. Each time Geo's response, although different than Arek's anger, bubbles over with chaos. His recovery seems to take longer and longer. They take breaks only to eat, then as the sun sets and Sassi and I are in the kitchen, we hear celebration from outside. Geo has finally, even if only one time, experienced Tri Planum.

After their success we sit around the table to eat, and belly laughter fills the room. The next morning, we begin the process for Sassi. At lunchtime, I watch her pull the rope until finally, she stops and Arek smiles. "That's intense," she whispers.

My curiosity grows. Even as the sun sets on the next day, I still have not been approached to try. Sassi, Geo, and Arek continually practice while Kilon and I watch from the porch, drinking tea at sunset.

"Why don't you want to try?" I ask him finally.

He hesitates, watching the sun fall behind the uneven horizon. "You know, all of this stuff . . . it's not for everyone. We could have forty people here, and those three could still be the only ones to accomplish it."

"You didn't answer my question," I whisper.

He chuckles. "You caught that, huh?" He runs his hands roughly through his hair. "I was afraid that I'd never be able to come back from it."

"From what?"

His eyes turn to look at me as the crickets and night life begin to wake. "There's a reason, Remy, that we shove things down so deep that even we don't know they are there. Nobody wants to visit a place that might tell us what we don't want to know about ourselves. It's too difficult to recognize which one is you."

"Sounds like my world over the last year," I say quietly.

He nods and lays his hand on mine. "Believe me, I'd love to revel in my true self, and be One with God, free of the buried layers. I don't know, Remy . . . you'll have to experience it yourself to understand."

When Sassi, Arek, and Geo come back into the house, Sassi takes a sip of Kilon's tea. "Maybe we should be done for the night?"

I stand. "No, I need to try."

No one seems surprised by this, and it shows in their calm reactions. Sassi shakes her head gently, "In all honesty, I'm not sure it'll be good for you right now. Not even the best can do this."

"I was able to put Kilon to sleep. I've been able to do everything you have asked and . . . I've done well."

They stay quiet for a bit until Geo looks at all of them. "Remy was always able to do this."

Arek is quiet from where he stands, leaning against the cottage post. I lean against the wall, keeping the space between us.

Sassi shrugs. "Maybe if she only works on the second and third level."

"No," I say quickly. "I want to do the entire thing. I believe I can do it."

We hear the ticking of the old clock that stands just inside the living room, since no one desires to break the silence.

"I'll take her in mine first." Arek watches Geo as though he's waiting to see if this is a good idea.

Geo nods. "Okay."

Minutes later, in the dark while the symphony of crickets puts on a concert for us, Geo, Arek, and I sit in a circle. I feel the rough rope in my hands and practice a couple of turns. Geo clears his throat, while Kilon brings out two lanterns and sets them beside our feet. Geo gets my attention, "Keep your eyes on me, but continue with the rope. Everything we experience here, right now, the feeling of the rope, the chair, the sounds, the smells . . . this is your actual conscious existence. Unfortunately, when the other levels get manipulated, this is the first to be affected. It will paralyze you."

"How do I make sure that doesn't happen?"

Geo admits, "That's what we teach you, right now."

"So, I will experience all three levels at once. How do I know which level is which?"

"We've taken you to your subconscious again and again. In all those trainings when things began to distort and change, looking nothing like reality . . . that is our fear turning our subconscious. And the unconscious . . . it's when the monsters stop and the authentic fears begin. I can try my best to explain it, but there's no better way than to just experience it. In order to be safe, I will only manipulate Arek's energy . . . not yours."

"Okay, let's go," I say confidently.

Arek and I begin to wrap the rope around our hands and elbows. Due to all the training we have been doing, I am more aware of my consciousness than ever before. Then, for the first time, as I listen for Arek's rhythm, something different happens—my awareness splits in two. In one reality, the chair is still hard beneath my body, the grass still tickles my feet, while Arek and I twist the rough material tightly yet simultaneously in another reality. I am standing on the edge of a mountain overlooking clouds traveling at a slow pace between more mountain peaks. I hear rustling behind me and when I turn, Arek is preparing rope around his waist that attaches to mine, as his chalked fingers grip tiny ridges on the mountain wall.

"You'd better get on quickly," he says to me with his hand out to help.

"Where do I grab?" I study the rock.

"There," he points to small edges. "You'd better hurry. It can drop out at any time."

I begin to climb up. "What can?" I say just as the ledge where I stood is gone and a thousand-foot drop is below me. Panic quakes within my body and my eyes shut tight. "Why are we doing this?"

"There's no rhyme or reason for our subconscious—the same way we have tsunami dreams when our life feels in chaos. Tomorrow it would give me something else . . ." His strong arms pull him higher. "Come on . . . look up at the stars. Find something to put your attention on that doesn't fester or change within your fear."

I finally open my eyes and pay attention to Arek, who climbs easily—his lantern is connected to his belt and lights the way. My heart slows and because I am aware of everything in my conscious level, as I sit across from Geo with my feet planted on firm ground—even Kilon clearing his throat at the cottage is within my awareness—I realize that even though this may feel very real, my body is not actually climbing this mountain.

Arek grabs tiny ledges using just his thumbs and fingertips. "Just be aware that things may change here, and you have to simply change with it."

"Okay." I grunt when pulling myself higher. "My muscles are burning?"

"You will feel everything. That's the power of our minds . . . and our biggest weakness." A few pebbles slip beneath Arek's toes and fall past my shoulder. "Okay, get comfortable here on this mountain. Once you do, we have to find the next level."

In my conscious, I wrap the rope around my hand and elbow, and at the same time climb inch by inch up the mountain in my subconscious. Recognizing the different sounds of each place is easy, even riding Arek's rhythm is possible after all the training I've gone through.

"Ready?" he asks.

"I think so."

As we climb higher something feels unsettling, a bit like floating or the hovering of your stomach as you take a quick fall. A third split takes place and instantly I can feel the difference within my mind. In the first consciousness I am strong and complete, there within the meadow around me. And in the second, as long as we work together it does not turn into the nightmares mine often become.

Now, this third level digs further within my spirit and immediately my body tenses in all three levels. The discomfort of a new irritatingly ticklish territory that isn't owned by one layer of consciousness alone. I want out immediately, which forces me to fumble on the mountain and my hand to stop wrapping the rope for just a moment.

In Arek's unconscious, we stand in a white stone archway that repeats for what seems to be miles, with hallways off each massive curve. The only things that aren't stone are the heavy curtains with gold ropes hanging from the sides. It reminds me of the artwork that hurt my brain as a child from M.C. Escher. Arek takes my hand in the third level.

"Keep your hands moving," Arek says in the first level; in the second level, at the same moment, he catches my hand to save me from falling and yells, "I've got you! Don't look down!" Meanwhile in the third level, our feet tap the cement floor, causing massive echoes within the stone walls.

In the third level, even Arek seems uncomfortable. "Does it always look like this?"

"No, this is mild compared to my first time exploring."

"Exploring? Is that what you want to call it?"

He smiles, but it goes away quickly when we hear something just ahead. "Stay close to me. I don't know what to expect."

"What lives here?"

"Everything I wish didn't." He looks around carefully as we continue to walk. "Geo is going to be working on something and he can manipulate anything that hides here."

Suddenly, a woman emerges from behind the thick molding on the stone archway just ahead. The graceful way she walks reveals that it is Holona, her long dark hair falling down her back. Arek squeezes my hand tighter as he watches her glide slowly across the white floor. I know this is not the same as my visions of her. Somewhere this is Arek's memory, fears, and subconscious all rolled into one. Just as she's about to turn, a heavy rumble shakes the ground and I look at him with confusion.

"What is that?" I ask, but I can see that he doesn't know.

Until the rumble turns to a large explosion. At the end of the hallway, just behind Holona, a massive wave of water comes barreling between the walls.

"Holona!" I yell, which makes her fearful face turn to me.

Arek is already running directly toward her, but Navin appears from the shadows. He strikes Arek so hard that Arek flies back and lands with a hard grunt on the ground. Before he can get up, Holona is swept into the water. Then it envelops Arek and Navin, and—even though I run—it overtakes me in seconds. Navin continues to hold Arek back from helping Holona, so I reach for her. We are just too far away.

Arek wraps his arm around Navin's neck as the water turns from a rushing river to stagnant water that continues to rise. Holona struggles to remain above it. Finally, Arek finds one of the ropes from the curtains below and wraps it around Navin's neck as he fights. As the water rises, Navin can't break free and is held below the water.

Soon the water is so high that there is only a sliver of air for us at the top. I can hear the fear in Holona's voice. "Arek, get Remy out of here."

As she drops below the surface, Arek yells and reaches for her. This place is real. No matter how much I want to tell myself that this is not truly happening, my lungs are aching and there is no end in sight. Arek comes up with a growl, without Holona in his arms.

"Arek!" I cry out.

He comes close; I can feel his panic. His strong hand emerges from the water, and he hits the stone ceiling angrily. Holona's body is struggling to breathe below us and Arek's fears have consumed his unconscious. We have only seconds before we have no more air, and a cry escapes my lips.

That's when I can feel the house of cards fall. As the water overwhelms us, my awareness as we climb the mountain fails and my hands slip. Arek catches me just in time and he cries out as his sweaty hand barely hangs on.

"Arek!" I yell as his palm has only my fingertips.

"Remy!" he yells back, but I realize it's not within the halls or on the mountain.

Suddenly my eyes open in the field beside the cottage and my hands haven't been moving. The blood has drained from them, and they are cold. Geo, Sassi, and Kilon have come closer with concern.

Just as I come out of it, I suck in a breath as though I have been drowning and falling all at once. My body is so tired and confused that I fall to the grass, sucking in air that just isn't enough.

Arek hurries to my side as Geo shakes his head. "What was that?" Geo asks.

"I couldn't do anything or get out," Arek says, clearly confused.

Geo sits on the wooden chair and lays his head back. "That was insane. Well, I guess we know now what truly happens with our biggest weakness."

37

My body is comfortably enveloped in the plush mattress and light blanket, but still, I've been unable to sleep. At nearly midnight, in the dark room, the energy of this cottage cradles me in feelings of both good and bad. Somehow, I know that something beautiful happened here, but strangely there is also sadness. It is especially loud when the world sleeps. "Arek?"

He takes in a breath as he wakes up, then turns to me. "You okay?"

"Tell me what happened here."

His silence is his apology as he comes closer. "I can't."

"Please, Arek. There is something so intense about this place. Please." A tear falls from the corner of my eye and I'm grateful that he probably won't see it.

Drawing his face to mine, his whisper is full of fight and angst. "I'm sorry, Remy, I can't."

I roll over to look at the tongue and groove ceiling. My chest rises and falls so that I can feel the satisfaction of a large breath. "There's so much pain within humans. We seem to suffer more than we experience joy."

"It doesn't have to be that way. The problem is simply that people don't know how to live in the present—we just visit it from time to time." A few moments of quiet pass, then he rolls to a seated position. "Come on. I have something to show you," he says quietly.

"Right now?"

"Yeah, right now." Before long, with a lantern in his hand, he leads us away from the cottage, somewhere I haven't gone. Sheep bleat in the distance and somewhere I can hear a strange call. From behind a grouping of trees, a lynx pops out.

"A lynx." I stop with surprise. "The only other time I saw one of these was in Switzerland."

"I remember that," Arek says and grins.

The large cat sniffs the air, as it carefully crosses from one tree to the safety of the next. I recollect a conversation with Gyre years before . . . *"The lynx," he says, "will show herself just before the revelation of hidden truths."*

Just ahead, I see the ruins of an historic church. There is beauty to it, of course, yet it is the warmth in my chest that tells me more exists within these walls than just brick and mortar. The lantern gives off only so much light, so I take it from his hand and head inside. My feet tap the old tile. Weathered pews fill the middle of the small sanctuary and the ceiling has caved in, in a couple of places. I'm drawn to touch the frescos on the wall even though the intricate details are hard to see in the dark. Somehow, I'm aware that within these walls there has been joy . . . there has been death . . . and elements of pain. My skin crawls from the back-and-forth emotions. "Why did you bring me here?" I turn to look at him.

"To show you that there is more to our unconscious than darkness." The floor creaks under his weight as he walks to me with a mission. His chest presses up against me until I'm knocked off balance and step back against the wall, to which he presses me harder. The lantern clangs against the red brick, almost on beat with my heart from the way he stares at me. It is times like these that turn my cheeks to fire and take my voice from me, and I wonder . . . if this feeling of flush and fever ever go away.

"No. It never does," he whispers. His height always forces him to bend his head to me, but this time, one arm reaches down to my waist, wraps about it, then lifts me so my eyes stare directly into his. "Being here, Remy, with you . . . has helped me realize that I don't care whether you remember everything. Because this . . ." He runs his other hand, the one that isn't lifting me on my toes, across my bare skin where my shirt is bunched up between us. My breath shakes just from his touch, and he nods. "That feeling. There's no one else." Then his hand glides down my arm and steals the lantern from my hand. As he squats down in front of me to rest the lantern on the floor, he makes sure to stay close enough that his lips and nose trace my body all the way down. Then again, as he stands, he kisses me everywhere making small but penetrating explosions. Finally, he presses me against the wall with his body and whispers in my ear. "Are you ready?"

"For what?" my strangled voice asks.

"To let me take you to all three." His mouth opens and presses against my lips, leaving a trail with his tongue. I've never been so willing to struggle for breath as my hands and arms wrap around his neck. Never in all my existence as an Epheme did I experience anything like this, as if when I look down at my skin there would be sprays of light where he has just touched. Just as he unbuttons my shirt, he says, "Wait for the split. It's coming." Even his voice shakes, reminding me that my essence does the same to his.

As his lips surround mine, with my eyes closed, I can sense something new—not in the church, not in our conscious existence, but once again, my conscious splits. Suddenly, while he carries me across the old, dilapidated church to one of the pews to lay me down, I am, at the same time, in a second part of my brain with him. Here, we visit moments from past centuries. Arek's perfect arms wrap around me while the background constantly changes every few moments through the archive of our love making. It reveals the millions of seconds we've spent wrapped around each other. Because the subconscious can change and swell with imagination, the sensations awaken to a level that your consciousness cannot experience. Thousands of memories, colors, echoes, and shapes abandon their safe place within me and come to light. It is better than any dream.

While he still travels down my body and kisses me within the church, we also are living within this second place of dreams rapidly watching the background change from beach, to rainforest, to under the night stars. There's a fragrance more perfect than any perfume in our conscious world. Rolling clouds pass overhead, nature does not exist in normal color as he drops his head and kisses my chest, then my ribs expand as his tongue brushes them.

"Hold on," Arek whispers, as the tides of the earth meet with perfect harmony.

Again, in the blink of an eye, there is another split to a third place. While it is not as dreamlike as the second, this one is denser within my spirit—a memory—to relive an experience together. This third place sits more aggressively in my spirit, forcing my emotions to the surface. It is a place of no limits, no boundaries. Only the purest joys we have felt in our lives swirl around us, within us, and between us. We are within the walls of our home in Switzerland, with the glass ceiling overhead. Lightning pierces the black sky as I look above Arek's shoulder. It's as if in this place—where everything feels absolute and complete from our bodies, minds, and spirits—we relive those milliseconds of pure joy.

We make love while desperately aware of all three realms.

Finally, when he pulls away, the experience comes to an end, and it takes me a moment to settle. I reach for Arek's face and stare into his eyes in silence as we both breathe heavily. He's studying me.

"Is it like that every time?" I whisper.

He kisses my fingertips and nods. "My life with you was always like this."

"No wonder you came looking for me."

He grins.

After a while we walk back through a foggy mist toward the cottage. I've never felt so connected to Arek or anyone else in all my

life. When we are within sight of the cottage, a vision or a memory
. . . I'm not sure which . . . comes to me swiftly.

Arek and I walk together, hand in hand, along these rolling hills.
We have spent the morning within the walls of the ancient church shar-
ing the air and our picnic with the birds. It is just us alone, which is
unusual. It feels as though I am drifting—floating above the weight of
life, experiencing pure joy. As we walk into the cottage, I stop at the sink
to arrange some flowers, as Arek reaches out and follows my pregnant
belly with his hand.

The vision ends and I gasp, refusing to walk any farther.

"What?" He turns to me with concern.

"I just had a vision or maybe a memory . . . I don't know. Here,
in this cottage . . . I am pregnant."

He's quiet for a moment.

"Arek? What does that mean? Is it the future? That is the Prophecy
. . . isn't it? Is this a vision of what is to come or what already was?" I
can tell by Arek's face that he won't answer.

38

After a peaceful morning, Arek gathers us together outside the cottage. "I couldn't sleep last night for multiple reasons." He subtly looks at me, bringing a smile to my lips. "It's important that we keep moving . . . not stay anywhere for too long. So, maybe it's time to take us all in."

Geo looks up with a question. "Multiple people mean more problems."

"Yeah, I suppose it does," Arek agrees. "It also means working together. It might give us one up on the Umbramanes."

"So, we all go in." Sassi lifts her chest, fixing her perfect posture and clears her throat. "Geo will throw at us what he has, whatever manipulation he can think of." She hesitates, then continues, "Is it safe for us all to go in?"

Arek looks at Geo as he nods. "I believe we can do it." Then he turns to Kilon, "We go in together."

Kilon nods. "Okay. Let's do it."

Minutes later, we all sit with ropes in our hands that we begin to wrap around our palms and elbows. Geo checks with everyone to make sure we are all ready to make the leap. Each one of us nods, as we listen for the rhythm. By now, this has become easy for me.

After a few moments of concentration, I can feel the split coming. In a blink, the divide happens, and we sit inside a long kayak beneath turquoise and green marble caves on crystal clear water. I've never been here before, but the beauty of it is astounding. The marble is lined with multiple colors, an ombre effect from top to bottom. We paddle through the calm water taking in the gorgeous caves.

"This is way better than my subconscious has ever been," I say quickly.

"This is mine." The smile on Sassi's face tells us of her nostalgia. "I would often visit these when I lived in Chile . . . just before I came to head your father's security."

"Hmmm, well sign me up for your subconscious anytime," I say as we glide through the perfectly clear water.

Sassi shakes her head. "Don't be fooled . . . be prepared. Geo can manipulate this somehow."

All of us grow uncomfortable as several quiet moments give us false security. Then, when looking closer, I notice the ocean water is moving just a bit more. It builds from small waves, to larger. Then unexpectedly, the marble caves begin to shake, forcing heavy boulders to break off the ceiling, nearly hitting us. The kayak rocks as we try to paddle through. A large wave suddenly towers over us. "Hold on!" Arek yells as it comes crashing down. I take in a mouthful of water as I plunge beneath the surface and roll repeatedly. When trying to swim, desperate for air, I kick my legs, but feel something below grab my ankle. I quickly look down while my lungs threaten to burst, and pain radiates through my chest. All I can see is a shadow that holds on and won't let go. I scream beneath the current sending bubbles up my nose.

My hips burn as I kick harder, but the shadow holds until the skin around my ankle burns. I am pulled down and pressed against the soft sand, looking up at a blurred vision of what's happening above the water. Rocks and boulders still fall around me.

In my conscious state, in the first level, I can feel my hand slow, as though I am becoming paralyzed. My head tells my hand to move and wrap the rope around my elbow, but it doesn't listen. Arek, Sassi, and Kilon start to scramble. "Remy it's your subconscious that is making this happen. You have to fight the urge to let Geo in." I try to respond but realize I can't speak. My mouth isn't working, and my muscles feel like cement.

In the caves, in Sassi's subconscious, I am drowning. Arek dives through the water toward me. He reaches me as my eyes roll to the back of my head. After a fight, he pulls me to the surface where I suck in a massive breath. Water pours out of my mouth and lungs as I lay on the hard surface of a narrow beach in the caves. The kayak is now at the sea bottom.

"I'm sorry. That was my fault," my voice barely makes it out.

"Until you get this, we can't move to the unconscious," Sassi says. "Maybe it's not time."

"No! I can do this." I cough up more water, but I'm determined. I am suddenly able to move like nothing ever happened in the conscious level.

"Arek," Sassi says, when looking at something behind me that gives her surprise. We all turn to a pathway through the marble walls that wasn't there just a moment ago. "This doesn't exist," she says.

"So, we know to expect something," Kilon whispers. "Lead us, baby," he says as he touches Sassi's hand.

"I don't recognize any of this," she admits.

She leads us through the ice-like caves, that seem more like mirrors than thick concrete walls. When I look back, the opening of the cave is no longer there. We are shut in. Everyone looks at one another, but no one seems as concerned as I feel.

Just beside me, a shadow within the wall catches my eye. It seems to glide across the marble, as everyone else continues paying no attention to it. I walk closer. As I do, the shadow darkens behind the turquoise; it is coming toward me. I reach out to touch it. Whatever is there mimics my movement and my fingertips land on the darkest part of the shadow. The marble is unexpectedly soft and sinks in like quicksand. It grabs hold of my fingertips and pulls me forward.

I reach out with my other hand to brace myself, but everywhere I touch disintegrates and my leverage is gone.

Arek races to my side and yanks me until we fall free to the ground. Sassi touches the wall, but it is solid rock again. Arek's chest rises and falls against my back, his arm protectively around my shoulders. He whispers in my ear, "Nothing here owns you and if you accept that these things are not your reality, they won't win. I promise. Keep your rhythm and let's get through this."

Once again, we travel through the caves until something begins to shift. In a flash, we suddenly return to the side of the mountain where Arek's subconscious seems to live. Everyone stops for a moment to adjust to the change. "Here again?" I ask him.

"I suppose since I love rock climbing it's the natural dropping point for my subconscious. Remember, our true loves, our true self is always there . . . it's our demons that turn it to nightmares."

"And others can manipulate that." It's all starting to make sense to me.

He nods. "That's right."

"We need to expect changes. I'm sure they will happen a lot." Sassi grins.

Kilon looks over the side of the mountain from the small ledge we stand on and I watch his panic. "Of course it had to be heights," he growls as he desperately searches for a place to grab.

"Afraid of heights, Kilon?" I try to hide a smile.

"It's natural," he quips. "It's common sense."

Sassi slaps his butt. "Oh relax, just hold on."

"Hold on, it could disappear at any time," I warn Sassi and Kilon.

Kilon swiftly turns to me, "What could disappear?"

"The ledge." Again, I find it hard not to laugh when Kilon tries to set his large-toed boots on a tiny section of cliff.

Before long, we follow Arek up the mountain. After several minutes, when he can keep things under control, he looks down at us. "Okay, we're ready to move on."

In our conscious world, we wrap and unwrap the rough rope without stopping while each of us climbs without hesitation. While Geo is there in the chairs outside the cottage, we cannot see him in the other level.

Soon, I feel the split, just as I did before. Faster than the blink of an eye, we stand within the massive white stone walls where the water swept Arek and I away the time before. When my eyes connect with his, I whisper, "No water this time, okay?"

He grins. "I'll do my best, but we're all here. The unconscious is never true to one person's buried secrets when we're all together."

Sassi explains, "Our true self is connection with God which we all are infinitely, but sometimes this true connection lies buried within the graves of our life and experiences. There aren't many of us who have successfully excavated all our demons, but if we did, our conscious would be a better place and our unconscious may not even exist. Can you imagine a life where there is nothing hiding?"

We walk beneath the fifty-foot-high ceiling within the white stone hallway. Only this time, there seem to be more shadows and hallways off the main thoroughfare. I notice a shadow again, just like the one that pulled me to the sea bottom and floated across the marble wall within Sassi's subconscious. It floats along the wall next to me as I walk. Nothing exists within this hall that should cast this darkness. I watch it carefully. When we pass, it gathers my curiosity. My heart jumps when the shadow looks up at me, with no human characteristics, and follows. There should be nothing about this, I mean, it's a shadow . . . however, there it is . . . following us down the hall. My chest flips uncomfortably, and my skin jumps when I notice it has eyes.

Suddenly we are at a dead end.

"Where do we go?" Sassi asks.

But just as the words leave her mouth, I take a step and have left the stone walls; my foot lands on soft grass. I look up to find myself under a night sky in a garden and instantly rain pours. A storm sends lightning followed by thunder overhead, and the temperature drops till my body shakes.

"Arek?" I ask as I look around. No one is there in the poorly tended garden. "Sassi?" I call out, but no one answers.

Smoke billows from somewhere in the distance, while the burned smell permeates my nose. Far away, I hear piercing screams.

"Sassi!" I yell, but still nothing.

It's hard to keep my eyes open due to the large drops of rain, but I rush through the garden maze. Somewhere in the distance the screams are mixed with angry hollering, and I run harder, sending mud flying against my skin. It looks to me like an English country-side and, just ahead, where the smoke swirls and rises, an old country house from the fifteenth century is on fire. Those piercing screams continue from somewhere inside and I rush across the grass, chasing the terror, until I'm forced to stop so fast my feet slide across the wet ground. A large mob, nearly all men, packs the front lawn, exiting from the front door to watch the flames rise.

"Burn in hell, you witch!" several of these men shout at the house. I see a side door and run to it, trying to hide behind the shrubbery and stone wall. The heat is overwhelming as I burst into the living room, which then leads to the kitchen. The smoke rushes through my lungs, forcing me to cough. Instantly my lungs ache. "Sassi!" I yell. Her scream is loud from upstairs, and I take two steps at a time.

At the top of the stairs, coming from the opposite direction, I see two men. Their skin is beat red and their hair soaking wet.

"Mother!" one of them says, his English accent rich.

My heart stops for longer than I expect, and my jaw drops when I realize what I'm looking at. "Arek," I whisper.

Just then, Sassi's voice whispers from just behind me, "It's Arek and Navin."

I look at her with shock and so much dread my head pulsates. "Sassi, you're okay! I thought it was you."

"I'm okay," she says.

The screams continue, but this time I recognize that they come from the backyard. Instantly, Arek and Navin—younger versions of them—run past us, as though they can't see anything but the work ahead. Kilon, Sassi, and I follow.

Before I step out the back door, the foul stench of burned flesh meets me. I cough and gag just as I step outside. The heat hits me first, before my eyes take in a large fire in the middle of the field beyond. It's only when her shrill voice fills the cold night air that I rush forward. "Is that Holona?" Through the flames, when the storm threatens to put out the fire, we can see her blistering hands, tied to the wood above her head. "Holona!" I cry out.

Navin's and Arek's painful yells make me want to cover my ears—anguish billowing from their depths. Instantly, they are on a rampage, angrily ripping apart the men and women with their bare hands and a knife. Sassi holds my arm to keep me from running to Arek.

"We're deep here, Remy. The monster within us, even though it can come from something terrible, is still a monster." Sassi turns to Kilon. "Is anyone watching him in his conscious or subconscious?"

I turn my attention to the subconscious, where we are climbing the mountain beneath the moon and stars. Each of us is sweating and groaning as we pull ourselves to the next level, but Arek seems okay. Sassi is below me on the mountain and shakes her head, "Our conscious is affected first. Arek! Be careful . . . you're lost!"

In our conscious, the rope is getting thicker around my arm and even though paying attention to Arek within these levels feels like it is separate, I realize all of this is happening at one time. There is no other way.

Arek sits on the wooden chair in the Vida field in Spain where our beautiful little cabin sits, and his eyes are glazed over. His hands are frozen in place. Sassi jumps to her feet and kneels in front of him. "Arek, listen to me, keep moving here. You're in hell right now. I know you are, but honestly, honey, if you can dig through this, dig."

Arek blinks and his hand begins to pull the rope around again. He says nothing and his eyes glisten at the bottom.

Sassi looks at me, "I'll work with him, you start pulling that rope again. You have to learn Remy."

I pass the rope over and under, while still climbing the mountain within our collective subconscious, and still watching Arek and Navin's rage in Arek's unconscious.

As Holona's screams rise to a peak, then begin to fall, I search the grounds for Arek. After the last man is dead and Arek looks at his red hands, he no longer is the younger version from before. His eyes look up in horror. I run to him. "Arek." My palms press against his stunned face. "We've seen her, Arek. Again and again. She's happy. She's not in pain and she doesn't remember the pain . . . not where she is. Okay? This is just a memory."

It takes him a moment, but he slowly returns. As he does, we are suddenly back within the white stone halls.

39

Arek has regained control.

"Geo's not holding back any punches," Kilon whispers.

We are distracted and almost don't notice a figure pass down one of the side hallways. It is a familiar man with gray hair and arthritic fingers. He holds the wrist of a young woman and is dragging her away from us. She cries and aggressively rips at his fingertips to let her go.

I swallow uncomfortably, and then notice Kilon's strange stance. Sassi is already at his side. "Kilon," Sassi says carefully. "Guard yourself. You know that's just your memory and it's not really happening."

Suddenly, Geo is running through the stone halls toward us. I look at Arek and it's obvious that this is not a good sign.

Arek's chest rises, "What are you doing here?"

"We've got trouble. This isn't me," Geo says pointing to Japha dragging the woman down the hall. "And I didn't take you back to your mother's death."

The woman within Japha's grasp, far down the hall, falls to her knees and cries out. Kilon's breathing increases. "No!" he bellows. Then he gives chase and disappears after Japha and this woman.

"Kilon!" Sassi yells.

"Who is it?" I ask as Sassi begins to chase after him.

"His sister and Japha," Arek says quickly. "The sister whom Japha killed. Sassi!" he yells. "We need to stay together. Don't chase him."

Sassi reluctantly stops and watches Kilon disappear down the hallway—the battle within her manifests into the curl and release of her fist.

"Check in! Now!" Geo says.

Instantly, I pay attention to my conscious self. All of us look around as we pull the ropes, except for Kilon. The evening has fallen upon us and we still sit in a circle. Geo and Arek stand, dropping their ropes to the ground. Dark figures are swarming the fields.

"Kilon!" Sassi yells. After a moment she slaps his face, but he still doesn't move. "Arek!" she cries.

"Get your weapons," Geo yells. "Now! I'll stay with Kilon. Get mine."

We rush to the cottage and pull out every weapon we have. Then together we drag Kilon to the cottage. His eyes blink, but it's as though the lights have turned off. He silently lays on the kitchen floor.

Within the second level, I look down below me, where Kilon has been climbing the mountain. He is frozen here as well. The stars start to shoot across the sky in big clumps of light, then the mountain begins to shake and crumble beneath our hands.

"Remy, don't let them get in," Sassi yells. "Guard yourself!"

Geo shakes his head from where he has suddenly joined us on the mountainside. "This isn't Remy. Remy isn't letting them in. They're manipulating Kilon."

"What?" Sassi turns her eyes and that's when Kilon finally looks up. His eyes no longer look like his own, and when he reaches out for Sassi's ankle, he begins to pull her down. "Kilon!" Sassi yells and kicks his hand away.

Arek and Geo quickly try to glide down their ropes to help Sassi. Geo looks at Sassi, "Get him back to awareness in his unconscious!"

Beneath my hands, where I hang on the mountain, it turns soft, crumbling under my fingertips, and I fall.

Geo catches me with one arm. "Get your mind right, Remy! Don't let them in!"

40

I hang precariously from the rock wall as Geo—his bicep bulging—tries to keep me from falling. I reach out my other hand, sliding it this way and that, finally finding an inch-wide crevice to stick my fingertips into. Not too long after, my toes find an equal amount of space and Geo is able to let go.

Meanwhile, at the cottage, dark figures slither like snakes through the grass and trees. Arek rushes to my side and pulls me back from the railing of the porch and under the dark overhang.

Sassi leans over a lifeless Kilon, lying on the kitchen floor, and yells, "Kilon!"

Geo returns from somewhere inside with arms full of guns. Both Geo and Arek wait silently, each pointing a gun into the darkness. I grab one as well and wait in unison with them. For several moments we see nothing—just a bit of fog emerging. My body pulses with energy as we wait.

Arek whispers, "They're going to come from everywhere."

Geo nods, "The wrap around."

Arek points to the back of the cottage with his head and Geo crawls away, taking the wrap-around porch to the back.

Something pulls my attention to the end of the porch, where a small bunch of bushes shakes with the breeze. My breathing deepens as I take a couple of steps toward it—it seems the energy is thickening.

Then suddenly I see him. A man, dressed in black, a mask pulled tightly over his face, jumps toward me and I shoot.

Simultaneously, Arek sees his own ghosts and begins to fire. One by one, if they even remotely show themselves, Arek catches them. Each shot hits the target, even as he leaves the porch and searches them out.

Sassi continues to work on Kilon. He blinks here and there, but that is all. We hear Geo taking shots on the other side of the cottage as Arek yells at Sassi. "We have to get him back in the unconscious."

As we run through the white stone halls of our collective unconscious looking for Kilon, something has changed. I now feel and see the difference between when we are training and when someone has infiltrated. The walls of this giant castle-like structure, which I know to be Arek's third state, are changing—at times seeming to lean one way and then the next. Water begins to trickle down the stone walls and I pray the tsunami that happened before doesn't happen again.

Just as we pass a corridor, the sound of a child catches my ear, and I peer down the hallway. Sassi does as well, and her reaction is surprising.

"No!" Sassi cries out from the depths of her soul, like I've never heard before.

The little girl looks at us and instantly I can see it. Her face is not much different than Sassi's, her skin perfect as well. The little girl reaches out her hand to Sassi, as Sassi steps toward her.

Arek hurriedly wraps his arms around her from behind, and he presses his cheek to her ear with compassion. "Sassi, it's not Nayo." Sassi holds on to Arek's arms and the pain resonates from her soul until I can feel it beneath my skin.

The little girl still has out her hand, at the level of her beautiful brown eyes. "Momma," she whispers.

From somewhere in the distance farther down the hall, we hear Kilon yelling. Immediately Sassi hears it and pulls herself together. She presses her hand to her lips and sends an emotional kiss to what I can only assume was once her daughter. Painfully turning her back to her daughter, she turns to Arek, who presses his palms on her cheeks and looks her in the eye. "She lives within you now, not here in these halls." Arek's voice is calm and reassuring.

Even though a tear writes her pain on her skin, with a resilient shine she drops her eyes and nods. Arek waits just a second longer to make sure she is truly ready to continue, then he leads us down the stone hall holding Sassi's hand in his own. The hall seems to grow longer and the doors multiply off it. Some of them shake on their hinges, when people bang from the inside. I never know which of us has conjured each situation.

One of the doors has a brass handle embedded with a blue jewel. Somebody from inside calls my name and the handle turns without help. I step a bit closer. The white door opens by itself to reveal a dark gloomy room. It belongs in the fourteenth century. A low fire in the corner fireplace dimly lights the room, casting shadows on the ancient furniture. I reach out and touch a wooden chair with thick cloth, but pull back when my hand is but a child's. I have been here before. This place instantly swaths me with discomfort, reminding my soul of an old memory. Strangely, my mind thinks like a child, afraid to make a wrong decision, and I quietly sit on a nearby settee. A heavy and ornate wooden door across the room creaks open. Japha enters. Evil resonates from his spirit, but as a child all I can think about are his cracking bones. He is a bit younger, but his hair is still white and his eyes are still yellow. I don't want to be here, but my mother brought me. In fact, I realize, this has happened again and again. The arthritic man glides to me and sits close, too close, until I try to move just an inch away. My tiny body shakes, knowing that he wants to dig within my soul. The indoctrination, the radiance of his righteousness is what he teaches, hoping that I will love him. Hoping that I will rise to be the One for him.

He reaches out and rubs my back until I desperately want to pull away.

"Remy!" Within the old room, I hear a voice that doesn't come from Japha. There are ghosts in here, I can feel them. There's an entire world beneath this darkness, screaming to find the light. This rumble vibrates my soul until my fingers tingle and ache.

"Remy!" Arek is there, but not visible.

I close my eyes, hoping to free myself of this place. Japha is dead. This is just a memory. I do not have to live here.

"Remy!" Arek calls again. This time when I open my eyes, I am no longer within that room and Arek is standing in front of me. "Okay," he says, "are you back?"

Sassi and Geo are already running ahead of us, and I nod. "Yes."

He pulls me by the hand through the white stone hall. We can't see Kilon, but he is yelling, his angry curses echoing.

"Kilon!" Sassi yells.

We rush through the halls, jumping from this one to that one, trying to find him.

"We are getting closer!" Geo yells.

Finally, we reach the door from which Kilon's voice resonates. Geo opens it.

Kilon is stuck in a small room the size of a closet as he bangs on a large window. Japha has locked the door so he cannot follow. The old man yanks the crying woman to her feet, while Kilon slams his fists again and again until they are bloody, his voice growing hoarse.

Geo turns to Arek, "This isn't working. We're trying to fight defensively, every one of us. We must fight them with their own game. We have to dig and direct them—not the other way around."

Meanwhile, within the subconscious, we climb. Kilon has begun to slow. He moves with more difficulty and his eyes seem empty.

Geo looks down at me from a higher position on the mountain crumbling beneath us and nods as the rock begins to break beneath my hands again. "Look for their rhythm. Once you find it, work hard to break their control. We have to take the offense here, otherwise we will never get ahead."

Men begin to descend from the top of the mountainside.

"Arek!" Geo yells, as he is the closest to the top.

Arek looks up and pulls his knife.

41

"Kilon!" Sassi yells. He lies paralyzed on the kitchen floor of the cottage, his mind falling further and further away from his physical body.

A man reaches me, coming from seemingly nowhere. He stabs me in my side, and I cry out with pain. He moves fast, effortlessly forcing me to be perfect, to read his move before he does it. His hands catch me off guard several times, but I am able to catch him as well. We fall to the ground, where I reach for a gun.

Arek and Geo show their savage abilities, one by one.

My face, hands, and body are cut up and bruised, however, I can feel myself moving better with every minute and finding my rhythm.

"Get Kilon out of it!" Geo yells.

In our unconscious, within the tiny room where the glass breaks beneath Kilon's strength, Sassi walks to him slowly. "Baby," she says. "Baby," she looks him in the eyes. "It's not her. This is you . . . this is all you." Kilon's eyes blink for the first time in a while. Sassi continues, "There is no Japha here, and that's not your sister, she's free . . . she's free of all that and you need to be too."

Tears fall from Kilon's eyes as his awareness comes around. Finally, he sees his wife and places a hand on her face as he kisses her. "I got you," Sassi reassures him, and he nods.

At the same time, in the kitchen in our consciousness, Kilon comes to life with a growl and jumps to his feet. He is a force, so big and sturdy that it puts fear into men's eyes—even those as skilled as the Umbramanes. Fighting beside him is the safest place in the world. His passion marks his body in sweat and fire as his hands glide through the air, countering every attack with precision.

And now, once again, he begins climbing under the stars on the mountain.

One of the Umbramanes tries to yank me from the rock wall by wrapping his sweaty arms around my neck. My body screams in pain, but I'm able to kick until he swings away. With agile hands, I pull a knife from my belt and when he swings back, I slice the rope in half. His eyes grow wide as he falls, disappearing into the night and clouds below.

Instantly, back on the cottage porch in my conscious existence, the man I fought in both levels turns to stone and falls to the ground. He doesn't seem to be dead, just comatose.

Kilon notices my confusion and nods, "It's too much damage if you experience death in the subconscious."

Another attacker stops Kilon from continuing.

Meanwhile in the unconscious, we run through the stone halls.

"Find them," Geo commands. "Their rhythm."

"What makes you feel we can get into their unconscious?" I ask.

We turn a corner and enter a large open room. It is so white there are no edges, so perhaps it doesn't even have a shape. Geo looks at me, sweat falling from his forehead. "We so easily fell into our own stories here. Their buried stories are somewhere because every human is connected. Whether we want them to be or not . . . we all were pulled from the same source and exist within the same world."

Sassi is breathing heavily as we stop for a moment to plan. "Only two of Alfonzo's men are here."

"Wait . . ." I put my hand up to quiet the others. "Do you hear that?"

Everyone looks at me, then stops to concentrate in the shapeless white room.

"I hear it," I say.

Like the heavy beat of a drum, an unfamiliar rhythm grows louder. A chill wafts, making my skin pucker and my hair stand on end. The room becomes so full of vibration that the walls shake, similar to when we returned to the Cellar. Only this time, the shaking is not caused by my fear—rather, our power, the group that has so selflessly led me here. All of us are listening. Each of us with our own rhythm, our own vibration, somehow living our unconscious worlds together. We are strangely free of the hauntings we just experienced from our past. Sassi has dropped her head to listen. Kilon and Geo have closed their eyes. Arek takes a few quiet steps and then slowly turns, taking in the large shapeless room—his concentration showing beneath his lowered brows. Silently we wait—perhaps for the unexpected. It is too quiet here. We fight the Umbramanes in every other level except this one, which is now empty but for the potent air telling me someone is near, their rhythm no longer hiding.

From the cottage in our consciousness, I toss a weapon to Arek as he fends off an attacker, but there are so many Umbramanes, dressed to blend in to the night sky, that he yells at all of us, "Get to the church!"

So, we run. We run across the fields toward the church, and while I know the Umbramanes are following us, I can only see glimpses of them in the shadows. Arek pulls me to hide within the tree line that runs along our property. "Follow me . . ." he whispers.

Together, in the dark, we zigzag through the wide-trunked trees. As we get closer to the dilapidated church, we slow down, our movements more strategic and meticulous. It's like I can hear the snap of twigs and movement of branches everywhere. Arek stops behind a large maple to listen. He jerks back when a bullet hits the bark just in front of him, then drops in kneeling position to take a shot. A hundred yards away, Arek's bullet forces one of Alfonzo's men to run from one tree to the next. "Stay here," Arek warns me.

He cautiously moves forward. The night is a greenish gray, with a slight chill to the air. Arek keeps the gun raised in front of him.

After a moment, he whistles softly to me.

Suddenly, someone runs from the shadows. And with that, Arek steps out into the open, walks toward the attacker, and empties his bullets into the night. The man falls.

We hurry on. As Arek reloads, an unexpected bullet hits his arm and he cries out. His gun drops to the ground, so I pick it up and shoot just as the man sneaks toward us. He falls instantly. Arek looks at me with surprise.

"Get that surprised look off your face," I whisper.

He quickly hurries to the man lying on the ground, then tosses his gun to me.

My lungs ache and my legs burn as we run inside the church. Geo, Kilon, and Sassi are already there, so they begin to barricade the door once we are in. With a mission, Arek walks to the corner of the church and begins to pull at the floorboards. They come up easy. Before long, Arek pulls an arsenal of weapons out and checks each one of them.

Sassi takes one of the guns. "We're in trouble."

Arek exhales heavily and nods.

Back in our unconscious, we stand within the open white stone room with no shape. I can feel something changing.

"Arek," Sassi yells suddenly, "watch your feet!" Arek stops moving and looks down. Perfectly cut rows of white stone have dropped out from beneath our feet, leaving limitless black holes around us.

I peer down into an endless pit. "I can't see the bottom!"

Geo's foot teeters on the edge and he loses his balance. He falls—catching himself by just his fingertips.

Each of us stands on our own ten-inch plank of stone. Kilon, with his big muscular body, has surprisingly good balance and must choose quickly to shift from both feet to one. Three-foot gaps are on each side.

Finally, Geo recovers and pulls himself back up. "Don't lose the rhythm," he says, then points to a door on the other side of the room. "That's ours. Get there."

Carefully, we all walk our own plank, still trying to concentrate on the beat. Geo opens the door and we are instantly ushered into an old brick building. All the stone has disappeared, and we stand on a staircase overlooking a bakery that has been torn apart until only segments of the ceiling are still overhead. Each of us studies the remains. The thick stench of oil fills my nose, while I can see a cloud of brick-and-mortar dust in the air. From somewhere in the distance, bombs are dropping and cannon are blasting.

"Be careful, we're in their unconscious," Arek says.

Geo looks around. "Are you sure? This is . . . we were all in the war." He points to a swastika poster on the wall. Just below this poster, we notice a little girl and her mom, who are hiding.

Arek shakes his head with confidence. "No. This is definitely one of theirs."

We begin to descend the stairs, but a large explosion blows my hair across my face. All of us drop to our knees for cover—when we look up, we see that the wall that once separated us from the outside is gone. When the dust settles, the end of a cannon stares at us from out in the rubble.

Arek continues down the broken stairs. From a doorway near the bottom, someone bursts through, throws his arms around Arek, and tumbles them down the rest of the stairs to the ground. They fight, ripping at each other's clothes. The man is in a uniform so dirty and bloody that it is nearly impossible to see what side he fights for. His face is charred from explosions. "Margo . . . take her out of here!" the dirty soldier yells.

The mother takes her daughter's hand and prepares to run . . . until Arek has control and pins the man to the ground, which makes the woman stop. Sassi hurries toward the mother and daughter with her hand out to stop them.

"Don't touch them!" the man yells from beneath Arek.

Arek grabs him by the collar, "Uri, look at me."

Just then two more soldiers rush in. Their eyes fall upon the woman and child, and they hurry down the stairs to them. It's as though they cannot see us, or even notice that Sassi stands nearby. The soldiers roughly grab the little girl and her mom.

Arek brings Uri's face close to his. "You and I know how this ends, don't we?"

"Don't touch them!" the man yells again, as he watches the soldiers abuse the mom and daughter.

I look at Sassi. "Does Arek know him?"

Sassi nods. "Seems to. I should have known he might know which of Alfonzo's men would be able to do Tri Planum. He led us here." She doesn't finish as she grins.

Again beneath Arek, Uri yells. This time Arek shakes him. "Uri, listen to me . . ."

But Uri keeps yelling at the soldiers as they harass his wife.

Arek shakes him and says, "Uri! Listen! You know how this works." Finally, with a heavy breath, Uri turns his pained eyes toward Arek. Arek lowers his voice but keeps the tension around his neck. "I found you . . . you either call off Alfonzo's men or you live through this again. We can make any of this worse, or we can make it better, but you either live through this again, or you call everyone off. Do you understand me?"

The soldiers grab the mother's hair, pulling her to her knees, and she cries out. One of them slides a gun across her cheek and chin. The soldiers both laugh. Again, Uri yells.

All I want to do is help them, but Sassi holds my arm back and shakes her head.

Meanwhile, within the church in our conscious level, at least five of Alfonzo's men have surrounded the building and point their guns through each window and door. One of them walks in and instantly pulls the black mask from his face. It is Uri.

"Arek!" he yells at the top of his lungs. He rushes to Arek and takes him to the ground. Their hands move fast, warding off weapons and strikes. Both are bloodied quickly.

"Shouldn't Uri have a hard time moving here?" I ask Sassi.

"I think that comes with the training. I'm sure it takes a lot more. That's why Arek has to do what he has to do."

"Arek!" Uri yells. He is thrown aside and grabs a gun nearby. He slowly stands with it out in front of him.

Arek quickly grabs his own and they are in a standoff. "Back off, Uri."

"Arek!" Uri yells again. "I have orders, Arek. My orders by the Powers and Prophets . . . and your own father . . . is that I don't stop until I bring you all in. If I don't do that . . ."

"Then what? If you don't do it, then what? Make a choice, Uri." Arek doesn't drop his guard and his knuckles are turning white as he squeezes the raised gun. "Listen to me. I have control and you understand what I will have to do if you do not let us go. You are giving me no choice. I don't want to do it, my friend."

Uri lets out a tormented yell. "I can't let you go!"

Arek's voice drops in intensity. "Yes, you can. You must. Otherwise, you will lose them again."

"Sir!" the other Umbramanes yell from their places around the church.

Uri thinks several moments longer than any of us expect in this situation. He shakes his head, as though that will help him battle each level happening at this moment, but it doesn't. Arek has control in the most important place . . . his most buried sadness.

"Sir!" several of the men call again.

"Back off," Uri yells at them. "We're backing off. All of us. You have an hour, but I have no choice after that."

"That's enough. One hour is enough. We'll be gone," Arek says, but still doesn't drop his gun.

With that, Uri backs away and whistles for the rest of his men to follow.

Within the unconscious, Arek still wrestles with a very different looking Uri. "It's the best choice," Arek says as the soldier places the gun to Uri's wife's head and is just about to pull the trigger; they both cry out.

Swiftly, Arek jumps up, raises his gun, and shoots twice. Both soldiers drop to the ground, just as Sassi reaches out and grabs the little girl for protection. Uri instantly races to his wife and daughter and wraps his arms around them.

42

I am relieved to once again be within my own mind and escaping Spain as quickly as we can before the Powers realize we've escaped.

Arek's hand sits heavily on his lap as we travel in the car away from the cottage. I reach out to wrap my fingers in his. He looks at me with a half-smile that doesn't do much to cover his concern. Then he pulls my hand to his lips and kisses it. This move transports me . . . I am sitting in a 1930s Studebaker listening to Bessie Smith. My dress is flowy and backless, while his tweed suit is dark as he presses my hand to his lips. The memory turns to saying goodbye outside a large train while he wears an Air Force uniform during World War II and he kisses my hand . . . again and again, in different times and places.

From the front seat, Sassi looks in her rearview mirror. "Are you two okay?"

"We are now," Arek says as he rubs the part of his arm that was hit.

"Let me get it," I say. While he lies back with a groan, I fish out the bullet while blood drips down his arm and clothes.

"There!" I say, as the metal piece finally releases from his skin.

Just an hour later, on a smaller jet than usual, Sassi turns to Arek. "Are you ready for some good news?"

"Always." Arek nods.

"Here, it's from Diem and Gal." Kilon pulls out a computer and hands it to Arek. A video plays when his finger presses the arrow.

The video shows someone moving through a dark house, with infra-red night vision. Vague whispers can be heard as they sneak from room to room in search of something. Even with their intention to be quiet, excitement forces their accents thicker.

"Where are they?" I ask.

Just as I say this, Diem and Gal run into trouble and the video gets a bit wild. We watch them fight, unable to see exactly what's happening from their chest cameras. Finally, they reach a locked room and anxiously yank on the handle, but it doesn't budge. So, they step away, then shoot it. Arek and I are motionless as we try to figure out what is happening. Then suddenly we see her. My eyes grow large, and my fingers touch my lips to cover my gasp. Even Arek shifts in his seat. Diem and Gal grab the woman from a bed where she sleeps.

"Please tell me that's Elizabeth," I whisper.

Kilon and Sassi are smiling at each other when the video stops. "They've been busy. They've taken her to a safehouse in Strausbourg, which is where we are headed."

Arek has stayed silent, but I can see a bit of relief within his green eyes. I lay a hand on his arm, and he looks at me with a smile.

"It's time for this to end," Arek whispers.

43

On the border of France and Germany, where the two cultures collide, Strasbourg sits as an unexpected or forgotten cosmopolitan center. It has a gothic cathedral, the Rhine River, and the Black Forest that snakes along the city's edge. Every sign is written in both German and French and the architecture is heavily storybook induced. I've been here before and, while I can't place one specific memory, even the city's tramline has my fingerprints on it, I'm certain of it.

Sassi points toward an alley where two cafés butt up against each other—flowers weave through wrought iron and hang from window boxes along the apartments that sit above these quaint restaurants. "The entrance is behind these buildings."

We find a place to park the ordinary car and cover ourselves up as best we can with layers of clothes and hats. I can smell the fresh-baked bread as we walk slowly down the sidewalk carefully hugging the building. A single green door with no number and no signage stands between the back of the cafés and a small flower shop. Everyone carefully looks around before Sassi opens it with a key.

The hallway we travel is dark and long, with another door at a dead end. Sassi knocks quietly.

"What happened to all the places with the fancy security and locks?" I ask, grinning.

After a moment, the door opens and a large man—nearly three

hundred pounds—answers the door. He speaks in French. I look at Arek with wide eyes. "Je comprends tout."

We enter a large office building decorated in the style of the Strasbourg quaintness, mainly in the art covering the walls. The lights overhead are barrack lights, and they seem to guide our way through this room and the next, lined with chairs and couches.

The large man who guides us quickly walks past without care, not bothering to introduce himself. He exits through the same door someone enters. Relief floods my body at the sight of Briston, healthy and strong. It takes a moment for this to sink in. Then, I run to him.

"Welcome to Strasbourg," he says as he holds me tight.

Dr. Hugh, Diem, Gal, and Prophet Jenner enter after him. The room becomes a reunion unlike anything we've had in a long time. My mind races back to moments of return throughout the years— men returning from war, centuries of voyages to explore—and I shake my head. The years are returning, and it must feel as it would if someone with Alzheimer's got the gift of a life forgotten being found again. I watch everyone: Kilon and Briston hug, and Sassi and Prophet Jenner laugh. We are living on a high from the success of Gal and Diem, yet the truth has not come out and I can feel the ball of dread begin to creep back in. It is my name that has been tarnished for years. Remy had the world against her.

Once again Gal catches me in her sights, sweeps confidently over to wrap her arm around me. "Hello, my wife." She winks at me, then moves on to Arek, doing the same to him, "Hello my husband," except she slaps his butt as he lets go.

"How did you heal my father?" I ask Dr. Hugh.

He throws one hand in the air, and the other drops on his hip. "I'm brilliant. Absolutely brilliant." He winks. "Gyre had a small bit to do with it. Good news is, we have it going to lab for more study and Navin will never be able to use it against anyone again."

Minutes later, we sit around a large table and the yellow chairs swivel so easily that Peter is already spinning around at high speed.

Again, the memories race back of so many moments like this, with friends around tables. I can't help but take it all in. After a few minutes, Caynan joins us wearing a perfect blue and pink plaid suit.

"The Prophets don't know that Lyneva is alive, which means that someone from the Fellows tipped Navin off when she was a baby," Caynan explains.

"The Fellows?" I ask.

"The group put together to make sure all possible Velieri and returns are known. They work specifically in hospitals and home-birth," Sassi explains. "Where is Elizabeth?" she asks eagerly.

Briston looks at her carefully. "Elizabeth . . . she's not the same." The entire group takes a hit as our excitement falls to the floor with a dull thud. He recognizes this and continues, "We'll work with her."

Kilon throws a plastic bag on the table with a bloody piece of cloth inside. "Lyneva's not Velieri." Everyone looks at him with surprise. "We tested her blood, and her levels don't show the possibility of a dual hypothalamus."

"So, what's the next step?" I ask impatiently.

"Take Elizabeth to Gyre. Let him help her," Briston admitted.

"How long will that take?" Peter asks.

Briston shakes his head. "I don't know."

"Do we have enough to take before the Prophets?" Sassi asks Caynan. "What Diem and Gal found? Is it enough?"

Caynan shakes his head. "I don't know. It's a lot. But we're battling unspoken rules. No one plays by the rules here."

As the sun warms my skin in a hotel in Strasbourg, I wake with Arek sleeping next to me. Feeling a strange sensation on my skin, I look around the room and find that someone very small is sitting in one of the chairs on the other side of the room, although I can't see her face because of the sun bursting in from the window behind her. Before I can say anything, she stands with her finger to her lips, telling me to be quiet. "I needed to let you know that I am okay."

She walks closer to the bed and her familiar smile instantly tells me who she is.

"Beckah?" I whisper.

With a quick wink, she dances over to me and hands me a book. "Make sure you look through this."

I notice that it is the book that Evette, the shopkeeper from Spain, gave me. "How did you . . ." I begin but stop when Beckah is no longer there. Just for a moment I thumb through the pages, until I find something stuffed within it. I pull out a small, blurry picture of Arek and me in Spain. My stomach curves out in front of me.

Before we know what is happening, the door bursts open. Arek flies for his guns but is unable to reach them quick enough. A large team of Protectors barges in, followed by Leigh. I stuff the picture down my pants.

"Good morning," Leigh says. "Enough running."

I watch Leigh's cold eyes, but something in me has changed since watching Holona's death.

"Arrest them," Leigh commands.

There is no more fighting and I look at Arek across the bed. As the soldiers cuff our hands and walk us to the door, Arek speaks. "I'll take care of this, Remy, I promise."

44

The five by eight cell is cold and empty with nothing but a place for me to sit while I wait. *Wait for what?* It is so quiet within these walls that I can hear the faint sound of dripping water—again and again.

Perhaps this is the way the Prophecy is supposed to play out. Do I even understand what it means to be the One? Is this world even capable of living peacefully? While humanity continues to create moments of greatness, it never seems to be empty of sadness and angst. Just as before, I am void of all thought, free of the unconscious depths that keep me from existing now. I close my eyes only to listen and be, since time does not exist in past or future.

The injustice of this world has existed from the beginning of time and there may never be a cure, no matter how much we desire it. However, is it human to continue to hope? No. The hope does not come from our humanity, but from our divinity.

Where Willow remains, Remy should no longer take space; where Remy has returned, Willow is no longer accepted. It is with both that my strength exists.

At least I am no longer running.

Down the hall, I hear the screech of a door, followed by footsteps. It's uncomfortable to have no idea where they've taken Arek or the others, who wait for their own sentencing to be carried out. Finally, my door opens and Meryl, with several other guards, enters.

"Stand up," he says without emotion.

"Don't I get a last meal or something?" I ask, sarcasm bubbling over.

"How about a last walk?" he asks.

Meryl cuffs my wrists so tight I cry out when my fingers lose feeling. Even though I am cold, my skin glistens as I walk through the dark halls of the courthouse. *Is this what it felt like the first time?* My heart aches for everything that hasn't been done. The Manchester Books that haven't been found, the world that strangely feels like it is imploding beyond these walls. They walk me through several halls of the old historical courthouse. We pass a curved archway and through a hallway that seems to lead to the end of the world—well, my world. I picture the many Velieri throughout the years who have walked these same steps to their death. Meryl is even strangely silent until he thinks of something to say.

"Remy, you ran as long as you could. The thing of it is, there are more of us than there are of you. More of us who have lost someone to the Ephemes or have been tortured by their power-hungry ways," Meryl explains quietly.

"That's what you don't understand. The oppressors are your own kind . . . they had a price, and we are the currency for as long as they are in Power."

"Maybe you're right. But I'd rather stand on the side of freedom," Meryl suggests.

I simply shake my head with a guarded laugh. "I'm beginning to understand, Meryl. Freedom is just a word that's misunderstood. You fight for freedom, and it takes mine away. I fight for freedom, and it takes yours away. True freedom is when you take responsibility for you and I take responsibility for me, all with one greater focus—peace."

We reach a large door and stop for a moment while he checks his phone. "Just in time," Meryl whispers and holds the phone to my ear.

"Remy." Navin is on the other end. "Do you need another chance?"

"I don't need your chances, Navin," I growl.

"Obviously you do. You say the word and I will put an end to all of this . . . right now."

"You believe you have the power to do that?"

"I do."

"Navin . . . watch your back. The moment this is over, they will come after you. Every single one of them."

"I'm ready for that, Remy. I promise you."

"Trust me when I tell you this . . . you will lose."

"Be brave, love. You can't come back again."

"Don't count on that." I hit the phone with my cheek so that it falls from Meryl's hand. The glass shatters, which makes Meryl curse as he picks it up and stuffs it back in his uniform.

One of the guards ushers us in.

Behind the two doors is a massive arena, filled to the brim. The crowd erupts the moment I step inside. Meryl pushes me through the crowd with a satisfied smile. People stomp the floor, yell, and throw things; others cry out "Free her," and "Let her go."

For the first time in a while, my hands shake, and I force myself to take a deep breath.

A large stage is set in front of the Powers and Prophets with the execution chair in the middle. Everyone watches me and Prophet Jenner gives a small nod.

Covey stands to gather everyone's attention. "Miss Landolin, do you have anything to say?"

As the guards begin to tie my hands and feet to the chair, I clear my throat. "The world is changing. Velieri are being discovered whether you want to accept it or not. Attacks are happening in every country around the world . . . right now. My death will do nothing to keep that quiet. I guess I just wonder who will ultimately win this war."

For the first time I notice familiar faces. My father stands next to Peter. Hok and others from the Gianda, Mak and Kenichi with Aita. Arek, Kilon, Sassi, and Geo aren't there. The Velieri media is there, and I quickly notice Andrew Vincent give me a meaningful but grave smile.

"We must begin," Covey demands.

A man I have never seen before steps up to the microphone and addresses the crowd. "If you all will quiet down, we will begin the proceedings." He speaks for a while, assuring every one of my guilt. "This is the only way we find justice," he says. "May you find reconciliation with your Maker."

A compassionless Covey motions to Leigh, who I didn't notice in the shadows. For the first time, I see regret in Leigh's eyes. Whether it is for Arek or me, I don't know.

"Wait just a minute." Prophet Jenner stands up with confidence and a smile.

"What?" Covey angrily turns to stare down the woman who has defied him at every turn.

"Guards." Prophet Jenner motions to the men in uniform. "Take Meryl, Davi, Cecil, and Kage in custody and let her go."

Suddenly the entire room—including many of the Prophets, Powers, and guards—is a melting pot of emotion. Meryl, Davi, and the others seem utterly confused and fight back when several men surround them with weapons drawn. That's when I notice the color of Meryl and Davi's eyes, and instantly the last night in the Cellar comes back to me.

"What's going on here?" Covey bellows.

"And guards," Prophet Jenner says, "please take Covey as well."

Covey laughs, until he doesn't. He suddenly realizes that all has changed, and he growls as the Protectors surround him. "Leigh?" Covey cries out.

Leigh steps forward. "Prophet Covey, you are hereby declared excommunicated by the department of the Velieri Powers and the Protectors. You will be taken to the Cellar." As Leigh speaks, Covey incessantly talks over him, but Leigh continues without pause. "There you will be tried for the crimes in connection with conspiracy, sabotage, and falsehoods regarding the Red Summit, working with the criminals Navin and Japha, and embezzlement in the name of the Prophets."

"What proof do you have?" he yells.

Leigh turns to Meryl. "Meryl, you and your men are hereby charged with the torture and assault of Remona Landolin within the walls of the Cellar."

Meryl is angry now and he lunges toward Leigh, forcing the guards surrounding him to interfere and hold him back. "Don't pretend, Leigh! Don't pretend you are not a part of this."

"What proof do you have?" Covey yells again.

Suddenly the heavy doors leading outside crash open. The crowd parts with surprise, leaving room for Caynan, Kilon, Diem, and Gal, followed by an army of their men and women. Someone walks beside them, wearing a hood that covers their face.

Covey explodes. "Leigh! What is happening?" He turns to Leigh's men, the Protectors, and commands them toward Kilon. "Stop this. Remove them. Take them into custody."

Prophet Jenner raises a hand to the guards, "Stand down. Don't touch a soul."

"Prophets and Powers," Kilon says forcefully. "I have the proof we need to free Remona today. It will be on your head to make another mistake." The masses cry out in clashing emotion.

"Remove them!" Covey yells.

The guards obey Prophet Jenner instead.

Fighting breaks out among the people, forcing Kilon and the others to surround whoever is under the hood.

"You are the Prophets who foretold that she would bring unity to our people when she was only a child," Caynan calls out. "Let me present the evidence."

Prophet Jenner stands tall and moves to the crowd. "Quiet down. This will all end today. Caynan, share what you have found."

When Prophet Hawking stands up to argue with Jenner, Jenner takes a step toward her with a raised eyebrow, which is enough to send the Prophet back to her seat.

Finally, they reach the podium and pull the hood. My mother, Lyneva, stands there with her head down. The place falls into stunned silence and many appear confused. This is the first that anyone has known of her return.

"Lyneva?" Prophet Hawking calls out with surprise. The rest of the Prophets and Powers stand to their feet. As I look around, I notice the divide. The reactions of those within the Powers and Prophets tell me instantly whether they knew of any of this, and it surprises me how many tell of a dark story.

"Yes," Lyneva says quietly.

"What is this?" Prophet Zelner asks. "How did we not know about this?"

Caynan nods, "That's a good question . . . and I'm going to help you understand. Covey, would you like to tell us how Navin knew of Lyneva's return and was able to hide it?"

Covey shakes his head. "I don't claim to know anything about this."

Caynan smiles, "That's all right. I have several documents that you sent to Navin Rykor back in September 1989 telling him of a code of DNA that matches Lyneva. In these documents, you tell him, and I quote, 'Take care of this immediately.' Lyneva is also willing to testify about everything Navin has told her. About how they set Remy up. It was Japha's and Lyneva's mission to blame Remy for the Red Summit, but Navin had different plans. I give to you everything here." Caynan hands the guard a large file of papers. "But I'm also sending everything to the phone of every Power and Prophet." Caynan raises his phone in the air and with his thumb touches send. Immediately, the courthouse fills with pings from everyone's electronic devices. Everyone's eyes are instantly distracted by the screen in front of them and what they can learn.

Caynan continues, "And the Red Summit. We've found many things leading up to that horrific day and it all trails back to Prophet Covey and Navin."

Lyneva looks at me, but I can't read anything beneath her calm exterior. Everyone continues to read their phones in near silence.

Just then, two people stand in the doorway of the court. My eyes follow the wave of curiosity and land on the sweetest eyes I've seen in a while. Arek and Elizabeth enter with Gyre beside them. The old man can barely walk, and people gasp at his appearance.

As Elizabeth walks toward us, she passes her sister. They do not look at each other or pretend. The crowd remains silent and Lyneva turns her eyes to me for the first time. She is a beautiful woman with eyes that seem to hold so much sadness and darkness. I hope that I will never carry the same burdens.

Suddenly, I see her in a vision.

Lyneva comes toward me. I'm not older than five and I smile. She runs her hand down my face. "You'll never be what they say you are." My impressionable eyes see the darkness within her. "Just remember," she whispers. "The world will be unkind. I can promise you that."

Prophet Jenner continues. "Take Lyneva into custody and take her away. We must figure out what to do with her—she has not returned as Velieri."

They remove Lyneva, followed by a fighting and kicking group of men who once felt invincible with power.

My hands are freed from the cuffs and that's when I see Arek standing just behind Elizabeth. He smiles at me and then I hurry to his side. He rests his hands on my face and stares into my eyes. "You're free. Free of what they think of you, what they told you that you were, and free to figure out who you are without chains."

He kisses me and then wraps me in his arms. After a moment, we notice Leigh leaving with a group of his men.

"Where are you going?" Arek calls out.

Leigh turns back. "To find my son." With that, he is gone.

Everyone walks to join together. Geo, Briston, Sassi, Kilon, Peter, Mak, Kenichi, Gyre, Arek, and I. Even Diem and Gal join us. "Our work is ahead. There is no safety—not yet. But you are free, Remy," Sassi says.

"How did you find Lyneva?" I ask.

Diem smiles and Gal explains, "She was there with Elizabeth. We just didn't want anyone to know."

"And she was going to testify?" I look at them with a raised eyebrow of suspicion.

Gal and Diem smile, which causes a wave through the group. Arek shrugs, "No. She was never going to testify. Navin has brainwashed her. Luckily, we had enough evidence without her." The chaos among the crowd is continuing to grow, so Arek turns to the door. "Let's get out of here."

All of us hurry down the steps of the courthouse, through the crowd, and outside, where a new mass of people has begun to form. I still see that many of them hate me. Several men and women representing the Fidelis nod.

A man holds up a sign in the crowd that reads, "We Won!"

I know that no one has won today. This is just the beginning. I hear the swell of voices begin, little by little, as Arek opens the back door of the car for me. Above the jeers of those who hate me, my followers chant my name: "Remy! Remy! Remy!"

I peer over the crowd. Their eyes are ablaze with promise of hope. They want their freedom—and I want it for them.

With one hand, I pound my chest three times. Instantly the crowd follows suit and roars to life with determination and hope.

We are ready.

45

Arek and I fly alone, for the first time realizing the freedom we have just been given. My name is cleared. Navin remains the threat, and the world is changing. The plane dips to the landing strip and I recognize it immediately. It has been so long since this all began. I look at Arek with a smile and he runs his hand down my back.

San Francisco, just as beautiful as I remember it, seems happy, as though it has been waiting for my return. Only now, Willow is a bit more like the stranger, not Remy. I realize as we drive through the winding and steep hills of this city that it is Willow's memory of this place that tells me every emotion and feeling that sweeps through my being. Remy and Willow will always be a part of me, yet it is the Right Now where I live. Needing not to answer the question of Who I am.

Arek holds my hand as he drives through the city. "Where are we going?" I ask.

"You'll see."

In just a few moments, we stand at the corner of an old building at a four-way stoplight in a beautiful and quaint part of the Mission District. He pulls me in for a kiss, then I look at him with a question. "Why are we here?"

He smiles and says, "Just wait a moment."

After several minutes of silence, as he leans against the building and I against him, his body suddenly perks up and he points to somewhere across the street. I try to zero in on whatever it is. Finally, two women, about my age, linked arm in arm, are talking as they walk down the sidewalk. At first, I wonder why he cares, but before I question him, their beauty calls to me. My chest burns and my heart takes a new rhythm. I step toward the street, but he holds my arm to keep me beneath the shadows. I study them, which only makes my questions build.

"They look like you," he says kindly.

My mind vacillates between sadness and joy, confusion and certainty.

The women turn the corner and take a seat at a café table, still engaged in perfect conversation. I study the curve of their faces, and the almond shape of their eyes—one of them with blue, and the other with green. The memory returns, as if lived yesterday, of Arek and me at the cottage in Spain. I feel the babies kicking inside my stomach and let Arek rest his hand there. I remember the pain of childbirth with no one but Arek to help me.

Tears fall from my eyes as I watch them.

"Arek?" When I turn to him, I realize what he has done.

"After you died, I had to bring them here so I could take care of all of you." So much of Arek's sadness and fear I now understand.

"How old are they?"

"Thirty-five."

Two years older than Willow.

"They're safe?" The fear wells within my soul.

He smiles. "Yes, I've raised them to know who their mother is. It was your idea to make them Fidelis and they now run the Gianda here in San Francisco, free of control of government. Free of anyone knowing what they are or who they are. Not even Sassi or Kilon know of them. Only your father, Prophet Jenner, and I."

Quickly, I pull the picture of Arek and me in Spain from my pocket. He is surprised that I have it and takes a closer look.

The pain of missing their lives, the pain of not knowing who they are, mixes with the joy of their existence. And the man next to me, who shares this moment, takes my head in his hands. "I love you," he says.

When we look back, one of them sees us as though she could feel us. She stands and walks forward. Across a busy street, within the heavy drum of San Francisco, she smiles and raises her hand in the air. Her sister comes to her side and the collision of our pain and joy rises in the air and meets with a dramatic clash over the city.

TO BE CONTINUED . . .

ACKNOWLEDGMENTS

First, I'd like to thank my family for believing in me more than I sometimes believe in myself. Ben, you are my rock, and we've been so very lucky in love. Evie, your kind heart, warrior's spirit, and crazy talent is everything that I hoped for you. Georgia, your genuine love, joy, and zest for life is contagious. You are my everything.

Mom, thank you for your talks as I walk through this publishing experience. Your support has been unwavering and I am so blessed to have it.

Dad, I miss you every single day! I hope you are proud!

To all of my clients for being the coolest, kindest, most loving people in the world. You have supported me even though I have often been tired. I can't thank you enough for your loyalty and love.

To the publishing team and the marketing team who helped me stand up from the depths of confusion. Without all of you, I might still be wide eyed and running away from my dreams. Thank you, Wayne, for actually reading Rachel Anne Praline and starting the chain of events that led us to here. Thank you, Jess, for loving the characters and story enough to take me on. Thank you, Natalie, for recognizing my vision and encouraging me to never stray from that. Thank you to Stephanie for your unbelievable encouragement and deeply connected spirituality. Everything you said was right on, whether I wanted to hear it or not.

STAY IN TOUCH
WITH TESSA VAN WADE

FACEBOOK
@TessaVanWadeAuthorPage

INSTAGRAM
@tessavanwade

YOUTUBE
@tessavanwade

WEBSITE
TessaVanWade.com

PODCAST
tessavanwade.com/podcast
or wherever you download your favorite podcasts